P9-CFG-819

"Haunting" (*Ch*... ...
"Hypnotic" (*Washington Post Book World*) . . .
"Eloquent" (*Orlando Sentinel*) . . .
"Breathtaking" (*Hartford Courant*) . . .
"Satisfying" (*Entertainment Weekly*) . . .
"Awesome" (*The Wall Street Journal*) . . .
"Stunning" (*The Boston Globe*) . . .
"Wonderful" (*Arizona Daily Star*)

Words of praise for James Lee Burke's crime fiction masterpiece—his sixth Dave Robicheaux novel

IN THE ELECTRIC MIST WITH CONFEDERATE DEAD

"Powerful . . . unsettling. . . . Burke is a master . . . a poet of the mystery novel."

—*Chicago Tribune*

"Vivid . . . first-rate."

—*Entertainment Weekly*

"Tough and soulful."

—*Ft. Wayne* (IN) *Journal-Gazette*

"A dazzling accomplishment. . . . A masterpiece. . . . Fine entertainment."

—*Mostly Murder*

"Rich and evocative. . . . Robicheaux's story will break your heart and free your spirit."

—*Worcester* (MA) *Magazine*

"Seductive . . . lyrical . . . lushly atmospheric."

—*The New York Times Book Review*

"A fine writer. . . . A real reading pleasure."

—*New Orleans Times-Picayune*

More acclaim for *In the Electric Mist with Confederate Dead*

"Masterful. . . . A taut, dark thriller."

—*Wichita* (KS) *Eagle*

"Thoughtfully written. . . . Mystery wrapped in eloquence."

—*USA Today*

"Outstanding. . . . A violent, somber, deeply satisfying novel."

—*Kirkus Reviews*

"Hallucinatory . . . Burke is one of the best stylists in the field."

—*Lexington* (KY) *Herald-Leader*

"A master . . . Burke writes prose as moody and memory-laden as his region."

—*Time*

"It's impossible to think of the Louisiana bayou . . . without conjuring up scenes from James Lee Burke's Dave Robicheaux books" (*Chicago Tribune*)—don't miss this new bestseller in the "landmark series" (*Booklist*)

THE GLASS RAINBOW

"Superlative. . . . A complex plot that repeatedly plumbs the depths of human depravity and the heights of nobility."

—*Publishers Weekly* (starred review)

"Magnificent."

—*Kirkus Reviews* (starred review)

"The suspense level is about as high as it gets in popular fiction."

—*Los Angeles Times*

"Arguably his finest. . . . Lush and lyrical, brutal and beautiful. . . . So powerful, so moving, that the reader is left in awe—and perhaps in tears."

—*Richmond Times-Dispatch*

"Burke writes with a vivid awareness of the human capacity for evildoing. . . . He is in top form in *The Glass Rainbow*."

—NPR.org

"A twisting, turning, suspense-filled thriller."

—*Seattle Post-Intelligencer*

"Burke should get [an award] for sustained literary brilliance in his Dave Robicheaux series. . . . In *The Glass Rainbow* he gets everything exactly right."

—*Cleveland Plain Dealer*

"Fans of *The Girl with the Dragon Tattoo* take note."

—*San Antonio Express-News*

"Unlike his forebears, Sam Spade and Philip Marlowe, Robicheaux . . . is an evolving, dynamic character whose story is as crucial to the turns of the novel as is the gathering of clues and elimination of suspects. . . . Gripping and tautly written . . . magnetic and captivating."

—*Missoula Independent*

By James Lee Burke

DAVE ROBICHEAUX NOVELS

The Glass Rainbow
Swan Peak
Tin Roof Blowdown
Pegasus Descending
Crusader's Cross
Last Car to Elysian Fields
Jolie Blon's Bounce
Purple Cane Road
Sunset Limited
Cadillac Jukebox
Burning Angel
Dixie City Jam
In the Electric Mist with Confederate Dead
A Stained White Radiance
A Morning for Flamingos
Black Cherry Blues
Heaven's Prisoners
The Neon Rain

BILLY BOB AND HACKBERRY HOLLAND NOVELS

In the Moon of Red Ponies
Bitterroot
Heartwood
Cimarron Rose
Lay Down My Sword and Shield
Rain Gods

OTHER FICTION

Jesus Out to Sea
White Doves at Morning
The Lost Get-Back Boogie
The Convict and Other Stories
Two for Texas
To the Bright and Shining Sun
Half of Paradise

JAMES LEE BURKE

IN THE ELECTRIC MIST WITH CONFEDERATE DEAD

POCKET BOOKS
New York London Toronto Sydney New Delhi

The sale of this book without its cover is unauthorized. If you purchased this book without a cover, you should be aware that it was reported to the publisher as "unsold and destroyed." Neither the author nor the publisher has received payment for the sale of this "stripped book."

Pocket Books
A Division of Simon & Schuster, Inc.
1230 Avenue of the Americas
New York, NY 10020

This book is a work of fiction. Names, characters, places, and incidents either are products of the author's imagination or are used fictitiously. Any resemblance to actual events or locales or persons, living or dead, is entirely coincidental.

Copyright © 1993 by James Lee Burke

Published by arrangement with Hyperion, an imprint of Buena Vista Books, Inc.

All rights reserved, including the right to reproduce this book or portions thereof in any form whatsoever. For information address Hyperion, 114 Fifth Avenue, New York, NY 10011.

First Pocket Books paperback edition November 2011

POCKET and colophon are registered trademarks of Simon & Schuster, Inc.

For information about special discounts for bulk purchases, please contact Simon & Schuster Special Sales at 1-866-506-1949 or business@simonandschuster.com.

The Simon & Schuster Speakers Bureau can bring authors to your live event. For more information or to book an event contact the Simon & Schuster Speakers Bureau at 1-866-248-3049 or visit our website at www.simonspeakers.com.

Cover design by John Vairo Jr., photo of swamp at night © Peter Rodger/Getty Images, photo of vault grave in New Orleans © Shutterstock

Manufactured in the United States of America

10 9 8 7 6 5 4

ISBN 978-1-4391-6760-1

For Frank and Tina Kastor
and Jerry and Maureen Hoag

CHAPTER 1

THE SKY HAD gone black at sunset, and the storm had churned inland from the Gulf and drenched New Iberia and littered East Main with leaves and tree branches from the long canopy of oaks that covered the street from the old brick post office to the drawbridge over Bayou Teche at the edge of town. The air was cool now, laced with light rain, heavy with the fecund smell of wet humus, night-blooming jasmine, roses, and new bamboo. I was about to stop my truck at Del's and pick up three crawfish dinners to go when a lavender Cadillac fishtailed out of a side street, caromed off a curb, bounced a hubcap up on a sidewalk, and left long serpentine lines of tire prints through the glazed pools of yellow light from the street lamps.

I was off duty, tired, used up after a day of searching for a nineteen-year-old girl in the woods, then finding her where she had been left in the bottom of a coulee, her mouth and wrists wrapped with electrician's tape. Already I had tried to stop thinking about the rest of it. The medical examiner was a kind man. He bagged the body before any news people or family members got there.

I don't like to bust drunk drivers. I don't like to listen to their explanations, watch their pitiful attempts to affect sobriety, or see the sheen of fear break out in their eyes when they realize they're headed for the drunk tank with little to look forward to in the morning except the appearance of their names in the newspaper. Or maybe in truth I just don't like to see myself when I look into their faces.

But I didn't believe this particular driver could make it another block without ripping the side off a parked car or plowing the Cadillac deep into someone's shrubbery. I plugged my portable bubble into the cigarette lighter, clamped the magnets on the truck's roof, and pulled him to the curb in front of the Shadows, a huge brick, white-columned antebellum home built on Bayou Teche in 1831.

I had my Iberia Parish Sheriff's Department badge opened in my palm when I walked up to his window.

"Can I see your driver's license, please?"

He had rugged good looks, a Roman profile, square shoulders, and broad hands. When he smiled I saw that his teeth were capped. The woman next to him wore her hair in blond ringlets and her body was as lithe, tanned, and supple-looking as an Olympic swimmer's. Her mouth looked as red and vulnerable as a rose. She also looked like she was seasick.

"You want driver's what?" he said, trying to

focus evenly on my face. Inside the car I could smell a drowsy, warm odor, like the smell of smoke rising from a smoldering pile of wet leaves.

"Your driver's license," I repeated. "Please take it out of your billfold and hand it to me."

"Oh, yeah, sure, wow," he said. "I was really careless back there. I'm sorry about that. I really am."

He got his license out of his wallet, dropped it in his lap, found it again, then handed it to me, trying to keep his eyes from drifting off my face. His breath smelled like fermented fruit that had been corked up for a long time in a stone jug.

I looked at the license under the street lamp.

"You're Elrod T. Sykes?" I asked.

"Yes, sir, that's who I am."

"Would you step out of the car, Mr. Sykes?"

"Yes, sir, anything you say."

He was perhaps forty, but in good shape. He wore a light-blue golf shirt, loafers, and gray slacks that hung loosely on his flat stomach and narrow hips. He swayed slightly and propped one hand on the door to steady himself.

"We have a problem here, Mr. Sykes. I think you've been smoking marijuana in your automobile."

"Marijuana . . . Boy, that'd be bad, wouldn't it?"

"I think your lady friend just ate the roach, too."

"That wouldn't be good, no, sir, not at all." He shook his head profoundly.

"Well, we're going to let the reefer business slide for now. But I'm afraid you're under arrest for driving while intoxicated."

"That's very bad news. This definitely was not on my agenda this evening." He widened his eyes and opened and closed his mouth as though he were trying to clear an obstruction in his ear canals. "Say, do you recognize me? What I mean is, there're news people who'd really like to put my ham hocks in the frying pan. Believe me, sir, I don't need this. I cain't say that enough."

"I'm going to drive you just down the street to the city jail, Mr. Sykes. Then I'll send a car to take Ms. Drummond to wherever she's staying. But your Cadillac will be towed to the pound."

He let out his breath in a long sigh. I turned my face away.

"You go to the movies, huh?" he said.

"Yeah, I always enjoyed your films. Ms. Drummond's, too. Take your car keys out of the ignition, please."

"Yeah, sure," he said, despondently.

He leaned into the window and pulled the keys out of the ignition.

"El, *do* something," the woman said.

He straightened his back and looked at me.

"I feel real bad about this," he said. "Can I make a contribution to Mothers Against Drunk Driving, or something like that?"

In the lights from the city park, I could see the rain denting the surface of Bayou Teche.

"Mr. Sykes, you're under arrest. You can remain

silent if you wish, or if you wish to speak, anything you say can be used against you," I said. "As a long-time fan of your work, I recommend that you not say anything else. Particularly about contributions."

"It doesn't look like you mess around. Were you ever a Texas ranger? They don't mess around, either. You talk back to those boys and they'll hit you upside the head."

"Well, we don't do that here," I said. I put my hand under his arm and led him to my truck. I opened the door for him and helped him inside. "You're not going to get sick in my truck, are you?"

"No, sir, I'm just fine."

"That's good. I'll be right with you."

I walked back to the Cadillac and tapped on the glass of the passenger's door. The woman, whose name was Kelly Drummond, rolled down the window. Her face was turned up into mine. Her eyes were an intense, deep green. She wet her lips, and I saw a smear of lipstick on her teeth.

"You'll have to wait here about ten minutes, then someone will drive you home," I said.

"Officer, I'm responsible for this," she said. "We were having an argument. Elrod's a good driver. I don't think he should be punished because I got him upset. Can I get out of the car? My neck hurts."

"I suggest you lock your automobile and stay where you are, Ms. Drummond. I also suggest you do some research into the laws governing the possession of narcotics in the state of Louisiana."

"Wow, I mean, it's not like we hurt anybody. This is going to get Elrod in a lot of trouble with Mikey. Why don't you show a little compassion?"

"Mikey?"

"Our *director*, the guy who's bringing about ten million dollars into your little town. Can I get out of the car now? I really don't want a neck like Quasimodo."

"You can go anywhere you want. There's a pay phone in the poolroom you can use to call a bondsman. If I were you, I wouldn't go down to the station to help Mr. Sykes, not until you shampoo the Mexican laughing grass out of your hair."

"Boy, talk about wearing your genitalia outside your pants. Where'd they come up with you?"

I walked back to my truck and got in.

"Look, maybe I can be a friend of the court," Elrod Sykes said.

"What?"

"Isn't that what they call it? There's nothing wrong with that, is there? Man, I can really do without this bust."

"Few people standing before a judge ever expected to be there," I said, and started the engine.

He was quiet while I made a U-turn and headed for the city police station. He seemed to be thinking hard about something. Then he said: "Listen, I know where there's a body. I saw it. Nobody'd pay me any mind, but I saw the dadburn thing. That's a fact."

"You saw what?"

"A colored, I mean a black person, it looked

like. Just a big dry web of skin, with bones inside it. Like a big rat's nest."

"Where was this?"

"Out in the Atchafalaya swamp, about four days ago. We were shooting some scenes by an Indian reservation or something. I wandered back in these willows to take a leak and saw it sticking out of a sandbar."

"And you didn't bother to report it until now?"

"I told Mikey. He said it was probably bones that had washed out of an Indian burial mound or something. Mikey's kind of hard-nosed. He said the last thing we needed was trouble with either cops or university archaeologists."

"We'll talk about it tomorrow, Mr. Sykes."

"You don't pay me much mind, either. But that's all right. I told you what I saw. Y'all can do what you want to with it."

He looked straight ahead through the beads of water on the window. His handsome face was wan, tired, more sober now, resigned perhaps to a booking room, drunk-tank scenario he knew all too well. I remembered two or three wire-service stories about him over the last few years—a brawl with a couple of cops in Dallas or Fort Worth, a violent ejection from a yacht club in Los Angeles, and a plea on a cocaine-possession bust. I had heard that bean sprouts, mineral water, and the sober life had become fashionable in Hollywood. It looked like Elrod Sykes had arrived late at the depot.

"I'm sorry, I didn't get your name," he said.

"Dave Robicheaux."

"Well, you see, Mr. Robicheaux, a lot of people don't believe me when I tell them I see things. But the truth is, I *see* things all the time, like shadows moving around behind a veil. In my family we call it 'touched.' When I was a little boy, my grandpa told me, 'Son, the Lord done touched you. He give you a third eye to see things that other people cain't. But it's a gift from the Lord, and you mustn't never use it otherwise.' I haven't ever misused the gift, either, Mr. Robicheaux, even though I've done a lot of other things I'm not proud of. So I don't care if people think I lasered my head with too many recreational chemicals or not."

"I see."

He was quiet again. We were almost to the jail now. The wind blew raindrops out of the oak trees, and the moon edged the storm clouds with a metallic silver light. He rolled down his window halfway and breathed in the cool smell of the night.

"But if that was an Indian washed out of a burial mound instead of a colored man, I wonder what he was doing with a chain wrapped around him," he said.

I slowed the truck and pulled it to the curb.

"Say that again," I said.

"There was a rusted chain, I mean with links as big as my fist, crisscrossed around his rib cage."

I studied his face. It was innocuous, devoid of intention, pale in the moonlight, already growing puffy with hangover.

"You want some slack on the DWI for your knowledge about this body, Mr. Sykes?"

"No, sir, I just wanted to tell you what I saw. I shouldn't have been driving. Maybe you kept me from having an accident."

"Some people might call that jailhouse humility. What do you think?"

"I think you might make a tough film director."

"Can you find that sandbar again?"

"Yes, sir, I believe I can."

"Where are you and Ms. Drummond staying?"

"The studio rented us a house out on Spanish Lake."

"I'm going to make a confession to you, Mr. Sykes. DWIs are a pain in the butt. Also I'm on city turf and doing their work. If I take y'all home, can I have your word you'll remain there until tomorrow morning?"

"Yes, sir, you sure can."

"But I want you in my office by nine A.M."

"Nine A.M. You got it. Absolutely. I really appreciate this."

The transformation in his face was immediate, as though liquified ambrosia had been infused in the veins of a starving man. Then as I turned the truck around in the middle of the street to pick up the actress whose name was Kelly Drummond, he said something that gave me pause about his level of sanity.

"Does anybody around here ever talk about Confederate soldiers out on that lake?"

"I don't understand."

"Just what I said. Does anybody ever talk about guys in gray or butternut-brown uniforms out there? A bunch of them, at night, out there in the mist."

"Aren't y'all making a film about the War Between the States? Are you talking about actors?" I looked sideways at him. His eyes were straight forward, focused on some private thought right outside the windshield.

"No, these guys weren't actors," he said. "They'd been shot up real bad. They looked hungry, too. It happened right around here, didn't it?"

"What?"

"The battle."

"I'm afraid I'm not following you, Mr. Sykes."

Up ahead I saw Kelly Drummond walking in her spiked heels and Levi's toward Tee Neg's poolroom.

"Yeah, you do," he said. "You *believe* when most people don't, Mr. Robicheaux. You surely do. And when I say you *believe*, you know exactly what I'm talking about."

He looked confidently, serenely, into my face and winked with one blood-flecked eye.

CHAPTER 2

My dreams took me many places: sometimes back to a windswept firebase on the top of an orange hill gouged with shell holes; a soft, mist-streaked morning with ducks rising against a pink sun while my father and I crouched in the blind and waited for that heart-beating moment when their shadows would race across the cattails and reeds toward us; a lighted American Legion baseball diamond, where at age seventeen I pitched a perfect game against a team from Abbeville and a beautiful woman I didn't know, perhaps ten years my senior, kissed me so hard on the mouth that my ears rang.

But tonight I was back in the summer of my freshman year in college, July of 1957, deep in the Atchafalaya marsh, right after Hurricane Audrey had swept through southern Louisiana and killed over five hundred people in Cameron Parish alone. I worked offshore seismograph then, and the portable drill barge had just slid its iron pilings into the floor of a long, flat yellow bay, and the jugboat crew had dropped me off by a chain of willow islands to roll up a long spool of recording cable that was strung through the trees and across the sand spits and sloughs. The sun was white in the sky, and the humidity was like the steam that rises from a pot of boiled vegetables. Once I was inside the shade of the trees, the mosquitoes swarmed around my ears and eyes in a gray fog as dense as a helmet.

The spool and crank hung off my chest by canvas straps, and after I had wound up several feet of cable, I would have to stop and submerge myself in the water to get the mosquitoes off my skin or smear more mud on my face and shoulders. It was our fifth day out on a ten-day hitch, which meant that tonight the party chief would allow a crew boat to take a bunch of us to the levee at Charenton, and from there we'd drive to a movie in some little town down by Morgan City. As I slapped mosquitoes into a bloody paste on my arms and waded across sand bogs that sucked over my knees, I kept thinking about the cold shower that I was going to take back on the quarter-boat, the fried-chicken dinner that I was going to eat in the dining room, the ride to town between the sugarcane fields in the cooling evening. Then I popped out of the woods on the edge of another bay, into the breeze, the sunlight, the hint of rain in the south.

I dropped the heavy spool into the sand, knelt in the shallows, and washed the mud off my skin. One hundred yards across the bay, I saw a boat with a cabin moored by the mouth of a narrow bayou. A Negro man stepped off the bow onto the bank, followed by two white men. Then I looked again and realized that something was terribly wrong. One of the white men had a pistol in his hand, and the black man's arms were pinioned at his sides with a thick chain that had been trussed around his upper torso.

I stared in disbelief as the black man started running along a short stretch of beach, his head twisting back over his shoulder, and the man with the pistol took aim and fired. The first round must have hit him in the leg, because it crumpled under him as though the bone had been snapped in two with a hammer. He half rose to his feet, stumbled into the water, and fell sideways. I saw the bullets popping the surface around him as his kinky head went under. The man with the pistol waded after him and kept shooting, now almost straight down into the water, while the other white man watched from the bank.

I didn't see the black man again.

Then the two white men looked across the flat expanse of bay and saw me. I looked back at them, numbly, almost embarrassed, like a person who had opened a bedroom door at the wrong moment. Then they walked calmly back to their boat, with no sign of apprehension or urgency, as though I were not even worthy of notice.

Later, I told the party chief, the sheriff's department, and finally anybody who would listen to me, about what I had seen. But their interest was short-lived; no body was ever found in that area, nor was any black man from around there ever reported as missing. As time passed, I tried to convince myself that the man in chains had eluded his tormentors, had held his breath for an impossibly long time, and had burst to the surface and a new day somewhere downstream. At age nineteen I did not want to accept the possibility that a man's murder could be treated with the social significance of a hangnail that had been snipped off someone's finger.

AT NINE SHARP the morning after I had stopped Elrod T. Sykes for drunk driving, a lawyer, not Elrod Sykes, was in my office. He was tall and had silver hair, and he wore a gray suit with red stones in his cuff links. He told me his name but it wouldn't register. In fact, I wasn't interested in anything he had to say.

"Of course, Mr. Sykes is at your disposal," he said, "and both he and I appreciate the courtesy which you extended to him last night. He feels very bad about what happened, of course. I don't know if he told you that he was taking a new prescription for his asthma, but evidently his system has a violent reaction to it. The studio also appreciates—"

"What is your name again, sir?"

"Oliver Montrose."

I hadn't asked him to sit down yet. I picked up several paper clips from a small tin can on my desk and began dropping them one by one on my desk blotter.

"Where's Sykes right now, Mr. Montrose?"

He looked at his watch.

"By this time they're out on location," he said. When I didn't respond, he shifted his feet and added, "Out by Spanish Lake."

"On location at Spanish Lake?"

"Yes."

"Let's see, that's about five miles out of town. It should take no longer than fifteen minutes to drive there from here. So thirty minutes should be enough time for you to find Mr. Sykes and have him sitting in that chair right across from me."

He looked at me a moment, then nodded.

"I'm sure that'll be no problem," he said.

"Yeah, I bet. That's why he sent you instead of keeping his word. Tell him I said that, too."

Ten minutes later the sheriff, with a file folder open in his hands, came into my office and sat down across from me. He had owned a dry-cleaning business and been president of the local Lions Club before running for sheriff. He wore rimless glasses, and he had soft cheeks that were flecked with blue and red veins. In his green uniform he always made me think of a nursery manager rather than a law officer, but he was an honest and decent man and humble enough to listen to those who had had more experience than he had.

"I got the autopsy and the photographs on that LeBlanc girl," he said. He took off his glasses and pinched the red mark on the bridge of his nose. "You know, I've been doing this stuff five years now, but one like this—"

"When it doesn't bother you anymore, that's when you should start to worry, Sheriff."

"Well, anyway, the report says that most of it was probably done to her after she was dead, poor girl."

"Could I see it?" I said, and reached out my hand for the folder.

I had to swallow when I looked at the photographs, even though I had seen the real thing only yesterday. The killer had not harmed her face. In fact, he had covered it with her blouse, either during the rape or perhaps before he stopped her young heart with an ice pick. But in the fourteen years that I had been with the New Orleans Police Department, or during the three years I had worked on and off for the Iberia Parish sheriff's office, I had seen few cases that involved this degree of violence or rage against a woman's body.

Then I read through the clinical prose describing the autopsy, the nature of the wounds, the sexual penetration of the vagina, the absence of any skin samples under the girl's fingernails, the medical examiner's speculation about the moment and immediate cause of death, and the type of instrument the killer probably used to mutilate the victim.

"Any way you look at it, I guess we're talking about a psychopath or somebody wired to the eyes on crack or acid," the sheriff said.

"Yeah, maybe," I said.

"You think somebody *else* would disembowel a nineteen-year-old girl with a scalpel or a barber's razor?"

"Maybe the guy wants us to think he's a meltdown. He was smart enough not to leave anything at the scene except the ice pick, and it was free of prints. There weren't any prints on the tape he used on her wrists or mouth, either. She went out the front door of the jukejoint, by herself, at one in the morning, when the place was still full of people, and somehow he abducted her, or got her to go with him, between the front door and her automobile, which was parked only a hundred feet away."

His eyes were thoughtful.

"Go on," he said.

"I think she knew the guy."

The sheriff put his glasses back on and scratched at the corner of his mouth with one fingernail.

"She left her purse at the table," I said. "I think she went outside to get something from her car and ran into somebody she knew. Psychopaths don't try to strongarm women in front of bars filled with drunk coonasses and oil-field workers."

"What do we know about the girl?"

I took my notebook out of the desk drawer and thumbed through it on top of the blotter.

"Her mother died when she was twelve. She quit school in the ninth grade and ran away from her father a couple of times in Mamou. She was arrested for prostitution in Lafayette when she was sixteen. For the last year or so she lived here with her grandparents, out at the end of West Main. Her last job was waitressing in a bar about three weeks ago in St. Martinville. Few close friends, if any, no current or recent romantic involvement, at least according to the grandparents. She didn't have a chance for much of a life, did she?"

I could hear the sheriff rubbing his thumb along his jawbone.

"No, she didn't," he said. His eyes went out the window, then refocused on my face. "Do you buy that about no romantic involvement?"

"No."

"Neither do I. Do you have any other theories except that she probably knew her killer?"

"One."

"What?"

"That I'm all wrong, that we *are* dealing with a psychopath or a serial killer."

He stood up to leave. He was overweight, constantly on a diet, and his stomach protruded over his gunbelt, but his erect posture always gave him the appearance of a taller and trimmer man than he actually was.

"I'm glad we operate out of this office with such a sense of certainty, Dave," he said. "Look, I want you to use everything available to us on this one. I want to nail this sonofabitch right through the breastbone."

I nodded, unsure of his intention in stating the obvious.

"That's why we're going to be working with the FBI on this one," he said.

I kept my eyes flat, my hands open and motionless on the desk blotter.

"You called them?" I said.

"I did, and so did the mayor. It's a kidnapping as well as a rape and murder, Dave."

"Yeah, that could be the case."

"You don't like the idea of working with these guys?"

"You don't *work* with the feds, sheriff. You take orders from them. If you're lucky, they won't treat you like an insignificant local douche bag in front of a television camera. It's a great learning exercise in humility."

"No one can ever accuse you of successfully hiding your feelings, Dave."

ALMOST THIRTY MINUTES from the moment the attorney, Oliver Montrose, had left my office, I looked out my window and saw Elrod T. Sykes pull his lavender Cadillac into a no-parking zone, scrape his white-walls against the curb, and step out into the bright sunlight. He wore brown striped slacks, shades, and a lemon-yellow short-sleeve shirt. The attorney got out on the passenger's side, but Sykes gestured for him to stay where he was. They argued briefly, then Sykes walked into the building by himself.

He had his shades in his hand when he stepped inside my office door, his hair wet and freshly combed, an uneasy grin at the corner of his mouth.

"Sit down a minute, please," I said.

The skin around his eyes was pale with hangover. He sat down and touched at his temple as though it were bruised.

"I'm sorry about sending the mercenary. It wasn't my idea," he said.

"Whose was it?"

"Mikey figures he makes the decisions on anything that affects the picture."

"How old are you, Mr. Sykes?"

He widened his eyes and crimped his lips.

"Forty. Well, actually forty-three," he said.

"Did you have to ask that man's permission to drive an automobile while you were drunk?"

He blinked as though I'd struck him, then made a wet noise in his throat and wiped his mouth with the backs of his fingers.

"I really don't know what to say to you," he said. He had a peculiar, north Texas accent, husky, slightly nasal, like he had a dime-sized piece of melting ice in his cheek. "I broke my word, I'm aware of that. But I'm letting other people down, too, Mr. Robicheaux. It costs ten thousand dollars an hour when you have to keep a hundred people standing around while a guy like me gets out of trouble."

"I hope y'all work it out."

"I guess this is the wrong place to look for aspirin and sympathy, isn't it?"

"A sheriff's deputy from St. Mary Parish is going to meet us with a boat at the Chitimacha Indian reservation, Mr. Sykes. I think he's probably waiting on us right now."

"Well, actually I'm looking forward to it. Did I tell you last night my grandpa was a Texas Ranger?"

"No, you didn't." I looked at my watch.

"Well, it's a fact, he was. He worked with Frank Hammer, the ranger who got Bonnie and Clyde right up there at Arcadia, Louisiana." He smiled at me. "You know what he used to tell me when I was a kid? 'Son, you got two speeds—wide-open and fuck it.' I swear he was a pistol. He—"

"I'd like to explain something to you. I don't want you to take offense at it, either."

"Yes, sir?"

"Yesterday somebody raped and murdered a nineteen-year-old girl on the south side of the parish. He cut her breasts off, he pulled her entrails out of her stomach, he pushed twigs up her vagina. I don't like waiting in my office for you to show up when it's convenient, I'm not interested in your film company's production problems, and on this particular morning I'd appreciate it if you'd leave your stories about your family history to your publicity people."

His eyes tried to hold on mine, then they watered and glanced away.

"I'd like to use your bathroom, please," he said. "I'm afraid I got up with a case of the purple butterflies."

"I'll be out front. I'll see you there in two minutes, Mr. Sykes."

The sky was bright and hazy, the wind hot as a flame as we drove toward the Atchafalaya River. I had to stop the truck twice to let Elrod Sykes vomit by the side of the road.

IT FELT STRANGE to go back into that part of the Atchafalaya Basin after so many years. In July of 1957, after the hurricane had passed through and the rains had finally stopped, the flooded woods and willow islands, the canals whose canopies were so thick that sunlight seldom struck the water, the stretches of beach along the bays had smelled of death for weeks. The odor, which was like the heavy, gray, salty stench from a decaying rat, hung in the heat all day, and at night it blew through the screen windows on the quarter-boat and awaited you in the morning when you walked through the galley into the dining room.

Many of the animals that did not drown starved to death. Coons used to climb up the mooring ropes and scratch on the galley screen for food, and often we'd take rabbits out of the tops of trees that barely extended above the current and carry them on the jugboat to the levee at Charenton. Sometimes at night huge trees with root systems as broad as barn roofs floated by in the dark and scraped the hull with their branches from the bow to the stern. One night when the moon was full and yellow and low over the willow islands, I heard something hit the side of the boat hard, like a big wood fist rolling its knuckles along the planks. I stood on my bunk and looked through the screen window and saw a houseboat, upside down, spinning in the current, a tangle of fishing nets strung out of one window like flotsam from an eye socket.

I thought about the hundreds of people who had either been crushed under a tidal wave or drowned in Cameron Parish, their bodies washed deep into the marshes along the Calcasieu River, and again I smelled that thick, fetid odor on the wind. I could not sleep again until the sun rose like a red molten ball through the mists across the bay.

It didn't take us long to find the willow island where Elrod Sykes said he had seen the skeletal remains of either an Indian or a black person. We crossed the wide sweep of the Atchafalaya in a sheriff's department boat with two outboard engines mounted on the stern, took a channel between a row of sandbars whose sun-dried crests looked like the backs of dolphin jumping in a school, crossed a long bay, and slid the boat onto a narrow strip of beach that bled back into a thick stand of willow trees and chains of flooded sinkholes and sand bogs.

Elrod Sykes stepped off the bow onto the sand and stared into the trees. He had taken off his shirt and he used it to wipe the sweat off his tanned chest and shoulders.

"It's back in yonder," he said, and pointed. "You can see my footprints where I went in to take a whiz."

The St. Mary Parish deputy fitted a cloth cap on his head and sprayed his face, neck, and arms with mosquito dope, then handed the can to me.

"If I was you, I'd put my shirt on, Mr. Sykes," he said. "We used to have a lot of bats down here. Till the mosquitoes ate them all."

Sykes smiled good-naturedly and waited for his turn to use the can of repellent.

"I bet you won't believe this," the deputy said, "but it's been so dry here on occasion that I seen a catfish walking down the levee carrying his own canteen."

Sykes's eyes crinkled at the corners, then he walked ahead of us into the gloom, his loafers sinking deep into the wet sand.

"That boy's a long way from his Hollywood poontang, ain't he?" the deputy said behind me.

"How about putting the cork in the humor for a while?" I said.

"What?"

"The man grew up down South. You're patronizing him."

"I'm wha—"

I walked ahead of him and caught up with Sykes just as he stepped out of the willows into a shallow, water-filled depression between the woods and a sandbar. The water was stagnant and hot and smelled of dead garfish.

"There," he said. "Right under the roots of that dead tree. I told y'all."

A barkless, sun-bleached cypress tree lay crossways in a sandbar, the water-smooth trunk eaten by worms, and gathered inside the root system, as though held by a gnarled hand, was a skeleton crimped in an embryonic position, wrapped in a web of dried algae and river trash.

The exposed bone was polished and weathered almost black, but sections of the skin had dried to the color and texture of desiccated leather. Just as Sykes had said, a thick chain encased with rust was wrapped around the arms and rib cage. The end links were fastened with a padlock as wide as my hand.

I tore a willow branch off a tree, shucked off the leaves with my Puma knife, and knelt down in front of the skeleton.

"How do you reckon it got up under those roots?" Sykes said.

"A bad hurricane came through here in '57," I said. "Trees like this were torn out of the ground like carrots. My bet is this man's body got caught under some floating trees and was covered up later in this sandbar."

Sykes knelt beside me.

"I don't understand," he said. "How do you know it happened in '57? Hurricanes tear up this part of the country all the time, don't they?"

"Good question, podna," I said, and I used the willow branch to peel away the dried web of algae from around one shinbone, then the other.

"That left one's clipped in half," Sykes said.

"Yep. That's where he was shot when he tried to run away from two white men."

"You clairvoyant or something?" Sykes said.

"No, I saw it happen. About a mile from here."

"You saw it happen?" Sykes said.

"Yep."

"What's going on here?" the deputy said behind us. "You saying some white people lynched somebody or something?"

"Yeah, that's exactly what I'm saying. When we get back we'll need to talk to your sheriff and get your medical examiner out here."

"I don't know about y'all over in Iberia Parish, but nobody around here's going to be real interested in nigger trouble that's thirty-five years old," the deputy said.

I worked the willow branch around the base of the bones and peeled back a skein of algae over the legs, the pelvic bones, and the crown of the skull, which still had a section of grizzled black hair attached to the pate. I poked at the corrugated, blackened work boots and the strips of rag that hung off the pelvis.

I put down the branch and chewed on the corner of my thumbnail.

"What are you looking for, Mr. Robicheaux?" Sykes said.

"It's not what's there, it's what isn't," I said. "He wasn't wearing a belt on his trousers, and his boots have no laces."

"Sonofabitch probably did his shopping at the Goodwill. Big fucking deal," the deputy said, slapped a mosquito on his neck, and looked at the red and black paste on his palm.

LATER THAT AFTERNOON I went back to work on the case of the murdered girl, whose full name was Cherry LeBlanc. No one knew the whereabouts of her father, who had disappeared from Mamou after he was accused of molesting a black child in his neighborhood, but I interviewed her grandparents again, the owner of the bar in St. Martinville where she had last worked, the girls she had been with in the clapboard jukejoint the night she died, and a police captain in Lafayette who had recommended probation for her after she had been busted on the prostitution charge. I learned little about her except that she seemed to have been an uneducated, unskilled, hapless, and fatally beautiful girl who thought she could be a viable player in a crap game where the dice for her kind were always shaved.

I learned that about her and the fact that she had loved zydeco music and had gone to the jukejoint to hear Sam "Hogman" Patin play his harmonica and bottleneck blues twelve-string guitar.

My desk was covered with scribbled notes from my note pad, morgue and crime-scene photos, interview cassettes, and Xeroxes from the LeBlanc family's welfare case history when the sheriff walked into my office. The sky outside was lavender and pink now, and the fronds on the palm trees out by the sidewalk were limp in the heat and silhouetted darkly against the late sun.

"The sheriff over in St. Mary Parish just called," he said.

"Yes?"

"He said thanks a lot. They really appreciate the extra work." He sat on the corner of my desk.

"Tell him to find another line of work."

"He said you're welcome to come over on your days off and run the investigation."

"What's he doing with it?"

"Their coroner's got the bones now. But I'll tell you the truth, Dave, I don't think it's going anywhere."

I leaned back in my swivel chair and drummed

my fingers on my desk. My eyes burned and my back hurt.

"It seems to me you've been vindicated," the sheriff said. "Let it go for now."

"We'll see."

"Look, I know you've got a big workload piled on you right now, but I've got a problem I need you to look into when you have a chance. Like maybe first thing tomorrow morning."

I looked back at him without speaking.

"Baby Feet Balboni," he said.

"What about him?"

"He's in New Iberia. At the Holiday Inn, with about six of his fellow greaseballs and their whores. The manager called me from a phone booth down the street he was so afraid one of them would hear him."

"I don't know what I can do about it," I said.

"We need to know what he's doing in town."

"He grew up here."

"Look, Dave, they can't even handle this guy in New Orleans. He cannibalized half the Giacano and Cardo families to get where he is. He's not coming back here. That's not going to happen."

I rubbed my face. My whiskers felt stiff against my palm.

"You want me to send somebody else?" the sheriff asked.

"No, that's all right."

"Y'all were friends in high school for a while, weren't you?"

"We played ball together, that's all."

I gazed out the window at the lengthening shadows. He studied my face.

"What's the matter, Dave?"

"It's nothing."

"You bothered because we want to bounce a baseball buddy out of town?"

"No, not really."

"Did you ever hear that story about what he did to Didi Giacano's cousin? Supposedly he hung him from his colon by a meat hook."

"I've heard that same story about a half-dozen wiseguys in Orleans and Jefferson parishes. It's an old N.O.P.D. heirloom."

"Probably just bad press, huh?"

"I always tried to think of Julie as nine-tenths thespian," I said.

"Yeah, and gorilla shit tastes like chocolate ice cream. Dave, you're a laugh a minute."

CHAPTER 3

JULIE BALBONI LOOKED just like his father, who had owned most of the slot and racehorse machines in Iberia Parish during the 1940s and, with an Assyrian family, had run the gambling and prostitution in the Underpass area of Lafayette. Julie was already huge, six and a half feet tall, when he was in the eleventh grade, thick across the hips and tapered at both ends like a fat banana, with tiny ankles and size-seven feet and a head as big as a buffalo's. A year later he filled out in serious proportions. That was also the year he was arrested for burglarizing a liquor store. His father walked him out into the woods at gunpoint and whipped the skin off his back with the nozzle end of a garden hose.

His hair grew on his head like black snakes, and because a physician had injured a nerve in his face when he was delivered, the corner of his mouth would sometimes droop involuntarily and give him a lewd or leering expression that repelled most girls. He farted in class, belched during the Pledge of Allegiance, combed his dandruff out on top of the desk, and addressed anyone he didn't like by gathering up his scrotum and telling them to bite. We walked around him in the halls and the locker room. His teachers were secretly relieved when his mother and father did not show up on parents' night.

His other nickname was Julie the Bone, although it wasn't used to his face, because he went regularly to Mabel White's Negro brothel in Crowley and the Negro cribs on Hopkins Avenue in New Iberia.

But Julie had two uncontested talents. He was both a great kick boxer and a great baseball catcher. His ankles twisted too easily for him to play football; he was too fat to run track; but with one flick of a thick thigh he could leave a kick-box opponent heaving blood, and behind the plate he could steal the ball out of the batter's swing or vacuum a wild pitch out of the dust and zip the ball to third base like a BB.

In my last time out as a high school pitcher, I was going into the bottom of the ninth against Abbeville with a shutout almost in my pocket. It was a soft, pink evening, with the smell of flowers and freshly cut grass in the air. Graduation was only three weeks away, and we all felt that we were painted with magic and that the spring season had been created as a song especially for us. Innocence, a lock on the future, the surge of victory in the loins, the confirmation of a girl's kiss among the dusky oak trees, like a strawberry bursting against the roof of the mouth, were all most assuredly our due.

We even felt an acceptance and camaraderie toward Baby Feet. Imminent graduation and the laurels of a winning season seemed to have melted away the differences in our backgrounds and experience.

Then their pitcher, a beanballer who used his elbows, knees, and spikes in a slide, hit a double and stole third base. Baby Feet called time and jogged out to the mound, sweat leaking out of his inverted cap. He rubbed up a new ball for me.

"Put it in the dirt. I'm gonna let that cocksucker have his chance," he said.

"I don't know if that's smart, Feet," I said.

"I've called a shutout for you so far, haven't I? Do what I tell you."

On the next pitch I glanced at the runner, then fired low and outside, into the dirt. Baby Feet vacuumed it up, then spun around, throwing dust in the air like an elephant, and raced toward the backstop as though the ball had gotten past him.

The runner charged from third. Suddenly Baby Feet reappeared at the plate, the ball never having left his hand, his mask still on his face. The runner realized that he had stepped into it and he tried to bust up Baby Feet in the slide by throwing one spiked shoe up in Feet's face. Baby Feet caught the runner's spikes in his mask, tagged him across the head with the ball, then, when it was completely unnecessary at that point, razored his own spikes into the boy's ankle and twisted.

The players on the field, the coaches, the people in the stands, stared numbly at home plate. Baby

Feet calmly scraped his spikes clean in the sand, then knelt and tightened the strap on a shin guard, his face cool and detached as he squinted up at the flag snapping on a metal pole behind the backstop.

IT WASN'T HARD to find him at the Holiday Inn. He and his entourage were the only people in and around the swimming pool. Their tanned bodies glistened as though they had rubbed them with melted butter. They wore wraparound sunglasses that were as black as a blind man's, reclined luxuriously on deck chairs, their genitalia sculpted against their bikinis, or floated on rubber mattresses, tropical drinks in holders at their sides, a glaze of suntan oil emanating from the points of their fingers and toes.

A woman came out the sliding door of a room with her two children, walked them to the wading pool, then obviously realized the nature of the company she was keeping; she looked around distractedly, as though she heard invisible birds cawing at her, and returned quickly to her room with her children's hands firmly in hers.

Julie the Bone hadn't changed a great deal since I had last seen him seven years ago in New Orleans. His eyes, which were like black marbles, were set a little more deeply in his face; his wild tangle of hair was flecked in places with gray; but his barrel chest and his washtub of a stomach still seemed to have the tone and texture of whale hide. When you looked at the ridges of scar tissue under the hair on his shoulders and back where his father had beaten him, at the nests of tendons and veins in his neck, and the white protrusion of knuckles in his huge hands, you had the feeling that nothing short of a wrecking ball, swung by a cable from a great height, could adequately deal with this man if he should choose to destroy everything in his immediate environment.

He raised himself on one elbow from his reclining chair, pushed his sunglasses up on his hair, and squinted through the haze at me as I approached him. Two of his men sat next to him at a glass table under an umbrella, playing cards with a woman with bleached hair and skin that was so tan it looked like folds of soft leather. Both men put down their cards and got to their feet, and one of them, who looked as though he were hammered together from boilerplate, stepped directly into my path. His hair was orange and gray, flattened in damp curls on his head, and there were pachuco crosses tattooed on the backs of his hands. I opened my seersucker coat so he could see the badge clipped to my belt. But recognition was already working in his face.

"What's happening, Cholo?" I said.

"Hey, Lieutenant, how you doin'?" he said, then turned to Baby Feet. "Hey, Julie, it's Lieutenant Robicheaux. From the First District in New Orleans. You remember him when—"

"Yeah, I know who it is, Cholo," Baby Feet said, smiling and nodding at me. "What you up to, Dave? Somebody knock a pop fly over the swimming-pool wall?"

"I was just in the neighborhood. I heard you were back in town for a short visit."

"No kidding?"

"That's a fact."

"You were probably in the barbershop and somebody said, 'The Bone's in town,' and you thought, 'Boy, that's great news. I'll just go say hello to ole Feet.' "

"You're a famous man, Julie. Word gets around."

"And I'm just here for a short visit, right?"

"Yeah, that's the word."

His eyes moved up and down my body. He smiled to himself and took a sip from a tall glass wrapped in a napkin, with shaved ice, fruit, and a tiny paper umbrella in it.

"You're a sheriff's detective now, I hear."

"On and off."

He pushed a chair at me with his foot, then picked it up and set it in a shady area across from him. I took off my seersucker coat, folded it on my arm, and sat down.

"Y'all worried about me, Dave?"

"Some people in New Iberia think you're a hard act to follow. How many guys would burn down their own father's nightclub?"

He laughed.

"Yeah, the old man lost his interest in garden hoses after that," he said.

"Everybody likes to come back to his hometown once in a while. That's a perfectly natural thing to do. No one's worried about that, Julie." I looked at his eyes. Under his sweaty brows, they were as shiny and full of light as obsidian.

He shook a cigarette out of a package on the cement and lit it. He blew smoke out into the sunlight and looked around the swimming-pool area.

"Except I've only got a visa, right?" he said. "I'm supposed to spread a little money around, stay on the back streets, tell my crew not to spit on the sidewalks or blow their noses on their napkins in the restaurants. Does that kind of cover it for you, Dave?"

"It's a small town with small-town problems."

"Fuck." He took a deep breath, then twisted his neck as though there were a crick in it. "Margot—" he said to the woman playing cards under the umbrella. She got up from her chair and stood behind him, her narrow face expressionless behind her sunglasses, and began kneading his neck with her fingers. He filled his mouth with ice, orange slices, and cherries from his glass and studied my face while he chewed.

"I get a little upset at these kind of attitudes, Dave. You got to forgive me," he said, and pointed into his breastbone with his fingertips. "But it don't seem to matter sometimes what a guy does *now*. It's always *yesterday* that's in people's minds. Like Cholo here. He made a mistake fifteen years ago and we're still hearing about it. What the fuck is that? You think that's fair?"

"He threw his brother-in-law off the roof of the Jax's brewery on top of a Mardi Gras float. That was a first even for New Orleans."

"Hey, Lieutenant, there was a lot of other things involved there. The guy beat up my sister. He was a fucking animal."

"Look, Dave, you been gone from New Orleans for a long time," Baby Feet said. "The city ain't anything like it used to be. Black kids with shit for brains are provoking everybody in the fucking town. People get killed in Audubon Park, for God's sake. You try to get on the St. Charles streetcar and there's either niggers or Japs hanging out the doors and windows. We used to have understandings with the city. Everybody knew the rules, nobody got hurt. Take a walk past the Desire or St. Thomas project and see what happens."

"What's the point, Julie?"

"The point is who the fuck needs it? I own a recording studio, the same place Jimmy Clanton cut his first record. I'm in the entertainment business. I talk on the phone every day to people in California you read about in *People* magazine. I come home to this shithole, they ought to have 'Welcome Back Balboni Day.' Instead, I get told maybe I'm like a bad smell in the air. You understand what I'm saying, that hurts me."

I rubbed one palm against the other.

"I'm just a messenger," I said.

"That laundry man you work for send you?"

"He has his concerns."

He waved the woman away and sat up in his chair.

"Give me five minutes to get dressed. Then I want you to drive me somewhere," he said.

"I'm a little tied up on time right now."

"I'm asking fifteen minutes of you, max. You think you can give me that much of your day, Dave?" He got up and started past me to his room. There were tufts of black hair like pig bristles on his love handles. He cocked his index finger at me. "Be here when I get back. You won't regret it."

The woman with the bleached hair sat back down at the table. She took off her glasses, parted her legs a moment, and looked into my face, her eyes neither flirtatious nor hostile, simply dead. Cholo invited me to play gin rummy with them.

"Thanks, I never took it up," I said.

"You sure took it up with horses, lieutenant," he said.

"Yep, horses and Beam. They always made an interesting combination at the Fairgrounds."

"Hey, you remember that time you lent me twenty bucks to get home from Jefferson Downs? I always remember that, Loot. That was all right."

Cholo Manelli had been born of a Mexican washerwoman, who probably wished she had given birth to a bowling ball instead, and fathered by a brain-damaged Sicilian numbers runner, whose head had been caved in by a cop's baton in the Irish Channel. He was raised in the Iberville welfare project across from the old St. Louis cemeteries, and at age eleven was busted with his brothers for rolling and beating the winos who slept in the empty crypts. Their weapons of choice had been sand-filled socks.

He had the coarse, square hands of a bricklayer,

the facial depth of a pie plate. I always suspected that if he was lobotomized you wouldn't know the difference. The psychiatrists at Mandeville diagnosed him as a sociopath and shot his head full of electricity. Evidently the treatment had as much effect as charging a car battery with three dead cells. On his first jolt at Angola he was put in with the big stripes, the violent and the incorrigible, back in the days when the state used trusty guards, mounted on horses and armed with double-barrel twelve-gauge shotguns, who had to serve the time of any inmate who escaped while under their supervision. Cholo went to the bushes and didn't come back fast enough for the trusty gunbull. The gunbull put four pieces of buckshot in Cholo's back. Two weeks later a Mason jar of prune-o was found in the gunbull's cell. A month after that, when he was back in the main population, somebody dropped the loaded bed of a dump truck on his head.

"Julie told me about the time that boon almost popped you with a .38," he said.

"What time was that?"

"When you were a patrolman. In the Quarter. Julie said he saved your life."

"He did, huh?"

Cholo shrugged his shoulders.

"That's what the man said, Lieutenant. What do I know?"

"Take the hint, Cholo. Our detective isn't a conversationalist," the woman said, without removing her eyes from her cards. She clacked her lacquered nails on the glass tabletop, and her lips made a dry, sucking sound when she puffed on her cigarette.

"You working on that murder case? The one about that girl?" he said.

"How'd you know about that?"

His eyes clicked sideways.

"It was in the newspaper," he said. "Julie and me was talking about it this morning. Something like that's disgusting. You got a fucking maniac on the loose around here. Somebody ought to take him to a hospital and kill him."

Baby Feet emerged resplendent from the sliding glass door of his room. He wore a white suit with gray pinstripes, a purple shirt scrolled with gray flowers, a half-dozen gold chains and medallions around his talcumed neck, tasseled loafers that seemed as small on his feet as ballet slippers.

"You look beautiful, Julie," Cholo said.

"Fucking A," Baby Feet said, lighting the cigarette in the corner of his mouth with a tiny gold lighter.

"Can I go with y'all?" Cholo asked.

"Keep an eye on things here for me."

"Hey, you told me last night I could go."

"I need you to take my calls."

"Margot don't know how to pick up a phone anymore?" Cholo said.

"My meter's running, Julie," I said.

"We're going out to dinner tonight with some interesting people," Baby Feet said to Cholo. "You'll enjoy it. Be patient."

"They're quite excited about the possibility of

meeting you. They called and said that, Cholo," the woman said.

"Margot, why is it you got calluses on your back? Somebody been putting starch in your sheets or something?" Cholo said.

I started walking toward my truck. The sunlight off the cement by the poolside was blinding. Baby Feet caught up with me. One of his other women dove off the board and splashed water and the smell of chlorine and suntan oil across my back.

"Hey, I live in a fucking menagerie," Baby Feet said as we went out onto the street. "Don't go walking off from me with your nose bent out of joint. Did I ever treat you with a lack of respect?"

I got in the truck.

"Where we going, Feet?" I said.

"Out by Spanish Lake. Look, I want you to take a message back to the man you work for. I'm not the source of any problems you got around here. The coke you got in this parish has been stepped on so many times it's baby powder. If it was coming from some people I've been associated with in New Orleans—and I'm talking about past associations, you understand—it'd go from your nose to your brain like liquid Drano."

I headed out toward the old two-lane highway that led to the little settlement of Burke and the lake where Spanish colonists had tried to establish plantations in the eighteenth century and had given Iberia Parish its name.

"I don't work narcotics, Julie, and I'm not good

at passing on bullshit, either. My main concern right now is the girl we found south of town."

"Oh, yeah? What girl's that?"

"The murdered girl, Cherry LeBlanc."

"I don't guess I heard about it."

I turned and looked at him. He gazed idly out the window at the passing oak trees on the edge of town and a roadside watermelon and strawberry stand.

"You don't read the local papers?" I said.

"I been busy. You saying I talk bullshit, Dave?"

"Put it this way, Feet. If you've got something to tell the sheriff, do it yourself."

He pinched his nose, then blew air through it.

"We used to be friends, Dave. I even maybe did you a little favor once. So I'm going to line it out for you and any of the locals who want to clean the wax out of their ears. The oil business is still in the toilet and your town's flat-ass broke. Frankly, in my opinion, it deserves anything that happens to it. But me and all those people you see back on that lake—" He pointed out the window. Through a pecan orchard, silhouetted against the light winking off the water, I could see cameras mounted on booms and actors in Confederate uniforms toiling through the shallows in retreat from imaginary federal troops. "We're going to leave around ten million dollars in Lafayette and Iberia Parish. They don't like the name Balboni around here, tell them we can move the whole fucking operation over to Mississippi. See how that floats with some of those coonass jackoffs in the Chamber of Commerce."

"You're telling me you're in the movie business?"

"Coproducer with Michael Goldman. What do you think of that?"

I turned into the dirt road that led through the pecan trees to the lake.

"I'm sure everyone wishes you success, Julie."

"I'm going to make a baseball movie next. You want a part in it?" He smiled at me.

"I don't think I'd be up to it."

"Hey, Dave, don't get me wrong." He was grinning broadly now. "But my main actor sees dead people out in the mist, his punch is usually ripped by nine A.M. on weed or whites, and Mikey's got peptic ulcers and some kind of obsession with the Holocaust. Dave, I ain't shitting you, I mean this sincerely, with no offense, with your record, you could fit right in."

I stopped the truck by a small wood-frame security office. A wiry man in a khaki uniform and a bill cap, with a white scar like a chicken's foot on his throat, approached my window.

"We'll see you, Feet," I said.

"You don't want to look around?"

"Adios, partner," I said, waited for him to close the door, then turned around in the weeds and drove back through the pecan trees to the highway, the sun's reflection bouncing on my hood like a yellow balloon.

IT HAPPENED MY second year on the New Orleans police force, when I was a patrolman in the

French Quarter and somebody called in a prowler report at an address on Dumaine. The lock on the iron gate was rusted and had been bent out of the jamb with a bar and sprung back on the hinges. Down the narrow brick walkway I could see bits of broken glass, like tiny rat's teeth, where someone had broken out the overhead lightbulb. But the courtyard ahead was lighted, filled with the waving shadows of banana trees and palm fronds, and I could hear a baseball game playing on a radio or television set.

I slipped my revolver out of its holster and moved along the coolness of the bricks, through a trickling pool of water, to the entrance of the courtyard, where a second scrolled-iron gate yawned back on its hinges. I could smell the damp earth in the flower beds, spearmint growing against a stucco wall, the thick clumps of purple wisteria that hung from a tile roof.

Then I smelled *him*, even before I saw him, an odor that was at once like snuff, synthetic wine, rotting teeth, and stomach bile. He was a huge black man, dressed in a Donald Duck T-shirt, filthy tennis shoes, and a pair of purple slacks that were bursting on his thighs. In his left hand was a drawstring bag filled with goods from the apartment he'd just creeped. He swung the gate with all his weight into my hand, snapped something in it like a Popsicle stick breaking, and sent my revolver skidding across the flagstones.

I tried to get my baton loose, but it was his show now. He came out of his back pocket with a worn one-inch .38, the grips wrapped with black electrician's tape, and screwed the barrel into my ear. There was a dark clot of blood in his right eye, and his breath slid across the side of my face like an unwashed hand.

"Get back in the walkway, motherfucker," he whispered.

We stumbled backward into the gloom. I could hear revelers out on the street, a beer can tinkling along the cement.

"Don't be a dumb guy," I said.

"Shut up," he said. Then, almost as an angry afterthought, he drove my head into the bricks. I fell to my knees in the water, my baton twisted uselessly in my belt.

His eyes were dilated, his hair haloed with sweat, his pulse leaping in his neck. He was a cop's worst possible adversary in that situation—strung-out, frightened, and stupid enough to carry a weapon on a simple B & E.

"Why'd you have to come along, man? Why'd you have to do that?" he said.

His thumb curled around the spur of the pistol's hammer and I heard the cylinder rotate and the chamber lock into place.

"There're cops on both ends of the street," I said. "You won't get out of the Quarter."

"Don't say no more, man. It won't do no good. You messed everything up."

He wiped the sweat out of his eyes, blew out his breath, and pointed the pistol downward at my chest.

Baby Feet had on only a bathrobe, his Jockey underwear, and a pair of loafers without socks when he appeared in the brick walkway behind the black man.

"What the fuck do you think you're doing here?" he said.

The black man stepped back, the revolver drifting to his thigh.

"Mr. Julie?" he said.

"Yeah. What the fuck you doing? You creeping an apartment in my building?"

"I didn't know you was living here, Mr. Julie."

Baby Feet took the revolver out of the black man's hand and eased down the hammer.

"Walter, if I want to, I can make you piss blood for six months," he said.

"Yes, suh, I knows that."

"I'm glad you've taken that attitude. Now, you get your sorry ass out of here." He pushed the black man toward the entrance. "Go on." He kept nudging the black man along the bricks, then he kicked him hard, as fast as a snake striking, between the buttocks. "I said go on, now." He kicked him again, his small pointed shoe biting deep into the man's crotch. Tears welled up in the man's eyes as he looked back over his shoulder. "Move it, Walter, unless you want balls the size of coconuts."

The black man limped down the Dumaine. Baby Feet stood in front of the sprung gate, dumped the shells from the .38 on the sidewalk, and flung the .38 into the darkness after the black man.

"Come on upstairs and I'll put your hand in some ice," he said.

I had found my hat and revolver.

"I'm going after that guy," I said.

"Pick him up in the morning. He shines shoes in a barbershop on Calliope and St. Charles. You sure you want to stay in this line of work, Dave?"

He laughed, lit a purple-and-gold cigarette, and put his round, thick arm over my shoulders.

The sheriff was right: Baby Feet might be a movie producer, but he could never be dismissed as a thespian.

CHAPTER 4

MY BRIEF VISIT with Julie Balboni should have been a forgettable and minor interlude in my morning. Instead, my conversation with him in the truck had added a disturbing question mark in the murder of Cherry LeBlanc. He said he had heard nothing about it, nor had he read about it in the local newspaper. This was ten minutes after Cholo Manelli had told me that he and Baby Feet had been talking about the girl's death earlier.

Was Baby Feet lying or was he simply not interested in talking about something that wasn't connected with his well-being? Or had the electroshock therapists in Mandeville overheated Cholo's brain pan?

My experience with members of the Mafia and sociopaths in general has been that they lie as a matter of course. They are convincing because they often lie when there is no need to. To apply some form of forensic psychology in attempting to understand how they think is as productive as placing your head inside a microwave oven in order to study the nature of electricity.

I spent the rest of the day retracing the geography of Cherry LeBlanc's last hours and trying to re-create the marginal world in which she had lived. At three that afternoon I parked my truck in the shade by the old wood-frame church in St. Martinville and looked at a color photograph of her that had been given to me by the grandparents. Her hair was black, with a mahogany tint in it, her mouth bright red with too much lipstick, her face soft, slightly plump with baby fat; her dark eyes were bright and masked no hidden thought; she was smiling.

Busted at sixteen for prostitution, dead at nineteen, I thought. And that's what we knew about. God only knew what else had befallen her in her life. But she wasn't born a prostitute or the kind of girl who would be passed from hand to hand until someone opened a car door for her and drove her deep into a woods, where he revealed to her the instruments of her denouement, perhaps even convinced her that this moment was one she had elected for herself.

Others had helped her get there. My first vote would be for the father, the child molester, in Mamou. But our legal system looks at nouns, seldom at adverbs.

I gazed at the spreading oaks in the church's graveyard, where Evangeline and her lover Gabriel were buried. The tombstones were stained with lichen and looked cool and gray in the shade. Beyond the trees, the sun reflected off Bayou Teche like a yellow flame.

Where was the boyfriend in this? I thought. A girl that pretty either has a beau or there is somebody in her life who would like to be one. She hadn't gone far in school, but necessity must have given her a survivor's instinct about people, about men in particular, certainly about the variety who drifted in and out of a south Louisiana jukejoint.

She had to know her killer. I was convinced of that.

I walked to the bar, a ramshackle nineteenth-century wooden building with scaling paint and a sagging upstairs gallery. The inside was dark and cool and almost deserted. A fat black woman was scrubbing the front windows with a brush and a bucket of soap and water. I walked the length of the bar to the small office in back where I had found the owner before. Along the counter in front of the bar's mirror were rows upon rows of bottles—dark green and slender, stoppered with wet corks; obsidian black with arterial-red wax seals; frosted-white, like ice sawed out of a lake; whiskey-brown, singing with heat and light.

The smell of the green sawdust on the floor, the wood-handled beer taps dripping through an aluminum grate, the Collins mix and the bowls of cherries and sliced limes and oranges, they were only the stuff of memory, I told myself, swallowing. They belong to your Higher Power now. Just like an old girlfriend who winks at you on the street one day, I thought. You already gave her up. You just walk on by. It's that easy.

But you don't think about it, you don't think about it, you don't think about it.

The owner was a preoccupied man who combed his black hair straight back on his narrow head and kept his comb clipped inside his shirt pocket. The receipts and whiskey invoices on his desk were a magnet for his eyes. My questions couldn't compete. He kept running his tongue behind his teeth while I talked.

"So you didn't know anything about her friends?" I said.

"No, sir. She was here three weeks. They come and they go. That's the way it is. I don't know what else to tell you."

"Do you know anything about your bartenders?"

His eyes focused on a spot inside his cigarette smoke.

"I'm not understanding you," he said.

"Do you hire a bartender who hangs around with ex-cons or who's in a lot of debt? I suspect you probably don't. Those are the kind of guys who set up their friends with free doubles or make change out of an open drawer without ringing up the sale, aren't they?"

"What's your point?"

"Did you know she had been arrested for prostitution?"

"I didn't know that."

"You hired her because you thought she was an honor student at USL?"

The corner of his mouth wrinkled slightly with the beginnings of a smile. He stirred the ashes in the ashtray with the tip of his cigarette.

"I'll leave you my card and a thought, Mr.

Trajan. One way or another we're going to nail the guy who killed her. In the meantime, if he kills somebody else and I find out that you held back information on me, I'll be back with a warrant for your arrest."

"I don't care for the way you're talking to me."

I left his office without replying and walked back down the length of the bar. The black woman was now outside, washing the front window. She put down her scrub brush, flung the whole bucket of soapy water on the glass, then began rinsing it off with a hose. Her skin was the color of burnt brick, her eyes turquoise, her breasts sagging like water-filled balloons inside her cotton-print dress. I opened my badge in my palm.

"Did you know the white girl Cherry LeBlanc?" I asked.

"She worked here, ain't she?" She squinted her eyes against the water spray bouncing off the glass.

"Do you know if she had a boyfriend, *tante*?"

"If that's what you want to call it."

"What do you mean?" I asked, already knowing the answer that I didn't want to hear.

"She in the bidness."

"Full time, in a serious way?"

"What you call sellin' out of your pants?"

"Was Mr. Trajan involved?"

"Ax him."

"I don't think he was, otherwise you wouldn't be telling me these things, *tante*." I smiled at her.

She began refilling the bucket with clear water. She suddenly looked tired.

"She a sad girl," she said. She wiped the perspiration off her round face with her palm and looked at it. "I tole her they ain't no amount of money gonna he'p her when some man make her sick, no. I tole her a pretty white girl like her can have anything she want—school, car, a husband wit' a job on them oil rig. When that girl dress up, she look like a movie star. She say, 'Jennifer, some people is suppose' to have only what other people let them have.' Lord God, her age and white and believing somet'ing like that."

"Who was her pimp, Jennifer?"

"They come here for her."

"Who?"

"The mens. When they want her. They come here and take her home."

"Do you know who they were, their names?"

"Them kind ain't got no names. They just drive their car up when she get off work and that po' girl get in."

"I see. All right, Jennifer, this is my card with my telephone number on it. Would you call me if you remember anything else that might help me?"

"I don't be knowin' anything else, me. She wasn't goin' to give the name of some rich white man to an old nigger."

"What white man?"

"That's what I tellin' you. I don't know, me."

"I'm sorry, I don't understand what you're saying."

"You don't understand English, you? Where you from? She say they a rich white man maybe gonna get her out of sellin' jellyroll. She say that the last time I seen her, right befo' somebody do them awful t'ings to that young girl. Mister, when they in the bidness, every man got a sweet word in his mouth, every man got a special way to keep jellyroll in his bed and the dollar in his pocket."

She threw the bucket of clear water on the glass, splashing both of us, then walked heavily with her brushes, cleaning rags, and empty bucket down the alley next to the bar.

THE RAIN FELL through the canopy of oaks as I drove down the dirt road along the bayou toward my house. During the summer it rains almost every afternoon in southern Louisiana. From my gallery, around three o'clock, you could watch the clouds build as high and dark as mountains out on the Gulf, then within minutes the barometer would drop, the air would suddenly turn cool and smell like ozone and gunmetal and fish spawning, the wind would begin to blow out of the south and straighten the moss on the dead cypress trees in the marsh, bend the cattails in the bayou, and swell and ruffle the pecan trees in my front yard; then a sheet of gray rain would move out of the marsh, across the floating islands of purple hyacinths in the bayou, my bait shop and the canvas awning over my boat-rental dock, and ring as loud on my gallery as marbles bouncing on corrugated tin.

I parked the truck under the pecan trees and ran up the incline to the front steps. My father, a trapper and oil-field roughneck who worked high on the derrick, on what they called the monkey board, built the house of cypress and oak back in the Depression. The planks in the walls and floors were notched and joined with wooden pegs. You couldn't shove a playing card in a seam. With age the wood had weathered almost black. I think rifle balls would have bounced off it.

My wife's car was gone, but through the screen door I could smell shrimp on the stove. I looked for Alafair, my adopted daughter, but didn't see her either. Then I saw that the horse lot and shed were empty and Alafair's three-legged coon, Tripod, was not in his cage on top of the rabbit hutches or on the chain that allowed him to run along a clothesline between two tree trunks.

I started to go inside, then I heard her horse paw the leaves around the side of the house.

"Alafair?"

Nothing.

"Alf, I've got a feeling somebody is doing something she isn't supposed to."

"What's that, Dave?" she said.

"Would you please come out here and bring your friends with you?"

She rode her Appaloosa out from under the eave. Her tennis shoes, pink shorts, and T-shirt were sopping, and her tanned skin glistened with water. She grinned under her straw hat.

"Alf, what happened the last time you took Tripod for a ride?"

She looked off reflectively at the rain falling in the trees. Tripod squirmed in her hands. He was a beautiful coon, silver-tipped, with a black mask and black rings on his thick tail.

"I told him not to do that no more, Dave."

"It's 'anymore.' "

"Anymore. He ain't gonna do it anymore, Dave."

She was grinning again. Tex, her Appaloosa, was steel gray, with white stockings and a spray of black and white spots on his rump. Last week Tripod had spiked his claws into Tex's rump, and Alafair had been thrown end over end into the tomato plants.

"Where's Bootsie?"

"At the store in town."

"How about putting Tex in the shed and coming in for some ice cream? You think you can handle that, little guy?"

"Yeah, that's a pretty good idea, Dave," she said, as though both of us had just thought our way through a problem. She continued to look at me, her dark eyes full of light. "What about Tripod?"

"I think Tripod probably needs some ice cream, too."

Her face beamed. She set Tripod on top of the hutches, then slid down off her horse into a mud puddle. I watched her hook Tripod to his chain and lead Tex back to the lot. She was eleven years old now. Her body was round and hard and full of energy, her Indian-black hair as shiny as a raven's wing; when she smiled, her eyes squinted almost completely shut. Six years ago I had pulled her from a wobbling envelope of air inside the submerged wreckage of a twin-engine plane out on the salt.

She hooked Tripod's chain on the back porch and went into her bedroom to change clothes. I put a small amount of ice cream in two bowls and set them on the table. Above the counter a telephone number was written on the small blackboard we used for messages. Alafair came back into the kitchen, rubbing her head with a towel. She wore her slippers, her elastic-waisted blue jeans, and an oversized University of Southwestern Louisiana T-shirt. She kept blowing her bangs out of her eyes.

"You promise you're going to eat your supper?" I said.

"Of course. What difference does it make if you eat ice cream before supper instead of after? You're silly sometimes, Dave."

"Oh, I see."

"You have funny ideas sometimes."

"You're growing up on me."

"What?"

"Never mind."

She brought Tripod's pan in from the porch and put a scoop of ice cream in it. The rain had slackened, and I could see the late sun breaking through the mist, like a pink wafer, above the sugarcane at the back of my property.

"Oh, I forgot, a man called," she said. "That's his number."

"Who was it?"

"He said he was a friend of yours. I couldn't hear because it was real noisy."

"Next time have the person spell his name and write it on the blackboard with his number, Alf."

"He said he wanted to talk with you about some man with one arm and one leg."

"What?"

"He said a soldier. He was mixing up his words. I couldn't understand him."

"What kind of soldier? That doesn't make too much sense, Alf."

"He kept burping while he talked. He said his grandfather was a Texas Ranger. What's a Texas Ranger?"

Oh, boy, I thought.

"How about Elrod T. Sykes?" I said.

"Yeah, that's it."

Time for an unlisted number, I thought.

"What was he talking about, Dave?"

"He was probably drunk. Don't pay attention to what drunk people say. If he calls again like that when Bootsie and I aren't here, tell him I'll call him and then hang up."

"Don't you like him?"

"When a person is drunk, he's sick, Alafair. If you talk to that person while he's drunk, in a funny way you become like him. Don't worry, I'll have a talk with him later."

"He didn't say anything bad, Dave."

"But he shouldn't be calling here and bothering little people," I said, and winked at her. I watched the concern in her face. The corners of her mouth were turned down, and her eyes looked into an empty space above her ice-cream dish. "You're right, little guy. We shouldn't be mad at people. I think Elrod Sykes is probably an all-right guy. He probably just opens too many bottles in one day sometimes."

She was smiling again. She had big, wide-set white teeth, and there was a smear of ice cream on her tan cheek. I hugged her shoulders and kissed her on the top of her head.

"I'm going to run now. Watch the shrimp, okay?" I said. "And no more horseback rides for Tripod. Got it, Alf?"

"Got it, big guy."

I put on my tennis shoes and running shorts and started down the dirt road toward the drawbridge over the bayou. The rain looked like flecks of spun glass in the air now, and the reflection of the dying sun was blood-red in the water. After a mile I was sweating heavily in the damp air, but I could feel the day's fatigue rise from my body, and I sprang across the puddles and hit it hard all the way to the bridge.

I did leg stretches against the rusted girders and watched the fireflies lighting in the trees and alligator gars turning in the shadows of a flooded canebrake. The sound of the tree frogs and cicadas in the marsh was almost deafening now.

At this time of day, particularly in summer, I always felt a sense of mortality that I could never adequately describe to another person. Sometimes it was like the late sun was about to burn itself into a dead cinder on the earth's rim, never to rise again. It made sweat run down my sides like snakes. Maybe it was because I wanted to believe that summer was an eternal song, that living in your fifty-third year was of no more significance than entering the sixth inning when your sidearm was still like a resilient whip and the prospect of your forkball made a batter swallow and step back from the plate.

And if it all ended tomorrow, I should have no complaint, I thought. I could have caught the bus any number of times years ago. To be reminded of that fact I only had to touch the punji-stick scar, coiled like a flattened, gray worm, on my stomach; the shiny, arrow-shaped welts from a bouncing Betty on my thigh; the puckered indentation below my collarbone where a .38 round had cored through my shoulder.

They were not wounds received in a heroic fashion, either. In each case I got them because I did something that was careless or impetuous. I also had tried to destroy myself in increments, a jigger at a time.

Get outside your thoughts, partner, I told myself. I waved to the bridge tender in his tiny house at the far end of the bridge and headed for home.

I poured it on the last half mile, then stopped at the dock and did fifty pushups and stomach crunches on the wood planks that still glowed with the day's heat and smelled of dried fish scales.

I walked up the incline through the trees and the layer of moldy leaves and pecan husks toward the lighted gallery of my house. Then I heard a car behind me on the dirt road and I turned and saw a taxicab stop by my mailbox. A man and woman got out, then the man paid the driver and sent him back toward town.

I rubbed the salt out of my eyes with my forearm and stared through the gloom. The man drained the foam out of a long-necked beer bottle and set the empty behind a tree trunk. Then the woman touched him on the shoulder and pointed toward me.

"Hey, there you are," Elrod Sykes said. "How you doin', Mr. Robicheaux? You don't mind us coming out, do you? Wow, you've got a great place."

He swayed slightly. The woman, Kelly Drummond, caught him by the arm. I walked back down the slope.

"I'm afraid I was just going in to take a shower and eat supper," I said.

"We want to take y'all to dinner," he said. "There's this place called Mulate's in Breaux Bridge. They make gumbo you could start a new religion with."

"Thanks, anyway. My wife's already fixed supper."

"Bad time of day to knock on doors, El," Kelly Drummond said, but she looked at me when she said it, her eyes fixed directly on mine. She wore tan slacks, flats, and a yellow blouse with a button open that exposed her bra. When she raised her hand to move a blond ringlet off her forehead, you could see a half-moon sweat stain under her arm.

"We didn't mean to cause a problem," Elrod said. "I'm afraid a drunk-front blew through the area this afternoon. Hey, we're all right, though. We took a cab. Did you notice that? How about that? Look, I tell you what, we'll just get us some liquids to go down at the bait shop yonder and call us a cab."

"Tell him why you came out, El," Kelly Drummond said.

"That's all right. We stumbled in at a bad time. I'm real sorry, Mr. Robicheaux."

"Call me Dave. Would you mind waiting for me at the bait shop a few minutes, then I'll shower and drive y'all home."

"You sure know how to avoid the stereotypes, don't you?" the woman said.

"I beg your pardon?" I said.

"Nobody can ever beat up on you for showing off your southern hospitality," she said.

"Hey, it's okay," Elrod said, turning her by the arm toward the bait shop.

I had gone only a short distance up the slope when I heard the woman's footsteps behind me.

"Just hold on a minute, Dick Tracy," she said.

Behind her I could see Elrod walking down the dock to the shop, where Batist, the black man who worked for me, was drawing back the canvas awning over the tables for the night.

"Look, Ms. Drummond—"

"You don't have to invite us into your house, you don't have to believe the stuff he says about what he sees and hears, but you ought to know that it took guts for him to come out here. He fucks up with Mikey, he fucks up with this film, maybe he blows it for good this time."

"You'll have to excuse me, but I'm not sure what that has to do with the Iberia Parish Sheriff's Department."

She carried a doeskin drawstring bag in her hand. She propped her hand on her hip. She looked up at me and ran her tongue over her bottom lip.

"Are you that dumb?" she asked.

"You're telling me a mob guy, maybe Baby Feet Balboni, is involved with your movie?"

"A mob guy? That's good. I bet y'all really send a lot of them up the road."

"Where are you from, Ms. Drummond?"

"East Kentucky."

"Have you thought about making your next movie there?"

I started toward the house again.

"Wait a minute, Mr. Smart Ass," she said. "Elrod respects you. Did you ever hear of the Chicken Ranch in LaGrange, Texas?"

"Yes."

"Do you know what it was?"

"It was a hot-pillow joint."

"His mother was a prostitute there. That's why he never talks about anyone in his family except his gran'daddy, the Texas Ranger. That's why he likes you, and you'd damn well better be aware of it."

She turned on her heel, her doeskin bag hitting her rump, and walked erectly down the slope toward the bait shop, where I could see Elrod opening a beer with his pocket knife under the lightbulb above the screen door.

Well, you could do a lot worse than have one like her on your side, Elrod, I thought.

I TOOK A shower, dried off, and was buttoning on a fresh shirt in the kitchen when the telephone rang on the counter. Bootsie put down a pan on the stove and answered it.

"It's Batist," she said, and handed it to me:

"*Qui t'as pr'est faire?*" I said into the receiver.

"Some drunk white man down here done fell in the bayou," he said.

"What's he doing now?"

"Sittin' in the middle of the shop, drippin' water on my flo'."

"I'll be there in a minute," I said.

"Dave, a lady wit' him was smokin' a cigarette out on the dock didn't smell like no tobacco, no."

"All right, podna. Thanks," I said, and hung up the phone.

Bootsie was looking at me with a question mark in the middle of her face. Her auburn hair, which she had pinned up in swirls on her head, was full of tiny lights.

"A man fell in the bayou. I have to drive him and his girlfriend home," I said.

"Where's their car?"

"They came out in a cab."

"A cab? Who comes fishing in a cab?"

"He's a weird guy."

"*Dave—*" she said, drawing my name out in exasperation.

"He's one of those actors working out at Spanish Lake. I guess he came out here to tell me about something."

"Which actor?"

"Elrod Sykes."

"*Elrod Sykes* is out at the bait shop?"

"Yep."

"Who's the woman with him?"

"Kelly Drummond."

"Dave, I don't believe it. You left Kelly Drummond and Elrod Sykes in the bait shop? You didn't invite them in?"

"He's bombed, Boots."

"I don't care. They came out to see you and you left them in the shop while you took a shower?"

"Bootsie, this guy's head glows in the dark, even when he's not on chemicals."

She went out the front door and down the slope to the bayou. In the mauve twilight I could see her touching at her hair before she entered the bait shop. Five minutes later Kelly Drummond was sitting at our kitchen table, a cup of coffee balanced in her fingers, a reefer-induced wistfulness on her face, while Elrod Sykes changed into dry clothes in our bedroom. He walked into the kitchen in a pair of my sandals, khaki trousers, and the Ragin' Cajuns T-shirt, with my name ironed on the back, that Alafair had given me for Father's Day.

His face was flushed with gin roses, and his gaze drifted automatically to the icebox.

"Would you like a beer?" Bootsie said.

"Yes, if you wouldn't mind," he said.

"Boots, I think we're out," I said.

"Oh, that's all right. I really don't need one," he said.

Bootsie's eyes were bright with embarrassment. Then I saw her face set.

"I'm sure there's one back in here somewhere," she said, then slid a long-necked Dixie out of the bottom shelf and opened it for him.

Elrod looked casually out the back door while he sipped from the bottle.

"I have to feed the rabbits. You want to take a walk with me, Elrod?" I said.

"The rice will be ready in a minute," Bootsie said.

"That's all it'll take," I said.

Outside, under the pecan trees that were now black-green in the fading light, I could feel Elrod watching the side of my face.

"Boy, I don't know quite what to say, Mr. Robicheaux, I mean Dave."

"Don't worry about it. Just tell me what it is you had on your mind all day."

"It's these guys out yonder on that lake. I told you before."

"Which guys? What are you talking about?"

"Confederate infantry. One guy in particular, with gold epaulets on his coat. He's got a bad arm and he's missing a leg. I think maybe he's a general."

"I'll be straight with you. I think maybe you're delusional."

"A lot of people do. I just didn't think I'd get the same kind of bullshit from you."

"I'd appreciate it if you didn't use profanity around my home."

"I apologize. But that Confederate officer was saying something. It didn't make sense to me, but I thought it might to you."

I filled one of the rabbit bowls with alfalfa pellets and latched the screen door on the hutch. I looked at Elrod Sykes. His face was absolutely devoid of guile or any apparent attempt at manipulation; in fact, it reminded me of someone who might have just been struck in the head by a bolt of lightning.

"Look, Elrod, years ago, when I was on the grog, I believed dead people called me up on the telephone. Sometimes my dead wife or members of my platoon would talk to me out of the rain. I was convinced that their voices were real and that maybe I was supposed to join them. It wasn't a good way to be."

He poured the foam out of his bottle, then flicked the remaining drops reflectively at the bark of a pecan tree.

"I wasn't drunk," he said. "This guy with the bad arm and one leg, he said to me, 'You and your friend, the police officer in town, must repel them.' He was standing by the water, in the fog, on a crutch. He looked right in my face when he said it."

"I see."

"What do you think he meant?"

"I'm afraid I wouldn't know, partner."

"I got the notion he thought you would."

"I don't want to hurt your feelings, but I think you're imagining all this and I'm not going to pursue it any further. Instead, how about your clarifying something Ms. Drummond said earlier?"

"What's that?"

"Why is it a problem to your director, this fellow Mikey, if you come out to my place?"

"She told you that?"

"That's what the lady said."

"Well, the way he put it was 'Stay out of that cop's face, El. Don't give him reason to be out here causing us trouble. We need to remember that a lot of things happened in this part of the country that are none of our business.' "

"He's worried about the dead black man you found?" I said. "That doesn't make too much sense."

"You got another one of these?" he said, and held up his empty bottle.

"Why is he worried about the black man?"

"When Mikey worries, it's about money, Mr. Robicheaux. Or actually about the money he needs to make the kind of pictures he wants. He did a miniseries for television on the Holocaust. It lost ten million dollars for the network. Nobody's lining up to throw money at Mikey's projects right now."

"Julie Balboni is."

"You ever heard of a college turning down money from a defense company because it makes napalm?"

He opened and closed his mouth as though he were experiencing cabin pressure in an airplane. The moon was up now, and in the glow of light through the tree branches the skin of his face looked pale and grained, stretched tight against the bone. "Mr. Robicheaux . . . Dave . . . I'm being honest with you, I need a drink."

"We'd better go inside and get you one, then. I'll make you a deal, though. Maybe you might want to think about going to a meeting with me. I don't necessarily mean that you belong there. But some people think it beats waking up like a chainsaw every morning."

He looked away at a lighted boat on the bayou.

"It's just a thought. I didn't mean to be intrusive," I said. "Let's go inside."

"You ever see lights out in the cypress trees at night?"

"It's swamp gas. It ignites and rolls across the water's surface like ball lightning."

"No, sir, that's not what it is," he said. "They had lanterns hanging on some of their ambulances. The horses got mired in the bogs. A lot of those soldiers had maggots in their wounds. That's the only reason they lived. The maggots ate out the infection."

I wasn't going to talk any more about the strange psychological terrain that evidently he had created as a petting zoo for all the protean shapes that lived in his unconscious.

I put the bag of alfalfa pellets on top of the hutches and turned to go back to the house.

"That general said something else," Elrod said behind me.

I waved my hand negatively and kept walking.

"Well, I cain't blame you for not listening," he said. "Maybe I *was* drunk this time. How could your father have his adjutant's pistol?"

I stopped.

"What?" I said.

"The general said, 'Your friend's father took the revolver of my adjutant, Major Moss.' . . . Hey, Mr. Robicheaux, I didn't mean to say the wrong thing, now."

I chewed on the corner of my lip and waited before I spoke again.

"Elrod, I've got the feeling that maybe I'm dealing with some kind of self-manufactured mojo-drama here," I said. "Maybe it's related to the promotion of your film, or it might have something to do with a guy floating his brain in alcohol too long. But no matter how you cut it, I don't want anyone, and I mean *anyone,* to try to use a member of my family to jerk me around."

He turned his palms up and his long eyelashes fluttered.

"I don't know what to say. I apologize to you, sir," he said. Then his eyes focused on nothing and he pinched his mouth in his hand as though he were squeezing a dry lemon.

AT ELEVEN THAT night I undressed and lay down on the bed next to Bootsie. The window fan billowed the curtains and drew the breeze across the sheets, and I could smell watermelons and night-blooming jasmine out in the moonlight. The closet door was open, and I stared at the wooden foot-locker that was set back under my hangered shirts and trousers. Bootsie turned her head on the pillow and brushed her fingers along the side of my face.

"Are you mad at me?" she said.

"No, of course not."

"They seem to be truly nice people. It would have been wrong not to invite them in."

"Yeah, they're not bad."

"But when you came back inside with Elrod, you looked bothered about something. Did something happen?"

"He says he talks with dead people. Maybe he's crazy. I don't know, Boots, I—"

"What is it, Dave?" She raised herself on her elbow and looked into my face.

"He said this dead Confederate general told him that my father took his adjutant's revolver."

"He had too much to drink, that's all."

I continued to stare at the closet. She smiled at me and pressed her body against me.

"You had a long day. You're tired," she said. "He didn't mean any harm. He probably won't remember what he said tomorrow."

"You don't understand, Boots," I said, and sat up on the edge of the bed.

"Understand what?" She put her hand on my bare back. "Dave, your muscles are tight as iron. What's the matter?"

"Just a minute."

I didn't want to fall prey to superstition or my own imaginings or Elrod Sykes's manipulations. But I did. I clicked on the table lamp and pulled my old footlocker out of the closet. Inside a half-dozen shoe boxes at the bottom were the memorabilia of my childhood years with my father back in the 1940s: my collections of baseball cards, Indian banner stones and quartz arrow points, and the minié balls that we used to find in a freshly plowed sugarcane field right after the first rain.

I took out a crushed shoe box that was tied with kite twine and sat back down on the bed with it. I slipped off the twine, removed the top of the box, and set it on the nightstand.

"This was the best gift my father ever gave me," I said. "On my brother's and my birthday he'd always fix *cush-cush* and sausage for our breakfast, and we'd always find an unusual present waiting for us by our plate. On my twelfth birthday I got this."

I lifted the heavy revolver out of the box and unwrapped the blackened oil rag from it.

"He had been laid off in the oil field and he took a job tearing down some old slave quarters on a sugar plantation about ten miles down the bayou. There was one cabin separate from the others, with a brick foundation, and he figured it must have belonged to the overseer. Anyway, when he started tearing the boards out of the walls he found some flattened minié balls in the wood, and he knew there had probably been a skirmish between some federals and Confederates around there. Then he tore out what was left of the floor, and in a crawl space, stuck back in the bricks, was this Remington .44 revolver."

It had been painted with rust and cobweb when my father had found it, the cylinder and hammer frozen against the frame, the wood grips eaten away by mold and insects, but I had soaked it for a week in gasoline and rubbed the steel smooth with emery paper and rags until it had the dull sheen of an old nickel.

"It's just an antique pistol your father gave you, Dave," she said. "Maybe you said something about it to Elrod. Then he got drunk and mixed it up with some kind of fantasy he has."

"No, he said the officer's name." I opened the nightstand drawer and took out a small magnifying glass. "He said it had belonged to a Major Moss."

"So what?"

"Boots, there's a name cut into the trigger guard. I haven't thought about it in years. I couldn't have mentioned it to him."

I rested the revolver across my thighs and looked through the magnifying glass at the soft glow of light off the brass housing around the trigger. The steel felt cold and slick with oil against my thighs.

"Take a look," I said, and handed her the glass and the revolver.

She folded her legs under her and squinted one eye through the glass.

"It says 'CSA,' " she said.

"Wrong place. Right at the back of the guard."

She held the pistol closer to the glass. Then she

looked up at me and there were white spots in her cheeks.

"J. Moss." Her voice was dry when she said it. Then she said the name again. "It says 'J. Moss.'"

"It sure does."

She wrapped the blackened oil cloth around the pistol and replaced it in the shoe box. She put her hand in mine and squeezed it.

"Dave?"

"Yes?"

"I think Elrod Sykes is a nice man, but we mustn't have him here again."

She turned out the light, lay back on the pillow, and looked out at the moonlight in the pecan trees, her face caught with a private, troubled thought like the silent beating of a bird's wings inside a cage.

CHAPTER 5

EARLY THE NEXT morning the sheriff stopped me in the corridor as I was on my way to my office.

"Special Agent Gomez is here," he said. A smile worked at the corner of his mouth.

"Where?"

"In your office."

"So?"

"I think it's a break the FBI's working with us on this one."

"You told me that before."

"Yeah, I did, didn't I?" His eyes grew brighter, then he looked away and laughed out loud.

"What's the big joke?" I asked.

"Nothing." He rubbed his lips with his knuckle, and his eyes kept crinkling at the corners.

"Let me ask you something between insider jokes," I said. "Why is the FBI coming in on this one so early? They don't have enough work to do with the resident wiseguys in New Orleans?"

"That's a good question, Dave. Ask Agent Gomez about that and give me feedback later." He walked off smiling to himself. Uniformed deputies in the corridor were smiling back at him.

I picked up my mail, walked through my office door, and stared at the woman who was sitting in my chair and talking on my telephone. She was looking out the window at a mockingbird on a tree limb while she talked. She turned her head long enough to point to a chair where I could sit down if I wished.

She was short and dark-skinned, and her thick, black hair was chopped stiffly along her neck. Her white suit coat hung on the back of my chair. There was a huge silk bow on her blouse of the sort that Bugs Bunny might wear.

Her eyes flicked back at me again, and she took the telephone receiver away from her ear and slipped her hand over the mouthpiece.

"Have a seat. I'll be right with you," she said.

"Thank you," I said.

I sat down, looked idly through my mail, and a moment later heard her put down the phone receiver.

"Can I help you with something?" she asked.

"Maybe. My name's Dave Robicheaux. This is my office."

Her face colored.

"I'm sorry," she said. "A call came in for me on your extension, and I automatically sat behind your desk."

"It's all right."

She stood up and straightened her shoulders. Her breasts looked unnaturally large and heavy for a woman her height. She picked up her purse and walked around the desk.

"I'm Special Agent Rosa Gomez," she said. Then she stuck her hand out, as though her motor control was out of sync with her words.

"It's nice to know you," I said.

"I think they're putting a desk in here for me."

"Oh?"

"Do you mind?"

"No, not at all. It's very nice to have you here."

She remained standing, both of her hands on her purse, her shoulders as rigid as a coat hanger.

"Why don't you sit down, Ms. . . . Agent Gomez?"

"Call me Rosie. Everyone calls me Rosie."

I sat down behind my desk, then noticed that she was looking at the side of my head. Involuntarily I touched my hair.

"You've been with the Bureau a long time?" I said.

"Not really."

"So you're fairly new?"

"Well, just to this kind of assignment. I mean, out in the field, that sort of thing." Her hands looked small on top of her big purse. I think it took everything in her to prevent them from clenching with anxiety. Then her eyes focused again on the side of my head.

"I have a white patch in my hair," I said.

She closed then opened her eyes with embarrassment.

"Someone once told me I have skunk blood in me," I said.

"I think I'm doing a lot of wrong things this morning," she said.

"No, you're not."

But somebody at Fart, Barf, and Itch is, I thought.

Then she sat erect in her chair and concentrated her vision on something outside the window until her face became composed again.

"The sheriff said you don't believe we're dealing with a serial killer or a random killing," she said.

"That's not quite how I put it. I told him I think she knew the killer."

"Why?"

"Her father appears to have been a child molester. She was streetwise herself. She had one prostitution beef when she was sixteen. Yesterday I found out she was still hooking—out of a club in St. Martinville. A girl like that doesn't usually get forced into cars in front of crowded jukejoints."

"Maybe she went off with a john."

"Not without her purse. She left it at her table. In it we found some—"

"Rubbers," she said.

"That's right. So I don't think it was a john. In her car we found a carton of cigarettes, a brand-new hairbrush, and a half-dozen joints in a Baggy in the trunk. I think she went outside to get some cigarettes, a joint, or the hairbrush, she saw somebody she knew, got in his car, and never came back."

"Maybe it was an old customer, somebody she trusted. Maybe he told her he just wanted to set something up for later."

"It doesn't fit. A john doesn't pay one time, then come back the next time with a razor blade or scalpel."

She put her thumbnail between her teeth. Her eyes were brown and had small lights in them.

"Then you think the killer is from this area, she knew him, and she trusted him enough to get in the car with him?"

"I think it's something like that."

"We think he's a psychopath, possibly a serial killer."

"*We?*"

"Well, actually *I*. I had a behavioral profile run on him. Everything he did indicates a personality that seeks control and dominance. During the abduction, the rape, the killing itself, he was absolutely in control. He becomes sexually aroused by power, by instilling fear and loathing in a woman, by being able to smother her with his body. In all probability he has ice water in his veins."

I nodded and moved some paper clips around on my desk blotter.

"You don't seem impressed," she said.

"What do you make of the fact that he covered her face with her blouse?" I said.

"Blindfolding humiliates the victim and inspires even greater terror in her."

"Yeah, I guess it does."

"But you don't buy the profile."

"I'm not too keen on psychoanalysis. I belong to a twelve-step fellowship that subscribes to the notion that most bad or evil behavior is generated by what we call a self-centered fear. I think our man was afraid of Cherry LeBlanc. I don't think he could look into her eyes while he raped her."

She reached for a folder she had left on the corner of my desk.

"Do you know how many similar unsolved murders of women have been committed in the state of Louisiana in the last twenty-five years?"

"I sent in an information-search request to Baton Rouge yesterday."

"We have an unfair advantage on you in terms of resources," she said. She leafed through the printouts that were clipped together at the top of the folder. Behind her, I saw two uniformed deputies grinning at me through the glass in my office partition.

"Excuse me," I said, got up, closed the door, and sat back down again.

"Is this place full of comedians?" she said. "I seem to make a lot of people smile."

"Some of them don't get a lot of exposure to the outside world."

"Anyway, narrowing it down to the last ten years, there are at least seventeen unsolved homicides involving females that share some similarity with the murder of Cherry LeBlanc. You want to take a look?" she said, and handed me the folder. "I have to go down to the sheriff's office and get my building keys. I'll be right back."

It was grim material to read. There was nothing abstruse about the prose. It was unimaginative, flat, brutally casual in its depiction of the bestial potential among the human family, like a banal rendering of our worst nightmares: slasher cases, usually involving prostitutes; the garroting of housewives who had been abducted in broad daylight in supermarket and bowling-alley parking lots; the roadside murders of women whose cars had broken down at night; prostitutes who had probably been set on fire by their pimps; the drowning of two black women who had been wrapped to an automobile engine block with barbed wire.

In almost all the cases rape, sodomy, or torture of some kind was involved. And what bothered me most was the fact that the perpetrators were probably still out there, unless they were doing time for other crimes; few of them had known their victims, and consequently few of them would ever be caught.

Then I noticed that Rosie Gomez had made check marks in the margins by six cases that shared more common denominators with the death of Cherry LeBlanc than the others: three runaways who had been found buried off highways in a woods; a high school girl who had been raped, tied to a tree in a fish camp at Lake Chicot, and shot at point-blank range; two waitresses who had gone off from their jobs without explanation and a few hours later had been thrown, bludgeoned to death, into irrigation ditches.

Their bodies had all showed marks, in one way or another, of having been bound. They had all been young, working class, and perhaps unsuspecting when a degenerate had come violently and irrevocably into their lives and had departed without leaving a sign of his identity.

My respect for Rosie Gomez's ability was appreciating.

She walked back through the door, clipping two keys onto a ring.

"You want to talk while we take a ride out to Spanish Lake?" I said.

"What's at Spanish Lake?"

"A movie director I'd like to meet."

"What's that have to do with our case?"

"Probably nothing. But it beats staying indoors."

"Sure. I have to make a call to the Bureau, then I'll be right with you."

"Let me ask you an unrelated question," I said.

"Sure."

"If you found the remains of a black man, and he had on no belt and there were no laces in his boots, what speculation might you make about him?"

She looked at me with a quizzical smile.

"He was poor?" she said.

"Could be. In fact, someone else told me about the same thing in a less charitable way."

"No," she said. She looked thoughtfully into space, puffed out one jaw, then the other, like a chipmunk might. "No, I'd bet he'd been in jail, in a parish or a city holding unit of some kind, where they were afraid he'd do harm to himself."

"That's not bad," I said. Not at all, I thought. "Well, let's take a ride."

I waited for her outside in the shade of the building. I was sweating inside my shirt, and the sunlight off the cement parking lot made my eyes film. Two of the uniformed deputies who had been grinning through my glass earlier came out the door with clipboards in their hands, then stopped when they saw me. The taller one, a man named Rufus Arceneaux, took a matchstick out of his mouth and smiled at me from behind his shades.

"Hey, Dave," he said, "does that gal wear a Bureau buzzer on each of her boobs or is she just a little top-heavy?"

They were both grinning now. I could hear bottleflies buzzing above an iron grate in the shade of the building.

"You guys can take this for what it's worth," I said. "I don't want you to hold it against me, either, just because I outrank you or something like that. Okay?"

"You gotta make plainclothes before you get any federal snatch?" Arceneaux said, and put the matchstick back in the corner of his mouth.

I put on my sunglasses, folded my seersucker coat over my arm, and looked across the street at a black man selling rattlesnake watermelons off the tailgate of a pickup truck.

"If y'all want to act like public clowns, that's your business," I said. "But you'd better wipe that stupid expression off your faces when you're around my partner. Also, if I hear you making remarks about her, either to me or somebody else, we're going to take it up in a serious way. You get my drift?"

Arceneaux rotated his head on his neck, then pulled the front of his shirt loose from his damp skin with his fingers.

"Boy, it's hot, ain't it?" he said. "I think I'm gonna come in this afternoon and take a cold shower. You ought to try it too, Dave. A cold shower might get the wrong thing off your mind."

They walked into the shimmering haze, their leather holsters and cartridge belts creaking on their hips, the backs of their shirts peppered with sweat.

ROSIE GOMEZ AND I turned off the highway in my pickup truck and drove down the dirt lane through the pecan orchard toward Spanish Lake, where we could see elevated camera platforms and camera booms silhouetted against the sun's reflection on the water. A chain was hung across the road between a post and the side of the wood-frame security building. The security guard, the wiry man with the white scar embossed on his throat like a chicken's foot, approached my window. His face looked pinched and heated in the shadow of his bill cap.

I showed him my badge.

"Yeah, y'all go on in," he said. "You remember me, Detective Robicheaux?"

His hair was gray, cut close to the scalp, and his skin was browned and as coarse as a lizard's from the sun. His blue eyes seemed to have an optical defect of some kind, a nervous shudder like marbles clicking on a plate.

"It's Doucet, isn't it?" I said.

"Yes, sir, Murphy Doucet. You got a good memory. I used to be with the Jefferson Parish Sheriff's Department when you were with N.O.P.D."

His stomach was as flat as a shingle. He wore a .357 chrome-plated revolver, and also a clip-on radio, a can of Mace, and a rubber baton on his belt.

"It looks like you're in the movie business now," I said.

"Just for a while. I own half of a security service now and I'm a steward for the Teamsters out of Lafayette, too. So I'm kind of on board both ways here."

"This is Special Agent Gomez from the FBI. We'd like to talk to Mr. Goldman a few minutes if he's not too busy."

"Is there been some kind of trouble?"

"Is Mr. Goldman here?"

"Yes, sir, that's him right up yonder in the trees. I'll tell him y'all on your way." He started to take his radio off his belt.

"That's all right. We'll find him."

"Yes, sir, anything you say."

He dropped the chain and waited for us to pass. In the rearview mirror I saw him hook it to the post again. Rosie Gomez was looking at the side of my face.

"What is it?" she said.

"The Teamsters. Why does a Hollywood production company want to come into a depressed rural area and contract for services from the Teamsters? They can hire labor around here for minimum wage."

"Maybe they do business with unions as a matter of course."

"Nope, they usually try to leave their unions back in California. I've got a feeling this has something to do with Julie Balboni being on board the ark."

I watched her expression. She looked straight ahead.

"You know who Baby Feet Balboni is, don't you?" I said.

"Yes, Mr. Balboni is well known to us."

"You know he's in New Iberia, too, don't you?"

She waited before she spoke again. Her small hands were clenched on her purse.

"What's your implication?" she said.

"I think the Bureau has more than one reason for being in town."

"You think the girl's murder has secondary importance to me?"

"No, not to you."

"But probably to the people I work under?"

"You'd know that better than I."

"You don't think well of us, do you?"

"My experience with the Bureau was never too good. But maybe the problem was mine. As the Bible says, I used to look through a glass darkly. Primarily because there was Jim Beam in it most of the time."

"The Bureau's changed."

"Yeah, I guess it has."

Yes, I thought, they hired racial minorities and women at gunpoint, and they stopped wire-tapping civil-rights leaders and smearing innocent people's reputations after their years of illegal surveillance and character assassination were finally exposed.

I parked the truck in the shade of a moss-hung live-oak tree, and we walked toward the shore of the lake, where a dozen people listened attentively to a man in a canvas chair who waved his arms while he talked, jabbed his finger in the air to make a point, and shrugged his powerful shoulders as though he were desperate in his desire to be understood. His voice, his manner, made me think of a hurricane stuffed inside a pair of white tennis shorts and a dark blue polo shirt.

"—the best fucking story editor in that fucking town," he was saying. "I don't care what those assholes say, they couldn't carry my fucking jockstrap. When we come out of the cutting room with this, it's going to be solid fucking gold. Has everybody got that? This is a great picture. Believe it, they're going to spot their pants big-time on this one."

His strained face looked like a white balloon that was about to burst. But even while his histrionics grew to awesome levels and inspired mute reverence in his listeners, his eyes drifted to me and Rosie, and I had a feeling that Murphy Doucet, the security guard, had used his radio after all.

When we introduced ourselves and showed him our identification, he said, "Do you have telephones where you work?"

"I beg your pardon?" I said.

"Do you have telephones where you work? Do you have people there who know how to make appointments for you?"

"Maybe you don't understand, Mr. Goldman. During a criminal investigation we don't make appointments to talk to people."

His face flexed as though it were made of white rubber.

"You saying you're out here investigating some crime? What crime we talking about here?" he said. "You see a crime around here?" He swiveled his head around. "I don't see one."

"We can talk down at the sheriff's office if you wish," Rosie said.

He stared at her as though she had stepped through a hole in the dimension.

"Do you have any idea of what it costs to keep one hundred and fifty people standing around while I'm playing pocket pool with somebody's *criminal* investigation?" he said.

"You heard what she said. What's it going to be, partner?" I asked.

"*Partner?*" he said, looking out at the lake with a kind of melancholy disbelief on his face. "I think I screwed up in an earlier incarnation. I probably had something to do with the sinking of the *Titanic* or the assassination of the Archduke Ferdinand. That's gotta be it."

Then he rose and faced me with the flat glare of a boxer waiting for the referee to finish with the ring instructions.

"You want to take a walk or go in my trailer?" he said. "The air conditioner in my trailer is broken. You could fry eggs on the toilet seat. What d'you want to do?"

"This is fine," I said.

"Fine, huh?" he said, as though he were addressing some cynical store of private knowledge within himself. "What is it you want to say, Mr. Robicheaux?"

He walked along the bank of the lake, his hair curling out of his polo shirt like bronze wire. His white tennis shorts seemed about to rip at the seams on his muscular buttocks and thighs.

"I understand that you've cautioned some of your people to stay away from me. Is that correct?" I said.

"What people? What are you talking about?"

"I believe you know what I'm talking about."

"Elrod and his voice out in the fog? Elrod and skeletons buried in a sandbar? You think I care about stuff like that? You think that's what's on my mind when I'm making a picture?" He stopped and jabbed a thick finger at me. "Hey, try to understand something here. I live with my balls in a skillet. It's a way of life. I got no interest, I got no involvement, in people's problems in a certain locale. Is that supposed to be bad? Is it all right for me to tell my actors what I think? Are we all still working on a First Amendment basis here?"

A group of actors in sweat-streaked gray and blue uniforms, eating hamburgers out of foam containers, walked past us. I turned and suddenly realized that Rosie was no longer with us.

"She probably stepped in a hole," Goldman said.

"I think you *are* worried about something, Mr. Goldman. I think we both know what it is, too."

He took a deep breath. The sunlight shone through the oak branches over his head and made shifting patterns of shadow on his face.

"Let me try to explain something to you," he said. "Most everything in the film world is an illusion. An actor is somebody who never liked what he was. So he makes up a person and that's what he becomes. You think John Wayne came out of the womb John Wayne? He and a screenwriter created a character that was a cross between Captain Bligh and Saint Francis of Assisi, and the Duke played it till he dropped.

"Elrod's convinced himself he has magic powers. Why? Because he melted his head five years ago and he has days when he can't tie his shoestrings without a diagram. So instead of admitting that maybe he's got baked mush between his ears, he's a mystic, a persecuted clairvoyant."

"Let's cut the dog shit, Mr. Goldman. You're in business with Baby Feet Balboni. *That's* your problem, not Elrod Sykes."

"Wrong."

"You know what a 'fall partner' is?"

"No."

"A guy who goes down on the same bust with you."

"So?"

"Julie doesn't have fall partners. His hookers do parish time for him, his dealers do it for him in Angola, his accountants do it in Atlanta and Lewisburg. I don't think Julie has ever spent a whole day in the bag."

"Neither have I. Because I don't break the law."

"I think he'll cannibalize you."

He looked away from me, and I saw his hands clench and unclench and the veins pulse in his neck.

"You look here," he said. "I worked nine years on a miniseries about the murder of six million people. I went to Auschwitz and set up cameras on the same spots the S.S. used to photograph the people being pulled out of the boxcars and herded with dogs to the ovens. I've had survivors tell me I'm the only person who ever described on film what they actually went through. I don't give a fuck what any critic says, that series will last a thousand years. You get something straight, Mr. Robicheaux. People might fuck me over as an individual, but they'll never fuck me over as a director. You can take that to the bank."

His pale eyes protruded from his head like marbles.

I looked back at him silently.

"There's something else?" he said.

"No, not really."

"So why the stare? What's going on?"

"Nothing. I think you're probably a sincere man. But as someone once told me, hubris is a character defect better left to the writers of tragedy."

He pressed his fingers on his chest.

"I got a problem with pride, you're saying?"

"I think Jimmy Hoffa was probably the toughest guy the labor movement ever produced," I said. "Then evidently he decided that he and the mob could have a fling at the dirty boogie together. I used to know a button man in New Orleans who told me they cut Hoffa into hundreds of pieces and used him for fish chum. I believe what he said, too."

"Sounds like your friend ought to take it to a grand jury."

"He can't. Three years ago one of Julie's hired lowlifes put a crack in his skull with a cold chisel. Just for kicks. He sells snowballs out of a cart in front of the K & B drugstore on St. Charles now. We'll see you around, Mr. Goldman."

I walked away through the dead leaves and over a series of rubber-coated power cables that looked like a tangle of black snakes. When I looked back at Mikey Goldman, his eyes were staring disjointedly into space.

CHAPTER 6

Rosie was waiting for me by the side of the pickup truck under the live-oak tree. The young sugarcane in the fields was green and bending in the wind. She fanned herself with a manila folder she had picked up off the truck seat.

"Where did you go?" I asked.

"To talk to Hogman Patin."

"Where is he?"

"Over there, with those other black people, under the trees. He's playing a street musician in the film."

"How'd you know to talk to him?"

"You put his name in the case file, and I recognized him from his picture on one of his albums."

"You're quite a cop, Rosie."

"Oh, I see. You didn't expect that from an agent who's short, Chicana, and a woman?"

"It was meant as a compliment. How about saving that stuff for the right people? What did Hogman have to say?"

Her eyes blinked at the abruptness of my tone.

"I'm sorry," I said. "I didn't mean to sound like

that. I still have my mind on Goldman. I think he's hiding some serious problems, and I think they're with Julie Balboni. I also think there might be a tie-in between Julie and Cherry LeBlanc."

She looked off at the group of black people under the trees.

"You didn't bother to tell me that earlier," she said.

"I wasn't sure about it. I'm still not."

"Dave, I'll be frank with you. Before I came here I read some of your history. You seem to have a way of doing things on your own. Maybe you've been in situations where you had no other choice. But I can't have a partner who holds out information on me."

"It's a speculation, Rosie, and I just told you about it."

"Where do you think there might be a tie-in?" she said, and her face became clear again.

"I'm not sure. But one of his hoods, a character named Cholo Manelli, told me that he and Julie had been talking about the girl's death. Then ten minutes later Julie told me he hadn't heard or read anything about it. So one of them is lying, and I think it's Julie."

"Why not the hood, what's his name, Cholo?"

"When a guy like Cholo lies or tries to jerk somebody around, he doesn't involve his boss's name. He has no doubt about how dangerous that can be. Anyway, what did you get from Hogman?"

"Not much. He just pointed at you and said, 'Tell that other one yonder ain't every person innocent, ain't every person listen when they ought to, either.' What do you make of that?"

"Hogman likes to be an enigma."

"Those scars on his arms—"

"He had a bunch of knife beefs in Angola. Back in the 1940s he murdered a white burial-insurance collector who was sleeping with his wife. Hogman's a piece of work, believe me. The hacks didn't know how to deal with him. They put him in the sweat box on Camp A for eighteen days one time."

"How'd he kill the white man?"

"With a cane knife on the white man's front gallery. In broad daylight. People around here talked about that one for a long time."

I could see a thought working in her eyes.

"He's not a viable suspect, Rosie," I said.

"Why not?"

"Hogman's not a bad guy. He doesn't trust white people much, and he's a little prideful, but he wouldn't hurt a nineteen-year-old girl."

"That's it? *He's not a bad guy?* Although he seems to have a lifetime history of violence with knives? Good God."

"Also the nightclub owner says Hogman never left the club that night."

She got in the truck and closed the door. Her shoulders were almost below the level of the window. I got in on the driver's side and started the engine.

"Well, that clears all that up, then," she said. "I guess the owner kept his eyes on our man all night. You all certainly have an interesting way of conducting an investigation."

"I'll make you a deal. I'll talk with Hogman again if you'll check out this fellow Murphy Doucet."

"Because he's with the Teamsters?"

"That's right. Let's find out how these guys developed an interest in the War Between the States."

"You know what 'transfer' is in psychology?"

"What's the point?"

"Earlier you suggested that maybe I had a private agenda about Julie Balboni. Do you think that perhaps it's you who's taking the investigation into a secondary area?"

"Could be. But you can't ever tell what'll fly out of the tree until you throw a rock into it."

It was a flippant thing to say. But at the time it seemed innocent and of little more consequence than the warm breeze blowing across the cane and the plum-colored thunderclouds that were building out over the Gulf.

SAM "HOGMAN" PATIN lived on the bayou south of town in a paintless wood-frame house overgrown with banana trees and with leaf-clogged rain gutters and screens that were orange with rust. The roof was patched with R.C. Cola signs, the yard a tangle of weeds, automobile and washing-machine parts, morning-glory vines, and pig bones; the gallery and one corner of the house sagged to one side like a broken smile.

I had waited until later in the day to talk to him at his house. I knew that he wouldn't have talked to me in front of other people at the movie set, and actually I wasn't even sure that he would tell me anything of importance now. He had served seventeen years in Angola, the first four of which he had spent on the Red Hat gang. These were the murderers, the psychotics, and the uncontrollable. They wore black-and-white stripes and straw hats that had been dipped in red paint, always ran double-time under the mounted gunbulls, and were punished on anthills, in cast-iron sweatboxes, or with the Black Betty, a leather whip that could flay a man's back to marmalade.

Hogman would probably still be in there, except he got religion and a Baptist preacher in Baton Rouge worked a pardon for him through the state legislature. His backyard was dirt, deep in shadow from the live-oak trees, and sloped away to the bayou, where a rotted-out pirogue webbed with green algae lay half-submerged in the shallows. He sat in a straight-backed wood chair under a tree that was strung with blue Milk of Magnesia bottles and crucifixes fashioned out of sticks and aluminum foil. When the breeze lifted out of the south, the whole tree sang with silver and blue light.

Hogman tightened the key on a new string he had just strung on his guitar. His skin was so black it had a purple sheen to it; and his hair was grizzled, the curls ironed flat against his head. His shoulders were an ax handle wide, the muscles in his upper arms the size of grapefruit. There wasn't a tablespoon of fat on his body. I wondered what it must have been like to face down Hogman Patin back in the days when he carried a barber's razor on a leather cord around his neck.

"What did you want to tell me, Sam?" I asked.

"One or two t'ings that been botherin' me. Get a chair off the po'ch. You want some tea?"

"No, that's fine, thank you."

I lifted a wicker chair off the back porch and walked back to the oak tree with it. He had slipped three metal picks onto his fingers and was running a blues progression up the neck of the guitar. He mashed the strings into the frets so that the sound continued to reverberate through the dark wood after he had struck the notes with his steel picks. Then he tightened the key again and rested the big curved belly of the twelve-string on his thigh.

"I don't like to have no truck with white folks' bidness," he said. "But it bother me, what somebody done to that girl. It been botherin' me a whole lot."

He picked up from the dirt a jelly glass filled with iced tea and drank out of it.

"She was messin' in somet'ing bad, wouldn't listen to me or pay me no mind about it, neither. When they that age, they know what they wanta do."

"Messing in what?"

"I talked to her maybe two hours befo' she left the juke. I been knowing that girl a long time. She love zydeco and blues music. She tell me, 'Hogman, in the next life me and you is gonna get married.' That's what she say. I tole her, 'Darlin', don't let them mens use you for no chicken.'

"She say, 'I ain't no chicken, Hogman. I going to New Orleans. I gonna have my own coop. Them others gonna be the chickens. I gonna have me a townhouse on Lake Pontchartrain.' "

"Wait a minute, Sam. She told you she was going to have other girls working for her?"

"That's what I just tole you, ain't I?"

"Yes, you did."

"I say, 'Don't be talkin' like that. You get away from them pimps, Cherry. Them white trash ain't gonna give you no townhouse. They'll use you up, t'row you away, then find some other girl just like you, I mean in five minutes, that quick.'

"She say, 'No, they ain't, 'cause I got the mojo on the Man, Hogman. He know it, too.'

"You know, when she say that, she smile up at me and her face look heart shape, like she just a little girl doin' some innocent t'ing 'stead of about to get herself killed."

"What man did she mean?"

"Probably some pimp tole her she special, she pretty, she just like a daughter to him. I seen the same t'ing in Angola. It ain't no different. A bunch take a young boy down on the flo', then when they get finish with him, he ready, he glad to put on a dress, makeup, be the punk for some wolf gonna take care of him, tell him he ain't just somebody's poke chops in the shower stall."

"Why'd you wait to tell me this?"

" 'Cause ain't nothin' like this ever happen 'round here befo'. I don't like it, me. No, suh."

"I see."

He splayed his long fingers on the belly of the guitar. The nails were pink against his black skin. His eyes looked off reflectively at the bayou, where fireflies were lighting in the gloom above the flooded cattails.

Finally he said, "I need to tell you somet'ing else."

"Go ahead, Sam."

"You mixed up with that skeleton they found over in the Atchafalaya, ain't you?"

"How'd you know about that?"

"When somebody find a dead black man, black people know about it. That man didn't have on no belt, didn't have no strings in his boots, did he?"

"That wasn't in the newspaper, podna."

"The preacher they call up to do the burial is my first cousin. He brought a suit of clothes to the mo'tuary to dress the bones in. They was a black man workin' there, and my cousin say, 'That fella was lynched, wasn't he?' The black man say, 'Yeah, they probably drug him out of bed to do it, too. Didn't even have time to put strings in his boots or run a belt through his britches.' "

"What are you telling me, Sam?"

"I remember somet'ing, a long time ago, maybe thirty, thirty-five years back." He patted one hand on top of the other and his eyes became muddy.

"Just say it, Sam."

"A bluejay don't set on a mockin'bird's nest. I ain't got no use for that stuff in people, neither. The Lord made people a different color for a reason."

He shook his head back and forth, as though he were dispelling a troubling thought.

"You're not talking about a rape, are you?"

"White folk call it rape when it fit what they want," he said. "They see what they need to see. Black folk cain't be choicy. They see what they gots to see. They was a black man, no, that ain't right, this is a nigger I'm talkin' about, and he was carryin' on with a white woman whose husband he worked for. Black folk knowed it, too. They tole him he better stop what he doin' befo' the cars start comin' down in the quarters and some innocent black man end up on a tree. I t'ink them was the bones you drug up in that sandbar."

"What was his name?"

"Who care what his name? Maybe he got what he ax for. But them people who done that still out there. I say past is past. I say don't be messin' in it."

"Are you cautioning me?"

"When I was in the pen, yo' daddy, Mr. Aldous, brought my mother food. He care for her when she sick, he pay for her medicine up at the sto'. I ain't forgot that, me."

"Sam, if you have information about a murder, the law requires that you come forward with it."

"Whose law? The law that run that pen up there? You want to find bodies, go dig in that levee for some of them boys the gunbulls shot down just for pure meanness. I seen it." He touched the corner of his eye with one long finger. "The hack get drunk on corn liquor, single out some boy on the wheelbarrow, holler out, 'Yow! You! Nigger! Run!' Then he'd pop him with his .45, just like bustin' a clay duck."

"What was the white woman's name?"

"I got to be startin' my supper now."

"Was the dead man in a jail?"

"Ain't nobody interested back then, ain't nobody interested now. You give it a few mo' years, we all gonna be dead. You ain't goin' change nothin' for a nigger been in the river thirty years. You want to do some good, catch the pimp tore up that young girl. 'Cause sho' as God made little green apples, he gonna do it again."

He squinted one eye in a shaft of sunlight that fell through the tree branches and lighted one half of his face like an ebony stage mask that was sewn together from mismatched parts.

IT WAS ALMOST dusk when I got home that evening, but the sky was still as blue as a robin's egg in the west and the glow of the late sun looked like pools of pink fire in the clouds. After I ate supper, I walked down to the bait shop to help Batist close up. I was pulling back the canvas awning on the guy wires over the spool tables when I saw the sheriff's car drive down the dirt road and park under the trees.

He walked down the dock toward me. His face looked flushed from the heat, puffy with fatigue.

"I guarantee you, it's been one scorcher of a day," he said, went inside the shop, and came back with a sweating bottle of orange pop in his hand. He sat down at a table and wiped the sweat off his neck with his handkerchief. Grains of ice slid down the neck of the pop bottle.

"What's up, Sheriff?" I said.

"Have you seen Rosie this afternoon?" He took a drink out of the bottle.

I sat down across from him. Waves from a passing boat slapped against the pilings under the dock.

"We went out to the movie location, then she went to Lafayette to check out a couple of things," I said.

"Yeah, that's why I'm here."

"What do you mean?"

"I've gotten about a half-dozen phone calls this afternoon. I'm not sure what you guys are doing, Dave."

"Conducting a murder investigation."

"Oh, yeah? What does the director of a motion picture have to do with the death of Cherry LeBlanc?"

"Goldman got in your face?"

"*He* didn't. But you seem to have upset a few other people around here. Let's see, I received calls from two members of the Chamber of Commerce; Goldman's lawyer, who says you seem to be taking an undue interest in our visiting film community; and the mayor, who'd like to know what the hell my people think they're doing. If that wasn't enough, I also got a call from a Teamster official in Lafayette and a guy named Twinky Hebert Lemoyne who runs a bottling plant over there. Are you two working on some kind of negative outreach program? What was she doing over in Lafayette Parish?"

"Ask her."

"I have a feeling she was sent over there."

"She was checking out the Teamsters' involvement with Goldman and Julie Balboni."

"What does that have to do with our investigation?"

"I'm not sure. Maybe nothing. What did this guy Twinky Lemoyne call about?"

"He owns half of a security service with a guy named Murphy Doucet. Lemoyne said Rosie came out to his bottling plant, asked him questions that were none of her business, and told him that he should give second thought to doing business with the mob. Do you know who Twinky Lemoyne is?"

"Not really."

"He's a wealthy and respected man in Lafayette. In fact, he's a decent guy. What are y'all trying to do, Dave?"

"You sent me to invite Julie Balboni out of town. But now we find that Julie has made himself a big part of the local economy. I think that's the problem, Sheriff, not me and Rosie."

He rubbed his whiskers with the backs of his fingers.

"Maybe it is," he said finally, "but there's more than one way to do things."

"What would you suggest that we do differently?"

His eyes studied a turkey buzzard that floated on the hot-air currents above the marsh.

"Concentrate on nailing this psychopath. For the time being forget about Balboni," he said. His eyes didn't come back to meet mine when he spoke.

"Maybe Julie's involved."

"He's not. Julie doesn't do anything unless it's for money."

"I'm getting the strong feeling that the Spanish Lake area is becoming off limits."

"No, I didn't say that. It's a matter of priorities. That brings up another subject, too—the remains of that black man you found out in the Atchafalaya Basin."

"Yes?"

"That's St. Mary Parish's jurisdiction. Let them work the case. We've got enough on our own plate."

"They're not going to work it."

"Then that's their choice."

I didn't speak for a moment. The twilight was almost gone. The air was heavy and moist and full of insects, and out in the cypress I could hear wood ducks fluttering across the surface of the water.

"Would you like another cold drink?" I asked.

"No, this is fine," he answered.

"I'd better help Batist lock up, then. We'll see you, Sheriff," I said, and went inside the bait shop. I didn't come back out until I heard his car start and head down the dirt road.

SAM "HOGMAN" PATIN was wrong. Cherry LeBlanc's killer would not merely find another victim in the future. He already had.

CHAPTER 7

I GOT THE CALL at eleven o'clock that night. A fisherman running a trotline by the levee, way down in the bottom of Vermilion Parish, almost to the salt water, had seen a lidless oil drum half submerged on its side in the cattails. He would have paid little attention to it, except for the fact that he saw the backs of alligator gars arching out of the water in the moonlight as they tore at something inside the barrel.

I drove down the narrow dirt track on top of the levee through the miles of flooded sawgrass that eventually bled into the Gulf. Strips of black cloud floated across the moon, and up ahead I could see an ambulance and a collection of sheriff's cars parked on the levee in a white and red glow of floodlamps, burning flares, and revolving emergency lights.

The girl was already in a body bag inside the ambulance. The coroner was a tired, overweight Jewish man with emphysema and a terrible cigarette odor whom I had known for years. There were deep circles under his eyes, and he kept rubbing mosquito repellent onto his face and fat arms.

Down the bank a Vermilion Parish plainclothes was interviewing the fisherman, whose unshaven face looked bloodless and gray in the glare of the floodlamps.

"You want to see her, Dave?" the coroner asked.

"Should I?"

"Probably."

We climbed into the back of the ambulance. Even with the air conditioner running, it was hot and stale-smelling inside.

"I figure she was in the water only a couple of days, but she's probably been dead several weeks," he said. "The barrel was probably on the side of the levee, then it rolled into the water. Otherwise, the crabs and the gars would have torn her up a lot worse."

He pulled the zipper from the girl's head all the way down to her ankles.

I took a breath and swallowed.

"I'd say she was in her early twenties, but I'm guessing," he said. "As you can see, we won't get much in the way of prints. I don't think an artist will be able to re-create what her face looked like, either. Cause of death doesn't appear to be a mystery—asphyxiation with a plastic bag taped around her neck. The same electrician's tape he used to bind her hands and ankles. Rape, sodomy, sexual degradation, that kind of stuff? When their clothes are gone, you can put it in the bank."

"No rings, bracelets, tattoos?"

He shook his head.

"Have they found anything out there?"

"Nothing."

"Tire tracks?"

"Not after all the rain we've had."

"Do y'all have any missing-persons reports that coincide with—"

"Nope."

A long strand of her blond hair hung outside the bag. For some reason it bothered me. I picked it up and placed it on her forehead. The coroner looked at me strangely.

"Why would he stuff her in a barrel?" I said.

"Dave, the day you can put yourself inside the head of a cocksucker like that, that's the day you eat your gun."

I stepped back outside into the humid brilliance of the floodlamps, then walked along the slope of the levee and down by the water's edge. The darkness throbbed with the croaking of frogs, and fireflies were lighting in the tops of the sawgrass. The weeds along the levee had been trampled by cops' feet; fresh cigarette butts floated in the water; a sheriff's deputy was telling two others a racial joke.

The Vermilion Parish plainclothes finished interviewing the fisherman, put his notebook in his shirt pocket, and walked up the slope to his car. The fisherman continued to stand by his pirogue, scratching at the mosquito bites on his arms, evidently unsure of what he was supposed to do next. Sweat leaked out of the band of his cloth cap and glistened on his jawbones. When I introduced myself, his handshake, like most Cajun men's, was effeminate.

"I ain't never seen nothing like that, me," he said. "I don't want to never see nothing like that again, neither."

The bottom of his pirogue was piled with mudcat. They quivered on top of each other, their whiskers pasted back against their yellow sides and bloated white bellies. On the seat of his pirogue was a headlamp with an elastic strap on it.

"When'd you first see that metal barrel?" I said.

"Tonight."

"Do you come down here often?" I asked.

"Not too often, no, suh."

"You've got a nice bunch of fish there."

"Yeah, they feed good when the moon's up."

I gazed into the bottom of his pirogue, at the wet shine of moonlight on the fish's sides, the tangles of trotlines and corks, and a long object wrapped in a canvas tarp under the seat.

I caught the pirogue by the gunwale and slid it partly up on the mudbank.

"Do you mind if I look at this?" I said, and flipped back the folds of the canvas tarp.

He didn't answer. I took a pen flashlight out of my shirt pocket and shone it on the lever-action .30-.30 rifle. The bluing was worn off and the stock was wrapped with copper wire.

"Walk down here a little ways with me," I said.

He followed me out to the edge of the lighted area, out of earshot of the Vermilion Parish deputies.

"We want to catch the guy who did this," I said. "I think you'd like to help us do that, wouldn't you?"

"Yes, suh, I sho' would."

"But there's a problem here, isn't there? Something that's preventing you from telling me everything you want to?"

"I ain't real sho' what you—"

"Are you selling fish to restaurants?"

"No, suh, that ain't true."

"Did you bring that .30-.30 along to shoot frogs?"

He grinned and shook his head. I grinned back at him.

"But you might just poach a 'gator or two?" I said.

"No, suh, I ain't got no 'gator. You can look."

I let my expression go flat.

"That's right. So you don't have to be afraid," I said. "I just want you to tell me the truth. Nobody's going to bother you about that gun, or your headlamp, or what you might be doing with your fish. Do we have a deal?"

"Yes, suh."

"When'd you first notice that barrel?"

"Maybe t'ree, fo' weeks ago. It was setting up on dry ground. I didn't have no reason to pay it no mind, no, but then I started to smell somet'ing. I t'ought it was a dead nutria, or maybe a big gar rotting up on the bank. It was real strong one night, then t'ree nights later you couldn't smell it 'less the wind blow it right across the water. Then it rained and the next night they wasn't no smell at all. I just never t'ought they might be a dead girl up there."

"Did you see anyone up there?"

"Maybe about a mont' ago, at evening, I seen a car. I 'member t'inking it was new and why would anybody bring his new car down that dirt road full of holes."

"What kind of car?"

"I don't remember, suh."

"You remember the color?"

"No, suh, I'm sorry."

His face looked fatigued and empty. "I just wish I ain't been the one to find her," he said. "I ain't never gonna forget looking inside that barrel."

I put my business card in his shirt pocket.

"Call me if you think of anything else. You did just fine, podna," I said, and patted him on the arm.

I turned my truck around in the middle of the levee and headed back toward New Iberia. Up ahead the glow of the red and blue emergency lights on the ambulance sped across the tops of the sawgrass, cattails, and bleached sandspits where the husks of dead gars boiled with fire ants.

WHAT HAD I learned from it all?

Not much.

But maybe in his cynical way my friend the sleepless coroner had cut right to the heart of the problem: How do you go inside the head of a homicidal sadist who prowls the countryside like a tiger turned loose in a schoolyard?

I've seen films that portray detectives who try to absorb the moral insanity of their adversaries in order to trap them inside their own maniacal design. It makes an interesting story. Maybe it's even possible.

But four years ago I had to go to Huntsville, Texas, to interview a man on death row who had confessed to almost three hundred murders throughout the United States. Suddenly, from all over the country, cops with unsolved homicide cases flocked to Huntsville like flies on pig flop. We were no exception. A black woman in New Iberia had been abducted out of her house, strangled to death, and thrown in the Vermilion River. We had no suspects, and the man in Huntsville, Jack Hatfield, had been through Louisiana many times in his red tracings across the map.

He turned out to be neither shrewd nor cunning; there was no malevolent light in his eyes, nothing hostile or driven about his behavior. His accent was peckerwood, his demeanor finally that of a simpleton. He told me about his religious conversion and glowing presences that appeared to him in his cell; it was quickly apparent that he wanted me to like him, that he would tell me anything I wanted to hear. All I had to do was provide him the details of a murder, and he would make the crime his own.

(Later, an unemployed oil-field roughneck would confess to murdering the black woman after being given title to a ten-year-old car by her husband.)

I asked Jack Hatfield if he was trying to trade off his cooperation for a commutation of his sentence. He answered, "Naw, I got no kick comin' about that, long as it's legal."

With a benign expression on his face, he chronicled his long list of roadside murders from Maine to southern California. He could have been talking about a set of embossed ceramic plates that he had collected from each state that he had visited. If he had indeed done what he told me, he was completely without remorse.

"My victims didn't suffer none," he said.

Then he began to talk about his mother and an incredible transformation took place in him. Tears streaked down his homely face, he trembled all over, his fingers left white marks on his arms. Evidently she had been not only a prostitute but perverse as well. When he was a little boy she had made him stand by the bed and watch her copulate with her johns. When he had tried to hide in the woods, she beat him with a quirt, brought him back to the house, and made him watch some more.

He spent fifteen years in the Wisconsin penitentiary for her murder.

Then he paused in his story, wiped his face with his hand, pulled his T-shirt out from his chest with his finger, and smelled himself.

"I killed three more people the day I come out of prison. I told them I was gonna do it, and I done it," he said, and began cleaning his fingernails with a toothpick as though I were not there.

When I walked back out into the autumn sunshine that afternoon, back into the smell of east Texas piney woods and white-uniformed convicts burning piles of tree stumps on the edge of a cottonfield, I was convinced that Jack Hatfield's story about his mother was true but that almost everything else he had told me would remain as demonstrably elusive as a psychotic dream. Perhaps the answer to Jack Hatfield lay with others, I thought. Perhaps we should ask those who would eventually strap him to the gurney in the execution room, poke the IV needle into the vein, tape it lovingly to the skin, and watch him through the viewing glass as the injection dulled his eyes, then hit his heart like a hammer. Would his life, his secret and dark knowledge, be passed on to them?

I'D HAD LITTLE sleep when I set out for the office the next morning. The sun had come up red and hot over the trees, and because I had left the windows down the night before, the inside of my truck was full of mosquitoes and dripping with humidity. I stopped at a traffic light on the east side of town and saw a purple Cadillac limousine, with tinted black windows, pull into a yellow zone by a restaurant and park squarely in front of the fireplug.

Cholo Manelli stepped out of the driver's door, stretched, rotated a crick out of his neck, looked up and down the street a couple of times, then walked around to the other side of the limo and opened the back door for Julie Balboni. Then the rest of Julie's entourage—three men and the woman named Margot—stepped out onto the sidewalk, their faces dour in the heat, their eyes sullen with the morning's early hour.

Cholo went up the sidewalk first, point man and

good soldier that he was, his head turning slightly from side to side, his simian shoulders rolling under his flowered shirt. He opened the front door of the restaurant, and Julie walked inside, with the others in single file behind him.

I didn't plan any of the events that followed.

I drove through the light and went almost two blocks before I made a U-turn, drove back to the restaurant, and parked under a live-oak tree across the street from the limo. The early sun's heat was already rising from the cement, and I could smell dead water beetles in the curb gutters.

My eyes burned from lack of sleep, and though I had just shaved, I could feel stubble, like grit, along the edge of my jaw. I got out of the truck, put my seersucker coat over my arm, and walked across the street to the limo. The waxed purple surface had the soft glow of hard candy; the tinted black windows swam with the mirrored images of oak trees and azalea bushes moving in the breeze.

I unfolded the blade of my Puma knife, walked from fender to fender, and sawed the air stems off all four tires. The limo went down on the rims like it had been dropped from a chain. A black kid who had been putting circulars on doors stopped and watched me as he would a fascinating creature inside a zoo cage.

I walked to the filling station on the corner, called the dispatcher, and told him to have a wrecker tow the limo into the pound.

Then I went inside the restaurant, which gleamed with chrome and silverware and Formica surfaces, and walked past the long table where two waitresses were in the process of serving Julie and his group their breakfast. Cholo saw me first and started to speak, but I looked straight ahead and continued on into the men's room as though they were not there.

I washed my face with cold water, dried it with paper towels, and combed my hair in the mirror. There were flecks of white in my mustache now, and lines around my eyes that I hadn't noticed only a week before. I turned on the cold water and washed my face again, as though somehow I could rinse time and age out of my skin. Then I crumpled up the damp paper towel in my hand, flung it into the trash can, fixed my tie, put on my coat and sunglasses, and walked back into the restaurant.

Showtime, Julie, I thought.

Even sitting down, he towered above the others at the head of the table, in a pink short-sleeve shirt, suspenders, and gray striped slacks, his tangled black hair ruffling on his brow in the breeze from the fan, his mouth full of food while he told the waitress to bring more coffee and to reheat Margot's breakfast steak. Cholo kept trying to smile at me, his false teeth as stiff as whale bone in his mouth. Julie's other hoods looked up at me, then at Julie; when they read nothing in his face, they resumed eating.

"Hey, Lieutenant, I thought that was you. You here for breakfast?" Cholo said.

"I was just passing by," I said.

"What's going on, Dave?" Julie said, his mouth chewing, his eyes fixed on the flower vase in front of him.

"I had a long night last night," I said.

"Yeah?" he said.

"We found a girl in a barrel down in south Vermilion Parish."

He continued to chew, then he took a drink of water. He touched his mouth with his napkin.

"You want to sit down, or are you on your way out?" he said.

Just then I heard the steel hook of the wrecker clang somewhere on the limo's frame and the hydraulic cables start to tighten on the winch. Cholo craned his head to look beyond the angle of the front window that gave onto the street.

"I always thought you were standup, Feet," I said.

"I appreciate the compliment, but that's a term they use in a place I've never been."

"That's all right, I changed my mind. I don't think you're standup anymore, Feet."

He blew up both his cheeks.

"What are you trying to say, Dave?"

"The man I work for got a bunch of phone calls yesterday. It looks like somebody dropped the dime on me with the Kiwanis Club."

"It ain't a bunch I got a lot of influence with. Talk with Mikey Goldman if you got that kind of problem."

"You use what works, Julie."

"Hey, get real, Dave. When I want to send a message to somebody, it don't come through Dagwood Bumstead."

Outside, the driver of the wrecker gunned his engine, pulled away from the curb, and dragged the limo past the front window. The limo's two front tires, which were totally deflated and still on the asphalt, were sliced into ribbons by the wheel rims.

Cholo's mouth was wide with unchewed scrambled eggs.

"Hey, a guy's got our car! A guy's driving off with the fucking limo, Julie!" he said.

Julie watched the wrecker and his limo disappear up the street. He pushed his plate away an inch with his thumb. One corner of his mouth drooped, and he pressed against it with his napkin.

"Sit down," he said.

Everyone had stopped eating now. A waitress came to the table with a pitcher of ice water and started to refill the glasses, then hesitated and walked back behind the counter. I pulled out a chair and sat at the corner of the table, a foot from Julie's elbow.

"You're pissed off about something and you have my fucking car towed in?" he said.

"Don't park in front of fireplugs."

"Fireplugs?"

"Right."

"I'm getting this kind of dog shit because of a fucking fireplug?"

"No, what I'm wondering, Julie, is why you and Cholo have to hit on a small-town teenage hooker. Don't y'all have enough chippies back in New Orleans?"

"What?"

"Cherry LeBlanc," I said.

"Who the fuck is Cherry LeBlanc?"

"Give it a break and stop acting like you just popped out of your mama's womb."

He folded his napkin, placed it carefully by the side of his plate, pulled a carnation out of the flower vase, and pinched off the stem.

"You calling me a pimp?" he said. "You trying to embarrass me in public. That's what this is about?"

"You didn't listen to what I said. We just found another murdered girl. Cholo knew about the murder of the LeBlanc girl, and he said you did, too. Except you lied about it when I mentioned her to you."

His eyes drifted lazily to Cholo's face. Cholo squeezed his hands on his wrists.

"I'm all lost here. I'm—" he began.

"You know what the real trouble is, Dave?" Julie said. He flipped the carnation onto the tablecloth. "You never understood how this town worked. You remember anybody complaining about the cathouses on Railroad and Hopkins? Or the slot machines that were in every bar and restaurant in town? Nobody complained 'cause my old man delivered an envelope to certain people at the end of every month. But those same people treated our family like we were spit on the sidewalk.

"So you and that FBI broad went around town stirring up the Bumstead crowd, shoving a broomstick up their ringus, and your boss man called you in to explain the facts of life. But it's no fun finding out that the guys you work for don't want to scare a few million dollars out of town. So you fuck my car and get in my face in a public place. I think maybe you should go back to work in New Orleans. I think maybe this shithole is starting to rub off on you."

The manager had come from behind the glass cashier's counter and was now standing three feet from me and Julie, his clip-on bow tie askew, his tongue wetting his lips.

"Sir, could you gentlemen lower your, I mean, could you not use that language in—" he began.

Julie's eyes, which were filled with a black light, flipped up into the manager's face.

"Get the fuck away from my table," he said.

"Sir—" the manager said.

"It's all right, Mr. Meaux. I'm leaving in just a second," I said.

"Oh, sad to hear it," the woman, Margot, said. Except Cholo, the other hoods at the table smiled at her humor. She wore a sundress, and her hair, which was bleached the color of ash, was pulled back tightly on her head. She smoked a cigarette and the backs of her arms were covered with freckles.

"You want to come down to the office and look at some morgue pictures? I think that'd be a good idea," I said. "Bring your girlfriend along if you like."

"I'm going to say this just once. I don't know none of these girls, I don't have nothing to do with your problems, you understand what I'm saying?

You said some ugly things to me, Dave, but we're old friends and I'm going to let it slide. I'll call a couple of cabs, I'll pay the fine on my car, I'll buy new tires, and I'll forget everything you been saying to me. But don't you never try to get in my face in a public place again."

One of his hoods was getting up, scraping back his chair, to use the restroom.

I folded my sunglasses, slipped them into my shirt pocket, and rubbed the burning sensation in my eyes with my thumb and forefinger.

"Feet, you're full of more shit than a broken pay toilet," I said quietly.

The hood rested his hand on my shoulder. He was perhaps twenty-eight or thirty, lithe and olive-skinned, his dark hair boxed on his neck. A long pink scar, as thick as a soda straw, ran down the inside of one arm.

"Everybody's been pretty polite here," he said.

I looked at his hand and at his face. I could smell the faint hint of his sweat through his deodorant, the nicotine on the backs of his fingers.

"But you keep offending people," he said. He raised his palm slightly, then set it on my shoulder again.

"Don't let your day get complicated," I said.

"It's time to let people alone, Mr. Robicheaux," he said. Then he began to knead my shoulder as a fellow ballplayer might out on the pitcher's mound.

I felt a balloon of red-black color rise out of my chest into my head, heard a sound behind my eyes like wet newspaper tearing, and for some reason saw a kaleidoscopic image of the blond girl in the black body bag, a long strand of algae-streaked hair glued to the gray flesh of her forehead.

I hit him so hard in the stomach that my fist buried itself up to the wrist right under his sternum and spittle flew from his mouth onto the tabletop. Then I came up out of the chair and hooked him in the eye, saw the skin break against the bone and well with blood. He tried to regain his balance and swing a sugar shaker at my face, but I spun him sideways, caught him in the kidney, and drove him to his knees between two counter stools. I didn't remember hitting him in the mouth, but his bottom lip was drooling blood onto his shirtfront.

I didn't want to stop. I heard the roar of wind in seashells, the wheels of rusted engines clanging cog against cog. Then I saw Cholo in front of me, his big square hands raised in placation, his mouth small with sound.

"What?" I said.

"It ain't your style, Loot," he was whispering hoarsely. "Ease off, the guy's new, he don't know the rules, Loot. Come on, this ain't good for nobody."

My knuckles were skinned, my palms ringing. I heard glass crunch under the sole of my shoe in the stunned silence, and looked down numbly at my broken sunglasses on the floor like a man emerging from a blackout.

Julie Balboni scraped back his chair, took his gold money clip from his slacks, and began counting out a series of ten-dollar bills on the table.

He didn't even look up at me when he spoke. But everybody in the restaurant heard what he said. "I think you're losing it, Dave. Stop being a hired dildo for the local dipshits or get yourself some better tranqs."

CHAPTER 8

IT WAS TEN A.M. Batist had gone after a boat with a fouled engine down the bayou, and the bait shop and dock were empty. The tin roof was expanding in the heat, buckling and pinging against the bolts and wood joists. I pulled a can of Dr Pepper out of the crushed ice in the cooler and sat outside in the hot shade by myself and drank it. Green dragonflies hung suspended over the cattails along the bayou's banks; a needlenose gar that had probably been wounded by a boat propeller turned in circles in the dead current, while a school of minnows fed off a red gash behind its gills; a smell like dead snakes, sour mud, and rotted hyacinth vines blew out of the marsh on the hot wind.

I didn't want to even think about the events of this morning. The scene in the restaurant was like a moment snipped out of a drunk dream, in which I was always out of control, publicly indecent or lewd in the eyes of others.

The soda can grew warm in my palm. The sky in the south had a bright sheen to it like blue silk. I hoped that it would storm that afternoon, that rain would thunder down on the marsh and bayou, roar like grapeshot on the roof of my house, pour in gullies through the dirt and dead leaves under the pecan trees in my yard.

I heard Bootsie behind me. She sat down in a canvas chair by a spool table and crossed her legs. She wore white shorts, sandals, and a denim shirt with the sleeves cut off. There were sweat rings under her arms, and the down on top of her thighs had been burned gold by the sun.

We met at a dance on Spanish Lake during the summer of 1957, and a short time later we lost our virginity together in my father's boathouse, while the rain fell out of the sunlight and dripped off the eaves and the willow trees into the lake and the inside of the boathouse trembled with a wet green-yellow light.

But even at that age I had already started my long commitment to sour mash straight up with a sweating Jax on the side. Bootsie and I would go separate ways, far from Bayou Teche and the provincial Cajun world in which we had grown up. I would make the journey to Vietnam as one of our new colonials and return with a junkyard in my hip and thigh and nocturnal memories that neither whiskey nor army hospital dope could kill. She would marry an oil-field pilot who would later tip a guy wire on an offshore rig and crash his helicopter right on top of the quarter-boat; then she would discover that her second husband, an accounting graduate from Tulane, was a bookkeeper for the Mafia, although his career with them became short-lived when they shotgunned him and his mistress to death in the parking lot of the Hialeah racetrack.

She had lupus disease that we had knocked into remission with medication, but it still lived in her blood like a sleeping parasite that waited for its moment to attack her kidneys and sever her connective tissue. She was supposed to avoid hard sunlight, but again and again I came home from work and found her working in the yard in shorts and a halter, her hot skin filmed with sweat and grains of dirt.

"Did something happen at work?" she said.

"I had some trouble at Del's."

"What?"

"I busted up one of Baby Feet Balboni's lowlifes."

"In the restaurant?"

"Yeah, that's where I did it."

"What did he do?"

"He put his hand on me." I set down my soda can and propped my forearms on my thighs. I looked out at the sun's reflection in the brown water.

"Have you been back to the office?" she said.

"Not yet. I'll probably go in later."

She was quiet a moment.

"Have you talked to the sheriff?" she asked.

"There's not really much to talk about. The guy could make a beef but he won't. They don't like to get messed up in legal action against cops."

She uncrossed her legs and brushed idly at her knee with her fingertips.

"Dave, is something else going on, something you're not telling me about?"

"The guy put his hand on my shoulder and I wanted to tear him apart. Maybe I would have done it if this guy named Manelli hadn't stepped in front of me."

I saw her breasts rise and fall under her shirt. Far down the bayou Batist was towing a second boat behind his outboard and the waves were slapping the floating hyacinths against the banks. She got up from her chair and stood behind me. She worked her fingers into my shoulders. I could feel her thigh touch my back.

"New Iberia is never going to be the same place we grew up in. That's just the way things are," she said.

"It doesn't mean I have to like it."

"The Balboni family was here a long time. We survived, didn't we? They'll make their movie and go away."

"There're too many people willing to sell it down the drain."

"Sell what?"

"Whatever makes a dollar for them. Redfish and *sac-a-lait* to restaurants, alligators to the Japanese. They let oil companies pollute the oyster beds and cut canals through the marsh so salt water can eat up thousands of square miles of wetlands. They take it on their knees from anybody who's got a checkbook."

"Let it go, Dave."

"I think a three-day open season on people would solve a lot of our problems."

"Tell the sheriff what happened. Don't let it just hang there."

"He's worried about some guys at the Chamber of Commerce, Bootsie. He's a good guy most of the time, but these are the people he's spent most of his life around."

"I think you should talk to him."

"All right, I'm going to take a shower, then I'll call him."

"You're not going to the office?"

"I'm not sure. Maybe later."

Batist cut the engine on his boat and floated on the swell into the dock and bumped against the strips of rubber tire we had nailed to the pilings. His shirt was piled on the board seat beside him, and his black shoulders and chest were beaded with sweat. His head looked like a cannonball. He grinned with an unlit cigar in the corner of his mouth.

I was glad for the distraction.

"I was up at the fo'-corners," he said. "A man there said you mopped up the restaurant flo' with one of them dagos."

Thanks, Batist, I thought.

I SHOWERED IN water that was so cold it left me breathless, changed clothes, and drove to the bottling works down by the Vermilion River in Lafayette. The two-story building was an old one, made of yellow brick, and surrounded by huge live-oak trees. In back was a parking lot, which was filled with delivery trucks, and a loading dock, where a dozen black men were rattling crates of soda pop out of the building's dark interior and stacking them inside the waiting trucks. Their physical strength was incredible. Some of them would pick up a half-dozen full cases at a time and lift them easily to eye level. Their muscles looked like water-streaked black stone.

I asked one of them where I could find Twinky Hebert Lemoyne.

"Mr. Twinky in yonder, in the office. Better catch him quick, though. He fixin' to go out on the route," he said.

"He goes out on the route?"

"Mr. Twinky do everyt'ing, suh."

I walked inside the warehouse to a cluttered, windowed office whose door was already open. The walls and corkboards were papered with invoices, old church calendars, unframed photographs of employees and fishermen with thick-bellied large-mouth bass draped across their hands. Lemoyne's face was pink and well-shaped, his eyebrows sandy, his gray hair still streaked in places with gold. He sat erect in his chair, his eyes behind his rimless glasses concentrated on the papers in his hands. He wore a short-sleeved shirt and a loose burnt-orange tie (a seersucker coat hung on the back of the chair) and a plastic pen holder in his pocket; his brown shoes were shined; his fingernails were trimmed and clean. But he had the large shoulders and hands of a workingman, and he radiated the kind of quiet, hard-earned physical power that in some men neither age nor extra weight seems to diminish.

There was no air conditioning in his office, and he had weighted all the papers on his desk to keep them from blowing away in the breeze from the oscillating fan.

After I had introduced myself, he gazed out at the loading dock a moment, then lifted his hands from the desk blotter and put them down again as though somehow we had already reached a point in our conversation where there was nothing left to be said.

"Can I sit down?" I said.

"Go ahead. But I think you're wasting your time here."

"It's been a slow day." I smiled at him.

"Mr. Robicheaux, I don't have any idea in the world why either you or that Mexican woman is interested in me. Could you be a little bit more forthcoming?"

"Actually, until yesterday I don't believe I ever heard your name."

"What should I make of that?"

"The problem is you and a few others tried to stick a couple of thumbtacks in my boss's head." I smiled again.

"Listen, that woman came into my office yesterday and accused me of working with the Mafia."

"Why would she do that?"

"You tell me, please."

"You own half of a security service with Murphy Doucet?"

"That's right, I surely do. Can you tell me what y'all are looking for, why y'all are in my place of business?"

"When you do business with a man like Julie Balboni, you create a certain degree of curiosity about yourself."

"I don't do business with this man, and I don't know anything about him. I bought stock in this motion picture they're making. A lot of business-people around here have. I've never met Julie Balboni and I don't plan to. Are we clear on this, sir?"

"My boss says you're a respected man. It looks like you have a good business, too. I'd be careful who I messed with, Mr. Lemoyne."

"I'm not interested in pursuing the subject." He fixed his glasses, squared his shoulders slightly, and picked up several sheets of paper in his hands.

I drummed my fingers on the arms of my chair. Outside I could hear truck doors slamming and gears grinding.

"I guess I didn't explain myself very well," I said.

"You don't need to," he said, and looked up at the clock on the wall.

"You're a solid businessman. There's nothing wrong with buying stock in a movie company. There's nothing wrong with providing a security service for it, either. But a lady who's not much taller than a fireplug asks you a couple of questions and you try to drop the dime on her. That doesn't seem to fit, Mr. Lemoyne."

"There're people out there committing rapes, armed robberies, selling crack to children, God only knows what else, but you and that woman have the nerve to come in here and question me because

I have a vague business relationship with a movie production. You don't think that's reason to make someone angry? What's wrong with you people?"

"Are your employees union?"

"No, they're not."

"But your partner in your security service is a Teamster steward. I think you're involved in some strange contradictions, Mr. Lemoyne."

He rose from his chair and lifted a set of keys out of his desk drawer.

"I'm taking a new boy out on his route today. I have to lock up now. Do you want to stay around and talk to anybody else?" he said.

"No, I'll be on my way. Here's my business card in case you might like to contact me later."

He ignored it when I extended it to him. I placed it on his desk.

"Thank you for your time, sir," I said, and walked back out onto the loading dock, into the heated liquid air, the blinding glare of light, the chalky smell of crushed oyster shells in the unsurfaced parking lot.

When I was walking out to my pickup truck, I recognized an elderly black man who used to work in the old icehouse in New Iberia years ago. He was picking up litter out by the street with a stick that had a nail in the end of it. He had a rag tied around his forehead to keep the sweat out of his eyes, and the rotted wet undershirt he wore looked like strips of cheesecloth on his body.

"How do you like working here, Dallas?" I said.

"I like it pretty good."

"How does Mr. Twinky treat y'all?"

His eyes glanced back toward the building, then he grinned.

"He know how to make the eagle scream, you know what I mean?"

"He's tight with a dollar?"

"Mr. Twinky so tight he got to eat a whole box of Ex-Lax so he don't squeak when he walk."

"He's that bad?"

He tapped some dried leaves off the nail of his stick against the trunk of an oak tree.

"That's just my little joke," he said. "Mr. Twinky pay what he say he gonna pay, and he always pay it on time. He good to black folks, Mr. Dave. They ain't no way 'round that."

WHEN I GOT back to New Iberia I didn't go to the office. Instead, I called from the house. The sheriff wasn't in.

"Where is he?" I said.

"He's probably out looking for you," the dispatcher said. "What's going on, Dave?"

"Nothing much."

"Tell that to the greaseball you bounced off the furniture this morning."

"Did he file a complaint?"

"No, but I heard the restaurant owner dug the guy's tooth out of the counter with a screwdriver. You sure know how to do it, Dave."

"Tell the sheriff I'm going to check out some stuff in New Orleans. I'll call him this evening or I'll see him in the office early in the morning."

"I got the impression it might be good if you came by this afternoon."

"Is Agent Gomez there?"

"Yeah, hang on."

A few seconds later Rosie picked up the extension.

"Dave?"

"How you doing?"

"*I'm* doing fine. How are you doing?"

"Everything's copacetic. I just talked with your man Twinky Lemoyne."

"Oh?"

"It looks like you put your finger in his eye."

"Why'd you go over there?"

"You never let them think they can make you flinch."

"Hang on a minute. I want to close the door." Then a moment later she scraped the receiver back up and said, "Dave, what happens around here won't affect my job or career to any appreciable degree. But maybe you ought to start thinking about covering your butt for a change."

"I had a bad night last night and I acted foolishly this morning. It's just one of those things," I said.

"That's not what I'm talking about, and I think you know it. When you chase money out of a community, people discover new depths in themselves."

"Have you gotten any feedback on the asphyxiated girl down in Vermilion Parish?"

"I just got back from the coroner's office. She's still Jane Doe."

"You think we're dealing with the same guy?"

"Bondage, humiliation of the victim, a prolonged death, probable sexual violation—it's the same creep, you'd better believe it." I could hear an edge in her voice, like a sliver of glass.

"I've got a couple of theories, too," she said. "He's left his last two victims where we could find them. Maybe he's becoming more compulsive, more desperate, less in control of his technique. Most psychopaths eventually reach a point where they're like sharks in feeding frenzy. They never satisfy the obsession."

"Or he wants to stick it in our faces?"

"You got it."

"Everything you say may be true, Rosie, but I think prostitution is connected with this stuff somewhere. You want to take a ride to New Orleans with me this afternoon?"

"A Vermilion Parish sheriff's detective is taking me out on the levee where you all found the girl last night. Do all these people spit Red Man?"

"A few of the women deputies don't."

I heard her laugh into the telephone.

"Watch out for yourself, slick," she said.

"You, too, Rosie."

Neither Bootsie nor Alafair was home. I left them a note, packed a change of clothes in a canvas bag in case I had to stay overnight, and headed for I-10 and New Orleans as the temperature climbed to one hundred degrees and the willows along the bayou drooped motionlessly in the heat as though all the juices had been baked out of their leaves.

• • •

I DROVE DOWN the elevated interstate and crossed the Atchafalaya Basin and its wind-ruffled bays dotted with oil platforms and dead cypress, networks of canals and bayous, sand bogs, willow islands, stilt houses, flooded woods, and stretches of dry land where the mosquitoes swarmed in gray clouds out of the tangles of brush and intertwined trees. Then I crossed the wide, yellow sweep of the Mississippi at Baton Rouge, and forty-five minutes later I was rolling through Jefferson Parish, along the shores of Lake Pontchartrain, into New Orleans. The lake was slate green and capping, the sky almost white in the heat, and the fronds on the palm trees were lifting and rattling dryly in the hot breeze. The air smelled of salt and stagnant water and dead vegetation among the sand bogs on the west side of the highway; the asphalt looked like it could fry the palm of your hand.

But there were no rain clouds on the horizon, no hint of relief from the scorching white orb in the sky or the humidity that crawled and ran on the skin like angry insects.

I was on the New Orleans police force for fourteen years, first as a beat cop and finally as a lieutenant in Homicide. I never worked Vice, but there are few areas in New Orleans law enforcement that don't eventually lead you back into it. Without its pagan and decadent ambiance, its strip shows, hookers, burlesque spielers, taxi pimps, and brain-damaged street dopers, the city would be as attractive to most tourists as an agrarian theme park in western Nebraska.

The French Quarter has two populations, almost two sensory climates. Early in the morning black children in uniforms line up to enter the Catholic elementary school by the park; parishioners from St. Louis Cathedral have coffee *au lait* and *beignets* and read the newspaper at the outdoor tables in the Café du Monde; the streets are still cool, the tile roofs and pastel stucco walls of the buildings streaked with moisture, the scrolled ironwork on the balconies bursting with flowers; families have their pictures sketched by the artists who set up their easels along the piked fence in Jackson Square; in the background the breeze off the river blows through the azalea and hibiscus bushes, the magnolia blossoms that are as big as fists, and the clumps of banana trees under the equestrian statue of Andy Jackson; and as soon as you head deeper into the Quarter, under the iron, green-painted colonnades, you can smell the cold, clean odor of fresh fish laid out on ice, of boxed strawberries and plums and rattlesnake watermelons beaded with water from a spray hose.

But by late afternoon another crowd moves into the Quarter. Most of them are innocuous—college kids, service personnel, Midwestern families trying to see past the spielers into the interiors of the strip houses, blue-suited Japanese businessmen hung with cameras, rednecks from dry counties in Mississippi. But there's another kind, too—grifters, Murphy artists, dips and stalls, coke and skag dealers, stables of hookers who work the hotel trade only, and strippers who hook out of taxicabs after 2 A.M.

They have the franchise on the worm's-eye view of the world. They're usually joyless, indifferent to speculations about mortality, bored with almost all forms of experience. Almost all of them either freebase, mainline, do coke, or smoke crack. Often they straighten out the kinks with black speed.

They view ordinary people as carnival workers do rubes; they look upon their victims with contempt, sometimes with loathing. Most of them cannot think their way out of a paper bag; but the accuracy of their knowledge about various bondsmen, the hierarchy of the local mob, the law as it applies to themselves, and cops and judges on a pad, is awesome.

As the streets began to cool and turn purple with shadow, I went from one low-rent club to the next amid the din of Dixieland and rockabilly bands, black kids with clip-on taps dancing on the sidewalk for the tourists, spielers in straw boaters and candy-striped vests hollering at college boys, "No cover, no minimum, you studs, come on in and get your battery charged."

Jimmie Ryan's red mustache and florid, good-humored face made you think of a nineteenth-century bartender. But he was also known as Jimmie the Dime, because with a phone call he could connect you, in one way or another, with any form of illegal activity in New Orleans.

Inside the crook of both his arms his veins were laced with scar tissue, like flattened gray garden snakes.

He tilted his straw boater back on his head and

drank from his beer. Above him, a topless girl in a sequined G-string danced barefoot on a runway, her hips moving like water to the music from the jukebox, her skin rippled with neon light, her mouth open in feigned ecstasy.

"How you been, Streak?" he said.

"Pretty good, Jimmie. How's the life?" I said.

"I ain't exactly in it anymore. Since I got off the superfluid, I more or less went to reg'lar employment, you know what I mean? Being a human doorbell for geeks and dipshits has got some serious negative drawbacks, I'm talking about self-esteem here, this town's full of sick people, Streak, who needs it is what I'm trying to say."

"I see. Look, Jimmie, do you know anybody who might be trying to recruit girls out of the parishes?"

He leaned his elbows back on the bar. His soft stomach swelled out of his striped vest like a water-filled bottom-heavy balloon.

"You mean somebody putting together his own stable?" he asked.

"Maybe."

"A guy who goes out looking for the country girls, the ones who's waiting for a big sugar daddy or is about to get run out of town, anyway?"

"Possibly."

"It don't sound right."

"Why?"

"New Orleans is full of them. Why bring in more and drive the prices down?"

"Maybe this guy does more than just pimp,

Jimmie. Maybe he likes to hurt them. You know a guy like that?"

"We're talking about another type of guy now, somebody who operates way down on the bottom of the food chain. When I was in the business of dimeing for somebody, making various kinds of social arrangements around the city, I made it a point not to know no guys like that, in fact, maybe I'm a little bit taken aback here you think I associate with them kind of people."

"I respect your knowledge and your judgment, Jimmie. That's why I came to you instead of someone else. My problem is two dead girls in Vermilion and Iberia parishes. The same guy may have killed others."

He removed something from the back of his teeth with his little finger.

"The city ain't like it used to be," he said. "It's turning to shit."

"Okay—"

"Years ago there were certain understandings with New Orleans cops. A guy got caught doing the wrong stuff, I'm talking about sick stuff, molesting a child, robbing and beating up old people, something like that, it didn't go to the jailhouse. They stomped the shit out of the guy right there, I mean they left him with his brains running out of his nose.

"Today, what'd you got? Try to take a stroll by the projects and see what happens. Look, Streak, I don't know what you're looking for, but there's one special kind of cocksucker that comes to mind here, a new kind of guy in the city, why somebody don't walk him outside, maybe punch his ticket real hard, maybe permanent, you know what I'm saying, I don't know the answer to that one, but when you go down to the bus depot, you might think about it, I mean you're from out of town, right, and there ain't nobody, I mean nobody, gonna be upset if this kind of guy maybe gets ripped from his liver to his lights."

"The bus depot?"

"You got it. There's three or four of them. One of them stands out like shit in an ice-cream factory. Nothing against colored people."

I had forgotten what a linguistic experience a conversation with Jimmie the Dime could be.

He suppressed a beer belch and stared up at the girl on the runway.

"Could Baby Feet Balboni be involved in this?" I asked.

He rolled a matchstick on his tongue, looked upward at an oblique angle to a spot on the ceiling.

"Take a walk with me, breathe the night air, this place is like the inside of an ashtray. Some nights I think somebody poured battery acid in my lungs," he said.

I walked outside with him. The sidewalks were filled with tourists and revelers drinking beer out of deep paper cups. Jimmie looked up and down the street, blew air out his nose, smoothed his mustache with one knuckle.

"You're using the names of local personalities now," he said.

"It stays with me, Jimmie. Nobody'll know where it came from."

"Anything I might know about this certain man is already public knowledge, so it probably won't do no good for me to be commenting on the issue here."

"There's no action around here that doesn't get pieced off to Julie one way or another. Why should procuring be any different?"

"Wrong. There's fifteen-year-old kids in the projects dealing rock, girls, guns, Mexican brown, crank, you name it, the Italians won't fool with it, it's too uncontrollable. You looking for a guy who kills hookers? It ain't Feet, Lieutenant. The guy's got sub-zero feelings about people. I saw him wipe up a barroom in Algiers with three guys from the Giacano family who thought they could come on like wise-asses in front of their broads. He didn't even break a sweat. He even stopped stomping on one guy just so he could blow a long fart."

"Thanks for your time, Jimmie. Get in touch if you hear anything, all right?"

"What do I know? We're living in sick times. You want my opinion? Open up some prison colonies at the North Pole, where those penguins live. Get rid of the dirtbags, bring back some decency, before the whole city becomes a toilet." He rocked on the balls of his feet. His lips looked purple in the neon glow from the bar, his face an electric red, as though it were flaming from sunburn.

I gave him my business card. When I was down the block, under the marquee of a pornographic theater, and looked back at him, he was picking his teeth with it.

I HIT TWO biker bars across the river in Algiers, where a few of the mamas hooked so their old men would have the money they needed to deal guns or dope. Why they allowed themselves to be used on that level was anybody's guess. But with some regularity they were chain-whipped, gang-raped, nailed through their hands to trees, and they usually came back for more until sometimes they were murdered and dumped in a swamp. One form of their sad, ongoing victimization probably makes about as much sense as another.

The ones who would talk to me all had the same odor, like sweaty leather, the warm female scent of unwashed hair, reefer smoke and nicotine, and engine grease rubbed into denim. But they had little knowledge or interest about anything outside of their tribal and atavistic world.

I found a mulatto pimp off Magazine who also ran a shooting gallery that specialized in black-tar heroin, which was selling at twenty-five dollars a hit and was back in fashion with adult addicts who didn't want to join the army of psychotic meltdowns produced by crack in the projects.

His name was Camel; he had one dead eye, like a colorless marble, and he wore a diamond clipped in one nostril and his hair shaved in ridges and dagger points. He peeled back the shell on a hard-boiled egg with his thumb at the sandwich counter of an old dilapidated grocery and package store with wood-bladed fans on the ceiling. His skin had the bright copper shine of a newly minted penny.

After he had listened to me for a while, he set his egg on a paper napkin and folded his long fingers reflectively.

"This is my neighborhood, place where all my friends live, and don't nobody here hurt my ladies," he said.

"I didn't say they did, Camel. I just want you to tell me if you've heard about anybody who might be recruiting out in the parishes. Maybe a guy who's seriously out of control."

"I don't get out of the neighborhood much no mo'. Age creeping up on me, I guess."

"It's been a hot day, partner. My tolerance for bullshit is way down. You're dealing Mexican skag for Julie Balboni, and you know everything that's going on in this town."

"What's that name again?"

I looked into his face for a long moment. He scraped at a bit of crust on the corner of his dead eye with his fingernail.

"You're a smart man, Camel. Tell me honestly, do you think you're going to jerk me around and I'm just going to disappear?"

He unscrewed the cap on a Tabasco bottle and began dotting drops of hot sauce on his egg.

"I heard stories about a white guy, they say a strange guy reg'lar peoples in the bidness don't like to fool with," he said.

"All right—"

"You're looking in the wrong place."

"What do you mean?"

"The guy don't live around here. He sets the girls up on the Airline Highway, in Jefferson Parish, puts one in charge, then comes back to town once in a while to check everything out."

"I see, a new kind of honor system. What are you trying to feed me, Camel?"

"You're not hearing me. The reg'lar peoples stay away from him for a reason. His chippies try to short him, they disappear. The word there is *disappear,* gone from the crib, blipped off the screen. Am I getting this acrost to you all right?"

"What's his name?"

"Don't know, don't want to know. Ax yourself something. Why y'all always come to a nigger to solve your problem? We ain't got nothing like that in a black neighborhood."

"We'll see you around, Camel. Thanks for your help. Say, what's the name of the black guy working the bus depot?"

"I travel by plane, my man. That's what everybody do today," he said, and licked the top of the peeled egg before he put it in his mouth.

FOR YEARS THE Airline had been the main highway between Baton Rouge and New Orleans. When I-10 was built, the Airline became a secondary road and was absorbed back into that quasi-rural slum culture that has always characterized the peckerwood South: ramshackle nightclubs with oyster-shell parking lots; roach-infested motels that feature water beds and pornographic movies and rent rooms by the day or week; truck stops with banks of rubber machines in the restrooms; all-night glaringly lit cafés where the smell of fried food permeates the counters and stools as tangibly as a film of grease.

I went to three clubs and got nowhere. Each time I walked through the door the bartender's eyes glanced up to meet me as they would somebody who had been expected all evening. As soon as I sat at the bar the girls went to the women's room or out the back door. The electronic noise of the country bands was deafening, the amplified squelch in the microphones like metal raking on a blackboard. When I tried to talk to someone, the person would nod politely in the din as though a man without vocal cords were speaking to him, then go back to his drink or stare in the opposite direction through the layers of cigarette smoke.

I gave up and walked back to my truck, which was parked between the clapboard side of a nightclub and a squat six-room motel with a small yellow lawn and a dead palm tree by the drive-in registration window. The air smelled of creosote and burnt diesel fuel from the railway tracks by the river, dust from the shell parking lot, liquor and beer from a trash barrel filled with empty bottles. The sky out over the Gulf trembled with dry lightning.

I didn't hear her behind me.

"Everybody on the strip knew you were coming two hours ago, cutie," she said.

I turned and squinted my eyes at her. She drank

out of her beer bottle, then puffed off her cigarette. Her face was porcine, her lipstick on crooked, her dyed red hair lacquered like tangled wire on her head. She put one hand on her hip and waited for me to recognize her.

"Charlotte?"

"What a memory. Have I tubbed up on you?"

"No, not really. You're looking good."

She laughed to herself and blew her cigarette smoke at an upward angle into the dark.

Thirty years ago she had been a stripper and hooker on Bourbon Street, then the mistress of a loan shark who blew his brains out, the wife of an alcoholic ex–police sergeant who ended up in Angola for doping horses at the Fairgrounds, and the last I heard the operator of a massage parlor in Algiers.

"What are you doing out here on the Airline?" I said.

"I run the dump next door," she said, and nodded toward the motel. "Hey, I got to sit down. I really got crocked tonight." She shook a wooden chair loose from the trash pile by the side of the nightclub and sat down in it with her knees splayed and took another drink from her beer bottle. An exhaust fan from a restroom was pinging above her head. "I already heard what you're looking for, Streak. A guy bringing the chickens in from the country, right?"

"Do you know who he is?"

"They come and they go. I'm too old to keep track of it anymore."

"I'd sure like to talk to this guy, Charlotte."

"Yeah, somebody ought to run an iron hook through his balls, all right, but it's probably not going to happen."

"Why not?"

"You got the right juice, the playpen stays open."

"He's connected?"

"What do you think?"

"With the Balboni family?"

"Maybe. Maybe he's got juice with the cops or politicians. There's lots of ways to stay in business."

"But one way or another, most of them go down. Right?"

She raised her beer bottle to her mouth and drank.

"I don't think anybody is going to be talking about this guy a whole lot," she said. "You hear stories, you know what I mean? That this guy you're looking for is somebody you don't want mad at you, that he can be real hard on his chippies."

"Is it true?"

She set her empty bottle down on the shells and placed her hands loosely in her lap. For a moment the alcoholic shine left her eyes and her expression became strangely introverted, as though she were focusing on some forgotten image deep inside herself.

"When you're in the life, you hear a lot of bad stories, cutie. That's because there aren't many good ones," she said.

"The man I'm looking for may be a serial killer, Charlotte."

"That kind of guy is a john, not a pimp, Streak." She leaned on her forearms, puffing on her cigarette, staring at the hundreds of bottle caps pressed into the dirt at her feet. Her lacquered hair was wreathed in smoke. "Go on back home. You won't change anything here. Everybody out on this road signed up for it one way or another."

"Nobody signed up to be dead."

She didn't reply. She scratched a mosquito bite on her kneecap and looked at a car approaching the motel registration window.

"Who's the main man working the bus depot these days?" I said.

"That's Downtown Bobby Brown. He went up on a short-eyes once. Now he's a pro, a real piece of shit. Go back to your family, Streak, before you start to like your work."

She flipped her cigarette away backhandedly, got to her feet, straightened her dress on her elephantine hips, winked at me as though she might be leaving a burlesque stage, and walked delicately across the oyster shells toward her motel and the couple who waited impatiently for her in the heat and the dust and the snapping of an electric bug killer over the registration window.

YOU CAN FIND the predators at the bus depot almost any time during the twenty-four-hour period. But they operate best during the late hours. That's usually when the adventurers from Vidalia or De Ridder or Wiggins, Mississippi, have run out of money, energy, and hope of finding a place to sleep besides an empty building or an official shelter where they'll be reported as runaways. It's not hard to spot the adventurers, either. The corners of their mouths are downturned, their hair is limp and lies like moist string on their necks; often their hands and thin arms are flecked with home-grown tattoos; they wash under their arms with paper towels and brush their teeth in the depot restroom.

I watched him walk across the waiting room, a leather satchel slung on a strap over his shoulder, his eyes bright, a rain hat at an angle on his head, his tropical white shirt hanging outside his khakis. A gold cross was painted on the side of his satchel.

The two girls were white, both blond, dressed in shapeless jeans, tennis shoes without socks, blouses that looked salt-faded and stiff with dried perspiration. When he talked with them, his happy face made me think of a mythical goat-footed balloonman whistling far and wee to children in springtime. Then from his satchel he produced candy bars and ham sandwiches, a thermos of coffee, plums and red apples that would dwarf a child's hand.

The girls both bent into their sandwiches, then he was sitting next to them, talking without stop, the smile as wide as an ax blade, the eyes bright as an elf's, the gold cross on his satchel winking with light under his black arm.

I was tired, used up after the long day, wired with too many voices, too many people on the hustle, too many who bought and sold others or ruined themselves for money that you could make with a Fuller Brush route. There was grit in my clothes;

my mouth tasted bad; I could smell my own odor. The inside of the depot reeked of cigar butts and the diesel exhaust that blew through the doors to the boarding foyer.

I took the receiver off a pay phone by the men's room and let it hang by its cord.

A minute later the ticket salesman stared down at my badge that I had slid across the counter.

"You want me to do what?" he said.

"Announce that there's a call at the pay phone for Mr. Bob Brown."

"We usually don't do that."

"Consider it an emergency."

"Yes, sir."

"Wait at least one minute before you do it. Okay, podna?"

"Yes, sir."

I bought a soft drink from a vending machine and looked casually out the glass doors while a bus marked "Miami" was being loaded underneath with luggage. The ticket salesman picked up his microphone, and Bob Brown's name echoed and resonated off the depot walls.

Downtown Bobby Brown's face became quizzical, impish, in front of the girls, then momentarily apologetic as he explained that he'd be right back, that somebody at his shelter probably needed advice about a situation.

I dropped my soda can into a trash bin and followed him to the pay phone. Downtown Bobby was streetwise, and he turned around and looked into my face. But my eyes never registered his glance, and I passed him and stopped in front of the *USA Today* machine.

He picked up the telephone receiver, leaning on one arm against the wall, and said, "This is Bobby. What's happenin'?"

"The end of your career," I said, and clenched the back of his neck, driving his face into the restroom door. Then I pushed him through the door and flung him inside the room. Blood drained from his nose over his lip; his eyes were wide, yellow-white—like a peeled egg—with shock.

A man at the urinal stood dumbfounded with his fly opened. I held up my badge in front of him.

"This room's in use," I said.

He zipped his trousers and went quickly out the door. I shot the bolt into the jamb.

"What you want? Why you comin' down on me for? You cain't run a shake on somebody, run somebody's face into a do' just because you—"

I pulled my .45 out of the back of my belt and aimed it into the center of his face.

He lifted his hands in front of him, as though he were holding back an invisible presence, and shook his head from side to side, his eyes averted, his mouth twisted like a broken plum.

"Don't do that, man," he said. "I ain't no threat to you. Look, I ain't got a gun. You want to bust me, do it. Come on, I swear it, they ain't no need for that piece, I ain't no trouble."

He was breathing heavily now. Sweat glistened like oil on his temples. He blotted drops of blood off his nose with the backs of his fingers.

I walked closer to him, staring into his eyes, and cocked the hammer. He backed away from me into a stall, his breath rife with a smell like sardines.

"I want the name of the guy you're delivering the girls to," I said.

"Nobody. I ain't bringing nobody to nobody."

I fitted the opening in the barrel to the point of his chin.

"Oh, God," he said, and fell backward onto the commode. The seat was up, and his butt plummeted deep into the bowl.

"You know the guy I'm talking about. He's just like you. He hunts on the game reserve," I said.

His chest was bent forward toward his knees. He looked like a round clothespin that had been screwed into a hole.

"Don't do this to me, man," he said. "I just had an operation. Take me in. I'll he'p y'all out any way I can. I got a good record wit' y'all."

"You've been up the road for child molesting, Bobby. Even cons don't like a short-eyes. Did you have to stay in lockdown with the snitches?"

"It was a statutory. I went down for nonconsent. Check it out, man. No shit, don't point that at me no more. I still got stitches inside my groin. They're gonna tear loose."

"Who's the guy, Bobby?"

He shut his eyes and put his hand over his mouth.

"Just give me his name, and it all ends right here," I said.

He opened his eyes and looked up at me.

"I messed my pants," he said.

"This guy hurts people. Give me his name, Bobby."

"There's a white guy sells dirty pictures or something. He carries a gun. Nobody fucks wit' him. Is that the guy you're talking about?"

"You tell me."

"That's all I know. Look, I don't have nothin' to do wit' dangerous people. I don't hurt nobody. Why you doin' this to me, man?"

I stepped back from him and eased down the hammer on the .45. He put the heels of his hands on the rim of the commode and pushed himself slowly to his feet. Toilet water dripped off the seat of his khakis. I wadded up a handful of paper towels, soaked them under a faucet, and handed them to him.

"Wipe your face," I said.

He kept sniffing, as though he had a cold.

"I cain't go back out there."

"That's right."

"I went to the bathroom in my pants. That's what you done, man."

"You're never coming back here, Bobby. You're going to treat this bus depot like it's the center of a nuclear test zone."

"I got a crib . . . a place . . . two blocks from here, man. What you—"

"Do you know who ——— is?" I used the name of a notorious right-wing racist beat cop from the Irish Channel.

His hand stopped mopping at his nose with the towels.

"I got no beef wit' that peckerwood," he said.

"He broke a pimp's trachea with his baton once. That's right, Bobby. The guy strangled to death in his own spit."

"What you talkin' 'bout, man? I ain't said nothing 'bout ———. I know what you're doin', man, you're—"

"If I catch you in the depot again, if I hear you're scamming runaways and young girls again, I'm going to tell ——— you've been working his neighborhood, maybe hanging around school grounds in the Channel."

"Who the fuck are you, man? Why you makin' me miserable? I ain't done nothing to you."

I unlocked the bolt on the door.

"Did you ever read the passage in the Bible about what happens to people who corrupt children?" I said.

He looked at me with a stupefied expression on his face.

"Start thinking about millstones or get into another line of work," I said.

I had seventeen dollars in my billfold. I gave twelve to the two runaway girls and the address of an AA street priest who ran a shelter and wouldn't report them.

Outside, the air tasted like pennies and felt like it had been superheated in an electric oven. Even the wind blew off the pavement like heat rising from a wood stove. I started my truck, unbuttoned my shirt to my waist, and headed toward I-10 and home.

When I passed Lake Pontchartrain, the moon was up and small waves were breaking against the rim of gray sandy beach by the highway. I wanted to stop the truck, strip to my skivvies, wade out to the drop-off, then dive down through the descending layers of temperature until I struck a cold, dark current at the bottom that would wash the last five hours out of my pores.

But Lake Pontchartrain, like the city of New Orleans, was deceptive. Under its slate-green, capping waves, its moon-glazed surfaces, its twenty-four-mile causeway glowing with electric light, waste of every kind lay trapped in the dark sediment, and the level of toxicity was so high that it was now against the law to swim in the lake.

I kept the truck wide open, the plastic ball on the floor stick shaking under my palm, all the way to the Mississippi bridge at Baton Rouge. Then I rolled down the elevated causeway through the Atchafalaya marsh and the warm night air that smelled of sour mud and hyacinths blooming back in the trees. Out over the pewter-colored bays, the dead cypress trunks were silhouetted against burning gas flares and the vast black-green expanse of sawgrass and flooded willow islands. Huge thunderclouds tumbled one upon another like curds of black smoke from an old fire, and networks of lightning were bursting silently all over the southern sky. I thought I could smell raindrops on the wind, as cool and clean and bright as the taste of white alcohol on the tip of the tongue.

CHAPTER 9

OUTSIDE OUR BEDROOM window the pecan trees were motionless and gray, soaked with humidity, in the false dawn. Then the early red sun broke above the treeline in the marsh like a Lucifer match being scratched against the sky.

Bootsie slept on her side in her nightgown, the sheet molded against her thigh, her face cool, her auburn hair ruffled on the pillow by the window fan. In the early morning her skin always had a glow to it, like the pale pink light inside a rose. I moved her body against mine and kissed her mouth lightly. Without opening her eyes she smiled sleepily, slipped her arms around my back, widened her thighs, and pressed her stomach against me.

Out on the bayou, I thought I heard a bass leap from the water in a wet arc and then reenter the surface, slapping his tail, as he slid deep into the roots of the floating hyacinths.

Bootsie put her legs in mine, her breath warm against my cheek, one hand in the small of my back, her soft rump rolling against the bed; then I felt that heart-twisting moment begin to grow inside me, past any point of control, like a log dam in a canyon resisting a flooded streambed, then cracking and bursting loose in a rush of white water and uprooted boulders.

I lay beside her and held one of her hands and kissed the thin film of perspiration on her shoulders.

She felt my face with her fingers and touched the white patch in my hair as though she were exploring a physical curiosity in me for the first time.

"Ole Streak," she said, and smiled.

"Cops get worse names."

She was quiet a moment, then she said my name with a question mark beside it the way she always did when she was about to broach a difficult subject.

"Yes?" I said.

"Elrod Sykes called while you were in New Orleans. He wanted to apologize for coming to our house drunk."

"Okay."

"He wants to go to an AA meeting with you."

"All right, I'll talk to him about it."

She looked at the revolving shadows the window fan made on the wall.

"He's rented a big boat," she said. "He wants to go fishing out on the salt."

"When?"

"Day after tomorrow."

"What'd you tell him?"

"That I'd have to check with you."

"You don't think we should go?"

"He troubles me, Dave."

"Maybe the guy *is* psychic. That doesn't mean he's bad news."

"I have a strange feeling about him. Like he's going to do something to us."

"He's a practicing alcoholic, Boots. He's a sick man. How's he going to harm us?"

"I don't know. It's just the way I feel. I can't explain it."

"Do you think he's trying to manipulate me?"

"How do you mean?"

I raised up on one elbow and looked into her face. I tried to smile.

"I have an obligation to help other alcoholics," I said. "Maybe it looks like Elrod's trying to pull some strings on me, that maybe instead of helping him I'll end up back on the dirty-boogie again."

"Let him find his own help, Dave."

"I think he's harmless."

"I should have listened to you. I shouldn't have invited them into the house."

"It's not good to do this, Boots. You're worrying about a problem that doesn't exist."

"He's too interested in you. There's a reason for it. I know it."

"I'll invite him to go to a meeting. We'll forget about the fishing trip."

"Promise me that, Dave."

"I do."

"You mean it, no going back on it?"

"You've got my word."

She cupped my fingers in her hand and put her

head under my chin. In the shadowy light I could see her heart tripping against her breast.

I PARKED IN the lot behind the office and walked toward the back door. Two uniformed deputies had just taken a black man in handcuffs into the building, and four others were drinking coffee out of foam cups and smoking cigarettes in the shade against the wall. I heard one of them use my name, then a couple of them laugh when I walked by.

I stopped and walked back to them.

"How y'all doing today?" I said.

"What's going on, Dave?" Rufus Arceneaux said. He had been a tech sergeant in the Marine Corps and he still wore his sun-bleached hair in a military crewcut. He took off his shades and rubbed the bridge of his nose.

"I'd better get back on it," one deputy said, flipped away his cigarette, and walked toward his cruiser.

"What's the joke about, Rufus?" I said.

"It's nothing I said, Dave. I was just quoting the boss man," Rufus said. His green eyes were full of humor as he looked at the other deputies.

"What did the sheriff have to say?"

"Hey, Dave, fair is fair. Don't lay this off on me," he said.

"Do you want to take the mashed potatoes out of your mouth and tell me what you're talking about?"

"Hey, come on, man," he said, chuckling.

"What the fuck, it's no big deal. Tell him," the deputy next to him said.

"The sheriff said if the governor of Lou'sana invited the whole department to dinner, Dave would be the one guy who'd manage to spit in the punch bowl."

Then the three of them were silent, suppressing their grins, their eyes roving around the parking lot.

"Drop by my office sometime today, Rufus," I said. "Anytime before five o'clock. You think you can work it in?"

"It's just a joke, Dave. I'm not the guy who said it, either."

"That's right. So it's nothing personal. I'd just like to go through your jacket with you."

"What for?"

"You've been here eight or nine years, haven't you?"

"That's right."

"Why is it that I always have the feeling you'd like to be an NCO again, that maybe you have some ambitions you're not quite telling us about?"

His lips became a tight, stitched line, and I saw a slit of yellow light in his eye.

"Think about it and I'll talk to you later, Rufus," I said, and went inside the building, into the air-conditioned odor of cigar butts and tobacco spittle, and closed the door behind me.

Ten minutes later the sheriff walked into my office and sat down in front of my desk with his arms propped stiffly on his thighs. In his red-faced concentration he reminded me of a football coach sitting on the edge of a bench.

"Where do you think we should begin?" he said.

"You got me."

"From what I hear about that scene in the restaurant, you tried to tear that fellow apart."

"Those guys think they're in the provinces and they can do what they want. Sometimes you have to turn them around."

"It looks like you got your message across. Balboni had to take the guy to the hospital. You broke his tooth off inside his gums."

"It was a bad morning. I let things get out of control. It won't happen again."

He didn't answer. I could hear him breathing through his nose.

"You want some coffee?" I said.

"No."

I got up and filled my cup from my coffee maker in the corner.

"I've had two phone calls already about your trip to New Orleans last night," he said.

"What about it?"

He took a folded-back notebook out of his shirt pocket and looked at the first page.

"Did you ever hear of a black guy named Robert Brown?" he asked.

"Yep, that's Downtown Bobby Brown."

"He's trying to file charges against you. He says you smashed his face into a men's-room door at the bus depot."

"I see."

"What the hell are you doing, Dave?"

"He's a pimp and a convicted child molester.

When I found him, he was scamming two girls who couldn't have been over sixteen years old. I wonder if he passed on that information when he filed his complaint."

"I don't give a damn what this guy did. I'm worried about a member of my department who might have confused himself with Wyatt Earp."

"This guy's charges aren't going anywhere and you know it."

"I wish I had your confidence. It looks like you got some people's attention over in Jefferson Parish, too."

"I don't understand."

"The Jefferson Parish Sheriff's Department seems to think we may have a loose cannon crashing around on our deck."

"What's their problem?"

"You didn't check in with them, you didn't coordinate with anybody, you simply went up and down the Airline Highway on your own, questioning hookers and bartenders about a pimp with no name."

"So?"

He rubbed the cleft in his round chin, then dropped the flat of his hand on his thigh.

"They say you screwed up a surveillance, that you blew a sting operation of some kind," he said.

"How?"

"I don't know."

"It sounds like bullshit to me, Sheriff. It sounds like cops on a pad who don't want outsiders walking around on their turf."

"Maybe that's true, Dave, but I'm worried about you. I think you're overextending yourself and you're not hearing me when I talk to you about it."

"Did Twinky Lemoyne call?"

"No. Why should he?"

"I went over to Lafayette and questioned him yesterday afternoon."

He removed his rimless glasses, wiped them with a Kleenex, and put them back on. His eyes came back to meet mine.

"This was after I talked to you about involving people in the investigation who seem to have no central bearing in it?" he asked.

"I'm convinced that somehow Baby Feet was mixed up with Cherry LeBlanc, Sheriff. Twinky Lemoyne has business ties to Feet. The way I read it, that makes him fair game."

"I'm really sorry to hear this, Dave."

"An investigation clears as well as implicates people. His black employees seem to think well of him. He didn't call in a complaint about my talking to him, either. Maybe he's an all-right guy."

"You disregarded my instructions, Dave."

"I saw the bodies of both those girls, sheriff."

"And?"

"Frankly I'm not real concerned about whose toes I step on."

He rose from his chair and tucked his shirt tightly into his gunbelt with his thumbs while his eyes seemed to study an unspoken thought in midair.

"I guess at this point I have to tell you something of a personal nature," he said. "I don't care for your tone, sir. I don't care for it in the least."

I picked up my coffee cup and sipped off it and looked at nothing as he walked out of the room.

ROSIE GOMEZ WAS down in Vermilion Parish almost all day. When she came back into the office late that afternoon her face was flushed from the heat and her dark hair stuck damply to her skin. She dropped her purse on top of her desk and propped her arms on the side of the air-conditioning unit so the windstream blew inside her sleeveless blouse.

"I thought Texas was the hottest place on earth. How did anyone ever live here before air conditioning?" she said.

"How'd you make out today?"

"Wait a minute and I'll tell you. Damn, it was hot out there. What happened to the rain?"

"I don't know. It's unusual."

"Unusual? I felt like I was being cooked alive inside wet cabbage leaves. I'm going to ask for my next assignment in the Aleutians."

"I'm afraid you'll never make the state Chamber of Commerce, Rosie."

She walked back to her desk, blowing her breath up into her face, and opened her purse.

"What'd you do today?" she asked.

"I tried to run down some of those old cases, but they're pretty cold now—people have quit or retired or don't remember, files misplaced, that sort of thing. But there's one interesting thing here—"

I spread a dozen National Crime Information Center fax sheets over the top of my desk. "If one guy committed several of these unsolved murders, it doesn't look like he ever operated outside the state. In other words, there don't seem to be any unsolved female homicides that took place during the same time period in an adjoining area in Texas, Arkansas, or Mississippi.

"So this guy may not only be homegrown but for one reason or another he's confined his murders to the state of Louisiana."

"That'd be a new one," she said. "Serial killers usually travel, unless they prey off a particular local community, like gays or streetwalkers. Anyway, look at what jumped up out of the weeds today."

She held up a plastic Ziploc bag with a wood-handled, brass-tipped pocket knife inside. The single blade was opened and streaked with rust.

"Where'd you find it?"

"A half mile back down the levee from where the girl was found in the barrel. It was about three feet down from the crest."

"You covered all that ground by yourself?"

"More or less."

I looked at her a moment before I spoke again. "Rosie, you're kind of new to the area, but that levee is used by fishermen and hunters all the time. Sometimes they drop stuff."

"All my work for nothing, huh?" She smiled and lifted a strand of hair off her eyebrow.

"I didn't say that—"

"I didn't tell you something else. I ran into an elderly black man down there who sells catfish and frog legs off the back of his pickup truck. He said that about a month ago, late at night, he saw a white man in a new blue or black car looking for something on the levee with a flashlight. Just like that alligator poacher you questioned, he wondered why anybody would be down there at night with a new automobile. He said the man with the light wasn't towing a boat trailer and he didn't have a woman with him, either. Evidently he thinks those are the only two reasonable explanations for anyone ever going down there."

"Could he give you a description of the white man?"

"No, he said he was busy stringing a trotline between some duck blinds. What's a trotline, anyway?"

"You stretch a long piece of twine above the water and tie it to a couple of stumps or flooded trees. Then intermittently you hang twelve-inch pieces of weighted line with baited hooks into the water. Catfish feed by the moon, and when they hook themselves, they usually work the hook all the way through their heads and they're still on the trotline when the fisherman picks it up in the morning."

I sat on the corner of her desk and picked up the plastic bag and looked at the knife. It was the kind that was made in Pakistan or Taiwan and could be purchased for two dollars on the counter of almost any convenience store.

"If that was our man, what do you think happened?" I said.

"Maybe that's where he bound her with the electrician's tape. He used the knife to slice the tape, then dropped it. He either searched for it that night or came back another night when he discovered it was missing."

"I don't want to mess up your day, Rosie, but our man doesn't seem to leave fingerprints. At least there were none on the electrician's tape in the two murders that we think he committed. Why should he worry about losing the knife?"

"He needs to orchestrate, to be in control. He can't abide accidents."

"He left the ice pick in Cherry LeBlanc."

"Because he meant to. He gave us the murder weapon; it'll never be found on him. But he didn't plan to give us his pocket knife. That bothers him."

"That's not a bad theory. Our man is all about power, isn't he?"

She stood her purse up straight and started to snap it shut. It clunked on the desk when she moved it. She reached inside and lifted out her .357 magnum revolver, which looked huge in her small hand, and replaced it on top of her billfold. She snapped the catch on the purse.

"I said the obsession is about power, isn't it?"

"Always, always, always," she said.

The concentration seemed to go out of her eyes, as though the day's fatigue had just caught up with her.

"Rosie?"

"What is it?"

"You feel okay?"

"I probably got dehydrated out there."

"Drop the knife off with our fingerprint man and I'll buy you a Dr Pepper."

"Another time. I want to see what's on the knife."

"This time of day our fingerprint man is usually backed up. He probably won't get to it until tomorrow."

"Then he's about to put in for some overtime."

She straightened her shoulders, slung her purse on her shoulder, and walked out the door into the corridor. A deputy with a girth like a hogshead nodded to her deferentially and stepped aside to let her pass.

When I was helping Batist clean up the shop that evening I remembered that I hadn't called Elrod Sykes about his invitation to go fishing out on the salt. Or maybe I had deliberately pushed it out of my mind. I knew that Bootsie was probably right about Elrod. He was one of the walking wounded, the kind for whom you always felt sympathy, but you knew eventually he'd rake a whole dustpan of broken glass into your head.

I called up to the house and got the telephone number that he had left with Bootsie. While Elrod's phone was ringing, I gazed out the screen window at Alafair and a little black girl playing with Tripod by the edge of a corn garden down the road. Tripod was on his back, rolling in the baked dirt, digging his claws into a deflated football. Even though there was still moisture in the root systems, the corn looked sere and red against the late sun, and when the breeze lifted in the dust the leaves crackled dryly around the scarecrow that was tilted at an angle above the children's heads.

Kelly Drummond answered the phone, then put Elrod on.

"You cain't go?" he said.

"No, I'm afraid not."

"Tomorrow's Saturday. Why don't you take some time off?"

"Saturday's a big day for us at the dock."

"Mr. Robicheaux . . . Dave . . . is there some other problem here? I guess I was pretty fried when I was at your house."

"We were glad to have you all. How about I talk with you later? Maybe we'll go to a meeting, if you like."

"Sure," he said, his voice flat. "That sounds okay."

"I appreciate the invitation. I really do."

"Sure. Don't mention it. Another time."

"Yes, that might be fine."

"So long, Mr. Robicheaux."

The line went dead, and I was left with the peculiar sensation that I had managed both to be dishonest and to injure the feelings of someone I liked.

Batist and I cleaned the ashes out of the barbecue pit, on which we cooked sausage links and split chickens with a *sauce piquante* and sold them at noon to fishermen for three-ninety-five a plate;

then we seined the dead shiners out of the bait tanks, wiped down the counters, swept the grained floors clean, refilled the beer and soda-pop coolers, poured fresh crushed ice over the bottles, loaded the candy and cigarette machines, put the fried pies, hard-boiled eggs, and pickled hogs' feet in the icebox in case Tripod got into the shop again, folded up the beach umbrellas on the spool tables, slid back the canvas awning that stretched on wires over the dock, emptied water out of all our rental boats, ran a security chain through a welded ring on the housing of all the outboard engines, and finally latched the board flaps over the windows and turned keys in all the locks.

I walked across the road and stopped by the corn garden where Alafair and the black girl were playing. A pickup truck banged over the ruts in the road and dust drifted across the cornstalks. Out in the marsh, a solitary frog croaked, then the entire vault of sky seemed to ache with the reverberation of thousands of other frogs.

"What's Tripod been into today?" I said.

"Tripod's been good. He hasn't been into anything, Dave," Alafair said. She picked Tripod up and thumped him down on his back in her lap. His paws pumped wildly at the air.

"What you got there, Poteet?" I said to the little black girl. Her pigtails were wrapped with rubber bands and her elbows and knees were gray with dust.

"Found it right here in the row," she said, and opened her hand. "What that is, Mr. Dave?"

"I told you. It's a minié ball," Alafair said.

"It don't look like no ball to me," Poteet said.

I picked it out of her hand. It was smooth and cool in my palm, oxidized an off-white, cone-shaped at one end, grooved with three rings, and hollowed at the base. The French contribution to the science of killing people at long distances. It looked almost phallic.

"These were the bullets that were used during the War Between the States, Poteet," I said, and handed it back to her. "Confederate and federal soldiers fought all up and down this bayou."

"That's the war Alafair say you was in, Mr. Dave?"

"Do I look that old to you guys?"

"How much it worth?" Poteet said.

"You can buy them for a dollar at a store in New Orleans."

"You give me a dollar for it?" Poteet said.

"Why don't you keep it instead, Po'?" I said, and rubbed the top of her head.

"I don't want no nasty minié ball. It probably gone in somebody," she said, and flung it into the cornstalks.

"Don't do that. You can use it in a slingshot or something," Alafair said. She crawled on hands and knees up the row and put the minié ball in the pocket of her jeans. Then she came back and lifted Tripod up in her arms.

"Dave, who was that old man?" she said.

"What old man?"

"He got a stump," Poteet said.

"A stump?"

"That's right, got a stump for a leg, got an arm look like a shriveled-up bird's claw," Poteet said.

"What are y'all talking about?" I said.

"He was on a crutch, Dave. Standing there in the leaves," Alafair said.

I knelt down beside them.

"You guys aren't making a lot of sense," I said.

"He was right up there in the corn leaves. Talking in the wind," Poteet said. "His mouth just a big hole in the wind without no sound coming out."

"I bet y'all saw the scarecrow."

"If scarecrows got B.O.," Poteet said.

"Where'd this old man go?" I said.

"He didn't go anywhere," Alafair said. "The wind started blowing real hard in the stalks and he just disappeared."

"Disappeared?" I said.

"That's right," Poteet said. "Him and his B.O."

"Did he have a black coat on, like that scarecrow there?" I tried to smile, but my heart had started clicking in my chest.

"No, suh, he didn't have no black coat on," Poteet said.

"It was gray, Dave," Alafair said. "Just like your shirt."

"Gray?" I said woodenly.

"Except it had some gold on the shoulders," she said.

She smiled at me as though she had given me a detail that somehow would remove the expression she saw on my face.

My knees popped when I stood up.

"You'd better come home for supper now, Alf," I said.

"You mad, Dave? We done something wrong?" Alafair said.

"Don't say 'we done,' little guy. No, of course I'm not mad. It's just been a long day. We'll see you later, Poteet."

Alafair swung on my hand as she held on to Tripod's leash, and we walked up the slope through the pecan trees toward the lighted gallery of our house. The thick layer of humus and leaves and moldy pecan husks cracked under our shoes. Behind the house the western horizon was still as blue as a robin's egg and streaked with low-lying pink clouds.

"You're real tired, huh?" she said.

"A little bit."

"Take a nap."

"Okay, little guy."

"Then we can go to Vezey's for ice cream," she said. She grinned up at me.

"Were they epaulets?" I said.

"What?"

"The gold you saw on his shoulders. Sometimes soldiers wear what they call epaulets on the shoulders of their coats."

"How could he be a soldier? He was on a crutch. You say funny things sometimes, Dave."

"I get it from a certain little fellow I know."

"That man doesn't hurt children, does he?"

"No, I'm sure he's harmless. Let's don't worry about it anymore."

"Okay, big guy."

"I'll feed Tripod. Why don't you go inside and wash your hands for supper?"

The screen door slammed after her, and I looked back down the slope under the overhang of the trees at the corn garden in the fading twilight. The wind dented and bent the stalks and straightened the leaves and swirled a column of dust around the blank cheesecloth visage of the scarecrow. The dirt road was empty, the bait shop dark, the gray clouds of insects hovering over the far side of the bayou almost like a metamorphic and tangible shape in the damp heat and failing light. I stared at the cornstalks and the hot sky filled with angry birds, then pinched the moisture and salt out of my eyes and went inside the house.

A TROPICAL STORM that had been expected to hit the Alabama coast changed direction and made landfall at Grand Isle, Louisiana. At false dawn the sky had been bone white, then a red glow spread across the eastern horizon as though a distant fire were burning out of control. The barometer dropped; the air became suddenly cooler; the bream began popping the bayou's darkening surface; and in less than an hour a line of roiling, lightning-forked clouds moved out of the south and covered the wetlands from horizon to horizon like an enormous black lid. The rain thundered like hammers on the wood dock and the bait shop's tin roof, filled our unrented boats with water, clattered on the islands of lily pads in the bayou, and dissolved the marsh into a gray and shapeless mist.

Then I saw a sleek white cabin cruiser approaching the dock, its windows beaten with rain, riding in on its own wake as the pilot cut back the throttle. Batist and I were under the awning, carrying the barbecue pit into the lee of the shop. Batist had two inches of a dead cigar in the corner of his mouth; he squinted through the rain at the boat as it bumped against the strips of rubber tire nailed to the dock pilings.

"Who that is?" he said.

"I hate to think."

"He wavin' at you, Dave. Hey, it's that drunk man done fell in the bayou the ot'er night. That man must surely love water."

We set the barbecue pit under the eave of the building and got back inside. The rain was whipping off the roof like frothy ropes. Through the screen window I could see Elrod and Kelly Drummond moving around inside the boat's cabin.

"Oh, oh, he trying to get out on the dock, Dave. I ain't goin' out there to pull him out of the bayou this time, me. Somebody ought to give that man swimmin' lessons or a big rock, one, give people some relief."

Our awning extended on wires all the way to the lip of the dock, and Elrod was trying to climb over the cruiser's gunwale into the protected area under the canvas. He was bare-chested, his white golf slacks soaked and pasted against his skin, his rubber-soled boat shoes sopping with water. His hand slipped off the piling, and he fell backward onto the deck, raked a fishing rod down with him and snapped it in half so that it looked like a broken coat hanger.

I put on my rain hat and went outside.

Elrod shielded his eyes with his hands and looked up at me in the rain. A purple and green rose was tattooed on his upper left chest.

"I guess I haven't got my sea legs yet," he said.

"Get back inside," I said, and jumped down into the boat.

"We're going after speckled trout. They always hit in the rain. At least they do on the Texas coast."

The rain was cold and stung like BBs. From two feet away I could smell the heavy surge of beer on his breath.

"I'm going inside," I said, and pulled open the cabin door.

"Sure. That's what I was trying to do. Invite you down for a sandwich or a Dr Pepper or a tonic or something," he said, and closed the cabin door behind us.

Kelly Drummond wore leather sandals, a pair of jeans, and the Ragin' Cajuns T-shirt with my name ironed on the back that Alafair had given to Elrod after he had fallen into the bayou. She picked up a towel and began rubbing Elrod's hair with it. Her green eyes were clear, her face fresh, as though she had recently awakened from a deep sleep.

"You want to go fishing with us?" she said.

"I wouldn't advise going out on the salt today. You'll probably get knocked around pretty hard out there."

She looked at Elrod.

"The wind'll die pretty soon," he said.

"I wouldn't count on that," I said.

"The guy who rented us the boat said it can take pretty heavy seas. This weather's not that big a deal, is it?" he said.

On the floor was an open cooler filled with cracked ice, long-necked bottles of Dixie, soda pop, and tonic water.

"I can outfit you with some fly rods and popping bugs," I said. "Why not wait until the rain quits and then try for some bass and goggle-eye perch?"

"When's the last time you caught freshwater fish right after a rain?" He smiled crookedly at me.

"Suit yourself. But I think what you're doing is a bad idea," I said. I looked at Kelly.

"El, we don't have to go today," she said. "Why don't we just drive down to New Orleans and mess around in the French Quarter?"

"I planned this all week."

"Come on, El. Give it up. It looks like Noah's flood out there."

"Sorry, we've got to do it. You can understand that, cain't you, Mr. Robicheaux?"

"Not really. Anyway, watch the bend in the channel about three miles south. The water's been low and there're some snags on the left."

"Three miles south? Yeah, I'll watch it," he said, his eyes refocusing on nothing. His suntanned, taut chest was beaded with water. His feet were wide spread to keep his balance, even though the boat was not moving. "You sure you don't want a tonic?"

"Thanks, anyway. Good luck to you all," I said.

Before I went out the cabin door, Kelly made her eyes jump at me, but I closed the door behind me and stepped up on the gunwale and onto the dock.

I began pushing huge balloons of water out of the awning with a broom handle and didn't hear her come up behind me.

"He'll listen to you. Tell him not to go out there," she said. There was a pinched indentation high up on her right cheek.

"I think you should tell him that yourself."

"You don't understand. He had a big fight with Mikey yesterday about the script and walked off the set. Then this morning he put the boat on Mikey's credit card. Maybe if we take the boat back now, the man'll tear up the credit slip. You think he might do that?"

"I don't know."

"El's going to get fired, Mr. Robicheaux."

"Tell Elrod you're staying here. That's about all I can suggest."

"He'll go anyway."

"I wish I could help you."

"That's it? *Au revoir*, fuck you, boat people?"

"In the last two days Elrod told both me and my wife he'd like to go to an AA meeting with me. Now it's ten in the morning and he's already ripped. What do you think the real problem is—the boat, your director, the rain, me, or maybe something else?"

She turned around as though to leave, then turned back and faced me again. There was a bright, painful light in her green eyes, the kind that comes right before tears.

"What do I do?" she said.

"Go inside the shop. I'll try again," I said.

I climbed back down into the boat and went into the cabin. He had his elbows propped on the instrument panel, while he ate a po'-boy sandwich and stared at the rain dancing in a yellow spray on the bayou.

His face had become wan and indolent, either from fatigue or alcoholic stupor, passive to all insult or intimidation. The more I talked, the more he yawned.

"She's a good lady, El," I said. "A lot of men would cut off their fingers with tin snips to have one like her."

"You got that right."

"Then why don't you quit this bullshit, at least for one day, and let her have a little serenity?"

Then his eyes focused on the cooler, on an amber, sweating bottle of Dixie nestled in the ice.

"All right," he said casually. "Let me borrow your fly rods, Mr. Robicheaux. I'll take good care of them."

"You're not going out on the salt?"

"No, I get seasick anyway."

"You want to leave the beer box with me?"

"It came with the boat. That fellow might get mad if I left it somewhere. Thanks for your thoughtfulness, though."

"Yeah, you bet."

After they were gone, I resolved that Elrod Sykes was on his own with his problems.

"Hey, Dave, that man really a big movie actor?" Batist said.

"He's big stuff out in Hollywood, Batist. Or at least he used to be."

"He rich?"

"Yeah, I guess he is."

"That's his reg'lar woman, too, huh?"

"Yep."

"How come he's so unhappy?"

"I don't know, Batist. Probably because he's a drunk."

"Then why don't he stop gettin' drunk?"

"I don't know, partner."

"You mad 'cause I ax a question?"

"Not in the least, Batist," I said, and headed for the back of the shop and began stacking crates of canned soda pop in the storeroom.

"You got some funny moods, you," I heard him say behind me.

A half hour later the phone rang.

"Hello," I said.

"We got a problem down here," a voice said.

There was static on the line and rain was throbbing on the shop's tin roof.

"Elrod?"

"Yeah. We hit some logs or a sandbar or something."

"Where are you?"

"At a pay phone in a little store. I waded ashore."

"Where's the boat?"

"I told you, it's messed up."

"Wait until the water rises, then you'll probably float free."

"There's a bunch of junk in the propeller."

"What are you asking me, Elrod?"

"Can you come down here?"

Batist was eating some chicken and dirty rice at the counter. He looked at my face and laughed to himself.

"How far down the bayou is the boat?" I said.

"About three miles. That bend you were talking about."

"The bend I was talking about, huh?"

"Yeah, you were right. There're some dead trees or logs in the water there. We ran right into them."

"We?"

"Yeah."

"I'll come after you, but I'm also going to give you a bill for my time."

"Sure thing, absolutely, Dave. This is really good of you. If I can—"

I put the receiver back on the hook.

"Tell Bootsie I'll be back in about an hour," I said.

Batist had finished his lunch and was peeling the cellophane off a fresh cigar. The humor had gone out of his face.

"Dave, I ain't one to tell you what to do, no," he said. "But there's people that's always gonna be axin' for somet'ing. When you deal with them kind, it don't matter how much you give, it ain't never gonna be enough."

He lit his cigar and fixed his eyes on me as he puffed on the smoke.

I put on my raincoat and hat, hitched a boat and trailer to my truck, and headed down the dirt road under the canopy of oak trees toward the general store where Elrod had made his call. The trailer was bouncing hard in the flooded chuckholes, and through the rearview mirror I could see the outboard engine on the boat's stern wobbling against the engine mounts. I shifted down to second gear, pulled to a wide spot on the road, and let a car behind me pass. The driver, a man wearing a shapeless fedora, looked in the opposite direction of me, out toward the bayou, as he passed.

Elrod was not at the general store, and I drove a quarter mile farther south to the bend where he had managed to put the cabin cruiser right through the limbs of a submerged tree and simultaneously scrape the bow up on a sandbar. The bayou was running high and yellow now, and gray nests of dead morning-glory vines had stuck to the bow and fanned back and forth in the current.

I backed my trailer into the shallows, then unwinched my boat into the water, started the engine, and opened it up in a shuddering whine against the steady clatter of the rain on the bayou's surface.

I came astern of the cabin cruiser and looped the painter on a cleat atop the gunwale so that my boat swung back in the lee of the cruiser. The current was swirling with mud and I couldn't see the propeller, but obviously it was fouled. From under the keel floated a streamer of torn hyacinth vines and lily pads, baited trotline, a divot ripped out of a conical fishnet, and even the Clorox marker bottle that went with it.

Elrod came out of the cabin with a newspaper over his head.

"How does it look?" he said.

"I'll cut some of this trash loose, then we'll try to back her into deeper water. How'd you hit a fish net? Didn't you see the Clorox bottle?"

"Is that how they mark those things?"

I opened my Puma knife, reached as deep below the surface as I could, and began pulling and sawing away the flotsam from the propeller.

"I 'spect the truth is I don't have any business out here," he said.

I flung a handful of twisted hyacinths and tangled fish line toward the bank and looked up into his face. The alcoholic shine had gone out of his eyes. Now they simply looked empty, on the edge of regret.

"You want me to get down in the water and do that?" he asked. Then he glanced away at something on the far bank.

"No, that's all right," I said. I stepped up on the bow of my boat and over the rail of the cabin cruiser. "Let's see what happens. If I can't shake her loose, I'll tie my outboard onto the bow and try to pull her sideways into the current."

We went inside the dryness of the cabin and closed the door. Kelly was sleeping on some cushions, her face nestled into one arm. When she woke, she looked around sleepily, her cheek wrinkled with the imprint of her arm; then she realized that little had changed in her and Elrod's dreary morning and she said, "Oh," almost like a child to whom awakenings are not good moments.

I started the engine, put it in reverse, and gave it the gas. The hull vibrated against the sandbar, and through the back windows I could see mud and dead vegetation boiling to the bayou's surface behind the stern. But we didn't move off the sandbar. I tried to go forward and rock it loose, then I finally cut the engine.

"It's set pretty hard, but it might come off if you push against the bow, Elrod," I said. "You want to do that?"

"Yeah, sure."

"It's not deep there. Just stay on the sandbar, close to the hull."

"Put on a life jacket, El," Kelly said.

"I swam across the Trinity River once at flood stage when houses were floating down it," he said.

She took a life jacket out of a top compartment, picked up his wrist, and slipped his arm through one of the loops. He grinned at me. Then his eyes looked out the glass at the far bank.

"What's that guy doing?" he said.

"Which guy?" I said.

"The guy knocking around in the brush out there."

"How about we get your boat loose and worry about other people later?" I said.

"You got it," he said, tied one lace on his jacket, and went out into the rain.

He held on to the rail on the cabin roof and worked his way forward toward the bow. Kelly watched him through the glass, biting down on the corner of his lip.

"He waded ashore before," I said, and smiled at her. "He's not in any danger there."

"El has accidents. Always."

"A psychologist might say there's a reason for that."

She turned away from the glass, and her green eyes moved over my face.

"You don't know him, Mr. Robicheaux. Not the gentle person who gives himself no credit for anything. You're too hard on him."

"I don't mean to be."

"You are. You judge him."

"I'd like to see him get help. But he won't as long as he's on the juice or using."

"I wish I had those kinds of easy answers."

"They're not easy. Not at all."

Elrod eased himself over the gunwale, sinking to his chest, then felt his way through the silt toward the slope on the sandbar.

"Can you stand in the stern? For the weight," I said to Kelly.

"Where?"

"In the back of the boat."

"Sure."

"Take my raincoat."

"I'm already sopped."

I restarted the engine.

"Just a minute," I said, and put my rain hat

on her head. Her wet blond curls were flattened against her brow. "I don't mean to be personal, but I think you're a special lady, Ms. Drummond, a real soldier."

She used both her hands to pull the hat's floppy brim down tightly on her hair. She didn't answer, but for the first time since I had met her, she looked directly into my eyes with no defensiveness or anger or fear and in fact with a measure of respect that I felt in all probability was not easily won.

I waved at Elrod through the front glass, kicked the engine into reverse, and opened the throttle. The exhaust pipes throbbed and blew spray high into the air at the waterline, the windows shook, the boards under my feet hummed with the vibrations from the engine compartment. I looked over my shoulder through the back glass and saw Kelly bent across the gunwale, pushing at the bottom of the bayou with a tarpon gaff; then suddenly the hull scraped backward in the sand, sliding out of a trench in a yellow and brown gush of silt and dead reeds, and popped free in the current.

Elrod was standing up on the sandbar, his balled fists raised over his head in victory.

I cut the gas and started out the cabin door to get the anchor.

Just as the rain struck my bare head and stung my eyes, just as I looked across the bayou and saw the man in the shapeless fedora kneeling hard against an oak tree, his shadowed face aimed along the sights of a bolt-action rifle, the leather sling twisted military style around the forearm, I knew that I was caught in one of those moments that will always remain forever too late, knew this even before I could yell, wave my arms, tell him that the person in the rain hat and Ragin' Cajuns T-shirt with my name on the back was not me. Then the rifle's muzzle flashed in the rain, the report echoing across the water and into the willow islands. The bullet cut a hole like a rose petal in the back of Kelly's shirt and left an exit wound in her throat that made me think of wolves with red mouths running through trees.

CHAPTER 10

IT WAS A strange week, for me as well as the town. Kelly's death brought journalists from all over the country to New Iberia. They filled all the motels, rented every available automobile in Lafayette, and dwarfed in both numbers and technical sophistication our small area news services.

Many of them were simply trying to do their jobs. But another kind came among us, too, those who have a voyeuristic glint in their eyes, whose real motivations and potential for callousness are unknown even to themselves.

I got an unlisted phone number for the house.

I began to be bothered by an odor, both in my sleep and during the late afternoon when the sun baked down on the collapsed barn at the back of our property. I noticed it the second day after Kelly's death, the day that Elrod escorted her body back to Kentucky for the burial. It smelled like dead rats. I scattered a bag of lime among the weeds and rotted boards and the smell went away. Then the next afternoon it was back, stronger than before, as invasive as a stranger's soiled palm held to your face.

I put our bedroom fan in the side window so it would draw air from the front of the house, but I would dream of turkey buzzards circling over a corrugated rice field, of sand-flecked winds blowing across the formless and decomposing shape of a large animal, of a woman's hair and fingernails wedging against the sides of a metal box.

On the seventh morning I woke early, walked past the duck pond in the soft blue light, soaked the pile of boards and strips of rusted tin with gasoline, and set it afire. The flames snapped upward in an enormous red-black handkerchief, and a cottonmouth moccasin, with a body as thick as my wrist, slithered out of the boards into the weeds, the hindquarters of an undigested rat protruding from its mouth.

The shooter left nothing behind, no ejected brass, no recoverable prints from the tree trunk where he had fired. The pocket knife Rosie had found on the levee turned out to be free of prints. Almost all of our work had proved worthless. We had no suspects; our theories about motivation were as potentially myriad as the time we were willing to invest in thinking about them. But one heart-sinking and unalterable conclusion remained in front of my eyes all day long, in my conversations with Rosie, the sheriff, and even the deputies who went out of their way to say good morning through my office door—Kelly Drummond was dead, and she was dead because she had been mistaken for me.

I DIDN'T EVEN see Mikey Goldman walk into my office. I looked up and he was standing there, flexing the balls of his feet, his protruding, pale eyes roving about the room, a piece of cartilage working in his jaw like an angry dime.

"Can I sit down?" he said.

"Go ahead."

"How you doing?"

"I'm fine, thanks. How are you?"

"I'm all right." His eyes went all over me, as though I were an object he was seeing for the first time.

"Can I help you with something?" I said.

"Who's the fucking guy who did this?"

"When we know that, he'll be in custody."

"In custody? How about blowing his head off instead?"

"What's up, Mr. Goldman?"

"How you handling it?"

"I beg your pardon?"

"How you handling it? I'm talking about you. I've been there, my friend. First Marine Division, Chosin Reservoir. Don't try to bullshit me."

I put down my fountain pen on the desk blotter, folded my hands, and stared at him.

"I'm afraid we're operating on two different wavelengths here," I said.

"Yeah? The guy next to you takes a round, and then maybe you start wondering if you aren't secretly glad it was him instead of you. Am I wrong?"

"What do you want?"

He rubbed the curly locks of salt-and-pepper hair on his neck and rolled his eyes around the room. The skin around his mouth was taut, his chin and jaw hooked in a peculiar martial way like a drill instructor's.

"Elrod's going to go crazy on me. I know it, I've seen him there before. He's a good kid, but he traded off some of his frontal lobes for magic mushrooms a long time ago. He likes you, he'll listen to you. Are you following me?"

"No."

"You keep him at your place, you stay out at his place, I don't care how you do it. I'm going to finish this picture."

"You're an incredible man, Mr. Goldman."

"What?" He began curling his fingers backward, as though he wanted to pull words from my chest. "You heard I got no feelings, I don't care about my actors, movie people are callous dipshits?"

"I never heard your name before you came to New Iberia. It seems to me, though, you have only one thing on your mind—getting what you want. Anyway, I'm not interested in taking care of Elrod Sykes."

"If I get my hands on the fuckhead who shot Kelly, you're going to have to wipe him off the wallpaper."

"Eventually we're going to get this guy, Mr. Goldman. But in the meantime, the vigilante histrionics don't float too well in a sheriff's department. Frankly, they're not too convincing, either."

"What?"

"Ask yourself a question: How many professional killers—and the guy who did this is a professional killer—could a rural parish like this have? Next question: Who comprises the one well-known group of professional criminals currently with us in New Iberia? Answer: Julie Balboni and his entourage of hired cretins. Next question: Who's in a movie partnership with these characters?"

He leaned back in his chair, bouncing his wrists lightly on the chair's arms, glancing about the room, his eyes mercurial, one moment almost amused, then suddenly focused on some festering inner concern.

"Mr. Goldman?" I said.

"Yeah? You got something else to say?"

"No, sir, not a thing."

"Good. That's good. You're not a bad guy. You've just got your head up your hole with your own problems. It's just human."

"I see. I'm going down the hall for a cup of coffee now," I said. "I suspect you'll be gone when I get back."

He rose to his feet and flexed a kink out of his back. He unwrapped a short length of peppermint candy and stuck it in his jaw.

"You want one?" he said.

"No, thanks."

"Don't pretend to be a Rotary man. I checked out your background before I asked you to babysit Elrod. You're as crazy as any of us. You're always just one step away from blowing up somebody's shit."

He cocked his finger, pointed it at me, and made a hollow popping sound with his mouth.

THAT NIGHT I dreamed that I was trying to save a woman from drowning way out on the Gulf of

Mexico. We were sliding down a deep trough, the froth whipping across her blond curls and bloodless face, her eyes sealed against the cobalt sky. Our heads protruded from the water as though they had been severed and placed on a plate. Then her body turned to stone, heavier than a marble statue, and there was no way I could keep her afloat. She sank from my arms, plummeting downward into a vortex of spinning green light, down into a canyon hundreds of feet below, a gush of air bubbles rising from a pale wound in her throat.

ROSIE CAME THROUGH the door, clunked her purse loudly on her desk, and began rummaging through the file cabinet. She had to stand on her toes to see down into the top drawer.

"You want to have lunch today?" she asked.

"What?"

"Lunch . . . do you want to have lunch? Come in, Earth."

"Thanks, I'll probably go home." Then as an afterthought I said, "You're welcome to join us."

"That's all right. Another time." She sat down behind her desk and began shifting papers around in a couple of file folders. But her eyes kept glancing up into my face.

"Have you got something on your mind?" I asked.

"Yeah, you."

"You must be having an uneventful day."

"I worked late last night. The dispatcher and I had a cup of coffee together. He asked me how I was getting along here, and I told him real good, no complaints. Then he asked me if I'd experienced any more smart-aleck behavior from some of the resident clowns in the department. I told him they'd been perfect gentlemen. I bet you can't guess what he said next."

"You got me."

She imitated a Cajun accent. "'Them guys give you any mo' trouble, you just tell Dave, Miz Rosie. He done tole 'em what's gonna happen the next time they bother you.'"

"He was probably exaggerating a little bit."

"You didn't need to do that for me, Dave."

"I apologize."

"Don't be a wise-ass, either."

"Boy, you're a pistol."

"How should I take that?"

"I don't know. How about easing up?"

She rested one small hand on top of the other. She had the same solid posture behind her desk that I remembered in the nuns at the elementary school I attended.

"You look tired," she said.

"I have bouts of insomnia."

"You want to talk about what happened out on the bayou?"

"No."

"Do you feel guilty about it?"

"What do you think I feel? I feel angry about it."

"Why?"

"What kind of question is that?"

"Do you feel angry because you couldn't control

what happened? Do you think somehow you're to blame for her death?"

"What if I said 'yes to all the above'? What difference would it make? She's dead."

"I think beating up on yourself has about as much merit as masturbation."

"You're a friend, Rosie, but let it go."

I busied myself with my paperwork and did not look back up for almost a minute. When I did, her eyes were still fixed on me.

"I just got some interesting information from the Bureau about Julie Balboni," she said. She waited, then said, "Are you listening?"

"Yes."

"This year N.O.P.D. Vice has closed up a half-dozen of his dirty movie theaters and two of his escort services. His fishing fleet just went into bankruptcy, too." When I didn't respond, she continued. "That's where he laundered a lot of his drug money. He'd declare all kinds of legitimate profits to the IRS that never existed."

"That's how all the wiseguys do it, Rosie. In every city in the United States."

"Except the auditors at the IRS say he just made a big mistake. He came up with millions of dollars for this Civil War movie and he's going to have a hard time explaining where he got it."

"Don't count on it."

"The IRS nails their butts to the wall when nobody else can."

I sharpened a pencil over the wastebasket with my pocket knife.

"I have the feeling I'm boring you," she said.

"No, you're just reviving some of my earlier misgivings."

"What?"

"I think your agency wants Julie's ass in a sling. I think these murders have secondary status."

"That's what you think, is it?"

"That's the way it looks from here."

She rose from her chair, closed the office door, then stood by my desk. She wore a white silk blouse with a necklace of black wooden beads. Her fingers were hooked in front of her stomach like an opera singer's.

"Julie's been a longtime embarrassment to the feds," I continued. "He's connected to half the crime in New Orleans and so far he's never spent one day in the bag."

"When I was sixteen something happened to me that I thought I'd never get over." There was a flush of color in her throat. "Not just because of what two drunken crew leaders did to me in the back of a migrant farmworkers' bus, either. It was the way the cops treated it. In some ways that was even worse. Have I got your attention, sir?"

"You don't need to do this, Rosie."

"Like hell I don't. The next day I was sitting with my father in the waiting room outside the sheriff's office. I heard two deputies laughing about it. They not only thought it was funny, one of them said something about pepper-belly poontang. I'll never forget that moment. Not as long as I live."

I folded up my pocket knife and stared at the

tops of my fingers. I brushed the pencil shavings off my fingers into the wastebasket.

"I'm sorry," I said.

"When I went to work for the Bureau, I swore I'd never see a woman treated the way I was. So I take severe exception to your remarks, Dave. I'd like to bust Julie Balboni, but that has nothing to do with the way I feel about the man who raped and murdered these women."

"Where'd this happen?"

"In a migrant camp outside of Bakersfield. It's not an unusual story. Ask any woman who's ever been on a crew bus."

"I think you're a solid cop, Rosie. I think you'll nail any perp you put in your sights."

"Then change your goddamn attitude."

"All right."

She was waiting for me to say something else, but I didn't.

Her shoulders sagged and she started back toward her desk. Then she turned around. Her eyes were wet.

"That's all you've got to say?" she asked.

"No, it's not."

"What, then?"

"I'm proud to be working with you. I think you're a standup lady."

She started to take a Kleenex out of her purse, then she snapped the purse shut again and took a breath.

"I'm going down the hall a minute," she said.

"All right."

"Are we both clear about the priority in this investigation, Dave?"

"Yeah, I think we are."

"Good. Because I don't want to have this kind of discussion again."

"Let me mention just one thing before you go. Several years ago my second wife was murdered by some drug dealers. You know that, don't you?"

"Yes."

"One way or another, the guys and the woman who killed her went down for it. But sometimes I wake up in the middle of the night and the old anger comes back. Even though these people took a heavy fall, for a couple of them the whole trip, sometimes it still doesn't seem enough. You know the feeling I'm talking about, don't you?"

"Yes."

"Fair enough." Then I said, "You're sure you don't want to come home and have lunch with us today?"

"This isn't the day for it, Dave. Thanks, anyway," she said, and went out the door with her purse clutched under her arm, her face set as impassively as a soldier's.

Elrod Sykes called the office just after I had returned from lunch. His voice was deep, his accent more pronounced.

"You know where there're some ruins of an old plantation house south of your boat dock?" he asked.

"What about it?"

"Can you meet me there in a half hour?"

"What for?"

"I want to talk to you, that's what for."

"Talk to me now, Elrod, or come into the office."

"I get nervous down there. For some reason police uniforms always make me think of a Breathalyzer machine. I don't know why that might be."

"You sound like your boat might have caught the early tide."

"Who cares? I want to show you something. Can you be there or not?"

"I don't think so."

"What the fuck is with you? I've got some information about Kelly's death. You want it or not?"

"Maybe you ought to give some thought as to how you talk to people."

"I left my etiquette in Kelly's family plot up in Kentucky. I'll meet you in thirty minutes. If you're not interested, fuck you, Mr. Robicheaux."

He hung up the phone. I had the feeling I was beginning to see the side of Elrod's personality that had earned him the attention of the tabloids.

Twenty minutes later I drove my pickup truck down a dirt lane through a canebrake to the ruins of a sugar planter's home that had been built on the bayou in the 1830s. In 1863 General Banks's federal troops had dragged the piano outside and smashed it apart in the coulee, then as an afterthought had torched the slave quarters and the second story of the planter's home. The roof and cypress timbers had collapsed inside the brick shell, the cisterns and outbuildings had decayed into humus, the smithy's forge was an orange smear in the damp earth, and vandals had knocked down most of the stone markers in the family cemetery and, looking for gold and silver coins, had pried up the flagstones in the fireplaces.

Why spend time with a rude drunk, particularly on the drunk's terms?

Because it's difficult to be hard-nosed or righteous toward a man who, for the rest of his life, will probably wake sweating in the middle of the night with a recurring nightmare or whose series of gray dawns will offer no promise of light except that first shuddering razor-edged rush that comes out of a whiskey glass.

I leaned against the fender of my truck and watched Elrod's lavender Cadillac come down the dirt lane and into the shade of the oak trees that grew in front of the ruined house. The security guard from the set, Murphy Doucet, was behind the wheel, and Elrod sat in the passenger's seat, his tanned arm balanced on the window ledge, a can of Coca-Cola in his hand.

"How you doing today, Detective Robicheaux?" Doucet said.

"Fine. How are you?"

"Like they say, we all chop cotton for the white man one way or another, you know what I mean?" he said, and winked.

He rubbed the white scar that was embossed like a chicken's foot on his throat and opened a newspaper on the steering wheel. Elrod came around the side of the Cadillac in blue swimming shorts, a beige polo shirt, and brand-new Nike running shoes.

He drank from his Coca-Cola can, set it on the hood of the car, then put a breath mint in his mouth. His eyes wandered around the clearing, then focused wanly on the sunlight winking off the bayou beyond the willow trees.

"Would you like to continue our conversation?" I said.

"You think I was out of line or something?"

"What did you want to tell me, Elrod?"

"Take a walk with me out yonder in those trees and I'll show you something."

"The old cemetery?"

"That isn't it. Something you probably don't know about."

We walked through a thicket of stunted oaks and hackberry trees, briars and dead morning-glory vines, to a small cemetery with a rusted and sagging piked iron fence around it. Pines with deep-green needles grew out of the graves. A solitary brick crypt had long ago collapsed in upon itself and become overgrown with wild roses and showers of four o'clocks.

Elrod stood beside me, and I could smell the scent of bourbon and spearmint on his breath. He looked out into the dazzling sunlight but his eyes didn't squint. They had a peculiar look in them, what we used to call in Vietnam the thousand-yard stare.

"There," he said, "in the shade, right on the edge of those hackberry trees. You see those depressions?"

"No."

He squeezed my arm hard and pointed.

"Right where the ground slopes down to the bayou," he said, and walked ahead of me toward the rear of the property. He pointed down at the ground. "There's four of them. You stick a shovel in here and you'll bring up bone."

In a damp area, where rainwater drained off the incline into a narrow coulee, there was a series of indentations that were covered with mushrooms.

"What's the point of all this?" I said.

"They were cooking mush in an iron pot and an artillery shell got all four of them. The general put wood crosses on their graves, but they rotted away a long time ago. He was a hell of an officer, Mr. Robicheaux."

"I'll be going now," I said. "I'd like to help you, Elrod, but I think you've marked your own course."

"I've been with these guys. I know what they went through. They had courage, by God. They made soup out of their shoes and rifle balls out of melted nails and wagonwheel rims. There was no way in hell they were going to quit."

I turned and began walking back to my truck. Through the shade I could see the security guard urinating by the open door of the Cadillac. Elrod caught up with me. His hand clenched on my arm again.

"You want to write me off as a wet-brain, that's your business," he said. "You don't care about what these guys went through, that's your business, too. I didn't bring you out here for this, anyway."

"Then why am I here?"

He turned me toward him with his hand.

"Because I don't like somebody carrying my oil can," he said.

"What?"

"That's a Texas expression. It means I don't want somebody else toting my load. You've convinced yourself the guy who killed Kelly thought he had you in his sights. That's right, isn't it?"

"Maybe."

"What makes you so goddamn important?"

I continued to walk toward my truck. He caught up with me again.

"You listen to me," he said. "Before she was killed I had a blowout with Mikey. I told him the script stinks, the screenwriters he's hired couldn't get jobs writing tampon ads, he's nickel-and-dime-ing the whole project to death, and I'm walking off the set unless he gets his head on straight. The greaseballs heard me."

"Which greaseballs?"

"Balboni's people. They're all over the set. They killed Kelly to keep me in line."

His facial skin high up on one cheek crinkled and seemed almost to vibrate.

"Take it easy, El."

"They made her an object lesson, Mr. Robicheaux."

I touched his arm with my hand.

"Maybe Julie's involved, maybe not," I said. "But if he is, it's not because of you. You've got to trust me on this one."

He turned his face away and pushed at one eye with the heel of his hand.

"When Julie and his kind create object lessons, they go right to the source of their problem," I said. "They don't select out innocuous people. It causes them too many problems."

I heard his breath in his throat.

"I made them keep the casket closed," he said. "I told the funeral director in Kentucky, if he let her parents see her like that, I'd be back, I'd—"

I put my arm over his shoulder and walked back through the cemetery with him.

"Let's go back to town and have something to eat," I said. "Like somebody said to me this morning, it's no good to kick ourselves around the block, is it? What do you think?"

"She's dead. I cain't see her, either. It's not right."

"I beg your pardon?"

"I see those soldiers but I cain't see her. Why's that? It doesn't make any sense."

"I'll be honest with you, partner. I think you're floating on the edge of delirium tremens. Put the cork in the jug before you get there, El. Believe me, you don't have to die to go to hell."

"You figure me for plumb down the road and around the bend, don't you? I don't blame you. I got my doubts about what I see myself."

"Maybe that's not a bad sign."

"When we were driving through that canebrake, I said to Murph, the security guy, 'Who's that standing behind Mr. Robicheaux?' Then I looked again and I knew who it was. Except I've never seen him in daylight before. When I looked again, he was gone. Which isn't the way he does things."

"I'm going to an AA meeting tonight. You want to come?"

"Yeah, why not? It cain't be worse than having dinner with Mikey and the greaseballs."

"You might be a little careful about your vocabulary when you're around those guys."

"Boy, I wonder what my grandpa would say if he saw me working with the likes of that bunch. I told you he was a Texas Ranger, didn't I?"

"You surely did."

"You know what he once told me about Bonnie Parker and Clyde Barrow? He said—"

"I have to get back to the office. How about I pick you up at your place at seven-thirty?"

"Sure. Thanks for coming out, Mr. Robicheaux. I'm sorry about my bad manners on the phone. I'm not given to using profanity like that. I don't know what got into me." He picked up his soda can off the hood of his Cadillac and started to drink out of it. "It's just Coca-Cola. That's a fact."

"You'd better drink it then."

He smiled at me.

"It rots your teeth," he said, and emptied the can into the dirt.

THAT NIGHT I sat alone in the bait shop, a glass of iced coffee in my hand, and tried to figure the connection between Kelly's death and the pursuit of a serial killer who might also be involved with prostitution. Nothing in the investigation seemed to fit. Was the serial killer also a pimp? Why did his crimes seem to be completely contained within the state of Louisiana? If he had indeed mistaken Kelly for me, what had I discovered in the investigation that would drive him to attempt the murder of a police officer? And what was Baby Feet Balboni's stake in all this?

Equally troubling was the possibility that Kelly's death had nothing to do with our hunt for a serial killer. Maybe the rifleman in the fedora had had another motivation, one that was connected with a rat's nest of bones, strips of dried skin, rotted clothing, and a patch of kinky hair attached to a skull plate. Did someone out there believe that somehow that gaping mouth, impacted with sand, strung with green algae, could whisper the names of two killers who thought they had buried their dark deed in water thirty-five years ago?

We live today in what people elect to call the New South. But racial fear, and certainly white guilt over racial injustice, die hard. Hogman Patin, who probably feared very little in this world, had cautioned me because of my discovery of the lynched black man out in the Atchafalaya. He had also suggested that the dead man had been involved with a white woman. To Hogman, those events of years ago were still alive, still emblematic of an unforgiven and collective shame, to be spoken about as obliquely as possible, in all probability because some of the participants were still alive, too.

Maybe it was time to have another talk with Hogman, I thought.

When I drove out to his house on the bayou, the interior was dark and the white curtains in his open windows were puffing outward in the breeze. In the back I could hear the tinkling of the Milk of Magnesia bottles and the silver crosses that he had hung all over the branches of a live oak.

Where are you, Hogman? I thought. I wedged my business card in the corner of his screen door.

The moon was yellow through the trees. I could smell the unmistakable odor of chitterlings that had been burned in a pot. Out on the blacktop I heard a car engine. The headlights bounced off the tree trunks along the roadside, then the driver slowed and I thought he was about to turn into the grove of trees at the front of Hogman's property. I thought the car was probably Hogman's, and I started to walk toward the blacktop. Then the driver accelerated and his headlights swept past me.

I would have given no more notice to the driver and his vehicle, except that just as I started to turn back toward my truck and leave, he cut his lights and really gave it the gas.

If his purpose had been to conceal his license number, he was successful. But two other details stuck in my mind: the car looked new and it was dark blue, the same characteristics as the automobile that two witnesses had seen on the levee in Vermilion Parish where the asphyxiated girl had been stuffed nude into a metal barrel.

Or maybe the car had simply contained a couple

of teenage neckers looking for a little nocturnal privacy. I was too tired to think about it anymore. I started my truck and headed home.

The night was clear, the constellations bursting against the black dome of sky overhead. There was no hint of rain, no sudden drop or variation in temperature to cause fog to roll off the water. But two hundred yards down from Hogman's house the road was suddenly white with mist, so thick my headlights couldn't penetrate it. At first I thought a fire was burning in a field and the wind had blown the smoke across the road. But the air smelled sweet and cool, like freshly turned earth, and was almost wet to the touch. The mist rolled in clouds off the bayou, covered the tree trunks, closed about my truck like a white glove, drifted in wisps through my windows. I don't know whether I deliberately stopped the truck or my engine killed. But for at least thirty seconds my headlights flickered on and off, my starter refused to crank, and my radio screamed with static that was like fingernails on a blackboard.

Then as suddenly as it had come, the mist evaporated from the road and the tree trunks and the bayou's placid surface as though someone had held an invisible flame to it, and the night air was again as empty and pristine as wind trapped under a glass bell.

In the morning I made do with mechanical answers in the sunlight and cleaned the terminals on my truck battery with baking soda, water, and an old toothbrush.

• • •

HOGMAN CALLED THE next afternoon from the movie set out on Spanish Lake.

"What you want out at my house?" he said.

"I need to talk with you about the lynched black man."

"I done already tole you what I know. That nigger went messin' in the wrong place."

"That's not enough."

"Is for me."

"You said my father helped your mother when you were in prison. So now I'm asking you to help me."

"I already have. You just ain't listen."

"Are you afraid of somebody, Sam? Maybe some white people?"

"I fear God. Why you talkin' to me like this?"

"What time will you be home today?"

"When I get there. You got your truck?"

"Yes."

"My car hit a tree last night. It ain't runnin' no mo'. Come out to the set this evenin' and give me a ride home. 'Bout eight or nine o'clock."

"We'll see you then, partner," I said, and hung up.

The sun was red and half below the horizon, the cicadas droning in the trees, when I drove down the lane through the pecan orchard to the movie set on Spanish Lake. But I soon discovered that I was not going to easily trap Hogman Patin alone. It was Mikey Goldman's birthday and the cast and crew were throwing him a party. A linen-covered buffet table was piled with catered food, a huge pink cake, and a bowl of champagne punch in the center. The tree trunks along the lake's edge were wrapped with paper bunting, and Goldman's director's chair must have had two dozen floating balloons tied to it.

It was a happy crowd. They sipped punch out of clear plastic glasses and ate boiled shrimp and thin slices of *boudin* off paper plates. Mikey Goldman's face seemed to almost shine in the ambiance of goodwill and affection that surrounded him.

In the crowd I saw Julie Balboni and his entourage, Elrod Sykes, the mayor of New Iberia, the president of the Chamber of Commerce, a couple of Teamster officials, a state legislator, and Twinky Hebert Lemoyne from Lafayette. In the middle of it all sat Hogman Patin on an upended crate, his twelve-string guitar resting on his crossed thighs. He was dressed like a nineteenth-century Negro street musician, except he also wore a white straw cowboy hat slanted across his eyes. The silver picks on his right hand rang across the strings as he sang,

Soon as day break in the mornin'
I gone take the dirt road home.
'Cause these blue Monday blues
Is goin' kill me sure as you're born.

"You ought to get yourself a plate."

It was Murphy Doucet, the security guard. He was talking to me but his eyes were looking at a blond girl in shorts and a halter by the punch bowl. He ate a slice of *boudin* off a toothpick, then slipped the toothpick into the corner of his mouth and sucked on it.

"It doesn't look like everybody's broken up about Kelly Drummond's death, does it?" I said.

"I guess they figure life goes on."

"You're in business with Mr. Lemoyne over there, Murph?"

"We own a security service together, if that's what you mean. For me it's a pretty good deal, but for him it's nothing. If there's a business around here making money, Twinky's probably got a piece of it. Lord God, that man knows how to make money."

Lemoyne sat by the lake in a canvas chair, a julep glass filled with bourbon, shaved ice, and mint leaves in his hand. He looked relaxed and cool in the breeze off the water, his rimless glasses pink with the sun's afterglow. His eyes fixed for a moment on my face, then he took a sip from his glass and watched some kids waterskiing out on the lake.

"Get something to eat, Dave. It's free. Hell, I'm going to take some home," Murphy Doucet said.

"Thanks, I've already eaten," I said, and walked over to where Hogman sat next to two local black women who had been hired as extras.

"You want a ride?" I said.

"I ain't ready yet. They's people want me to play."

"It was your idea for me to come out here, Sam."

"I'll be comin' directly. That's clear, ain't it? Mr. Goldman fixin' to cut his cake."

Then he began singing,

I ax my bossman, Bossman, tell me what's right.
He whupped my left, said, Boy, now you know what's right.
I tole my bossman, Bossman, just give me my time.
He say, Damn yo' time, boy,
Boy, you time behind.

I waited another half hour as the twilight faded, the party grew louder, and someone turned on a bank of floodlamps that lit the whole area with the bright unnatural radiance of a phosphorus flare. The punch bowl was now empty and had been supplanted by washtubs filled with cracked ice and canned beer, a portable bar, and two white-jacketed black bartenders who were making mint juleps and martinis as fast as they could.

"I've got to head for the barn, Hogman," I said.

"This lady axin' me somet'ing. Give me ten minutes," he said.

A waiter came by with a tray and handed Hogman and the black woman with him paper cups streaming with draft beer. Then he handed me a frosted julep glass packed with shaved ice, mint leaves, orange slices, and candied cherries.

"I didn't order this," I said.

"Gentleman over yonder say that's what you drink. Say bring it to you. It's a Dr Pepper, suh."

"Which gentleman?"

"I don't rightly remember, suh."

I took the cup off the tray and drank from it. The ice was so cold it made my throat ache.

The lake was black now, and out in the darkness, above the noise of the revelers, I could hear somebody trying to crank an outboard engine.

I finished my drink and set the empty glass on the buffet table.

"That's it for me, Sam," I said. "You coming or not?"

"This lady gonna carry me home," he said. His eyes were red from drinking. They looked out at nothing from under the brim of his straw cowboy hat.

"Hogman—" I said.

"This lady live down the road from my house. Some trashy niggers been givin' her trouble. She don't want to go home by herself. That's the way it is. I be up to yo' office tomorrow mornin'."

I tried to look into his face, but he occupied himself with twisting the tuning pegs on his guitar. I turned and walked back through the shadows to my pickup truck. When I looked back at the party through my windshield, the blond girl in shorts and a halter was putting a spoonful of cake into Mikey Goldman's mouth while everyone applauded.

IT RAINED HARD as I approached the drawbridge over the bayou south of town. I could see the bridge tender in his lighted window, the wet sheen and streaks of rust on the steel girders, the green and red running lights of a passing boat in the mist. I was only a few minutes from home. I simply had to cross the bridge and follow the dirt road down to my dock.

But that was not what I did or what happened.

A bolt of lightning exploded in a white ball by the side of the road and blew the heart of a tree trunk, black and smoking, out into my headlights. I swallowed to clear my ears, and for just a second, in the back of my throat, I thought I could taste black cherries, bruised mint leaves, and orange rind. Then I felt a spasm go through me just as if someone had scratched a kitchen match inside my skull.

The truck veered off the shoulder, across a collapsed barbed-wire cattle gate, onto the levee that dissected the marsh. I remember the wild buttercups sweeping toward me out of the headlights, the rocks and mud whipping under the fenders, then the fog rolling out of the dead cypress trees and willow islands, encircling the truck, smothering the windows. I could hear thunder crashing deep in the marsh, echoing out of the bays, like distant artillery.

I knew that I was going off the levee, but I couldn't unlock my hands from the steering wheel or move my right foot onto the brake pedal. I felt myself trembling, my insides constricting, my back teeth grinding, as though all my nerve endings had been severed and painted with iodine. Then I heard lightning pop the levee and blow a spray of muddy water across my windshield.

Get out, I thought. *Knock the door handle with your elbow and jump.*

But I couldn't move.

The mist was as pink and thick as cotton candy and seemed to snap with electric currents, like a kaleidoscopic flickering of snakes' tongues. I felt the front wheels of the truck dip over the side of the levee, gain momentum with the weight in the rear end, then suddenly I was rumbling down an incline through weeds and broken cane, willow saplings and cattails, until the front wheels were embedded up to the axle in water and sand.

I don't know how long I sat there. I felt a wave of color pass through me, like nausea or the violent shudder that cheap bourbon gives you when you're on the edge of delirium tremens; then it was gone and I could see the reflection of stars on the water, the tips of the dead cypress silhouetted against the moon, and a campfire, where there should have been no fire, burning in a misty grove of trees on high ground thirty yards out from the levee.

And I knew that was where I was supposed to go.

As I waded through the lily pads toward the trees, I could see the shadows of men moving about in the firelight and hear their cracker accents and the muted sound of spoons scraping on tin plates.

I walked up out of the shallows into the edge of the clearing, dripping water, hyacinth vines stringing from my legs. The men around the fire paid me little notice, as though, perhaps, I had been expected. They were cooking tripe in an iron pot, and they had hung their haversacks and wooden canteens in the trees and stacked their rifle-muskets in pyramids of fives. Their gray and butternut-brown uniforms were sunbleached and stiff with dried salt, and their unshaved faces had the lean and hungry look of a rifle company that had been in the field a long time.

Then from the far side of the fire a bearded man with fierce eyes stared out at me from under a gray hat with gold cord around the crown. His left arm was pinned up in a black sling, and his right trouser leg flopped loosely around a shaved wooden peg.

He moved toward me on a single crutch. I could smell tobacco smoke and sweat in his clothes. Then he smiled stiffly, the skin of his face seeming almost to crack with the effort. His teeth were as yellow as corn.

"I'm General John Bell Hood. Originally from Kentucky. How you do, suh?" he said, and extended his hand.

CHAPTER 11

"*D*O YOU OBJECT *to shaking hands?*" he said.

"No. Not at all. Excuse me."

The heel of his hand was half-mooned with calluses, his voice as thick as wet sand. A holstered cap-and-ball revolver hung on his thigh.

"You look puzzled," he said.

"Is this how it comes? Death, I mean."

"Ask them."

Some of his men were marked with open, bloodless wounds I could put my fist in. Beyond the stacked rifles, at the edge of the firelight, was an ambulance wagon. Someone had raked a tangle of crusted bandages off the tailgate onto the ground.

"Am I dead?" I said.

"You don't look it to me."

"You said you're John Bell Hood."

"That's correct."

His face was narrow, his cheeks hollow, his skin grained with soot.

"I've read a great deal about you."

"I hope it met your approval."

"You were at Gettysburg and Atlanta. You com-

manded the Texas Brigade. They could never make you quit."

"My political enemies among President Davis's cabinet sometimes made note of that fact."

"What's the date?" I asked.

"It's April 21, 1865."

"I don't understand."

"Understand what?"

"Lee has already surrendered. The war's over. What are you doing here?"

"It's never over. I would think you'd know that. You were a lieutenant in the United States Army, weren't you?"

"Yes, but I gave my war back to the people who started it. I did that a long time ago."

"No, you didn't. It goes on and on."

He eased himself down on an oak stump, his narrow eyes lighting with pain. He straightened his artificial leg in front of him. The hand that hung out of his sling had wasted to the size of a monkey's paw. A corporal threw a log into the campfire, and sparks rose into the tree branches overhead.

"It's us against them, my friend," he said. *"There're insidious men abroad in the land."* He swept his crutch at the marsh. *"My God, man, use your eyes."*

"The federals?"

"Are your eyes and ears stopped with dirt?"

"I think this conversation is not real. I think all of this will be gone with daylight."

"You're not a fool, Mr. Robicheaux. Don't pretend to be one."

"I've seen your grave in New Orleans. No, it's in Metairie. You died of the yellowjack."

"That's not correct. I died when they struck the colors, suh." He lifted his crutch and pointed it at me as he would a weapon. The firelight shone on his yellow teeth. *"They'll try your soul, son. But don't give up your cause. Occupy the high ground and make them take it foot by bloody foot."*

"I don't know what we're talking about."

"For God's sakes, what's wrong with you? Venal and evil men are destroying the world you were born in. Can't you understand that? Why do I see fear in your face?"

"I think maybe I'm drunk again. I used to have psychotic episodes when I went on benders. I thought dead men from my platoon were telephoning me in the rain."

"You're not psychotic, Lieutenant. No more than Sykes is."

"Elrod is a wet-brain, general."

"The boy has heart. He's not afraid to be an object of ridicule for his beliefs. You mustn't be either. I'm depending on you."

"I have no understanding of your words."

"Our bones are in this place. Do you think we'll surrender it to criminals, to those who would use our teeth and marrow for landfill?"

"I'm going now, general."

"Ah, you'll simply turn your back on madness, will you? The quixotic vision is not for you, is it?"

"Something's pulling me back. I can feel it."

"They put poison in your system, son. But you'll

get through it. You've survived worse. The mine you stepped on, that sort of thing."

"*Poison?*"

He shrugged and put a cigar in his mouth. A corporal lit it with a burning stick from the fire. In the shadows a sergeant was putting together a patrol that was about to move out. Their faces were white and wrinkled like prunes with exhaustion and the tropical heat.

"*Come again,*" he said.

"*I don't think so.*"

"*Then goodnight to you, suh.*"

"*Goodnight to you, General. Goodnight to your men, too.*"

He nodded and puffed on his cigar. There were small round hollows in his cheeks.

"*General?*"

"*Yes, suh?*"

"*It's going to be bad, isn't it?*"

"*What?*"

"*What you were talking about, something that's waiting for me down the road.*"

"*I don't know. For one reason or another I seem to have more insight into the past than the future.*" He laughed to himself. Then his face sobered and he wiped a strand of tobacco off his lip. "*Try to keep this in mind. It's just like when they load with horseshoes and chain. You think the barrage will last forever, then suddenly there's a silence that's almost louder than their cannon. Please don't be alarmed by the severity of my comparison. Goodnight, Lieutenant.*"

"Goodnight, General."

I waded through the shallows, into deeper water, back toward the levee. The mist hung on the water in wisps that were as dense as thick-bodied snakes. I saw ball lightning roll through the flooded trees and snap apart against a willow island; it was as bright and yellow as molten metal dipped from a forge. Then rain began twisting out of the sky, glistening like spun glass, and the firelight behind me became a red smudge inside a fog bank that billowed out of the marsh, slid across the water, and once again closed around my truck.

The air was so heavy with ozone I could almost taste it on my tongue; I could hear a downed power line sparking and popping in a pool of water and smell a scorched electrical odor in the air like the metallic, burnt odor the St. Charles streetcar makes in the rain. I could hear a nutria crying in the marsh for its mate, a high-pitched shriek like the scream of a hysterical woman. I remember all these things. I remember the mud inside my shoes, the hyacinth vines binding around my knees, the gray-green film of algae that clung to my khaki trousers like cobweb.

When a sheriff's deputy and two paramedics lifted me out of the truck cab in the morning, the sun was as white as an arc welder's flame, the morning as muggy and ordinary as the previous day, and my clothes as dry as if I had recently taken them from my closet. The only physical change the supervising paramedic noted in me was an incised lump the size of a darning sock over my right eye. That and one other cautious, almost humorous observation.

"Dave, you didn't fall off the wagon on your head last night, did you?" he asked. Then, "Sorry. I was just kidding. Forget I said that."

Our family physician, Dr. Landry, sat on the side of my bed at Iberia General and looked into the corner of my eye with a small flashlight. It was late afternoon now, Bootsie and Alafair had gone home, and the rain was falling in the trees outside the window.

"Does the light hurt your eyes?" he asked.

"A little. Why?"

"Because your pupils are dilated when they shouldn't be. Tell me again what you felt just before you went off the road."

"I could taste cherries and mint leaves and oranges. Then I felt like I'd bitten into an electric wire with my teeth."

He put the small flashlight in his shirt pocket, adjusted his glasses, and looked at my face thoughtfully. He was an overweight, balding, deeply tanned golf player, with rings of blond hair on his forearms.

"How do you feel now?" he said.

"Like something's torn in my head. The way wet cardboard feels when you tear it with your hands."

"Did you eat anything?"

"I threw it up."

"You want the good news? The tests don't show any booze in your system."

"How could there be? I didn't drink any alcohol."

"People have their speculations sometimes, warranted or not."

"I can't help that."

"The bad news is I don't know what did this to you. But according to the medics you said some strange things, Dave."

I looked away from his face.

"You said there were soldiers out there in the marsh. You kept insisting they were hurt."

The wind began gusting, and rain and green leaves blew against the window.

"The medics thought maybe somebody had been with you. They looked all over the levee," he said. "They even sent a boat out into those willow islands."

"I'm sorry I created so much trouble for them."

"Dave, they say you were talking about Confederate soldiers."

"It was an unusual night."

He took a breath, then made a sucking sound with his lips.

"Well, you weren't drunk and you're not crazy, so I've got a theory," he said. "When I was an intern at Charity Hospital in New Orleans back in the sixties, I treated kids who acted like somebody had roasted their brains with a blowtorch. I'm talking about LSD, Dave. You think one of those Hollywood characters might have freshened up your Dr Pepper out there at Spanish Lake?"

"I don't know. Maybe."

"It didn't show up in the tests, but that's not unusual. To really do a tox screen for LSD, you need a gas chromatograph. Not many hospitals have one. We sure don't, anyway. Has anything like this ever happened to you before?"

"When my wife was killed, I got drunk again and became delusional for a while."

"Why don't we keep that to ourselves?"

"Is something being said about me, doc?"

He closed his black bag and stood up to go.

"When did you start worrying about what people say?" he said. "Look, I want you to stay in here a couple of days."

"Why?"

"Because you didn't feel any gradual effects, it hit you all at once. That indicates to me a troubling possibility. Maybe somebody really loaded you up. I'm a little worried about the possibility of residual consequences, Dave, something like delayed stress syndrome."

"I need to get back to work."

"No, you don't."

"I'll talk with the sheriff. Actually I'm surprised he hasn't been up yet."

Dr. Landry rubbed the thick hair on his forearm and looked at the water pitcher and glass on my nightstand.

"What is it?" I said.

"I saw him a short while ago. He said he talked with you for a half hour this morning."

I stared out the window at the gray sky and the rain falling in the trees. Thunder boomed and echoed out of the south, shaking the glass in the window, and for some reason in my mind's eye I saw rain-soaked enlisted men slipping in the mud around a cannon emplacement, swabbing out the smoking barrel, ramming home coils of chain and handfuls of twisted horseshoes.

I COULDN'T SLEEP that night, and in the morning I checked myself out of the hospital and went home. The doctor had asked me how I felt. My answer had not been quite accurate. I felt empty, washed-out inside, my skin rubbery and dead to the touch, my eyes jittering with refracted light that seemed to have no source. I felt as if I had been drinking sour mash for three days and had suddenly become disconnected from all the internal fires that I had nourished and fanned and depended upon with the religious love of an acolyte. There was no pain, no broken razor blades were twisting inside the conscience; there was just numbness, as though wind and fleecy clouds and rain showers marching across the canefields were a part of a curious summer phenomenon that I observed in a soundless place behind a glass wall.

I drank salt water to make myself throw up, ate handfuls of vitamins, made milkshakes filled with strawberries and bananas, did dozens of pushups and stomach crunches in the backyard, and ran wind sprints in the twilight until my chest was heaving for breath and my gym shorts were pasted to my skin with sweat.

I showered with hot water until there was none left in the tank, then I kept my head under the cold water for another five minutes. Then I put on a fresh pair of khakis and a denim shirt and walked outside into the gathering dusk under the pecan trees. The marsh across the road was purple with haze, sparkling with fireflies. A black kid in a pirogue was cane fishing along the edge of the lily pads in the bayou. His dark skin seemed to glow with the sun's vanishing red light. His body and pole were absolutely still, his gaze riveted on his cork bobber. The evening was so quiet and languid, the boy so transfixed in his concentration, that I could have been looking at a painting.

Then I realized, with a twist of the heart, that something was wrong—there was no sound. A car passed on the dirt road, the boy scraped his paddle along the side of the pirogue to move to a different spot. But there was no sound except the dry resonance of my own breathing.

I went into the house, where Bootsie was reading under a lamp in the living room. I was about to speak, with the trepidation a person might have if he were violating the silence of a church, just to see if I could hear the sound of my own voice, when I heard the screen door slam behind me like a slap across the ear. Then suddenly I heard the television, the cicadas in the trees, my neighbor's sprinkler whirling against his myrtle bushes, Batist cranking an outboard down at the dock.

"What is it, Dave?" Bootsie said.

"Nothing."

"Dave?"

"It's nothing. I guess I got some water in my ears." I opened and closed my jaws.

"Your dinner is on the table. Do you want it?"

"Yeah, sure," I said.

Her eyes studied mine.

"Let me heat it up for you," she said.

"That'd be fine."

When she walked past me she glanced into my face again.

"What's the deal, Boots? Do I look like I just emerged from a hole in the dimension?" I said, following her into the kitchen.

"You look tired, that's all."

She kept her back to me while she wrapped my dinner in plastic to put it in the microwave.

"What's wrong?" I said.

"Nothing, really. The sheriff called. He wants you to take a week off."

"Why didn't he tell *me* that?"

"I don't know, Dave."

"I think you're keeping something from me."

She put my plate in the microwave and turned around. She wore a gold cross on a chain, and the cross hung at an angle outside her pink blouse. Her fingers came up and touched my cheek and the swelling over my right eye.

"You didn't shave today," she said.

"What did the sheriff say, Boots?"

"It's what some other people are saying. In the mayor's office. In the department."

"What?"

"That maybe you're having a breakdown."

"Do you believe I am?"

"No."

"Then who cares?"

"The sheriff does."

"That's his problem."

"A couple of deputies went out to the movie location and questioned some of the people who were at Mr. Goldman's birthday party."

"What for?"

"They asked people about your behavior, things like that."

"Was one of those deputies Rufus Arceneaux?"

"Yes, I think so."

"Boots, this is a guy who would sell his mother to a puppy farm to advance one grade in rank."

"That's not the point. Some of those actors said you were walking around all evening with a drink in your hand. People believe what they want to hear."

"I had blood and urine tests the next morning. There was no alcohol in my system. It's a matter of record at the hospital."

"You beat up one of Julie Balboni's hoods in a public place, Dave. You keep sending local businessmen signals that you just might drive a lot of big money out of town. You tell the paramedics that there're wounded Confederate soldiers in the marsh. What do you think people are going to say about you?"

I sat down at the kitchen table and looked out the back screen at the deepening shadows on the lawn. My eyes burned, as though there were sand under my eyelids.

"I can't control what people say," I said.

She stood behind me and rested her palms on my shoulders.

"Let's agree on one thing," she said. "We just can't allow ourselves to do anything that will help them hurt us. Okay, Dave?"

I put my right hand on top of hers.

"I won't," I said.

"Don't try to explain what you think you heard or saw in the marsh. Don't talk about the accident. Don't defend yourself. You remember what you used to say? 'Just grin and walk through the cannon smoke. It drives them crazy.' "

"All right, Boots."

"You promise?"

"I promise."

She folded her arms across my chest and rested her chin on the top of my head. Then she said, "What kind of person would try to do this to us, Dave?"

"Somebody who made a major mistake," I said.

But it was a grandiose remark. The truth was that I had taken the drink at the party incautiously and that I had walked right into the script someone else had written for me.

Later that night, in bed, I stared at the ceiling and tried to recreate the scene under the oak trees at Spanish Lake. I wanted to believe that I could reach down into my unconscious and retrieve a photographic plate on which my eye had engraved an image of someone passing his hand over the glass of Dr Pepper, black cherries, orange slices, and bruised mint that a waiter was about to serve me.

But the only images in my mind were those of a levee extending out into gray water and an electrically charged fog bank rolling out of the cypress trees.

Bootsie turned on her side and put her arm across my chest. Then she moved her hand down my stomach and touched me.

I stared up into the darkness. The trees were motionless outside the window. I heard a 'gator flop in the marsh.

Then her hand went away from me and I felt her weight turn on the mattress toward the opposite wall.

An hour later I dressed in the darkness of the living room, slipped my pickup truck into neutral, rolled it silently down the dirt lane to the dock, and hooked my boat and trailer to the bumper hitch.

I PUT MY boat into the water at the same place I had driven my truck off the levee. I used the paddle to push out into deeper water, past the cattails and lily pads that grew along the bank's edge, then I lowered the engine and jerked it alive with the starter rope.

The wake off the stern looked like a long V-shaped trench roiling with yellow mud, bobbing with dead logs. Then the moon broke through the clouds, gilding the moss in the cypress with a silver light, and I could see cottonmouths coiled on the lower limbs of willow trees, the gnarled brown-green head of a 'gator in a floating island of leaves and sticks, the stiffened, partly eaten body of a coon on a sandbar, and a half-dozen wood ducks that skittered across the water in front of the high ground and the grove of trees where I had met the general.

I cut the throttle and let the boat ride on its wake until the bow slid up on the sand. Then I walked into the trees with a six-battery flashlight and a GI entrenching tool.

The ground was soft, oozing with moisture, matted with layers of dead leaves and debris left by receding water. Tangles of abandoned trotlines were strung about the tree trunks; Clorox marker bottles from fish traps lay half-buried in the sand.

In the center of the clearing I found the remains of a campfire.

A dozen blackened beer cans lay among the charred wood. Crushed into the grass at the edge of the fire was a used rubber.

I kicked the wood, ashes, and cans across the ground, propped my flashlight in the weeds, folded the E-tool into the shape of a hoe, screwed down and locked the socket at the base of the blade, and started chopping into the earth.

Eighteen inches down I hit what archaeologists call a "fireline," a layer of pure black charcoal sediment from a very old fire. I sifted it off the blade's tip a shovelful at a time. In it was a scorched brass button and the bottom of a hand-blown bottle, one that had tiny air bubbles inside the glass's green thickness.

But what did that prove? I asked myself.

Answer: That perhaps nineteenth-century trappers, cypress loggers, or even army surveyors had built a campfire there.

Then I thought about the scene the other night: the stacked rifle muskets, the haversacks suspended in the trees, the exhaustion in the men who were about to move out on patrol, the dry, bloodless wounds that looked like they had been eaten clean by maggots, the ambulance wagon and the crusted field dressings that had been raked out onto the ground.

The ambulance wagon.

I picked up my flashlight and moved to the far side of the clearing. The water was black under the canopy of flooded trees out in the marsh. I knelt and started digging out a two-by-four-foot trench. The clearing sloped here, and the ground was softer and wetter, wrinkled with small eroded gullies. I scraped the dirt into piles at each end of the hole; a foot down, water began to run from under the shovel blade.

I stopped to reset the blade and begin digging back toward the top of the incline. Then I saw the streaks of rust and bits of metal, like small red teeth, in the wet piles of dirt at each end of the hole. I shined the flashlight into the hole, and protruding from one wall, like a twisted snake, was a rusted metal band that might have been the rim of a wagon wheel.

Five minutes later I hit something hard, and I set the E-tool on the edge of the hole and used my fingers to pry up the hub of a wagon wheel with broken spokes the length of my hand radiating from it. I placed it on the slope, and in the next half hour I created next to it a pile of square nails, rotted wood as light as balsa, metal hinges, links of chain, a rusted wisp of a drinking cup, and a saw. The wood handle and the teeth had been almost totally eaten away by groundwater, but there was no mistaking the stubby, square, almost brutal shape; it was a surgeon's saw.

I carried everything that I had found back to the boat. My clothes were streaked with mud; I stunk of sweat and mosquito repellent. My palms rang with popped water blisters. I wanted to wake up Bootsie, call Elrod or perhaps even the sheriff, to tell anybody who would listen about what I had found.

But then I had to confront the foolishness of my thinking. How sane was any man, at least in the view of others, who would dig for Civil War artifacts in a swamp in the middle of the night in order to prove his sanity?

In fact, that kind of behavior was probably not unlike a self-professed extraterrestrial traveler showing you his validated seat reservations on a UFO as evidence of his rationality.

When I got back home I covered my boat with a tarp, took a shower, ate a ham-and-onion sandwich in the kitchen while night birds called to each other under the full moon, and decided that the general and I would not share our secrets with those whose lives and vision were defined by daylight and a rational point of view.

CHAPTER 12

I SLEPT LATE THE next morning, and when I awoke, I found a note from Bootsie on the icebox saying that she had taken Alafair shopping in town. I fixed chicory coffee and hot milk, Grape-Nuts, and strawberries on a tray and carried it out to the redwood table under the mimosa tree in the backyard. The morning was not hot yet, and blue jays flew in and out of the dappled shade and my neighbor's sprinkler drifted in an iridescent haze across my grass.

Then I saw Rosie Gomez's motor-pool government car slow by our mailbox and turn into our drive. Her face was pointed at an upward angle so she could see adequately over the steering wheel. I got up from the table and waved her around back.

She wore a white blouse and white skirt with black pumps, a wide black belt, and a black purse.

"How you feeling?" she asked.

"Pretty good. In fact, great."

"Yeah?"

"Sure."

"You look okay."

"I am okay, Rosie. Here, I'll get you some coffee."

When I came back outside with the pot and another cup and saucer, she was sitting on the redwood bench, looking out over my duck pond and my neighbor's sugarcane fields. Her face looked cool and composed.

"It's beautiful out here," she said.

"I'm sorry Bootsie and Alafair aren't here. I'd like you to meet them."

"Next time. I'm sorry I didn't come see you in the hospital. I'd left for New Orleans early that morning. I just got back."

"What's up?"

"About three weeks ago an old hooker in the Quarter called the Bureau and said she wanted to seriously mess up Julie Balboni for us. Except she was drunk or stoned and the agent who took the call didn't give it a lot of credence."

"What'd she have to offer?"

"Nothing, really. She just kept saying, 'He's hurting these girls. Somebody ought to fix that rotten dago. He's got to stop hurting these girls.' "

"So what happened?"

"Three days ago there was a power failure at the woman's apartment building on Ursulines. With the air conditioner off it didn't take long for the smell to leak through the windows to the courtyard. The M.E. says it was suicide."

I watched her face. "You don't think it was?" I said.

"How many women shoot themselves through the head with a .38 special?"

"Maybe she was drunk and didn't care how she bought it."

"Her refrigerator and cupboards were full of food. The apartment was neat, all her dishes were washed. There was a sack of delicatessen items on the table she hadn't put away yet. Does that suggest the behavior of a despondent person to you?"

"What do they say at N.O.P D.?"

"They don't. They yawn. They've got a murder rate as high as Washington, D.C.'s. You think they want to turn the suicide of a hooker into another open homicide case?"

"What are you going to do?"

"I don't know. I think you've been right about a tie with Balboni. The most common denominator that keeps surfacing in this case is prostitution in and around New Orleans. There isn't a pimp or chippy working in Jefferson or Orleans parishes who don't piece off their action to Julie Balboni."

"That doesn't mean Julie's involved with killing anyone, Rosie."

"Be honest with me. Do I continue to underwhelm you as a representative of Fart, Barf, and Itch?"

"I'm not quite sure I—"

"Yeah, I bet. What do pimps call the girls in the life? 'Cash on the hoof,' right?"

"That's right."

"Do you think anybody kills one of Balboni's hookers and gets away with it without his knowledge and consent?"

"Except there's a bump in the road here. The man who murdered Kelly Drummond probably thought he was shooting at me. The mob doesn't kill cops. Not intentionally, anyway."

"Maybe he's a cowboy, out of control. We've got rogue cops. The wiseguys have rogue shitheads."

I laughed. "You're something else," I said.

"Cut the patronizing attitude, Dave."

"Sorry," I said, still smiling.

Her eyes looked into mine and darkened.

"I'm worried about you. You don't know how to keep your butt down," she said.

"Everything's copacetic. Believe me."

"Sure it is."

"You know something I don't?"

"Yes, human beings and money make a very bad combination," she said.

"I'd appreciate it if you could stop speaking to me in hieroglyphics."

"Few people care about the origins of money, Dave. All they see is a president's picture on a bill, not Julie Balboni's."

"Let's spell it out, okay?"

"A few of the locals have talked to the sheriff about your taking an extended leave. At least that's what I've heard."

"He's not a professional cop, but he's a decent man. He won't give in to them."

"He's an elected official. He's president of the Lions Club. He eats lunch once a week with the Chamber of Commerce."

"He knows I wasn't drinking. The people in my AA group know it, too. So do the personnel at the hospital. Dr. Landry thinks somebody zapped me with LSD. What else can I say?"

Her face became melancholy, and she looked out at the sunlight on the field with a distant, unfocused expression in her eyes.

"What's the trouble?" I asked.

"You don't hear what you're saying. Your reputation, maybe your job, are hanging in the balance now, and you think it's acceptable to tell people that somebody loaded your head with acid."

"I never made strong claims on mental health, anyway."

I tried to smile when I said it. But the skin around my mouth felt stiff and misshaped.

"It isn't funny," she said. She stood up to go, and the bottom of her purse, with the .357 magnum inside, sagged against her hip. "I'm not going to let them do this to you, Dave."

"Wait a minute, Rosie. I don't send other people out on the firing line."

She began walking through the sideyard toward her car, her back as square and straight as a small door.

"Rosie, did you hear me?" I said. "Rosie? Come back here and let's talk. I appreciate what you're trying to—"

She got into her automobile, gave me the thumbs-up sign over the steering wheel, and backed out onto the dirt road by the bayou. She dropped the transmission into low and drove down the long tunnel of oaks without glancing back.

REGARDLESS OF ROSIE'S intentions about my welfare, I still had not resolved the possibility that the racial murder I had witnessed in 1957 and the sack of skin and polished bones Elrod Sykes had discovered in the Atchafalaya Basin were not somehow involved in this case.

However, where do you start in investigating a thirty-five-year-old homicide that was never even reported as such?

Although southern Louisiana, which is largely French Catholic, has a long and depressing record of racial prejudice and injustice, it never compared in intensity and violence to the treatment of black people in the northern portion of the state or in Mississippi, where even the murder of a child, Emmett Till, by two Klansmen in 1955 not only went unpunished but was collectively endorsed after the fact by the town in which it took place. There was no doubt that financial exploitation of black people in general and sexual exploitation of black women in particular were historically commonplace in our area, but lynching was rare, and neither I nor anyone I spoke to remembered a violent incident, other than the one I witnessed, or a singularly bad racial situation from the summer of 1957.

The largest newspapers in Louisiana are the Baton Rouge *Morning Advocate* and the New Orleans *Times-Picayune*. They also have the best libraries, or "morgues," of old newspapers and cross-referenced clippings. However, I started my strange odyssey into the past on the microfilm in the morgue of the *Daily Iberian*.

Actually I had little hope of finding any information that would be helpful. During that era little was published in Louisiana newspapers about people of color, except in the police report or perhaps on a separate page that was designated for news about black marriages.

But in my mind's eye I kept seeing the dead man's stringless boots and the rotted strips of rag about his pelvis instead of a belt. Had he been in custody? Was he being transported by a couple of cops who had decided to execute him? If that was the case, why wasn't he in handcuffs? Maybe they had locked the chain on him to sink his body, I thought. No, that couldn't be right. If the victim was being transported by cops, they would have kept him in cuffs until they had murdered him, *then* they would have removed the cuffs and weighted down the body. Also, why would cops want to sink the body in the Atchafalaya, anyway? They could have claimed that they stopped the car to let him relieve himself, he had taken off for the woods, and they had been forced to shoot him. That particular explanation about a prisoner's death was one that was seldom challenged.

Then I found it, on the area news page dated July 27, 1957. A twenty-eight-year-old Negro man by the name of DeWitt Prejean had been arrested in St. Landry Parish, north of Lafayette, for breaking into the home of a white family and threatening the wife with a butcher knife. There was no mention of motivation or intent. In fact, the story was not about his arrest but about his escape. He had been in custody only eleven hours, had not even been formally charged, when two armed men wearing gloves and Halloween masks entered the parish prison at four in the morning, locked the night jailer in the restroom, and took DeWitt Prejean out of a downstairs holding cell.

The story was no more than four column inches.

I rolled the microfilm through the viewer, looking for a follow-up story. If it was there, I didn't find it, and I went through every issue of the *Daily Iberian* to February 1958.

Every good cop who spends time in a newspaper morgue, particularly in the rural South, knows how certain kinds of news stories were reported or were not reported in the pre-civil-rights era. "The suspect was subdued" usually meant that somebody had had his light switch clicked off with a baton or blackjack. Cases involving incest and child molestation were usually not treated at all. Stories about prisoners dying in custody were little more than obituaries, with a tag line to the effect that an autopsy was pending.

The rape or attempted rape of a white woman by a black man was a more complicated issue, however. The victim's identity was always protected by cops and prosecutors, even to the extent that sometimes the rapist was charged with another crime, one that the judge, if at all possible, would punish as severely as he would rape. But the level of white fear and injury was so collectively intense, the outrage so great, that the local paper would be compelled to report the story in such a way that no one would doubt what really happened, or what the fate of the rapist would be.

Also, the 1957 story in the *Iberian* had mentioned that DeWitt Prejean had been taken from a holding cell eleven hours after his arrest.

People didn't stay in holding cells eleven hours, particularly in a rural jail where a suspect could be processed into lockdown in twenty minutes.

I left Bootsie a note, then drove to Lafayette and continued on north for another twenty miles into St. Landry Parish and the old jailhouse in Opelousas.

THE TOWN HAD once been the home of James Bowie before he became a wealthy cotton merchant and slave trader in New Orleans. But during the 1950s it acquired another kind of notoriety, namely for its political corruption, an infamous bordello named Margaret's that had operated since the War Between the States, and its gambling halls, which were owned or controlled by the sheriff and which were sometimes raided by the state police when a legislative faction in Baton Rouge wanted to force a change in the parish representatives' vote.

I parked my truck at the back of the courthouse square, right next to the brick shell of the old jail, whose roof had caved in on top of the cast-iron tank, perforated with small square holes, that had served as the lockdown area. As I walked under the live oaks toward the courthouse entrance, I looked through the jail's glassless windows at the mounds of soft, crumbled brick on the floor, the litter of moldy paper, and wondered where the two gloved men in Halloween masks had burst inside and what dark design they had planned for the Negro prisoner DeWitt Prejean.

I got nowhere at the courthouse. The man who had been sheriff during the fifties was dead, and no one now in the sheriff's department remembered the case or the escape; in fact, I couldn't even find a record of DeWitt Prejean's arrest.

"It *happened*. I didn't make it up," I said to the sheriff, who was in his late thirties. "I found the account in a 1957 issue of the *Daily Iberian*."

"That might be," he answered. He wore his hair in a military crewcut and his jaws were freshly shaved. He was trying to be polite, but the light of interest kept fading from his eyes. "But they didn't always keep good records back then. Maybe some things happened that people don't want to remember, too, you know what I mean?"

"No."

He twirled a pencil around on his desk blotter.

"Go talk to Mr. Ben. That is, if you want to," he said. "That's Mr. Ben Hebert. He was the jailer here for thirty years."

"Was he the jailer in 1957?"

"Yeah, he probably was."

"You don't sound enthusiastic."

He rubbed the calluses on his hands without looking up at me.

"Put it this way," he said. "His only son ended up in Angola, his wife refused to see him on her deathbed, and there're still some black people who cross the street when they see him coming. Does that help form a picture for you?"

I left the courthouse and went to the local newspaper to look for a follow-up story on the jailbreak. There was none. Twenty minutes later I found the old jailer on the gallery of his weathered wood-frame home across from a Popeye's fast-food restaurant. His yard was almost black with shade, carpeted with a wet mat of rotted leaves, his side-walks inset with tethering rings, cracked and pyra-mided from the oak roots that twisted under them. The straw chair he sat in seemed about to burst from his huge bulk.

I had to introduce myself twice before he re-sponded. Then he simply said, "What you want?"

"May I sit down, sir?"

His lips were purple with age, his skin covered with brown spots the size of dimes. He breathed loudly, as though he had emphysema.

"I ax you what you want," he said.

"I wondered if you remembered a black man by the name of DeWitt Prejean."

He looked at me carefully. His eyes were clear-blue, liquid, elongated, red along the rims.

"A nigger, you say?" he asked.

"That's right."

"Yeah, I remember that sonofabitch. What about him?"

"Is it all right if I sit down, Mr. Hebert?"

"Why should I give a shit?"

I sat down in the swing. He put a cigarette in his mouth and searched in his shirt pocket for a match while his eyes went up and down my body. Gray hair grew out of his nose and on the back of his thick neck.

"Were you on duty the night somebody broke him out of jail?" I said.

"I was the jailer. A jailer don't work nights. You hire a man for that."

"Do you remember what that fellow was charged with?"

"He wasn't charged with nothing. It never got to that."

"I wonder why he was still in a holding cell eleven hours after he was arrested."

"They busted him out of the tank."

"Not according to the newspaper."

"That's why a lot of people use newspaper to wipe their ass with."

"He went into a white woman's home with a butcher knife, did he?"

"Find the nigger and ax him."

"That's what puzzles me. Nobody seems to know what happened to this fellow, and nobody seems to care. Does that make sense to you?"

He puffed on his cigarette. It was wet and splayed when he took it out of his mouth. I waited for him to speak but he didn't.

"Did y'all just close the books on a jailbreak, Mr. Hebert?" I asked.

"I don't remember what they done."

"Was DeWitt Prejean a rapist?"

"He didn't know how to keep his prick in his pants, if that's what you mean."

"You think her husband broke him out?"

"He might have."

I looked into his face and waited.

"That is, if he could," he said. "He was a cripple-man. He got shot up in the war."

"Could I talk to him?"

He tipped his cigarette into an ashtray and looked out toward the bright glare of sunlight on the edge of his yard. Across the street black people were going in and out of the Popeye's restaurant.

"Talk to him all you want. He's in the cemetery, out by the tracks east of town," he said.

"What about the woman?"

"She moved away. Up North somewhere. What's your interest in nigger trouble that's thirty-five years old?"

"I think I saw him killed. Where's the man who was on duty the night of the jailbreak?"

"Got drunk, got hisself run over by a train. Wait a minute, what did you say? You saw what?"

"Sometimes rivers give up their dead, Mr. Hebert. In this instance it took quite a while. Y'all took his boot strings and his belt, didn't you?"

"You do that with every prisoner."

"You do it when they're booked and going into the tank. This guy was never booked. He was left in a holding cell for two armed men to find him. You didn't even leave him a way to take his own life."

He stared at me, his face like a lopsided white cake.

"I think one of the men who killed Prejean tried to kill me," I said. "But he murdered a young woman instead. A film actress. Maybe you read about it."

He stood up and dropped his cigarette over the gallery railing into a dead scrub. He smelled like Vicks VapoRub, nicotine, and an old man's stale sweat. His breath rasped as though his lungs were filled with tiny pinholes.

"You get the fuck off my gallery," he said, and walked heavily on a cane into the darkness of his house, and let the screen slam behind him.

I STOPPED AT Popeye's on Pinhook Road in Lafayette and ate an order of fried chicken and dirty rice, then I drove down Pinhook through the long corridor of oak trees, which had been planted by slaves, down toward the Vermilion River bridge and old highway 90, which led through the little sugar town of Broussard to New Iberia.

Just before the river I passed a Victorian home set back in a grove of pecan trees. Between the road and the wide, columned porch a group of workmen were trenching a water or sewer line of some kind. The freshly piled black dirt ran in an even line past a decorative nineteenth-century flatbed wagon that was hung with baskets of blooming impatiens. The bodies and work clothes of the men looked gray and indistinct in the leafy shade, then a hard gust of wind blew off the river through the trees, the dappled light shifted back and forth across the ground like a bright yellow net, and when I looked back at the workmen I saw them dropping their tools, straightening their backs, fitting on their military caps that were embroidered with gold acorns, picking up their stacked muskets, and forming into ranks for muster.

The general sat in the spring seat of the wagon, his artificial leg propped stiffly on the iron rim of a wheel, a cigar in his mouth, the brim of his campaign hat set at a rakish angle over one eye.

He screwed his body around in the wagon seat and raised his hat high over his head in salute to me.

Gravel exploded like a fusillade of lead shot under my right fender. I cut the wheel back off the shoulder onto the pavement, then looked back at the wide sweep of leafy lawn under the pecan trees. A group of workmen were lowering a long strip of flexible plastic pipe into the ground like a white worm.

Back in New Iberia I parked behind the sheriff's department and started inside the building. Two deputies were on their way out.

"Hey, Dave, you're supposed to be in sick bay," one of them said.

"I'm out."

"Right. You look good."

"Is the skipper in?"

"Yeah. Sure. Hey, you look great. I mean it."

He gave me the thumbs-up sign.

His words were obviously well intended, but I remembered how I was treated after I stepped on a bouncing Betty in Vietnam—with a deference and kindness that not only separated me from those who had a lock on life but constantly reminded me that the cone of flame that had illuminated my bones had also given me a permanent nocturnal membership in a club to which I did not want to belong.

The dispatcher stopped me on my way to the sheriff's office. He weighed over three hundred pounds and had a round red face and a heart condition. His left-hand shirt pocket was bursting with cellophane-wrapped cigars. He had just finished writing out a message on a pink memo slip. He folded it and handed it to me.

"Here's another one," he said. He had lowered his voice, and his eyes were hazy with meaning.

"Another what?"

"Call from this same party that keeps bugging me."

"Which party?"

His eyebrows went up in half-moons.

"The Spanish broad. Or Mexican. Or whatever she is."

I opened the memo and looked at it. It read, *Dave, why don't you return my calls? I'm still waiting at the same place. Have I done wrong in some way?* It was signed "Amber."

"*Amber?*" I said.

"You got eight or nine of them in your mailbox," he said. "Her last name sounded Spanish."

"Who is she?"

"How should I know? You're the guy she's calling."

"All right, thanks, Wally," I said.

I took all my mail out of my box, then shuffled through the pink memo slips one at a time.

The ones from "Amber" were truly an enigma. A few examples:

I've done what you asked. Please call.

Dave, leave a message on my answering machine.

It's me again. Am I supposed to drop dead?

You're starting to piss me off. If you don't want me to bother you again, say so. I'm getting tired of this shit.

I'm sorry, Dave. I was hurt when I said those things. But don't close doors on me.

I walked back to the dispatcher's cage.

"There's no telephone number on any of these," I said.

"She didn't leave one."

"Did you ask her for one?"

"No, I got the impression y'all were buddies or something. Hey, don't look at me like that. What is she, a snitch or something?"

"I don't have any idea."

"She sounds like she's ready to bump uglies, though."

"Why don't you give some thought to your language, Wally?"

"Sorry."

"If she calls again, get her telephone number. If

she doesn't want to give it to you, tell her to stop calling here."

"Whatever you say."

I wadded up the memo slips, dropped them into a tobacco-streaked brass cuspidor, and walked into the sheriff's office.

A manila folder was open on his desk. He was reading from it, with both his elbows propped on the desk blotter and his fingertips resting lightly on his temples. His mouth looked small and down-turned at the corners. On his wall was a framed and autographed picture of President Bush.

"How you doing?" I said.

"Oh, hello, Dave," he said, looking up at me over his glasses. "It's good to see you. How do you feel today?"

"Just fine, Sheriff."

"You didn't need to come in. I wanted you to take a week or so off. Didn't Bootsie tell you?"

"I went up to Opelousas this morning. I think I found out who those bones out in the Atchafalaya might belong to."

"What?"

"A couple of armed men broke a black prisoner named DeWitt Prejean out of the St. Landry Parish jail in 1957. The guy was in for threatening a white woman with a butcher knife. But it sounds like an attempted rape. Or maybe there's a possibility that something was going on with consent. The old jailer said something about Prejean not being able to keep his equipment in his pants. Maybe the woman and Prejean just got caught and

Prejean got busted on a phony charge and set up for a lynching."

The sheriff's eyes blinked steadily and he worked his teeth along his bottom lip.

"I don't understand you," he said.

"Excuse me?"

"I've told you repeatedly that case belongs to St. Mary Parish. Why is it that you seem to shut your ears to whatever I say?"

"Kelly Drummond's death doesn't belong to St. Mary Parish, Sheriff. I think the man who killed her was after me because of that lynched black man."

"You don't know that. You don't know that at all."

"Maybe not. But what's the harm?"

He rubbed his round cleft chin with his thumb. I could hear his whiskers scraping against the skin.

"An investigation puts the right people in jail," he said. "You don't throw a rope around half the people in two or three parishes. And that's what you and that woman are doing."

"That's the problem, is it?"

"You damn right it is. Thirty minutes ago Agent Gomez marched into my office with all her findings." He touched the edge of the manila folder with his finger. "According to Agent Gomez, New Iberia has somehow managed to become the new Evil Empire."

I nodded.

"The New Orleans mob is laundering its drug money through Bal-Gold Productions," he said. "Julie Balboni is running a statewide prostitution operation from Spanish Lake, he's also having prostitutes killed, and maybe he laced your Dr Pepper with LSD when he wasn't cutting illegal deals with the Teamsters. Did you know we had all those problems right here in our town, Dave?"

"Julie's a walking shit storm. Who knows what his potential is?"

"She also called some of our local business people moral weenies and chicken-hearted buttheads."

"She has some eloquent moments."

"Before she left my office she said she wanted me to know that she liked me personally but in all honesty she had to confess that she thought I was full of shit."

"I see," I said, and fixed my eyes on a palm tree outside the window.

The room was quiet. I could hear a jail trusty mowing the grass outside. The sheriff turned his Southwestern class ring on his finger.

"I want you to understand something, Dave," he said. "*I* was the one who wanted that fat sonofabitch Balboni out of town. *You* were the one who thought he was a source of humor. But now we're stuck with him, and that's the way it is."

"Why?"

"Because he has legitimate business interests here. He's committed no crime here. In fact, there's no outstanding warrant on this man anywhere. He's never spent one day in jail."

"I think that's the same shuck his lawyers try to sell."

He exhaled his breath through his nose.

"Go home. You've got the week off," he said.

"I heard my leave might even be longer."

He chewed on a fingernail.

"Who told you that?" he said.

"Is it true or not?"

"You want the truth? The truth is your eyes don't look right. They bother me. There's a strange light in them. Go home, Dave."

"People used to tell me that in bars. It doesn't sound too good to hear it where I work, Sheriff."

"What can I say?" he said, and held his hands up and turned his face into a rhetorical question mark.

When I walked back down the corridor toward the exit, I stuffed my mail back into my mailbox, unopened, and continued on past my own office without even glancing inside.

My clothes were damp with sweat when I got home. I took off my shirt, threw it into the dirty-clothes hamper, put on a fresh T-shirt, and took a glass of iced tea into the backyard where Bootsie was working chemical fertilizer into the roots of the tomato plants by the coulee. She was in the row, on her hands and knees, and the rump of her pink shorts was covered with dirt.

She raised up on her knees and smiled.

"Did you eat yet?" she asked.

"I stopped in Lafayette."

"What were you doing over there?"

"I went to Opelousas to run down a lead on that '57 lynching."

"I thought the sheriff had said—"

"He did. He didn't take well to my pursuing it."

I sat down at the redwood picnic table under the mimosa tree. On the table were a pad of lined notebook paper and three city library books on Texas and southern history.

"What's this?" I said.

"Some books I checked out. I found out some interesting things."

She got up from the row of tomato plants, brushing her hands, and sat down across from me. Her hair was damp on her forehead and flecked with grains of dirt. She picked up the note pad and began thumbing back pages. Then she set it down and looked at me uncertainly.

"You know how dreams work?" she said. "I mean, how dates and people and places shift in and out of a mental picture that you wake up with in the morning? The picture seems to have no origin in your experience, but at the same time you're almost sure you lived it, you know what I mean?"

"Yeah, I guess."

"I looked up some of the things that, well, maybe you believe you saw out there in the mist."

I drank out of my iced tea and looked down the sloping lawn at the duck pond and the bright, humid haze on my neighbor's sugarcane.

"You see, Dave, according to these books, John Bell Hood never had a command in Louisiana," she said. "He fought at Gettysburg and in Tennessee and Georgia."

"He was all through this country, Boots."

"He lived here but he didn't fight here. You see,

what's interesting, Dave, is that part of your information is correct but the rest you created from associations. Look here—"

She turned the notebook around so I could see the notes she had taken. "You're right, he commanded the Texas Brigade," she said. "It was a famous cavalry outfit. But look here at this date. When you asked the general what the date was, he told you it was April 21, 1865, right?"

"Right."

"April 21 is Texas Independence Day, the day the battle of San Jacinto was fought between the Mexican army and the Texans in 1836. Don't you see, your mind mixed up two historical periods. Nothing happened out in that mist, Dave."

"Maybe not," I said. "Wait here a minute, will you?"

I walked to the front of the house, where my boat trailer was still parked, pulled back the tarp, which was dented with pools of rainwater, reached down inside the bow of the boat, and returned to the backyard.

"What is it?"

"Nothing."

"Why'd you go out front?"

"I was going to show you some junk I found out in the marsh."

"What junk?"

"Probably some stuff left by an old lumber crew. It's not important."

Her face was puzzled, then her eyes cleared and she put her hand on top of mine.

"You want to go inside?" she said.

"Where's Alf?"

"Playing over at Poteet's house."

"Sure, let's go inside."

"I'm kind of dirty."

She waited for me to say something but I didn't. I stared at my iced-tea glass.

"What is it, babe?" she said.

"Maybe it's time to start letting go of the department."

"Let go how?"

"Hang it up."

"Is that what you want?"

"Not really."

"Then why not wait awhile? Don't make decisions when you're feeling down, *cher.*"

"I think I've already been cut loose, Boots. They look at me like I have lobotomy stitches across my forehead."

"Maybe you read it wrong, Dave. Maybe they want to help but they just don't know how."

I didn't answer. Later, after we had made love in the warm afternoon gloom of our bedroom, I rose from the softness of her body and sat listlessly on the side of the bed. A moment later I felt her nails tick lightly on my back.

"Ask the sheriff if he wants your resignation," she said.

"It won't solve the problem."

"Why won't it? Let them see how well they'll do without you."

"You don't understand. I'm convinced Kelly

Drummond's killer was after me. It's got something to do with that dead black man. That's the only thing that makes sense."

"Why?"

"We've gotten virtually nowhere in trying to find this serial killer or psychopath or whatever he is. So why would *he* want to come after me? But the lynched black man is another matter. I'm the only one making noise about it. That's the connection. Why doesn't the sheriff see that?"

I felt her nails trace my vertebrae.

"You want to believe that all people are good, Dave," she said. "When your friends don't act the way they should, you feel all this anger and then it turns inward on you."

"I'm going to take down that guy, Boots. Even if I have to do it outside the department."

It was quiet for a long time. Then I felt her weight shift on the mattress and I thought she was getting up to get dressed. Instead, she rose to her knees, pressed her body hard against my back, and pulled my head against her breasts.

"I'll always love you, Dave," she said. "I don't care if you're a cop or a commercial fisherman or if you hunt down this bastard and kill him, I'll always love you for the man you are."

How do you respond to a statement like that?

THE PHONE CALL came at 9:30 that night. I answered it in the kitchen.

"You're a hard man to catch," she said.

"Who's this?"

"The lady who's been trying to catch you, sugar."

"How about giving me a name?"

"It's Amber. Who else, darlin'?" Her voice sounded sleepy, indolent, in slow motion.

"Ah, the lady of the mysterious phone messages."

"You don't remember me? Don't hurt my feelings."

"No, I'm sorry, I don't recall who you are. What can I do for you?"

"It's me that's going to do you a big favor, darlin'. It's because I like you. It's because I remember you from New Orleans a long time ago."

"I appreciate all this, but how about we cut to it?"

"I'm gonna give you the guy you want, sweetheart."

"Which guy are we talking about?"

"He's a nasty ole pimp and he's been doin' some nasty things to his little girls."

Through the back window I could see my neighbor burning field stumps in the dark. The sparks spun upward against the black sky.

"What's his name, Amber?"

"I've got a temporary problem, though. I want to go back to Florida for a little while, you know what I mean?"

"What do you need?"

"Just the air ticket and a little pin money. Three or four hundred dollars. That's not a lot to ask, is it?"

"We might be able to arrange that. Would you like to come into my office?"

"Oh, I don't know if I should do that. All those handsome men make me self-conscious. Do you know where Red's Bar is in Lafayette?"

"On the north side?"

"You got it, sugar. How about in an hour? I'll be at the bar, right by the door."

"You wouldn't try to take me over the hurdles, would you, Amber?"

"Tell me you don't recognize me and break my heart. Ooou, ooou," she said, and hung up.

Who was she? The rhetoric, the flippant cynicism, the pout in the voice, the feigned little-girlishness, all spelled hooker. And the messages she had left at my office were obviously meant to indicate to others that there was a personal relationship between us. It sounded like the beginning of a good scam. But she had also sounded stoned. Or maybe she was simply crazy, I thought. Or maybe she was both stoned and crazy and simply running a hustle. Why not?

There are always lots of possibilities when you deal with that vast army of psychological mutants for whom police and correctional and parole officers are supposed to be lifetime stewards. I once knew a young psychiatrist from Tulane who wanted to do volunteer counseling in the women's prison at St. Gabriel. He lasted a month. The inkblot tests he gave his first subjects not only drove him into clinical depression but eventually caused him to drop his membership in the ACLU and join the National Rifle Association.

I made a call to the home of an AA friend

named Lou Girard who was a detective sergeant in Vice at the Lafayette Police Department. He was one of those who drifted in and out of AA and never quite let go of the old way of life, but he was still a good cop and he would have made lieutenant had he not punched out an obnoxious local politician at Democratic headquarters.

"What's her name again?" he said.

I told him.

"Yeah, there's one broad around calls herself Amber, but she's a Mexican," he said. "You said this one sounds like she's from around here?"

"Yep."

"Look, Dave, these broads got about two dozen names they trade around—Ginger, Consuela, Candy, Pepper, there's even a mulatto dancer named Brown Sugar. Anyway, there're three or four hookers that float in and out of Red's. They're low-rent, though. Their johns are oil-field workers and college boys, mostly."

"I'm going to drive over there in a few minutes. Can you give me some backup?"

"To check out a snitch?"

"Maybe she's not just a snitch."

"What about your own guys?"

"I'm supposed to be on sick leave right now."

"Is something wrong over there, Dave?"

"Things could be better."

"All right, I'll meet you behind the bar. I'll stay in my car, though. For some reason my face tends to empty out a place. Or maybe I need a better mouthwash."

"Thanks for doing this."

"It beats sitting at home listening to my liver rot."

RED'S BAR WAS located in a dilapidated, racially mixed neighborhood of unsurfaced streets, stagnant rain ditches coated with mosquitoes, and vacant lots strewn with lawn trash and automobile parts. Railway tracks intersected people's dirt yards at crazy angles, and Southern Pacific freight cars often lumbered by a few feet from clotheslines and privies and bedroom windows.

I parked my truck in the shadows behind the bar. The shell parking lot was covered with hundreds of flattened beer cans, and the bushes that bordered the neighbor's property stank from all the people who urinated into them nightly. The owner of Red's had built his bar by knocking out the front wall of a frame house and attaching a neon-lit house trailer to it perpendicularly. Originally he had probably intended it to be the place it looked like—a low-bottom bar where you didn't have to make comparisons or where you could get laid and not worry about your own inadequacies.

But the bar became a success in ways that the owner didn't anticipate. He hired black musicians because they were cheap, and through no fault of his own he ended up with one of the best new *zydeco* bands in southwestern Louisiana. And on Saturday nights he french-fried potatoes in chicken fat and served them free on newspaper to enormous crowds that spilled out into the parking lots.

But tonight wasn't Saturday, there was no band; little sound except the jukebox's came from the bar; and the dust from my truck tires floated in a cloud across the bushes that were sour with urinated beer.

Lou Girard got out of his car and walked over to my window. He was a huge man, his head as big as a basketball, who wore cowboy boots with his suits and a chrome-plated .357 magnum in a hand-tooled belt holster. He also carried a braided slapjack in his back pocket and handcuffs that he slipped through the back of his belt.

"It's good to see you, Streak," he said.

"You too, Lou. How's everything at home?"

"My wife finally took off with her beautician. A woman, I'm talking about. I guess I finally figured out why she seemed a little remote in the sack. What are we doing tonight?"

"I'll go inside and look around. I'd like you to be out here to cover my back. It's not a big deal."

He looked at the clapboard back of the bar, at the broken windows and the overflow of the garbage cans, and hooked his thumb in his belt.

"When'd you start needing backup for bullshit like this?"

"Maybe I'm getting over the hill for it."

"Be serious, my friend."

"You know about Kelly Drummond being killed?"

"That actress? Yeah, sure."

"I think maybe the shooter was after me. I don't want to walk into a setup."

"This is a weird fucking place for a setup, Dave. Why would a guy want to bring a cop to a public place in Lafayette for a whack?"

"Why do these guys do anything?"

"You have any idea who the shooter might be?"

"Maybe a guy who was in on a lynching thirty-five years ago."

He nodded and his eyes became veiled.

"That doesn't sound plausible to you?" I asked.

"What's plausible? I try to get off the booze and my liver swells up like a football, my wife turns out to be a dyke, and for kicks I'm standing by a bunch of bushes that stink like somebody with a kidney disease pissed on them."

I pulled my tropical shirt out of my khakis, stuck my .45 inside the back of my belt, and walked through the rear entrance of the building.

The inside smelled like refrigerated bathroom disinfectant and tobacco smoke. The wood floors were warped and covered with cigarette burns that looked like black insects. Some college boys were playing the jukebox and drinking pitcher beer at the bar, and two or three couples were dancing in the adjacent room. A lone biker, with a lion's mane of blond hair and arms wrapped with jailhouse art, hit the cue ball so hard on the pool table that it caromed off the side of the jukebox. But it was a dead night at Red's, and the only female at the bar was an elderly woman who was telling a long tale of grief and discontent to a yawning bartender.

"What'll you have?" he said to me.

"Has Amber been in?"

He shook his head to indicate either that she had not or he had no idea whom I was talking about.

"She hasn't been here?" I said.

"What do you want to drink?"

"A 7Up."

He opened it and poured it into a glass full of ice. But he didn't serve it to me. He walked to the rear of the long bar, which was empty, set it down, and waited for me. When he leaned on the bar, the biceps of his brown arms ridged with muscles like rocks. I walked down the length of the bar and sat on the stool in front of him.

"Which Amber you looking for?" he asked.

"I only know one."

"She don't come in here reg'lar. But I could call somebody who probably knows where she's at. I mean if we're talking about the same broad."

"A Mexican?"

"Yeah, that's right."

"She talks like a Mexican?"

"Yeah. What's a Mexican supposed to talk like?"

"That's not the one I'm looking for, then."

"Enjoy your 7Up," he said, and walked away from me.

I waited a half hour. The biker went out and I heard him kick-start his motorcycle and peel down the dirt street in a roar of diminishing thunder. Then the college boys left and the bar was almost deserted. The bartender brought me another 7Up. I reached for my billfold.

"It's on the house," he said.

"It's my birthday?" I said.

"You're a cop."

"I'm a cop?"

"It don't matter to me. I like having cops in. It keeps the riffraff out."

"Why do you think I'm a cop, partner?"

"Because I just went out back for a breath of air and Lou Girard was taking a leak on our banana trees. Tell Lou thanks a lot for me."

So I gave it up and walked back outside into the humid night, the drift of dust off the dirt road, and the heat lightning that flickered silently over the Gulf.

"I'm afraid it's a dud," I said to Lou through his car window. "I'm sorry to get you out for nothing."

"Forget it. You want to get something to eat?"

"No, I'd better head home."

"This hooker, Amber, her full name is Amber Martinez. I heard she was getting out of the life. But I can pick her up for you."

"No, I think somebody was just jerking me around."

"Let me know if I can do anything, then."

"All right. Thanks again. Goodnight, Lou."

"Goodnight, Dave."

I watched him drive around the side of the building and out onto the dirt street. Raindrops began to ping on the top of my truck.

But maybe I was leaving too early, I thought. If the bartender had made Lou Girard, maybe the woman had, too.

I went back inside. All the bar stools were empty. The bartender was rinsing beer mugs in a tin sink. He looked up at me.

"She still ain't here. I don't know what else to tell you, buddy," he said.

I put a quarter in the jukebox and played an old Clifton Chenier record, *Hey 'Tite Fille,* then I walked out onto the front steps. The rain was slanting across the neon glow of the Dixie beer sign and pattering in the ditches and on the shell parking lot. Across the street were two small frame houses, and next to them was a vacant lot with a vegetable garden and three dark oaks in it and an old white Buick parked in front. Then somebody turned on a light inside the house next to the lot, and I saw the silhouette of somebody in the passenger seat of the Buick. I saw the silhouette as clearly as if it had been snipped out of tin, and then I saw the light glint on a chrome or nickel-plated surface as brightly as a heliograph.

The shots were muffled in the rain—*pop, pop,* like Chinese firecrackers under a tin can—but I saw the sparks fly out from the pistol barrel through the interior darkness of the Buick. The shooter had fired at an odd angle, across the seat and through the back window, but I didn't wait to wonder why he had chosen an awkward position to take a shot at me.

I pulled the .45 from under my shirt, dropped to my knees behind the bumper of a pickup truck, and began firing with both hands extended in front of me. I let off all eight rounds as fast as I could pull the trigger. The roar was deafening, like someone had slapped both his palms violently against my eardrums. The hollow-points exploded the glass out of the Buick's windows, cored holes like a cold chisel through the doors, *whanged* off the steering wheel and dashboard, and blew the horn button like a tiddly-wink onto the hood.

The slide locked open on the empty magazine, and the last spent casing tinkled on the flattened beer cans at my feet. I stood erect, still in the lee of the pickup truck, slipped the empty magazine out of the .45's butt, inserted a fresh one, and eased a round into the chamber. The street was quiet except for the pattering of the rain in the ditches. Then I heard a siren in the distance and the bar door opening behind me.

"What the fuck's going on?" the bartender said, his whole body framed in the light. "You fucking crazy or something?"

"Get back inside," I said.

"We never had trouble here. Where the fuck are you from? People lose licenses because of bullshit like this."

"Do you want to get shot?"

He slammed the door shut, locked it, and pulled the blinds.

I started across the street just as an electrical short in the Buick caused the horn to begin blowing nonstop. I kept the .45 pointed with both hands at the Buick's windows and moved in a circle around the front of the car. No one was visible above the level of the windows nor was there any movement inside. The hollow-points had cut exit holes the size of half-dollars in the passenger door.

A Lafayette city police car came hard around the corner, its emergency lights whirling in the rain. The police car stopped twenty yards from the Buick and both front doors sprang open. I could see the cop in the passenger's seat pulling his pump shotgun out of its vertical mount on the dashboard. I got my badge holder out of my back pocket and held it high over my head.

"Lay your weapon on the ground and step back from the car," the driver said, aiming his revolver at me between the door and the jamb.

I held my right arm at a ninety-degree angle, the barrel of the .45 pointing into the sky.

"I'm Detective Dave Robicheaux, Iberia Parish Sheriff's Department," I said. "I'm complying with your request."

I crouched in the beam of their headlights, laid my .45 by the front tire of the Buick, and raised back up again.

"Step away from it," the driver said.

"You got it," I said, and almost lost my balance in the rain ditch.

"Walk this way. Now," the driver said.

People were standing on their front porches and the rain was coming down harder in big drops that stung my eyes. I kept my badge turned outward toward the two Lafayette city cops.

"I've identified myself. Now how about jacking it down a couple of notches?" I said.

The cop with the shotgun pulled my badge holder out of my hand and looked at it. Then he flexed the tension out of his shoulders, made a snuffing sound in his nose, and handed me back my badge.

"What the hell's going on?" he said.

"Somebody took two shots at me. In that Buick. I think maybe he's still inside."

They looked at each other.

"You're saying the guy's still in there?" the driver said.

"I didn't see him go anywhere."

"Fuck, why didn't you say so?"

I didn't get a chance to answer. Just then, Lou Girard pulled abreast of the police car and got out in the rain.

"Damn, Dave, I thought you'd gone home. What happened?"

"Somebody opened up on me," I said.

"You know this guy?" the cop with the shotgun said.

"Hell, yes, I do. Put your guns away. What's wrong with you guys?" Lou said.

"Lou, the shooter fired at me twice," I said. "I put eight rounds into the Buick. I think he's still in there."

"What?" he said, and ripped his .357 from his belt holster. Then he said to the two uniformed cops, "What have you fucking guys been doin' out here?"

"Hey, Lou, come on. We didn't know who this—"

"Shut up," he said, walked up to the Buick, looked inside, then jerked open the passenger door. The interior light went on.

"What is it?" the cop with the shotgun said.

Lou didn't answer. He replaced his revolver in his holster and reached down with his right hand and felt something on the floor of the automobile.

I walked toward him. "Lou?" I said.

His hands felt around on the seat of the car, then he stepped back and studied the ground and the weeds around his feet as though he were looking for something.

"Lou?"

"She's dead, Dave. It looks like she caught one right through the mouth."

"She?" I said. I felt the blood drain from my heart.

"You popped Amber Martinez," he said.

I started forward and he caught my arm. The headlights of the city police car were blinding in the rain. He pulled me past the open passenger door, and I saw a diminutive woman in an embryonic position, a white thigh through a slit in a cocktail dress, a mat of brown hair that stuck wetly to the floor carpet.

Our faces were turned in the opposite direction from the city cops'. Lou's mouth was an inch from my ear. I could smell cigarettes, bourbon, and mints on his breath.

"Dave, there's no fucking gun," he whispered hoarsely.

"I saw the muzzle flashes. I heard the reports."

"It's not there. I got a throw-down in my glove compartment. Tell me to do it."

I stared woodenly at the two uniformed cops, who stood in hulking silhouette against their head-lights like gargoyles awaiting the breath of life.

CHAPTER 13

THE SHERIFF CALLED me personally at 5 A.M. the next morning so there would be no mistake about my status with the department: I was suspended without pay. Indefinitely.

It was 7 A.M. and already hot and muggy when Rosie Gomez and I pulled up in front of Red's Bar in her automobile. The white Buick was still parked across the street. The bar was locked, the blinds closed, the silver sides of the house-trailer entrance creaking with heat.

We walked back and forth in front of the building, feeling dents in the tin, scanning the improvised rain gutters, even studying the woodwork inside the doorjamb.

"Could the bullets have struck a car or the pickup truck you took cover behind?" she said.

"Maybe. But I didn't hear them."

She put her hands on her hips and let her eyes rove over the front of the bar again. Then she lifted her hair off the back of her neck. There was a sheen of sweat above the collar of her blouse.

"Well, let's take a look at the Buick before they tow it out of here," she said.

"I really appreciate your doing this, Rosie."

"You'd do the same for me, wouldn't you?"

"Who knows?"

"Yeah, you would." She punched me on the arm with her little fist.

We walked across the dirt street to the Buick. On the other side of the vacant lot I could hear freight cars knocking together. I opened all four doors of the Buick and began throwing out the floor mats, tearing up the carpet, raking trash out from under the seats while Rosie hunted in the grass along the rain ditch.

Nothing.

I sat on the edge of the backseat and wiped the sweat out of my eyes. I felt tired all over and my hands were stiff and hard to open and close. In fact, I felt just like I had a hangover. I couldn't keep my thoughts straight, and torn pieces of color kept floating behind my eyes.

"Dave, listen to me," she said. "What you say happened is what happened. Otherwise you would have taken up your friend on his offer."

"Maybe I should have."

"You're not that kind of cop. You never will be, either."

I didn't answer.

"What'd your friend call it?" she asked.

"A 'throw-down.' Sometimes cops call it a 'drop.' It's usually a .22 or some other piece of junk with the registration numbers filed off." I got up off the seat and popped the trunk. Inside, I found a jack handle. I drove the tapered end into the inside panel of the back door on the driver's side.

"What are you doing?" Rosie said.

I ripped the paneling away to expose the sliding frame and mechanism on which the window glass had been mounted.

"Let me show you something," I said and did the same to the inside panel on the driver's door. "See, both windows on this side of the car were rolled partially up. That's why my first rounds blew glass all over the place."

"Yes?"

"Why would the shooter try to fire through a partially opened window?"

"Good question."

I walked around to the passenger side of the Buick. The carpet had a dried brown stain in it, and a roach as long and thick as my thumb was crawling across the stiffened fibers.

"But *this* window is all the way down," I said. "That doesn't make any sense. It had already started to rain. Why would this woman sit by an open window in the rain, particularly in the passenger seat of her own car?"

"It's registered to Amber Martinez?"

"That's right. According to Lou Girard, she was a hooker trying to get out of the life. She also did speedballs and was ninety pounds soaking wet. Does that sound like a hit artist to you?"

"Then why was she in the car? What was she doing here?"

"I don't know."

"What did the homicide investigator have to say last night?"

"He said, 'A .45 sure does leave a hole, don't it?'"

"What else?"

"He said, 'Did you have to come over to Lafayette to fall in the shithouse?'"

"Look at me," she said.

"What?"

"How much sleep did you get last night?"

"Two or three hours."

I threw the tire iron on the front seat of the Buick.

"What do you feel now?" she said.

"What do you mean?" I was surprised at the level of irritation in my voice.

"You *know* what I mean."

My eyes burned and filmed in the haze. I saw the three oaks in the vacant lot go out of focus, as though I were looking at them inside a drop of water.

"Everyone thinks I killed an unarmed woman. What do you think I feel?" I said. I had to swallow when I said it.

"It was a setup, Dave. We both know it."

"If it was, what happened to the gun? Why aren't there any holes in the bar?"

"Because the guy behind this is one smart perp. He got a woman, probably a chippy, to make calls to your dispatcher to give the impression your fly was open, then he got you out of your jurisdiction and involved you in another hooker's death. I think this guy's probably a master at control."

"Somehow that doesn't make me feel a lot better, Rosie."

I looked at the stain on the Buick's carpet. The heat was rising from the ground now and I thought I could smell a salty odor like dead fish. I closed the passenger door.

"I really walked into it, didn't I?" I said.

"Don't worry, we're going to bust the guy behind this and lose the key on him." Her eyes smiled, then she winked at me.

I had brought a garden rake from home. I took it out of Rosie's car and combed a pile of mud and soggy weeds from the bottom of the ditch next to the Buick. Then Rosie said, "Dave, come over here and look at this."

She stood next to the vegetable patch that was located on the edge of the vacant lot. She pointed at the ground.

"Look at the footprints," she said. "Somebody ran through the garden. He broke down the tomato stakes."

The footprints were deep and wide-spaced in the soft earth. The person had been moving away from the street toward the three oak trees in the center of the lot. Some of the tomato and eggplant bushes were crushed down flat in the rows.

A wrecker came around the corner with two men in it and stopped behind the Buick. The driver got out and began hooking up the rear end of the Buick. A middle-aged plainclothes detective in short sleeves with his badge on his belt got out with him. His name was Doobie Patout, a wizened and xenophobic man, with faded blue tattoos on his forearms; some people believed he'd once been the official executioner at Angola.

He didn't speak. He simply stared through the heat at me and Rosie.

"What's happening, Doobie?" I said.

"What y'all doin' out here?" he said.

"Looking for a murder weapon," I said.

"I heard you were suspended."

"Word gets around."

"You're not supposed to be messin' 'round the crime scene."

"I'm really just an observer."

"Who's she?" He raised one finger in Rosie's direction.

"Special Agent Gomez," Rosie said. "This is part of an FBI investigation. Do you have a problem with that?"

"You got to coordinate with the city," he said.

"No, I don't," she said.

The driver of the wrecker began winching the Buick's weight off its back wheels.

"I wouldn't hang around here if I was you," Doobie said to me.

"Why not?" Rosie said.

"Because he don't have legal authority here. Because he made a mistake and nobody here'll probably hold it against him. Why piss people off, Robicheaux?"

"What are you saying, Doobie?"

"So you got to go up against Internal Affairs in your own department. That don't mean you're gonna get indicted in Lafayette Parish. Why put dog shit on a stick and hold it under somebody's nose?"

Behind us, an elderly fat mulatto woman in a print dress came out on her porch and began gesturing at us. Doobie Patout glanced at her, then opened the passenger door to the wrecker and paused before getting in.

"Y'all can rake spinach out of that ditch all you want," he said. "I ran a metal detector over it last night. There's no gun in it. So don't go back to New Iberia and be tellin' people you got a bad shake over here."

"Y'all gonna do somet'ing 'bout my garden, you?" the woman shouted off the porch.

The wrecker drove off with the Buick wobbling on the winch cable behind it. At the corner the wrecker turned and a hubcap popped off the Buick and bounced on its own course down the empty dirt road.

"My, what a nasty little man," Rosie said.

I looked back at the footprints in the vegetable patch. They exited in the Johnson grass and disappeared completely. We walked into the shade of the oaks and looked back at the road, the bits of broken glass that glinted in the dirt, the brilliant glare of sunlight on the white shell parking lot. I felt a weariness that I couldn't find words for.

"Let's talk to some of the neighbors, then pack it in," I said.

We didn't have to go far. The elderly woman whom we had been ignoring labored down her porch steps with a cane and came toward us like a determined crab. Her legs were bowed and popping with varicose veins, her body ringed with fat, her skin gold and hairless, her turquoise eyes alive with indignation.

"Where that other one gone?" she said.

"Which one?" I said.

"That po-liceman you was talkin' to."

"He went back to his office."

"Who gonna pay for my li'l garden?" she asked. "What I gone do wit' them smush tomato? What I gone do wit' them smush eggplant, me?"

"Did you see something last night, auntie?" I said.

"You ax me what I seen? Go look my li'l garden. You got eyes, you?"

"No, I mean did you see the shooting last night?"

"I was in the bat'room, me."

"You didn't see anything?" Rosie said.

The woman jabbed at a ruined eggplant with her cane.

"I seen *that*. That look like a duck egg to you? They don't talk English where y'all come from?"

"Did you see a woman in a white car outside your house?" I said.

"I seen her. They put her in an ambulance. She was dead."

"I see," I said.

"What you gone do 'bout my garden?"

"I'm afraid I can't do anything," I said.

"He can put his big feet all over my plants and I cain't do nothin' 'bout it?"

"Who?" I said.

"The man that run past my bat'room. I just tole you. You hard of hearin' just like you hard of seein'? I got up to go to the bat'room."

My head was swimming.

"Listen, auntie, this is very important," I said. "You're telling me you saw a man run past your window?"

"That's right. I seen him smush my li'l plants, break down my tomato pole, keep on runnin' right out yonder t'rough them tree, right on 'cross the tracks till he was gone. I seen the light on that li'l gun in his hand, too."

Rosie and I looked at each other.

"Can you describe this fellow, auntie?" I said.

"Yeah, he's a white man who don't care where he put his big muddy feet."

"Did the gun look like this one?" Rosie said, opened her purse, and lifted out her .357 magnum.

"No, it mo' li'l than that."

"Why didn't you tell this to the police last night?" I asked.

"I tole them. I be talkin' and they be carryin' on with each other like I ain't here, like I some old woman just in they way. It ain't changed, no."

"What hasn't?" I said.

"When the last time white people 'round here ax us what we t'ink about anyt'ing? Ain't nobody ax me if I want that juke 'cross from my li'l house, no. Ain't nobody worried 'bout my li'l garden. Black folk still black folk, livin' out here without no pave, with dust blowin' off the road t'rough my screens. Don't be pretendin' like it ain't so."

"You've helped us a great deal, auntie," I said.

She leaned over on her cane, wrapped a tangle of destroyed tomato vines around her hand, and flung them out into the grass. Then she began walking back toward her porch, the folds of skin in her neck and shoulders creasing like soft tallow.

"Would you mind if we came to see you again?" I asked.

"Waste mo' of my day, play like you care what happen down here on the dirt road? Why you ax me? You comin' when you want, anyway, ain't you?"

Her buttocks swelled like an elephant's against her dress when she worked her way up the steps. On the way out of town we stopped at a nursery and I paid cash to have a dozen tomato plants delivered to her address.

"Not smart giving anything to a potential witness, Slick," Rosie said when we were back on the highway.

"You're used to operating in the normal world, Rosie. Did you hear what Doobie Patout said? Lafayette Homicide has given that girl's death the priority of a hangnail. Welcome to the New South."

WHEN I GOT back home I turned on the window fan in the bedroom, undressed, and lay down on top of the sheets with my arm across my eyes. The curtains, which were printed with small pink flowers, lifted and fell in the warm breeze, and I could hear Tripod running back and forth on his chain in the dead leaves under the pecan trees.

In my sleep I thought I could feel the .45 jumping in my palm, the slide slamming down on a fresh cartridge, the recoil climbing up my forearm like the reverberation from a jackhammer. Then, as though in slow motion, I saw a woman's face bursting apart; a small black hole appeared right below the mouth, then the fragile bone structure caved in upon itself, like a rubber mask collapsing, and the back of her head suddenly erupted in a bloody mist.

I wanted to wake from my dream, force myself even inside my sleep to realize that it was indeed only a dream, but instead the images changed and I heard the ragged popping of small-arms and saw the border of a hardwood forest in autumn, the leaves painted with fire, and a contingent of Confederate infantry retreating into it.

No, I didn't simply see them; I was in their midst, under fire with them, my throat burning with the same thirst, my hands trembling as I tried to reload my weapon, my skin twitching as though someone were about to peel it away in strips. I heard a toppling round *throp* close to my ear and whine away deep in the woods, saw the long scarlet streaks in the leaves where the wounded had been dragged behind tree trunks, and was secretly glad that someone else, not me, had crumpled to his knees, had cried out for his mother, had tried futilely to press his blue nest of entrails back inside his stomach.

The enemy advanced across an open field out of their own cannon smoke, their bayonets fixed, their artillery arching over their heads and exploding behind us in columns of dirt and flame. The light was as soft and golden as the season, but the air inside the woods was stifling, filled with dust and particles of leaves, the smell of cordite and bandages black with gangrene, the raw odor of blood.

Then I knew, even in sleep, what the dream meant. I could see the faces of the enemy now, hear the rattle of their equipment, their officers yelling, "Form up, boys, form up!" They were young, frightened, unknowledgeable of politics or economics, trembling as much as I was, their mouths too dry now even to pray, their sweaty palms locked on the stocks of their rifles. But I didn't care about their innocence, their beardless faces, the crimson flowers that burst from their young breasts. I just wanted to live. I wanted every round we fired to find a target, to buckle bone, to shatter lungs and explode the heart; I wanted their ranks to dissolve into a cacophony of sorrow.

My head jerked erect on the pillow. The room was hot and close and motes of dust spun in the columns of weak light that shone through the curtains. My breath rasped in my throat, and my chest and stomach were slick with perspiration.

The general sat in a straight-backed chair by the foot of my bed, with his campaign hat resting on one knee. His beard was trimmed and he wore a brushed gray coat with a high gold collar. He was gazing out the window at the shifting patterns of light made by the pecan and oak trees.

"*You!*" I said.

"*I hope you don't mind my being here.*"

"*No, I—you simply surprised me.*"

"*You shouldn't have remorse about the kinds of feelings you just experienced, Mr. Robicheaux. A desire to live doesn't mean you lack humanity.*"

"*I opened up on the Buick too soon. I let off the whole magazine without seeing what I was shooting at.*"

"*You thought your life was at risk, suh. What were you supposed to do?*"

"*They say I killed an unarmed woman, General.*"

"*Yes, I think that would probably trouble me, too.*" He turned his hat in a circle on his knee. "*I have the impression that you were very fond of your father, the trapper.*"

"*Excuse me?*"

"*Didn't he once tell you that if everyone agrees on something, it's probably wrong?*"

"*Those were his words.*"

"*Then why not give them some thought?*"

"*General, somebody has done a serious mind fuck on me. I can't trust what I see or hear anymore.*"

"*I'm sorry. Someone has done what?*"

"*It's the same kind of feeling I had once in Golden Gloves. A guy hooked me after the bell, hard, right behind the ear. For two or three days I felt like something was torn loose from the bone, like my brain was floating in a jar."*

"Be brave."

"I see that woman, the back of her head. . . . Her hair was glued to the carpet with her own blood."

"Think about what you just said."

"What?"

"You're a good police officer, an intelligent man. What does your eye tell you?"

"I need some help, General."

"You belong to the quick, you wake in the morning to the smell of flowers, a woman responds to the touch of your fingers, and you ask help of the dead, suh?"

He lifted himself to his feet with his crutch.

"I didn't mean to offend you," I said.

"In your dream you saw us retreating into a woods and you saw the long blue line advancing out of the smoke in the field; didn't you?"

"Yes."

"Were you afraid?"

"Yes."

"Because you thought time had run out for you, didn't you?"

"Yes, I knew it had."

"We should have died there but we held them. Our thirst was terrible. We drank rainwater from the hoof prints of livestock. Then that night we tied sticks in the mouths of our wounded so they wouldn't cry out while we slipped out of the woods and joined the rest of our boys."

The wind began blowing hard in the trees outside the window. Last fall's leaves swirled off the ground and blew against the house.

"I sense resentment in you," he said.

"I already paid my dues. I don't want—"

"You don't want what?" He pared a piece of dirt from under his fingernail.

"To be the only man under a flag."

"Ah, we never quit paying dues, my friend. I must be going now. The wind's out of the south. There'll be thunder by this afternoon. I always have a hard time distinguishing it from Yankee cannon."

He made a clucking sound with his tongue, fitted his campaign hat on his head, took up his crutch, and walked through the blades of the window fan into a spinning vortex of gold and scarlet leaves.

WHEN I FINALLY woke from my sleep in midafternoon, like rising from the warm stickiness of an opium dream, I saw Alafair watching me through the partly opened bedroom door. Her lips were parted silently, her round, tan face wan with incomprehension. The sheets were moist and tangled around my legs. I tried to smile.

"You okay, Dave?"

"Yeah, I'm fine."

"You were having a dream. You were making all kinds of sounds."

"It's probably not too good to sleep in the daytime, little guy."

"You got malaria again?"

"No, it doesn't bother me much anymore."

She walked into the room and placed one hand on the bedstead. She looked at the floor.

"What's the matter, Alf?" I said.

"I went to the grocery down at the four-corners with Bootsie. A man had the newspaper open on the counter and was reading something out loud. A lady saw us and touched the man on the arm. Then both of them just stared at us. Bootsie gave them a real mean look."

"What was the man saying?"

"A lady got shot." Her palm was cupped tightly on the knob of the bedstead. She stared at the floor, and there were small white discolorations in her cheeks like slivers of ice. "He said you shot the lady. You shot the lady, Dave."

I sat up on the edge of the bed.

"I had some trouble last night, Alafair. Somebody fired a pistol at me and I shot back. I'm not sure who fired at me or what this lady was doing there. But the situation is a lot more complex than maybe some people think. The truth can be real hard to discover sometimes, little guy."

"Did you do what they say, Dave?" I could see the shine of fear in her brown eyes.

"I don't know. But I never shot at anybody who didn't try to hurt me first. You have to believe me on that, Alf. I'm not sure what happened last night, but sooner or later I probably will. In the meantime, guys like you and me and Bootsie have to be standup and believe in each other."

I brushed her bangs away from her eyes. She looked for a long time at the whirling blades of the window fan and the shadows they made on the bed.

"They don't have any right," she said.

"Who?"

"Those people. They don't have the right to talk about you like that."

"They have the right to read what's in the newspaper, don't they?"

"The lady at the counter was saying something just before we walked in. I heard her through the screen. She said, 'If he's gone back to drinking, it don't surprise me he done that, no.' That's when the man started reading out loud from the newspaper."

I picked her up by the waist and sat her on the bed. Her muscular body felt as compact as a small log.

"Look, little guy," I said, "drinking isn't part of my life anymore. I gave it to my Higher Power."

I stroked her hair and saw a smile begin to grow at the edge of her mouth and eyes.

"Dave?"

"What?"

"What's it mean when you say somebody's got to be standup?"

"No matter what the other side does to you, you grin and walk through the cannon smoke. It drives them crazy."

She was grinning broadly now, her wide-set teeth white in the shadows of the room.

"Where's Bootsie?" I asked.

"Fixing supper."

"What are we having?"

"*Sac-a-lait* and dirty rice."

"Did you know they run freight trains on that in Louisiana?"

She started bouncing on the edge of the bed, then my words sank in. "What? Freight . . . what?" she said.

"Let me get dressed, little guy, then we'll check out the food situation."

My explanation to Alafair was the best I could offer, but the truth was I needed to get to an AA meeting. Since the night I had seen the general and his soldiers in the mist, I had talked once over the phone to my AA sponsor but had not attended a meeting, which was the place I needed to be most. What might be considered irrational, abnormal, aberrant, ludicrous, illogical, bizarre, schizoid, or schizophrenic to earth people (which is what AAs call nonalcoholics) is usually considered fairly normal by AA members.

The popular notion exists that Catholic priests become privy to the darkest corners of man's soul in the confessional. The truth is otherwise. Any candid Catholic minister will tell you that most people's confessions cause eye-crossing boredom in the confessor, and the average weekly penitent usually owns up to a level of moral failure on par with unpaid parking violations and overdue library books.

But at AA meetings, I've heard it all at one time

or another: extortion, theft, forgery, armed robbery, child molestation, sodomy with animals, arson, prostitution, vehicular homicide, and the murder of prisoners and civilians in Vietnam.

I went to an afternoon meeting on the second floor of an Episcopalian church. I knew almost everyone there: a few housewives, a black man who ran a tree nursery, a Catholic nun, an ex-con bartender named Tee Neg who was also my sponsor, a woman who used to hook in the Column Hotel Bar in Lafayette, a psychologist, a bakery owner, a freight conductor on the Southern Pacific, and a man who was once a famous aerialist with Ringling Brothers.

I told them the whole story about my psychohistorical encounters and left nothing out. I told them about the electricity that snapped and flickered like serpents' tongues in the mist, my conversations with the general, even the unwashed odor that rose from his clothes, the wounds in his men that maggots had eaten as slick as spoons.

As is usual with one's dramatic or surreal revelations at an AA meeting, the response was somewhat humbling. They listened attentively, their eyes sympathetic and good-natured, but a number of the people there at one time or another had ripped out their own wiring, thought they had gone to hell without dying, tried to kill themselves, or been one step away from frontal lobotomies.

When I had finished, the leader of the meeting, a pipeline welder, said, "Damn, Dave, that's the best endorsement of Dr Pepper I ever heard. You ought to call up them sonsofbitches and get that one on TV."

Then everyone laughed and the world didn't seem so bad after all.

WHEN I LEFT the meeting I bought a spearmint snowball in the city park on Bayou Teche and used the outdoor pay phone by the recreation building. Through the moss-hung oak trees I could see kids diving into the public pool, their tan bodies glistening with water in the hot sunlight.

It took a couple of minutes to get the Lafayette coroner on the line. He was a hard-nosed choleric pathologist named Sollie Rothberg, whom cops quickly learned to treat diplomatically.

"I wondered what you had on the Amber Martinez shooting," I said.

I could hear the long-distance wires humming in the receiver.

"Robicheaux?" he said.

"That's right."

"Why are you calling me?"

"I just told you."

"It's my understanding you're suspended."

"So what? Your medical findings are a matter of public record, aren't they?"

"When they become public they are. Right now they aren't public."

"Come on, Sollie. Somebody's trying to deep-fry my *cojones* in a skillet."

In my mind's eye I could see him idly throwing paper clips at his wastebasket.

"What's the big mystery I can clear up for you?" he said.

"What caliber weapon killed her?"

"From the size of the wound and the impact of the round, I'd say a .45."

"What do you mean 'size'?"

"Just what I said."

"What about the round?"

"It passed through her. There wasn't much to recover. It was a clean exit wound."

"It was a copper-jacketed round?"

"That's my opinion. In fact, I know it was. The exit hole wasn't much larger in diameter than the entry."

I closed and opened my eyes. I could feel my heart beating in my chest.

"You there?" he said.

"Yes."

"What's wrong?"

"Nothing, Sollie. I use hollow-points."

I could hear birds singing in the trees, and the surface of the swimming pool seemed to be dancing with turquoise light.

"Anything else?" he asked.

"Yeah, time of death."

"You're crowding me."

"Sollie, I keep seeing the back of her head. Her hair had stuck to the carpet. The blood had already dried, hadn't it?"

"I can't tell you about that because I wasn't there."

"Come on, you know what I'm asking you."

"Did she die earlier, you want to know?"

"Look, partner, you're my lifeline. Don't be jerking me around."

"How about I go you one better? Did she die in that car, you want to ask me?"

I had learned long ago not to interfere with or challenge Sollie's moods, intentions, or syntax.

"It's gravity," he said. "The earth's always pulling on us, trying to suck us into the ground."

"What?"

"It's what the shooter didn't think about," he said. "Blood's just like anything else. It goes straight down. You stop the heart, in this case the brain and then the heart, and the blood takes the shortest course to the ground. You with me?"

"Not quite."

"The blood settles out in the lowest areas of where the body is lying. The pictures show the woman curled up on her side on the floor of the Buick. Her head was higher than her knees. But the autopsy indicates that she was lying full length on her back at the time of death. She also had high levels of alcohol and cocaine in her blood. I suspect she may have been passed out when she died."

"She was shot somewhere else and moved?"

"Unless the dead are walking around on their own these days."

"You've really been a friend, Sollie."

"Do you ever carry anything but a .45? A nine-millimeter or a .357 sometimes?"

"No, I've always carried the same Colt .45 auto I brought back from Vietnam."

"How many people know that?"

"Not many. Mostly cops, I guess."

"That thought would trouble me. So long, Robicheaux."

But the moment was not one for brooding. I walked back to the hot-dog stand and bought snowballs for a half-dozen kids. When a baseball bounced my way from the diamond, I scooped it up in my palms, rubbed the roughness of the horsehide, fitted my fingers on the stitches, and whipped a sidearm slider into the catcher's glove like I was nineteen years old and could blow a hole through the backstop.

THAT NIGHT I called Lou Girard at his home in Lafayette, told him about my conversations with the coroner and the mulatto woman across from the bar, and asked him if anyone had vacuumed the inside of the Buick.

"Dave, I'm afraid this case isn't the first thing on everybody's mind around here," he said.

"Why's that?"

"The detective assigned to it thinks you're a pain in the ass and you should have stayed in your own territory."

"When's the last time anyone saw Amber Martinez?"

"Three or four days ago. She was a bender drinker and user. She was supposed to be getting out of the life, but I think she'd work up a real bad Jones and find a candy man to pick up her tab until she ended up in a tank or a detox center somewhere."

"Who was her pimp?"

"Her husband. But he's been in jail the last three weeks on a check-writing charge. Whoever killed her probably got her out of a bar someplace."

"Yeah, but he knew her before. He used another woman to keep leaving Amber's name on messages at my office."

"If I can get the Buick vacuumed, what are we looking for?"

"I know I saw gun flashes inside the car. But there weren't any holes in the front of the bar. See what you come up with."

"Like what?"

"I don't know."

"Why don't you forget the forensic bullshit and concentrate on what your nose tells you?"

"What's that?"

"This isn't the work of some lone fuckhead running around. It has the smell of the greaseballs all over it. One smart greaseball in particular."

"You think this is Julie's style?"

"I worked two years on a task force that tried to get an indictment on the Bone. When he gets rid of a personal enemy, he puts a meat hook up the guy's rectum. If he wants a cop or a judge or a labor official out of the way, he does it long distance, with a whole collection of lowlifes between him and the target."

"That sounds like our man, all right."

"Can I give you some advice?"

"Go ahead."

"If Balboni is behind this, don't waste your time

trying to make a case against him. It doesn't work. The guy's been oiling jurors and judges and scaring the shit out of witnesses for twenty years. You wait for the right moment, the right situation, and you smoke him."

"I'll see you, Lou. Thanks for your help."

"All right, excuse me. Who wants to talk about popping a cap on a guy like Balboni? Amber Martinez probably did herself. Take it easy, Dave."

At six the next morning I took a cup of coffee and the newspaper out on the gallery and sat down on the steps. The air was cool and blue with shadow under the trees and the air smelled of blooming four o'clocks and the pecan husks that had moldered into the damp earth.

While I read the paper I could hear boats leaving my dock and fishermen's voices out on the water. Then I heard someone walking up the incline through the leaves, and I lowered the newspaper and saw Mikey Goldman striding toward me like a man in pursuit of an argument.

He wore shined black loafers with tassels on them, a pink polo shirt that hung out of his gray slacks, and a thick gold watch that gleamed like soft butter on his wrist. His mouth was a tight seam, down-turned at the corners, his jaw hooked forward, his strange, pale, bulging eyes flicking back and forth across the front of my house.

"I want a word with you," he said.

"How are you today, Mr. Goldman," I said.

"It's 6 A.M., I'm at your house instead of at work; I got four hours' sleep last night. Guess."

"Do I have something to do with your problem?"

"Yeah, you do. You keep showing up in the middle of my problem. Why is that, Mr. Robicheaux?"

"I don't have any idea."

"I do. It's because Elrod had got some kind of hard-on for you and it's about to fuck my picture in a major way."

"I'd appreciate it if you didn't use that kind of language around my home."

"You got a problem with language? That's the kind of stuff that's on your mind? What's wrong with you people down here? The mosquitoes pass around clap of the brain or something?"

"What is it you want, sir?"

"He asks me what *I* want?" he said, looking around in the shadows as though there were other listeners there. "Elrod doesn't like to see you get taken over the hurdles. Frankly I don't either. Maybe for other reasons. Namely nobody carries my load, nobody takes heat for me, you understand what I'm saying?"

"No."

He cleared something from a nostril with his thumb and forefinger.

"What is it with you, you put your head in a bucket of wet cement every morning?" he asked.

"Can I be frank, too, Mr. Goldman?"

"Be my guest."

"A conversation with you is a head-numbing experience. I don't think any ordinary person is ready for it."

"Let me try to put it in simple words that you can understand," he said. "You may not know it, but I try to be a fair man. That means I don't like somebody else getting a board kicked up his ass on my account. I'm talking about you. Your own people are dumping on you because they think you're going to chase some big money out of town. I leave places or I stay in places because I want to. Somebody gets in my face, I deal with it, personal. You ask anybody in the industry. I don't rat-fuck people behind their back."

I set down my coffee cup, folded the newspaper on the step, and walked out into the trees toward his parked automobile. I waited for him to follow me.

"Is there anything else you wanted to tell me?" I said.

"No, of course not. I'm just out here to give you my personal profile. Listen to me, I'm going to finish this picture, then I'm never coming back to this state. In fact, I'm not even going to fly over it. But in the meantime no more of my people are going to the hospital."

"What?"

"Good, the flashbulb went off."

"What happened?" I said.

"Last night we'd wrapped it up and everybody had headed home. Except Elrod and this kid who does some stunt work got loaded and Elrod decides he's going to 'front Julie Balboni. He picks up a Coke bottle and starts banging on Julie's trailer with it. Julie opens the door in his Jockey undershorts, and there's a twenty-year-old local broad trying to put on her clothes behind him. So Elrod calls him a coward and a dago bucket of shit and tells him he can fix him up in L.A. with Charlie Manson's chippies, like they got hair under their arms and none on their heads and they're more Julie's speed. Then El tells him that Julie had better not cause his buddy Robicheaux any more grief or El's going to punch his ticket for him, and if he finds out Julie murdered Kelly he's going to do it anyway, big time, with a shotgun right up Balboni's cheeks.

"I don't know what Balboni was doing with the broad, but he had some handcuffs. He walked outside, clamped one on El's wrist, the other on a light pole, and said, 'You're a lucky man, Elrod. You're a valuable piece of fruit. But your friend there, he don't have any luck at all.' Then he stomped the shit out of the stunt kid. 'Stomped' is the word, Mr. Robicheaux, I mean with his feet. He busted that kid's nose, stove in his ribs, and ripped his ear loose from his head."

"Why didn't you stop it?"

"I wasn't there. I got all this from the kid at the hospital. That's why I didn't get any sleep last night."

"Is the kid pressing charges?"

"Get real. He was on a flight back to Los Angeles this morning with enough dope in him to tranquilize a rhinoceros."

"What do you want with me?"

"I want you to take care of Elrod. I don't want him hurt."

"Tell me the truth. Do you have any concerns at all except making your pictures?"

"Yeah, human beings. If you don't accept that, I say fuck you."

His tense, protruding eyes reminded me of hard-boiled eggs. I looked away from him, felt my palm close and unclose against my trousers. The sunlight on the bayou was like a yellow flare burning under the water.

"I'm not in the baby-sitting business, Mr. Goldman," I said. "My advice is that you tell all this to the sheriff's department. Right now I'm still suspended. I'm going back and finish my coffee now. We'll see you around."

"It's Dogpatch. I'm in a cartoon. I talk, nobody hears me." He tapped himself on the cheek. "Maybe I'm dead and this is hell."

"What else do you want to say?" I heard the heat rising in my own voice.

"You accuse me of not having any humanity. Then I tell you Elrod's striking matches on Balboni's balls on your account and you blow me off. You want Balboni to put his foot through El's face?"

"He's your business partner. You brought him here. You didn't worry about the origins of his money till you—"

"That's all true. The question is what do we do now?"

"We?"

"Right. I'm getting through. Everybody around here doesn't have meatloaf for brains after all."

"There's no *we* in this. I'll talk to Elrod, I'll take him to AA meetings, but he's not my charge."

"Good. Tell him that. I'm on my way to work. Dump him in a cab."

"What?"

"He's down there in your bait shop. Drunk. I think you have a serious hearing problem. Get some help."

He stuck a peppermint candy cane in the corner of his mouth and walked back down the slope to his automobile, his shoulders rolling under his polo shirt, his jaws cracking the candy between his teeth, his profile turned into the freshening breeze like a gladiator's.

CHAPTER 14

"YOU DID WHAT?" Bootsie said. She stared at me open-mouthed across the kitchen table.

I told her again.

"You *threw* him in the bayou? I don't believe it," she said.

"He's used to it. Don't worry about him."

"Mr. Sykes started fighting with Dave on the dock, Bootsie," Alafair said. "He was drunk and making a lot of noise in front of the customers. He wouldn't come up to the house like Dave told him."

Way to go, Alf, I thought.

"Where is he now?" Bootsie said, wiping her mouth with her napkin and starting to rise from her chair.

"Throwing up on the rose bushes, the last I saw him."

"Dave, that's disgusting," she said, and sat back down.

"Tell Elrod."

"Batist said he drank five beers without paying for them," Alafair said.

"What are you going to do about him?" Bootsie said. Then she turned her head and looked out the back screen. "Dave, he just went across the backyard."

"I think El has pulled his suction cups loose for a while, Boots."

"Suction cups?" Alafair said, her cereal spoon poised in front of her mouth.

"He's crawling around on his hands and knees. Do something," Bootsie said.

"That brings up a question I was going to ask you."

I saw the recognition grow in her eyes.

"The guy went up against Julie Balboni because of me," I said. "Or at least partly because of me."

"You want him to stay *here*? Dave, this is our home," she said.

"The guy's in bad shape."

"It's still our home. We can't open it up to every person who has a problem."

"The guy needs an AA friend or he's not going to make it. Look at him. He's pitiful. Should I take him down to the jail?"

Bootsie rested her fingers on her temples and stared at the sugar container.

"I'll make him a deal," I said. "The first time he takes a drink, he gets eighty-sixed back to Spanish Lake. He pays his share of the food, he doesn't tie up the telephone, he doesn't come in late."

"Why's he squirting the hose in his mouth?" Alafair said.

"All right, we can try it for a couple of days,"

Bootsie said. "But, Dave, I don't want this man talking anymore about his visions or whatever it is he thinks he sees out on the lake."

"You think that's where I got it from, huh?" I smiled.

"In a word, yes."

"He's a pretty good guy when he's not wired. He just sees the world a little differently than some."

"Oh, wonderful."

Alafair got up from her chair and peered at an angle through the screen into the backyard.

"Oooops," she said, and put her hand over her mouth.

"What is it?" Bootsie said.

"Mr. Sykes just did the rainbow yawn."

"What?" I said.

"He vomited on the picnic table," Alafair said.

I waited until Bootsie and Alafair had driven off to the grocery store in town, then I went out into the backyard. Elrod's slacks and shirt were pasted to his skin with water from the bayou and grimed with mud and grass stains. He had washed down the top of the picnic table with the garden hose, and he now sat slack-jawed on the bench with his knees splayed, his shoulders stooped, his hands hanging between his thighs. His unshaved face had the gray color of spoiled pork.

I handed him a cup of coffee.

"Thanks," he said.

I winced at his breath.

"If you stay on at our house, do you think you can keep the cork in the jug?" I said.

"I can't promise it. No, sir, I surely can't promise it."

"Can you try?"

He lifted his eyes up to mine. The iris of his right eye had a clot of blood in it as big as my fingernail.

"Nothing I ever tried did any good," he said. "Antabuse, psychiatrists, a dry-out at the navy hospital, two weeks hoeing vegetables on a county P-farm. Sooner or later I always went back to it, Mr. Robicheaux."

"Well, here's the house rules, partner," I said, and I went through them one at a time with him. He kept rubbing his whiskers with the flat of his hand and spitting between his knees.

"I guess I look downright pathetic to you, don't I?" he said.

"Forget what other people think. Don't drink, don't think, and go to meetings. If you do that, and you do it for yourself, you'll get out of all this bullshit."

"I got that kid beat up real bad. It was awful. Balboni kept jumping up in the air, spinning around, and cracking the sole of his foot across the kid's head. You could hear the skin split against the bone."

He placed his palms over his ears, then removed them.

"You stay away from Balboni," I said. "He's not your problem. Let the law deal with him."

"Are you kidding? The guy does whatever he wants. He's even getting his porno dirt bag into the film."

"What porno dirt bag?"

"He brought up some guy of his from New Orleans, some character who thinks he's the new Johnny Wadd. He's worked the guy into a half-dozen scenes in the picture. Look, Mr. Robicheaux, I'm getting the shakes. How about cutting me a little slack? Two raw eggs in a beer with a shot on the side. That's all I'll need. Then I won't touch it."

"I'm afraid not, partner."

"Oh man, I'm really sick. I've never been this sick. I'm going into the D.T.s."

I put my hand on his shoulder. His muscles were as tight and hard as cable wire and quivering with anxiety. Then he covered his eyes and began weeping, his wet hair matted with dirt, his body trembling like that of a man whose soul was being consumed by its own special flame.

I DROVE OUT to Spanish Lake to find Julie Balboni. No one was in the security building by the dirt road that led into the movie location, and I dropped the chain into the dirt and parked in the shade, close by the lake, next to a catering truck. The sky was darkening with rain clouds, and the wind off the water blew leaves across the ground under the oak trees. I walked through a group of actors dressed as Confederate infantry. They were smoking cigarettes and lounging around a freshly dug rifle pit and ramparts made out of huge stick-woven baskets filled with dirt. Close by, a wheeled canon faced out at the empty lake. I could smell the drowsy, warm odor of reefer on the breeze.

"Could y'all tell me where to find Julie Balboni?" I said.

None of them answered. Their faces had turned dour. I asked again.

"We're just the hired help," a man with sergeant's stripes said.

"If you see him, would you tell him Dave Robicheaux is looking for him?"

"You'd better tell him yourself," another actor said.

"Do you know where Mr. Goldman is?"

"He went into town with some lawyers. He'll be back in a few minutes," the sergeant said.

"Thank you," I said.

I walked back to my truck and had just opened the door when I heard someone's feet in the leaves behind me.

"I need a moment of your time, please," Twinky Lemoyne said. He had been walking fast, holding his ballpoint pens in his shirt pocket with one hand; a strand of hair hung over his rimless glasses and his face was flushed.

"What can I do for you?"

"I'd like to know what your investigation has found out."

"You would?"

"Yes. What have you learned about these murders?"

I shouldn't have been surprised at the presumption and intrusiveness of his question. Successful businessmen in any small town usually think of policemen as extensions of their mercantile fraternity, dedicated in some ill-defined way to the financial good of the community. But previously he had stonewalled me, had even been self-righteous, and it was hard to accept him now as an innocuous Rotarian.

"Maybe you should call the sheriff's office or the FBI, Mr. Lemoyne. I'm suspended from the department right now."

"Is this man Balboni connected with the deaths of these women?"

"Did someone tell you he was?"

"I'm asking you an honest question, sir."

"And I'm asking you one, Mr. Lemoyne, and I advise you to take it quite seriously. Do you have some personal knowledge about Balboni's involvement with a murder?"

"No, I don't."

"You don't?"

"No, of course not. How could I?"

"Then why your sense of urgency, sir?"

"You wouldn't keep coming out here unless you suspected him. Isn't that right?"

"What difference should it make to you?"

The skin of his face was grained and red, and his eyelashes fluttered with his frustration.

"Mr. Robicheaux, I think . . . I feel . . ."

"What?"

"I believe you've been treated unfairly."

"Oh?"

"I believe I've contributed to it, too. I've complained to others about both you and the FBI woman."

"I think there's another problem here, Mr. Lemoyne. Maybe it has to do with the price of dealing with a man like Julie Balboni."

"I've tried to be honest with you."

"That's fine. Get away from Balboni. Divest yourself of your stock or whatever it takes."

"Then maybe he *was* involved with those dead girls?" His eyes were bright and riveted on mine.

"You tell me, Mr. Lemoyne. Would you like Julie for your next-door neighbor? Would you like your daughter around him? Would you, sir?"

"I find your remark very offensive."

"*Offensive* is when a stuntman gets his nose and ribs broken and an ear torn loose from his head as an object lesson."

I could see the insult and injury in his eyes. His lips parted and then closed.

"Why are you out here, Mr. Lemoyne?"

"To see Mr. Goldman. To find out what I can."

"I think your concern is late in coming."

"I have nothing else to say to you. Good day to you, sir."

He walked to his automobile and got in. As I watched him turn onto the dirt road and head back toward the security building, I had to wonder at the self-serving naïveté that was characteristic of him and his kind. It was as much a part of their personae as the rows of credit and membership cards they carried in their billfolds, and when the proper occasion arose they used it with a collective disingenuousness worthy of a theatrical award.

At least that was what I thought—perhaps in

my own naïveté—about Twinky Hebert Lemoyne at the time.

When I reached the security building Murphy Doucet, the guard, was back inside, and the chain was down in the road. He was bent over a table, working on something. He waved to me through the open window, then went back to his work. I parked my truck on the grass and walked inside.

It was hot and close inside the building and smelled of airplane glue. Murphy Doucet looked up from a huge balsa-wood model of a B-17 Flying Fortress that he was sanding. His blue eyes jittered back and forth behind a pair of thick bifocals.

"How you doing, Dave?" he said.

"Pretty good, Murph. I was looking for Julie Balboni."

"He's playing ball."

"Ball?"

"Yeah, sometimes he takes two or three guys into town with him for a pepper game."

"Where?"

"I think at his old high school. Say, did you get Twinky steamed up about something."

"Why's that?"

"I saw you talking to him, then he went barreling-ass down the road like his nose was out of joint."

"Maybe he was late for lunch."

"Yeah, probably. It don't take too much to get Twinky's nose out of joint, anyway. I've always suspected he could do with a little more pussy in his life."

"He's not married?"

"He used to be till his wife run off on him. Right after she emptied his bank account and all the money in his safe. I didn't think Twinky was going to survive that one. That was a long time ago, though."

He used an X-Acto knife to trim away a tiny piece of dried glue from one of the motors on his model airplane. He blew sawdust off the wings and held the plane aloft.

"What do you think of it?" he asked.

"It looks good."

"I've got a whole collection of them. All the planes from World War II. I showed Mikey Goldman my B-17 and he said maybe he could use my collection in one of his films."

"That sounds all right, Murph."

"You kidding? He meant I should donate them. I figured out why that stingy Jew has such a big nose. The air's free."

"He seems like an upfront guy to me," I said.

"Try working for one of them."

I looked at him. "You say Julie's at his old high school?" I said.

"Yeah, him and some actor and that guy named Cholo."

He set his bifocals on the work table and rubbed his hands on the smooth blond surface of his plane. His skin was wrinkled and brown as a cured tobacco leaf.

"Thanks for your time," I said.

"Stop by more often and have coffee. It's lonely sitting out here in this shack."

"By the way, do you know why Goldman might be with a bunch of attorneys?"

"Who knows why these Hollywood sonsofbitches do anything? You're lucky, Dave. I wish I was still a real cop. I do miss it."

He brushed with the backs of his fingers at the starch-white scar on his throat.

A HALF HOUR later, as rain clouds churned thick and black overhead, like curds of smoke from an oil fire, I parked my truck by the baseball diamond of my old high school, now deserted for the summer, where Baby Feet and I had played ball as boys. He stood at home plate, wearing only a pair of spikes and purple gym shorts, the black hair on his enormous body glistening with sweat, his muscles rippling each time he belted a ball deep into the outfield with a shiny blue aluminum bat.

I walked past the oak trees that were carved with the names of high school lovers, past the sagging, paintless bleachers, across the worn infield grass toward the chicken-wire backstop and the powerful swing of his bat, which arched balls like tiny white dots high over the heads of Cholo and a handsome shirtless man whose rhythmic movements and smooth body tone reminded me of undulating water. A canvas bag filled with baseballs spilled out at Julie's feet. There were drops of moisture in his thick brows, and I could see the concentrated, hot lights in his eyes. He bent over effortlessly, in spite of his great weight, picked up a ball with his fingers, and tossed it in the air; then

I saw his eyes flick at me, his left foot step forward in the batter's box, just as he swung the aluminum bat and ripped a grounder like a rocket past my ankles.

I watched it bounce between the oak trees and roll into the street.

"Pretty good shot for a foul ball," I said.

"It looked right down the line to me."

"You were never big on rules and boundaries, Feet."

"What counts is the final score, my man."

Another ball rang off his metal bat and arched high into the outfield. Cholo wandered around in a circle, trying to get his glove under it, his reddish-gray curls glued to his head, his glove outstretched like an amphibian's flipper. The ball dropped two feet behind him.

"I hear you've been busy out at the movie set," I said.

"How's that?"

"Tearing up a young guy who didn't do anything to you."

"There's two sides to every story."

"This kid hurt you in some way, Julie?"

"Maybe he keeps bad company."

"Oh, I see. Elrod Sykes gave you a bad time? He's the bad company? You're bothered by a guy who's either drunk or hungover twenty-four hours a day?"

"Read it like you want." He flipped a ball into the air and lined it over second base. "What's your stake in it, Dave?"

"It seems Elrod felt he had to come to my defense with you. I wish he hadn't done that."

"So everybody's sorry."

"Except it bothers me that you seriously hurt a man, maybe because of me."

"Maybe you flatter yourself." He balanced himself on one foot and began tapping the dirt out of his spikes with his bat.

"I don't think so. You've got a big problem with pride, Julie. You always did."

"Because of you? If my memory hasn't failed me, some years ago a colored shoe-shine man was about to pull real hard on your light chain. I don't remember you minding when I pulled your butt out of the fire that night."

"Yesterday's box score, Feet."

"So don't take everything so serious. There's another glove in the bag."

"The stuntman left town. He's not going to file charges. I guess you already know that."

He rubbed his palm up and down the tapered shank of the bat.

"It was a chickenshit thing to do," I said.

"Maybe it was. Maybe I got my point of view, too. Maybe like I was with a broad when this fucking wild man starts beating on the side of my trailer."

"He's staying at my house now, Julie. I want you to leave him alone. I don't care if he gets in your face or not."

He flipped another ball in the air and *whanged* it to the shirtless man deep in left field. Then he took a hard breath through his nostrils.

"All right, I got no plans to bother the guy," he said. "But not because you're out here, Dave. Why would I want to have trouble with the guy who's the star of my picture? You think I like headaches with these people, you think I like losing money? . . . We clear on this now? . . . Why you keep staring at me?"

"A cop over in Lafayette thinks you set me up."

"You mean that shooting in front of Red's Bar? Get serious, will you?" He splintered a shot all the way to the street, then leaned over and picked up another ball, his stomach creasing like elephant hide.

"It's not your style, huh?" I said.

"No, it's not."

"Come on, Julie, fair and square—look back over your own record. Even when we were kids, you always had to get even, you could never let an insult or an injury pass. Remember the time you came down on that kid's ankle with your spikes?"

"Yeah, I remember it. I remember him trying to take my eyes out with *his.*"

The sky had turned almost black now, and the wind was blowing dust across the diamond.

"You're a powerful and wealthy man. Why don't you give it up?"

"Give what up? What the fuck are you talking about?"

"Carrying around all that anger, trying to prove you're big shit, fighting with your old man, whatever it is that drives you."

"Where do you think you get off talking to me like this?"

"Come on, Julie. We grew up together. Save the hand job for somebody else."

"That's right. That's why maybe I overlook things from you that I don't take from nobody else."

"What's to take? Your father used to beat you with a garden hose. I didn't make that up. You burned down his nightclub."

"It's starting to rain. I think it's time for you to go." He picked up another ball and bounced it in his palm.

"I tried, partner."

"Oh, yeah? What's that mean?"

"Nothing."

"No, you mean you came out here and gave me a warning."

"Why do you think every pitch is a slider, Julie?"

He looked away at the outfield, then back at me.

"You've made remarks about my family. I don't like that," he said. "I'm proud to be Italian. I was even proud of my old man. The people who ran this town back then weren't worth the sweat off his balls. In New Iberia we were always 'wops,' 'dagos,' and 'guineas' because you coonasses were too fucking stupid to know what the Roman Empire was. So you get your nose out of the air when you talk about my family, or about my problems, or anything about my life, you understand what I'm saying, Dave?"

"Somebody made you become a dope dealer? That's what you're telling me?"

"I'm telling you to stay the fuck away from me."

"You don't make a convincing victim, Julie. I'll see you around. Tell your man out there not to spit on the ball."

"What?"

"Isn't that your porno star? I'd be careful. I think AIDS is a lot more easily transmitted than people think."

I saw the rain pattering in the dust as I walked away from him toward the bleachers behind first base. Then I heard a ball ring off the aluminum bat and crash through the tree limbs overhead. I turned around in time to see Julie toss another ball into the air and swing again, his legs wide spread, his torso twisting, his wrists snapping as the bat bit into the ball and laced it in a straight white line toward my face.

WHEN I OPENED my eyes I could see a thick layer of black clouds stretched across the sky from the southern horizon to a silken stretch of blue in the north. The rain had the warm amber color of whiskey, but it made no sound and it struck against my skin as dryly as flower petals in a windstorm.

The general sat on the bottom bench in the bleachers, coatless, the wind flowing through his shirt, a holstered cap-and-ball revolver hanging loosely from his right shoulder. The polished brass letters CSA gleamed softly on the crown of his gray hat. I could smell horses and hear teamsters shouting and wagons creaking in the street. Two enlisted men separated themselves from a group in the oak trees, lifted me to my feet, and sat me down on the wood plank next to the general.

He pointed toward first base with his crutch. My body lay on its side in the dirt, my eyes partially rolled. Cholo and the pornographic actor were running toward home plate from the outfield while Julie was fitting the aluminum bat back in the canvas ball bag. But they were all moving in slow motion, like creatures that were trying to burst free from an invisible gelatinous presence that encased their bodies.

The general took a gold watch as thick as a buttermilk biscuit from his pants pocket, snapped open the cover, glanced at the time, then twisted around in his seat and looked at the soldiers forming into ranks in the street. They were screwing their bayonets on the ends of their rifles, sliding their pouches of paper cartridges and minié balls to the centers of their belts, tying their haversacks and rolled blankets across their backs so their arms would be unencumbered. I saw a man put rolls of socks inside his coat and over his heart. I saw another man put a Bible in the same place. A boy not over sixteen, his cap crimped tightly on his small head, unfurled the Stars and Bars from its wooden staff and lifted it popping into the wind.

Then in the north, where the sky was still blue and not sealed by storm clouds, I saw bursts of black smoke, like birds with ragged wings, and I heard thunder echoing in the trees and between the wooden buildings across the street.

"*What's that?*" I asked him.

"*You've never heard that sound, the electric snap, before?*"

"*They're air bursts, aren't they?*"

"*It's General Banks's artillery firing from down the Teche. He's targeted the wrong area, though. There's a community of darkies under those shells. Did you see things like that in your war?*"

"*Yes, up the Mekong. Some villagers tried to run away from a barrage. They got caught out in the rice field. When we buried them, their faces all looked like they had been inside a terrible wind.*"

"*Then you know it's the innocent about whom we need to be most concerned?*"

Before I could answer I saw Cholo and the man without a shirt staring down at my body, their faces beaded with rain. Julie pulled the drawstring tight on the ball bag and heaved it over his shoulder.

"Get in the Caddy, you guys," he said.

"What happened, Julie?" Cholo said. He wore tennis shoes without socks, a tie-dyed undershirt, and a urine-yellow bikini knotted up tightly around his scrotum. Hair grew around the edges of his bikini like tiny pieces of copper wire.

"He got in the way of the ball," Julie said.

"The guy's got a real goose egg in his hair," the shirtless man said. "Maybe we ought to take him to a hospital or something."

"Leave him alone," Julie said.

"We just gonna leave him here?" Cholo said.

"Unless you want to sit around out here in the rain," Julie said.

"Hey, come on, Feet," Cholo said.

"What's the problem?" Julie said.

"He's not a bad guy for a cop. Y'all go back, right?"

"He's got diarrhea of the mouth. Maybe he learned a lesson this time," Julie said.

"Yeah, but that don't mean we can't drop the guy off at the hospital. I mean, it ain't right to leave him in the fucking rain, Julie."

"You want to start signing your own paychecks? Is that what you're telling me, Cholo?"

"No, I didn't say that. I was just trying to act reasonable. Ain't that what you're always saying? Why piss off the locals?"

"We're not pissing off anybody. Even his own department thinks he's a drunk and a pain in the ass. He got what he deserved. Are you guys coming or not?" Julie said.

He opened the trunk of the purple Cadillac limousine and threw the ball bag clattering inside. The porn actor followed him, wiping his chest and handsome face with his balled-up shirt. Cholo hesitated, stared after them, then pulled the first-base pad loose from its anchor pins and rested it across the side of my face to protect it from the rain. Then he ran after the others.

The blue strip of sky in the north was now filled with torn pieces of smoke. I could hear a loud *snap* each time a shell burst over the distant line of trees.

"*What were you going to tell me?*" I said to the general.

"*That it's the innocent we need to worry about. And when it comes to their protection, we shouldn't hesitate to do it under a black flag.*"

"*I don't understand.*"

"*I feel perhaps I've deceived you.*"

"*How?*"

"*Perhaps I gave you the indication that you had been chosen as part of some chivalric cause.*"

"*I didn't think that, General.*"

His face was troubled, as though his vocabulary was inadequate to explain what he was thinking. Then he looked out into the rain and his eyes became melancholy.

"*My real loss wasn't in the war,*" he said. "*It came later.*"

He turned slowly and looked into my face. "*Yellowjack took not only my life but also the lives of my wife and daughter, Mr. Robicheaux.*"

He waited. The rain felt like confetti blowing against my skin. I searched his eyes, and my heart began to beat against my ribs.

"*My family?*" I said.

"*If you're brave and honorable and your enemies can't destroy you personally, they'll seek to destroy what you love.*"

He gestured with his crutch to a sergeant, who led a saddled white gelding around the side of the bleachers.

"*Wait a minute, General. That's not good enough,*" I said.

"It's all I have," he answered, now seated in the saddle, his back erect, the reins wrapped around his gloved fist.

"Who would try to hurt them? What would they have to gain?"

"I don't know. Keep the Sykes boy with you, though. He's a good one. You remember what Robert Lee once said: 'Texans move them every time.' Good day to you, Lieutenant. It's time we go give Bonnie Nate Banks his welcome to southwestern Louisiana." Then he cut the spur on his left boot into his horse's flank, galloped to the head of his infantry, and hollered out brightly, *"Hideeho, boys! It's a fine day for it! Let's make religious fellows of them all!"*

SOMETIME LATER, I sat up on the ground in the rain, my clothes soaked, the base pad in my lap, a knot as hard and round as a half-dollar throbbing three inches behind my ear. An elderly black yardman bent over me, his face filled with concern. Down the street I could see an ambulance coming toward me through the rain.

"You okay, mister?" the black man said.

"Yes, I think so."

"I seen you there and I t'ought you was drunk. But it look like somebody done gone upside yo' head."

"Would you help me up, please?"

"Sho. You all right?"

"Why, yes, I'm sure I am. Did you see a man on horseback?"

"The Popsicle man gone by. His li'l cart got a horse. That's what you talkin' about?"

The black man eased me down on the bottom plank of the bleachers. It was starting to rain hard now, but right next to me, where the general had been sitting, was a pale, dry area in the wood that was as warm to the touch as living tissue.

CHAPTER 15

THE SKY WAS clear when I woke in the morning, and I could hear gray squirrels racing across the bark of the trees outside the window. The icebag I had put on the lump behind my ear fell to the floor when I got out of bed to answer the phone.

"I called your office and found out you're still suspended," Lou Girard said. "What's going on over there?"

"Just that. I'm still suspended."

"It sounds like somebody's got a serious bone on for you, Dave. Anyway, I talked to this FBI agent, what's her name, Gomez, as well as your boss. We vacuumed the Buick. Guess what we found?"

"I don't know."

"Paper wadding. The kind that's used to seal blank cartridges. It looks like somebody fired a starter's gun at you. He probably leaned down through the passenger window, let off a couple of rounds, then bagged out."

"What'd the sheriff have to say when you told him?"

"Not much. I got the feeling that maybe he was

a little uncomfortable. He doesn't look too good, right, when one of his own men has to be cleared by a cop and a pathologist in another parish? I thought I could hear a little Pontius Pilate tap water running in the background."

"He's always been an okay guy. He just got too close to a couple of the oil cans in the Chamber of Commerce."

"Your friends don't stand around playing pocket pool while civilians kick a two-by-four up your butt, either."

"Anyway, that's real good news, Lou. I owe you a red-fishing trip out to Pecan Island."

"Wait a minute, I'm not finished. That Gomez woman has some interesting theories about serial killers. She said these guys want control and power over people. So I got to thinking about the LeBlanc girl. If your FBI friend is right and the guy who killed her is from around here, what kind of work would he be in?"

"He may be just a pimp, Lou."

"Yeah, but she got nailed on a prostitution charge when she was sixteen, right? That means the court gave somebody a lot of control over her life. What if a probation or parole officer had her selling out of her pants?"

"I saw the body. I think the guy who mutilated her has a furnace instead of a brain. I think he'd have a hard time hiding inside a white-collar environment."

"It was the pencil pushers who gave the world Auschwitz, Dave. Anyway, her prostitution bust was in Lafayette. I'll find out if her P.O. or social worker is still around."

"Okay, but I still believe we're after a pimp of some kind."

"Dave, if this guy's just a pimp, particularly if he's mobbed-up, he would have been in custody a long time ago. These are dumb guys. That's why they do what they do. Most of them couldn't get jobs cleaning gum off movie seats."

"So maybe Balboni's got a smart pimp working for him."

"No, this guy knows how things work from the inside. He sucked us both in on that deal at Red's Bar."

Lou had never gotten along with white-collar authority, in fact, was almost obsessed about it, and I wasn't going to argue with him.

"Let me know what you come up with," I said.

But he wasn't going to let it drop that easily.

"I've been in law enforcement for thirty-seven years," he said. "I've lost count of the lowlifes I've helped send up the road. Is Louisiana any better for it? You know the answer to that one. Face it. The real sonsofbitches are the ones we don't get to touch."

"Don't be too down, Lou." I told him about Julie line-driving a ball off the side of my head. Then I told him the rest of it. "I asked the paramedics who called in the report. They said it was anonymous. So I went down later and listened to the 911 tapes. It was a guy named Cholo Manelli. He's a—"

"Yeah, I know who he is. Cholo did that?"

"There's no mistaking that broken-nose Irish Channel accent."

"He owes you or something?"

"Not really. But he's an old-time mob soldier. He knows you don't antagonize cops unnecessarily. Maybe Julie's starting to lose control of his people."

"It's a thought. But stay away from Balboni till you get your shield back. Stay off baseball diamonds, too. For a sober guy you sure have a way of spitting in the lion's mouth."

After I hung up the phone I showered, dressed in a pair of seersucker slacks, brown loafers, a charcoal shirt with a gray and red striped tie, and got a haircut and a shoe shine in town. My scalp twitched when the barber's scissors clipped across the lump behind my ear. Through the front window I saw Julie Balboni's purple limo drive down Main Street. The barber stopped clipping. The shop was empty except for the shoe-shine man.

"Dave, how come that man's still around here?" the barber said. His round stomach touched lightly against my elbow.

"He hasn't made the right people mad at him."

"He ain't no good, that one. He don't have no bidness here."

"I think you're right, Sid."

He started clipping again. Then, almost as a casual afterthought, he said, "Y'all gonna get him out of town?"

"There're some business people making a lot of money off of Julie. I think they'd like to keep him around awhile."

His hands paused again, and he stepped around the side of the chair so I could see his face.

"That ain't the rest of us, no," he said. "We don't like having that man in New Iberia. We don't like his dope, we don't like his criminals he bring up here from New Orleans. You tell that man you work for we gonna 'member him when we vote, too."

"Could I buy you a cup of coffee and a doughnut this morning, Sid?"

A little later, with my hair still wet and combed, I walked out of the heat into the air-conditioned coolness of the sheriff's department and headed toward the sheriff's office. I glanced inside my office door as I passed it. Rosie was not inside but Rufus Arceneaux was, out of uniform now, dressed in a blue suit and tie and a silk shirt that had the bright sheen of tin. He was sitting behind my desk.

I leaned against the door jamb.

"The pencil sharpener doesn't work very well, but there's a pen knife in my drawer that you can use," I said.

"I wasn't bucking for plainclothes. The old man gave it to me," he said.

"I'm glad to see you're moving on up, Rufe."

"Look, Dave, I'm not the one who went out and got fucked up at that movie set."

"I hear you were out there, though. Looking into things. Probably trying to clear me of any suspicion that I got loaded."

"I got a GED in the corps. You're a college graduate. You were a homicide lieutenant in New Orleans. You want to blame me for your troubles?"

"Where's Rosie?"

"Down in Vermilion Parish."

"What for?"

"How would I know?"

"Did she say anything about Balboni having legal troubles with Mikey Goldman?"

"What legal—" His eyes clouded, like silt being disturbed in dark water.

"When you see her, would you ask her to call me?"

"Leave a message in her box," he said, positioned his forearms on my desk blotter, straightened his back, and looked out the window as though I were not there.

When I walked into the sheriff's office he was pouring a chalky liquid from a brown prescription bottle into a water glass. A dozen sheets of paper were spread around on his desk. The "hold" light was flashing on his telephone. He didn't speak. He drank from the glass, then refilled it from the water cooler and drank again, his throat working as though he were washing out an unwanted presence from his metabolism.

"How you doin', podna?" he said.

"Pretty good now. I had a talk with Lou Girard this morning."

"So did I. Sit down," he said, then picked up the phone and spoke to whoever was on hold. "I'm not sure *what* happened. When I am, I'll call you.

In the meantime, Rufus is going to be suspended. Just hope we don't have to pass a sales tax to pay the bills on this one."

He hung up the phone and pressed the flat of his hand against his stomach. He made a face like a small flame was rising up his windpipe.

"Did you ever have ulcers?" he asked.

"Nope."

"I've got one. If this medicine I'm drinking doesn't get rid of it, they may have to cut it out."

"I'm sorry to hear that."

"That was the prosecutor's office I was talking to. We're being sued."

"Over what?"

"A seventy-six-year-old black woman shot her old man to death last night, then killed both her dogs and shot herself through the stomach. Rufus in there handcuffed her to the gurney, then came back to the office. He didn't bother to give the paramedics a key to the cuffs either. She died outside the emergency room."

I didn't say anything.

"You think we got what we deserved, huh?" he said.

"Maybe he would have done it even if he hadn't been kicked up to plainclothes, Sheriff."

"No, he wouldn't have been the supervising officer. He wouldn't have had the opportunity."

"What's my status this morning?"

He brushed at a nostril with one knuckle.

"I don't know how to say this," he said. "We messed up. No, *I* messed up."

I waited.

"I did wrong by you, Dave," he said.

"People make mistakes. Maybe you made the best decision you could at the time."

He held out his hands, palms front.

"Nope, none of that," he said. "I learned in Korea a good officer takes care of his men. I didn't get this ulcer over Rufus Arceneaux's stupidity. I got it because I was listening to some local guys I should have told to butt out of sheriff's department business."

"Nobody's supposed to bat a thousand, Sheriff."

"I want you back at work today. I'll talk to Rufus about his new status. That old black woman is part my responsibility. I don't know why I made that guy plainclothes. You don't send a warthog to a beauty contest."

I shook hands with him, walked across the street to a barbecue stand in a grove of live oaks, ate a plate filled with dirty rice, pork ribs, and red beans, then strolled back to the office, sipping an ice-cold can of Dr Pepper. Rufus Arceneaux was gone. I clipped my badge on my belt, sat in the swivel chair behind my desk, turned the air-conditioner vents into my face, and opened my mail.

ROSIE WAS BEAMING when she came through the office door an hour later.

"What's that I see?" she said. "With a haircut and a shoe shine, too."

"How's my favorite fed?"

"Dave, you look wonderful!"

"Thanks, Rosie."

"I can't tell you how fine it is to have you back."

Her face was genuinely happy, to such an extent that I felt vaguely ill at ease.

"I owe you and Lou Girard a lot on this one," I said.

"Have you had lunch yet?"

"Yeah, I did."

"Too bad. Tomorrow I'm taking you out, though. Okay?"

"Yeah, that'd be swell."

She sat down behind her desk. Her neck was flushed and her breasts rose against her blouse when she breathed. "I got a call this morning from an old Frenchman who runs a general store on Highway 35 down in Vermilion Parish. You know what he said? 'Hey, y'all catch the man put dat young girl in dat barrel?' "

I filled a water glass for her and put it on her desk.

"He knows something?" I said.

"Better than that. I think he saw the guy who did it. He said he remembers a month or so ago a blond girl coming in his store at night in the rain. He said he became worried about her because of the way a man in the store was watching her." She opened her notebook pad and looked at it. "These are the old fellow's words: 'You didn't need but look at that man's face to know he had a dirty mind.' He said the girl had a canvas backpack and she went back out in the rain to the highway with it. The man followed her, then he came back in a few minutes and asked the old fellow if he had any red balloons for sale."

"Balloons?"

"If you think that sounds weird, how about this? When the old fellow said no, the man found an old box of Valentine candy on the back shelf and said he wanted that instead."

"I'm not making connections here," I said.

"The store owner watched the man with the candy box through the window. He said just before he pulled out of the parking lot he threw the candy box in the ditch. In the morning the old fellow went out and found it in the weeds. The cellophane wrapping was gone." She watched my face. "What are you thinking?"

"Did he see the man pick up the girl?"

"He's not sure. He remembers the man was in a dark blue car and he remembers the brake lights going on in the rain." She continued to watch my face. "Here's the rest of it. I looked around on the back shelves of the store and found another candy box that the owner says is like the one the man in the blue car bought. Guess what tint the cellophane was."

"Red or purple."

"You got it, slick," she said, and leaned back in her chair.

"He wrapped it around a spotlight, didn't he?"

"That'd be my bet."

"Could the store owner describe this guy?"

"That's the problem." She tapped a ballpoint pen on her desk blotter. "All the old fellow remembers is that the man had a rain hood."

"Too bad. Why didn't he contact us sooner?"

"He said he told all this to somebody, he doesn't know who, in the Vermilion Parish Sheriff's Department. He said when he called again yesterday, they gave him my number. Is your interagency cooperation always this good?"

"Always. Does he still have the candy box?"

"He said he gave the candy to his dog, then threw the box in the trash."

"So maybe we've got a guy impersonating a cop?" I said.

"It might explain a lot of things."

Unconsciously I fingered the lump behind my ear.

"What's the matter?" she said.

"Nothing. Maybe our man is simply a serial killer and psychopath after all. Maybe he doesn't have anything to do with Julie Balboni."

"Would that make you feel good or bad?"

"I honestly can't say, Rosie."

"Yeah, you can," she said. "You're always hoping that even the worst of them has something of good in him. Don't do that with Balboni. Deep down inside all that whale fat is a real piece of shit, Dave."

Outside, a jail trusty cutting the grass broke the brass head off a sprinkler with the lawnmower. A violent jet of water showered the wall and ran down the windows. In the clatter of noise, in the time it takes the mind's eye to be distracted by shards of wet light, I thought of horses fording a stream, of sun-browned men in uniform looking back over their shoulders at the safety of a crimson and gold hardwood forest, while ahead of them dirty puffs of rifle fire exploded from a distant treeline that swarmed with the shapes of the enemy.

It's the innocent we need to worry about, he had said. *And when it comes to their protection, we shouldn't hesitate to do it under a black flag.*

"Are you all right?" she said.

"Yeah, it's a fine day. Let's go across the street and I'll buy you a Dr Pepper."

THAT EVENING, AT sunset, I was sprinkling the grass and the flower beds in the backyard while Elrod and Alafair were playing with Tripod on top of the picnic table. The air was cool in the fading light and smelled of hydrangeas and water from the hose and the fertilizer I had just spaded into the roots of my rosebushes.

The phone rang inside, and a moment later Bootsie brought it and the extension cord to the back screen. I sat down on the step and put the receiver to my ear.

"Hello," I said.

I could hear someone breathing on the other end.

"Hello?"

"I want to talk to you tonight."

"Sam?"

"That's right. I'm playing up at the black juke in St. Martinville. You know where that's at?"

"The last time I had an appointment with you, things didn't work out too well."

"That was last time. I was drinkin' then. Then them womens was hangin' around, made me forget what I was supposed to do."

"I think you let me down, partner."

He was quiet except for the sound of his breathing.

"Is something wrong?" I said.

"I got to tell you somet'ing, somet'ing I ain't tole no white man."

"Say it."

"You come up to the juke."

"I'll meet you at my office tomorrow morning."

"What I got to say can put me back on the farm. I sure ain't gonna do it down there."

Elrod picked Tripod up horizontally in his arms, then bounced him up and down by tugging on his tail.

"I'll be there in an hour or so," I said. "Don't jerk me around again, Sam."

"You might be a po-liceman, you might even be different from most white folks, but you still white and you ain't got no idea 'bout the world y'all give people of color to live in. That's a fact, suh. It surely is," he said, and hung up.

I should have known that Hogman would not be outdone in eloquence.

"Don't pull his tail," Alafair was saying.

"He likes it. It gets his blood moving," Elrod said.

She sighed as though Elrod were unteachable, then took Tripod out of his arms and carried him around the side of the house to the hutch.

"Can you take yourself to the meeting tonight?" I asked Elrod.

"You cain't go?"

"No."

"How about I just wait till we can go together?" He rubbed the top of the table with his fingers and didn't look up.

"What if I drop you off and then come back before the meeting's over?"

"Look, this is a, what do you call it, a step meeting?"

"That's right."

"You said it's about amends, about atoning to people for what you did wrong?"

"Something like that."

"How do I atone for Kelly? How do I make up for that one, Dave?" He stared out at the late red sun over the canefield so I couldn't see his eyes.

"You get those thoughts out of your head. Kelly's dead because we have a psychopath in our midst. Her death doesn't have anything to do with you."

"You can say that all you want, but I know better."

"Oh, yeah?"

"Yeah."

I could see the clean, tight line of his jaw and a wet gleaming in the corner of his eye.

"Tell me, did you respect Kelly?" I asked.

He swiveled around on the picnic bench. "What kind of question is that?"

"I'm going to be a little hard on you, El. I think you're using her death to feel sorry for yourself."

"What?" His face was incredulous.

"When I lost my wife I found out that self-pity and guilt could be a real rush, particularly when I didn't have Brother Jim Beam to do the job."

"That's a lousy fucking thing to say."

"I was talking about myself. Maybe you're different from me."

"What the hell's the matter with you? You don't think it's natural to feel loss, to feel grief, when somebody dies? I tried to close the hole in her throat with my hands, her blood was running through my fingers. She was still alive and looking straight into my eyes. Like she was drowning and neither one of us could do anything about it." He pressed his forehead against his fist; his flexed thigh trembled against his slacks.

"I got four of my men killed on a trail in Vietnam. Then I got drunk over it. I used them, I didn't respect them for the brave men they were. That's the way alcoholism works, El."

"I'd appreciate it if you'd leave me be for a while."

"Will you go to the meeting?"

He didn't answer. There was a pained light in his eyes like someone had twisted barbed wire around his forehead.

"You don't have to talk, just listen to what these guys have to say about their own experience," I said.

"I'd rather pass tonight."

"Suit yourself," I said.

I told Bootsie where I was going and walked

out to the truck. The cicadas droned from horizon to horizon under the vault of plum-colored sky. Then I heard Elrod walking through the leaves and pecan husks behind me.

"If I sit around here, I'll end up in the beer joint," he said, and opened the passenger door to the truck. Then he raised his finger at me. "But I'm going to ask you one thing, Dave. Don't ever accuse me of using Kelly again. If you do, I'm going to knock your teeth down your goddamn throat."

There were probably a number of things I could have said in reply—but you don't deny a momentary mental opiate to somebody who has made an appointment in the Garden of Gethsemane.

THE BLACK JUKEJOINT in St. Martinville was set back in a grove of trees off a yellow dirt road not far from Bayou Teche. It was one of those places that could be dropped by a tornado in the middle of an Iowa cornfield and you would instantly know that its origins were in the Deep South. The plank walls and taped windows vibrated with noise from Friday afternoon until late Sunday night. Strings of Christmas-tree lights rimmed the doors and windows year round; somebody was barbecuing ribs on top of a tin barrel, only a few feet from a pair of dilapidated privies that were caked under the eaves with yellowjacket and mud-dauber nests; people copulated back in the woods against tree trunks and fought in the parking lot with knives, bottles, and razors. Inside, the air was always thick with the smell of muscatel, smoke, cracklings, draft beer and busthead whiskey, expectorated snuff, pickled hogs' feet, perfume, body powder, sweat, and homegrown reefer.

Sam Patin sat on a small stage with a canopy over it hung with red tassels and miniature whiskey bottles that clinked in the backdraft from a huge ventilator fan. His white suit gleamed with an electric purple glow from the floor lamps, and the waxed black surfaces of his twelve-string guitar winked with tiny lights. The floor in front of him was packed with dancers. When he blew into the harmonica attached to a wire brace on his neck and began rolling the steel picks on his fingers across an E-major blues run, the crowd moaned in unison. They yelled at the stage as though they were confirming a biblical statement he had made at a revival, pressed their loins together with no consciousness of other people around them, and roared with laughter even though Hogman sang of a man who had sold his soul for an ox-blood Stetson hat he had just lost in a crap game:

Stagolee went runnin'
In the red-hot boilin' sun,
Say look in my chiffro drawer, woman,
Get me my smokeless .41.
Stagolee tole Miz Billy,
You don't believe your man is dead,
Come down to the barroom,
See the .41 hole in his head.
That li'l judge found Stagolee guilty

And that li'l clerk wrote it down,
On a cold winter morning,
Stagolee was Angola-bound.
Forty-dollar coffin,
Eighty-dollar hack,
Carried that po' man to the burying ground,
Ain't never comin' back.

Two feet away from me the bartender filled a tray with draft beers without ever looking at me. He was bald and had thick gray muttonchop sideburns that looked like they were pasted on his cheeks. Then he wiped his hands on his apron and lit a cigar.

"You sho' you in the right place?" he said.

"I'm a friend of Hogman's," I said.

"So this is where you come to see him?"

"Why not?"

"What you havin', chief?"

"A 7Up."

He opened a bottle, placed it in front of me without a glass, and walked away. The sides of the bottle were warm and filmed with dust. Twenty minutes later Hogman had not taken a break and was still playing.

"You want another one?" the bartender said.

"Yeah, I would. How about some ice or a cold one this time?" I said.

"The gentleman wants a cold one," he said to no one in particular. Then he filled a tall glass with cracked ice and set it on the bar with another dusty bottle of 7Up. "Why cain't y'all leave him alone? He done his time, ain't he?"

"I look like the heat?" I said.

"You *are* the heat, Chief. You and that other one out yonder."

"What other one? What are you talking about, partner?"

"The white man that was out yonder in that blue Mercury."

I got off the stool and looked into the parking lot through the Venetian blinds and the scrolled neon tubing of a Dixie beer sign.

"I don't see any blue Merc," I said.

"'Cause he gone now, Chief. Like it's a black people's club, like he figured that out, you understand what I'm sayin'?"

"What'd this guy look like?" I said.

"White. He look white. That he'p you out?" he said, tossed a towel into the tin sink, and walked down the duckboards toward the far end of the bar.

Finally Hogman slipped his harmonica brace and guitar strap off his neck, looked directly at me, and went through a curtained door into a back storage room. I followed him inside. He sat on a wood chair, among stacks of beer cases, and had already started eating a dinner of pork chops, greens, and cornbread from a tin plate that rested on another chair.

"I ain't had a chance to eat today. This movie-star life is gettin' rough on my time. You want some?" he said.

"No, thanks." I leaned against a stack of beer cartons.

"The lady fix me these chops don't know how to season, but they ain't too bad."

"You want to get to it, Sam?"

"You t'ink I just messin' with you, huh? All right, this is how it play. A long time ago up at Angola I got into trouble over a punk. Not my punk, you understand, I didn't do none of that unnatural kind of stuff, a punk that belong to a guy name Big Melon. Big Melon was growin' and sellin' dope for a couple of the hacks. Him and his punk had a whole truck patch of it behind the cornfield."

"Hogman, I'm afraid this sounds a little remote."

"You always *know,* you always got somet'ing smart to say. That's why you runnin' around in circles, that's why them men laughin' at you."

"Which men?"

"The ones who killed that nigger you dug up in the Atchafalaya. You gonna be patient now, or you want to go back to doin' it your way?"

"I'm looking forward to hearing your story, Hogman."

"See, these two hacks had them a good bidness. Big Melon and the punk growed the dope, cured it, bagged it all up, and the hacks sold it in Lafayette. They carried it down there themselves sometimes, or the executioner and another cop picked it up for them. They didn't let nobody get back there by that cornfield. But I was half-trusty then, livin' in Camp I, and I used to cut across the field to get to the hog lot. That's how come I found out they was growin' dope back there. So Big Melon tole the hack I knowed what they was doin', that I was gonna snitch them off, and then the punk planted a jar of julep under my bunk so I'd lose my trusty job and my good-time.

"I tole the hack it ain't right, I earn my job. He say, 'Hogman, you fuck with the wrong people in here, you goin' in the box and you goin' stay in there till you come out a white man.' That's what the bossman say. I tole him it don't matter how long they keep me in there, it still ain't right. They wrote me up for sassin' and put me to pickin' cotton. When I get down in a thin patch and come up short, they make me stand up all night on an oil barrel, dirty and smellin' bad and without no supper.

"I went to the bossman in the field, say I don't care what Big Melon do, what them hacks do, it ain't my bidness, I just want my job back on the hog lot. He say, 'You better keep shut, boy, you better fill that bag, you better not put no dirt clods in it when you weigh in, neither, like you tried to do yesterday.' I say, 'Boss, what's I gonna do? I ain't put no dirt clods in my bag, I ain't give nobody trouble, I don't be carin' Big Melon want to grow dope for the hacks.' He knock me down with a horse quirt and put me in the sweatbox on Camp A for three days, in August, with the sun boilin' off them iron sides, with a bucket between my knees to go to the bat'room in."

He had stopped eating now and his face looked solitary and bemused, as though his own experience had become strange and unfamiliar in his recounting of it.

"You were a standup guy, Hogman. I always admired your courage," I said.

"No, I was scared of them people, 'cause when I come out of the box I knowed the gunbulls was gonna kill me. I seen them do it befo', up on the levee, where they work them Red Hat boys double-time from cain't-see to cain't-see. They shot and buried them po' boys without never missin' a beat, just the way somebody run over a dog with a truck and keep right on goin'.

"I had me a big Stella twelve-string guitar, bought it off a Mexican on Congress Street in Houston. I used to keep it in the count-man's cage so nobody wouldn't be foolin' with it while I was workin' or sleepin'. When I come out of the box and taken a shower and eat a big plate of rice and beans, I ax the count-man first thing for my guitar. He say, 'I'm sorry, Sam, but the bossman let Big Melon take it while you was in the box.'

"I waited till that night and went to Big Melon's 'hunk,' that's what we call the place where a wolf stay with his punk. There's that big fat nigger sittin' naked on his mattress, like a big pile of black inner tubes, while the punk is playin' my guitar on the floor, lipstick and rouge all over his face and pink panties on his li'l ass.

"I say, 'Melon, you or your punk fuck wit' my guitar again and I gone cut that black dick off. It don't matter if I go to the electric chair for it or not. I'm gonna joog you in the shower, in the chow line, or while you pumpin' your poke chops here. They's gonna be one fat nigger they gonna have to haul in a piano crate down to the graveyard.'

"Melon smile at me and say, 'We just borrowed it, Hogman. We was gonna give it back. Here, you want Pookie to rub your back for you?'

"But I knowed they was comin'. Two nights later, right befo' lockup, I was goin' to the toilet and I turn around and his punk is standin' in the do'. I say, 'What you want, Pookie?' He say, 'I'm sorry I was playin' your guitar, Hogman. I wanta be yo' friend, maybe come stay up at your hunk some nights.'

"When I reached down to pull up my britches, he come outta his back pocket with a dirk and aim it right at my heart. I catched him around the neck and bent him backwards, then I kept bendin' him backwards and squeezin' acrost his windpipe, and he was floppin' real hard, shakin' all over, he shit in his pants, 'cause I could smell it, then it went *snap*, just like you bust a real dry piece of firewood acrost your knee.

"I look up and there's one of the hacks who's selling the dope. He say, 'Hogman, we ain't gonna let this be a problem. We'll just stuff this li'l bitch out yonder in the levee with them others. Won't nobody care, won't make no difference to nobody, not even to Big Melon. It'll just be our secret.'

"All that time they'd been smarter than me. They sent Pookie to joog me, but they didn't care if he killed me or if I killed him. It worked out for them just fine. They knew I'd never cause them no trouble. They was right, too. I didn't sass, I done what they tole me, I even he'ped hoe them dope plants a couple of times."

"I don't understand, Sam. You're telling me that the lynched black man was killed by one of these guards?"

"I ain't said that. I said they was a bunch of them sellin' that dope. They was takin' it out of the pen in a police car. What was the name of that nigger you dug out of the sandbar?"

"DeWitt Prejean."

"I'll tell you this. He was fuckin' a white man's wife. Start axin' what he done for a livin', you'll find the people been causin' you all this grief."

"Who's the guy I'm looking for?"

"I said all I can say."

"Look, Sam, don't be afraid of these gunbulls or cops from years ago. They can't harm you now."

He put a toothpick in the corner of his mouth, then took a pint bottle of rum from his coat pocket and unscrewed the cap with his thumb. He held the bottle below his mouth. His long fingers were glistening with grease from the pork chops he had eaten.

"This still the state of Lou'sana, or are we livin' somewhere else these days?" he said.

I COULDN'T SLEEP that night. I poured a glass of milk and walked down by the duck pond in the starlight. A pair of mudhens spooked out of the flooded reeds and skittered across the water's surface toward the far bank. The pieces of the case wouldn't come together. Were we looking for a serial killer who had operated all over the state, a local psychopath, a pimp, or perhaps even a hit man from the mob? Were cops involved? Hogman thought so, and even believed there was someone out there with the power to send him back to prison. But his perspective was colored by his own experience as a career recidivist. And what about the lynched black man, DeWitt Prejean? Would the solution to his murder in 1957 lead us to the deviate who had mutilated Cherry LeBlanc?

No, the case was not as simple as Hogman had wanted me to think, even though he was obviously sincere and his fears about retribution were real. But I had no answers, either.

Unfortunately, they would come in a way that I never anticipated. I saw Elrod come out of the lighted kitchen and walk down the slope toward the pond. He was shirtless and barefoot and his slacks were unbuttoned over his skivvies. He clutched a sheet of lined notebook paper in his right hand. He looked at me uncertainly, and his lips started to form words that obviously he didn't want to speak.

"What's wrong?" I said.

"The phone rang while I was in the kitchen. I answered it so y'all wouldn't get woke up."

"Who was it? What's that in your hand?"

"The sheriff . . ." He straightened the piece of paper in his fingers and read the words to himself, then looked up into my face. "It's a friend of yours, Lou Girard, Dave. The sheriff says maybe you should go over to Lafayette. He says, I'm sorry, man, he says your friend got drunk and killed himself."

Elrod held the sheet of paper out toward me, his eyes looking askance at the duck pond. The moonlight was white on his hand.

CHAPTER 16

HE DID IT with a dogleg twenty-gauge in his little garage apartment, whose windows were overgrown with bamboo and banana trees. Or at least that's what the investigative officer, Doobie Patout, was telling me when I got there at 4 A.M., just as the photographer was finishing and the paramedics were about to lift Lou's body out of a wide pool of blood and zipper it inside a black bag.

"There's a half-empty bottle of Wild Turkey on the drainboard and a spilled bottle of Valium on the coffee table," Doobie said. "I think maybe Lou just got real down and decided to do it."

The single-shot twenty-gauge lay at the foot of a beige-colored stuffed chair. The top of the chair, the wall behind it, and the ceiling were streaked with blood. One side of Lou's face looked perfectly normal, the eye staring straight ahead like a blue marble pressed into dough. The opposite side of his face, where the jawbone should have been, had sunk into the rug like a broken pomegranate. Lou's right arm was pointed straight out onto the wood floor. At the end of his fingers, painted in red, were the letters *SI*.

"You guys are writing it off as suicide?" I said.

"That's the way it looks to me," Doobie said. The tops of his jug ears were scaled with sunburn. "He was in bad shape. The mattress is covered with piss stains, the sink's full of raw garbage. Go in the bedroom and take a whiff."

"Why would a suicide try to write a note in his own blood?"

"I think they change their minds when they know it's too late. Then they want to hold on any way they can. They're not any different from anybody else. It was probably for his ex-wife. Her name's Silvia."

"Where's his piece?"

"On his dresser in the bedroom."

"If Lou wanted to buy it, why wouldn't he use his .357?" I said. I scratched at a lead BB that had scoured upward along the wallpaper. "Why would he do it with twenty-gauge birdshot, then botch it?"

"Because he was drunk on his ass. It wasn't an unusual condition for him."

"He was helping me on a case, Doobie."

"And?"

"Maybe he found out something that somebody didn't want him to pass along."

The paramedics lifted Lou's body off the rug, then lowered it inside the plastic bag, straightened his arms by his sides, and zipped the bag over his face.

"Look, his career was on third base," Doobie said, as the medics worked the gurney past him.

"His wife dumped him for another dyke, he was getting freebies from a couple of whores down at the Underpass, he was trembling and eating pills in front of the whole department every morning. You might believe otherwise, but there's no big mystery to what happened here tonight."

"Lou had trouble with booze, but I think you're lying about his being on a pad with hookers. He was a good cop."

"Think whatever you want. He was a drunk. That fact's not going to go away. I'm going to seal the place now. You want to look at anything else?"

"Is it true you were an executioner up at Angola?"

"None of your goddam business what I was."

"I'm going to look around a little more. In the meantime I want to ask you a favor, Doobie. I'd appreciate your waiting outside. In fact, I'd really appreciate your staying as far away from me as possible."

"You'd appreciate it—"

"Yes. Thanks very much."

His breath was stale, his eyes liquid and resentful. Then the interest went out of them and he glanced outside at the pale glow of the sun on the eastern horizon. He stuck a cigarette in the corner of his mouth, walked out onto the porch, and watched the paramedics load Lou's body into the back of the ambulance, not out of fear of me or even personal humiliation; he was simply one of those law officers for whom insensitivity, cynicism, cruelty, and indifference toward principle eventually become normal and interchangeable attitudes, one having no more value or significance than another.

In the sink, on top of a layer of unwashed dishes, was a pile of garbage—coffee grounds, banana peels, burned oatmeal, crushed beer cans, cigarette butts, wadded newspapers. The trash can by the icebox was empty, except for a line of wet coffee grounds that ran from the lip of the can to the bottom, where a solitary banana peel rested.

In the bedroom one drawer was open in the dresser. On top of the dresser were a roll of white socks, a framed photograph of Lou and his wife at a Las Vegas wedding chapel, Lou's holstered revolver, and the small notebook with a pencil attachment that he always carried in his shirt pocket. The first eight pages were filled with notes about an accidental drowning and a stabbing in a black nightclub. The next few pages had been torn out. Tiny bits of paper clung to the wire spirals, and the first blank page had no pencil impressions on it from the previous one.

In his sock drawer I found a bottle of vodka and his "throw-down," an old .32 revolver with worn bluing, taped wooden grips, and serial numbers that had been eaten and disfigured with acid. I flipped open the cylinder. Five of the chambers were loaded, and the sixth had been left empty for the hammer to rest on.

I started to replace the revolver in the drawer; instead, I pushed the drawer shut and dropped the revolver into my pants pocket.

On the way out of the apartment I looked again

at Lou's blood on the floor. Doobie Patout's shoes had tracked through the edge of it and printed the logo of his rubber heel brightly on the wood.

What a way to exit thirty-seven years of law enforcement, I thought. You died facedown in a rented garage apartment that wouldn't meet the standards of public housing; then your colleagues write you off as a drunk and step in your blood.

I looked at the smudged letters *SI* again. What were you trying to tell us, Lou?

Doobie Patout locked the door behind me when I walked outside. A red glow was spreading from the eastern horizon upward into the sky.

"This is what I think happened, Doobie. You can do with it what you want," I said. "Somebody found Lou passed out and tossed the place. After he ripped some pages out of Lou's notebook, he put Lou's twenty-gauge under his chin."

"If he tossed the place first, he would have found Lou's .357, right? Why wouldn't he use it? That's the first thing you jumped on, Robicheaux."

"Because he would have had to put it in Lou's hand. He didn't want to wake him up. It was easier to do it with the shotgun."

His eyes fixed on mine; then they became murky and veiled as they studied a place in the air about six inches to the right of my face. A dead palm tree in the small yard clattered in the warm morning breeze.

IT WAS SATURDAY, and I didn't have to go to the office, but I called Rosie at the motel where she was living and told her about Lou's death.

At noon of the same day Cholo Manelli drove a battered fire-engine-red Cadillac convertible down the dirt road by the bayou and parked by the dock just as I was headed up to the house for lunch. The left front fender had been cut away with an acetylene torch and looked like an empty eye socket. The top was down, and the backseat and the partly opened trunk were filled with wrought-iron patio furniture, including a glass-topped table and a furled beach umbrella.

He wore white shorts and a green Hawaiian shirt with pink flamingoes printed on it. He squinted up at me from under his white golf cap, which was slanted over one eye. When he grinned I saw that an incisor tooth was broken off in his lower mouth and there was still blood in the empty space above his gum.

"I wanted to say good-bye," he said. "Give you something, too."

"Where you going, Cholo?"

"I thought I might go to Florida for a while, take it easy, maybe open up a business like you got. Do some marlin fishing, stuff like that. Look, can we talk someplace a minute?"

"Sure. Come on inside the shop."

"No, you got customers around and I got a bad problem with language. It don't matter what I say, it comes out sounding like a toilet flushing. Take a ride with me, lieutenant."

I got into the passenger's seat, and we drove down to the old grocery store with the wide gallery at the four-corners. The white-painted iron patio furniture vibrated and rattled in the backseat. On the leg of one chair was the green trademark of Holiday Inn. Cholo parked in the shade of the huge oak tree that stretched over the store's gallery.

"What's with the furniture?" I said.

"The owner wanted me to take it when I checked out. He said he's been needing some new stuff, it's a write-off, anyway, and I'm kind of doing him a favor. They got po'-boys in here? It's on me."

Before I could answer he went inside the store and came back with two shrimp-and-fried-oyster sandwiches dripping with mayonnaise, lettuce, and sliced tomatoes. He unwrapped the wax paper on his and chewed carefully on one side of his mouth.

"What's going on, Cholo?" I said.

"Just like I said, it's time to hang it up."

"You had some problems with Baby Feet?"

"Maybe."

"Because you called an ambulance for me?"

He stopped chewing, removed a piece of lettuce from his teeth, and flicked it out onto the shell parking lot.

"Margot told him. She heard me on the phone," he said. "So last night we was all having dinner at this class place out on the highway, with some movie people there, people who still think Julie's shit don't stink, and Julie says, 'Did y'all know Cholo thinks he's Florence Nightingale? That it's his job to take care of people who get hurt on ball fields, even though that means betraying his old friends?'

"I say, 'What are you talking, Julie? Who's fucking Florence Nightingale or whatever?'

"He don't even look at me. He says to all the others, 'So we're gonna get Cholo another job 'cause he don't like what he's doing now. He's gonna start work in one of my restaurants, down the street from the Iberville project. Bus dishes for a little while, get the feel of things, make sure the toilets are clean, 'cause a lot of middle-class niggers eat in there and they don't like dirty toilets. What d'you say, Cholo?'

"Everybody at the table's grinning and I go, 'I ain't done anything wrong, Julie. I made a fucking phone call. What if the guy'd died out there?'

"Julie goes, 'There you go again, Cholo. Always opening your face when you ain't supposed to. Maybe you ought to leave the table. You got wax in your ears, you talk shit, you rat-fuck your friends. I don't want you around no more.'

"When I walked out, everybody in the restaurant was looking at me, like I was a bug, like I was somebody didn't have no business around regular people. Nobody ever done anything like that to me."

His face was bright with perspiration in the warm shade. He rubbed his nose on the back of his wrist.

"What happened to your tooth, Cholo?" I asked.

"I went down to Julie's room last night. I told him that he was a douche bag, I wouldn't work for him again if he begged me, that just like Cherry

LeBlanc told him, he's a needle-dick and the only reason a broad like Margot stays with him is because what she's got is so wore out it's like the Grand Canyon down there and it don't matter if he's a needle-dick or not. That's when he comes across my mouth with this big glass ashtray, the sonofabitch.

"Here, you want to see what he's into, lieutenant," he said, pulled a videocassette out of the glove box, and put it in my hand. "Go to the movies."

"Wait a minute. What's this about Cherry LeBlanc?"

"If he tells you he never knew her, ask him about this. Julie forgot he told me to take some souvenir pictures when we drove over to Biloxi once. Is that her or not?"

He slipped a black-and-white photograph from his shirt pocket and placed it in my hand. In it, Julie and Cherry LeBlanc sat at an outdoor table under an umbrella. They wore swimsuits and held napkin-wrapped drinks in their hands; both were smiling. The background was hazy with sunshine and out of focus. An indistinct man at another table read a newspaper; his eyes looked like diamonds embedded in his flesh.

"I want you to be straight with me, Cholo. Did Feet kill her?" I said.

"I don't know. I'll tell you what happened the night she got killed, though. They had a big blowup in the motel room. I could hear it coming through the walls. She said she wasn't nobody's chicken, she wanted her own action, her own girls, a place out on Lake Pontchartrain, maybe a spot in a movie. So he goes, 'There's broads who'd do an awful lot just to be in the same room with me, Cherry. Maybe you ought to count your blessings.' That's when she started to make fun of him. She said he looked like a whale with hair on it, and besides that, he had a putz like a Vienna sausage.

"The next thing I know she's roaring out of the place and Julie's yelling into the phone at somebody, I don't know who, all I heard him say was Cherry is a fucking nightmare who's snorting up six hundred dollars' worth of his coke a day and he don't need any more nightmares in his life, particularly a teenage moron who thinks she can go apeshit any time she feels like it."

"Who killed her, Cholo?"

He tossed his unfinished po'-boy sandwich at a rusted trash barrel. He missed, and the bread, shrimp, and oysters broke apart on the ground.

"Come on, Lieutenant. You know how it works. A guy like Julie don't do hits. He says something to somebody, then he forgets it. If it's a special kind of job, maybe somebody calls up a geek, a guy with real sick thoughts in his head.

"Look, you remember a street dip in New Orleans named Tommy Figorelli, people used to call him Tommy Fig, Tommy Fingers, Tommy Five? Used to be a part-time meat cutter in a butcher shop on Louisiana Avenue? He got into trouble for something besides picking pockets, he molested a couple of little girls, and one of them turned out to be related to the Giacano family. So the word went out that Tommy Fig was anybody's fuck, but it wasn't supposed to be no ordinary hit, not for what he done. Did I ever tell you I worked in the kitchen up at Angola? That's right. So when Tommy got taken out, three guys done it, and when that butcher shop opened on Monday morning, it was the day before Christmas, see, Tommy was hung in parts, freeze-dried and clean, all over the shop like tree ornaments.

"That sounds sick, don't it, but the people who ran the shop didn't have no use for a child molester, either, and to show how they felt, they called up some guys from the Giacano family and they had a party with eggnog and fruitcake and music and Tommy Fig twirling around in pieces on the blades of the ceiling fan.

"What I'm saying, Lieutenant, is I ain't gonna get locked up as a material witness and I ain't going before no grand jury, I been that route before, eight months in the New Orleans city prison, with a half-dozen guys trying to whack me out, even though I was standup and was gonna take the fall for a couple of guys I wouldn't piss on if they was burning to death."

"You're sure Julie didn't catch up with Cherry LeBlanc later that same night?"

"It ain't his style. But then—" He poked his tongue into the space where his incisor tooth was broken off—"who knows what goes on in Julie's head? He had the hots for the LeBlanc broad real bad, and she knew how to kick a Coke bottle up his ass. Go to the movies, lieutenant, make up your own mind. Hey, but remember something, okay? I didn't have nothing to do with this movie shit. You seen my rap sheet. When maybe I done something to somebody, I ain't saying I did, the guy had it coming. The big word there is the *guy,* Lieutenant, you understand what I'm saying?"

I clicked my nails on the plastic cassette that rested on my thigh.

"A Lafayette detective named Lou Girard was killed last night. Did you hear anything about it?" I said.

"Who?" he said.

I said Lou's name again and watched Cholo's face.

"I never heard of him. Was he a friend of yours or something?"

"Yes, he was."

He yawned and watched two black children sailing a Frisbee on the gallery of the grocery store. Then the light of recognition worked its way into his eyes and he looked back at my face.

"Hey, Loot, old-time lesson from your days at the First District," he said. "Nobody, and I mean *nobody,* from the New Orleans families does a cop. The guy who pulls something like that ends up a lot worse than Tommy Fig. His parts come off while he's still living."

He nodded like a sage delivering a universal truth, then hawked, sucked the saliva out of his mouth, and spat a bloody clot out onto the shell.

• • •

A HALF HOUR later I closed the blinds in the sheriff's empty office and used his VCR to watch the cassette that Cholo had given me. Then I clicked it off, went to the men's room, rinsed my face in the lavatory, and dried it with paper towels.

"Something wrong, Dave?" a uniformed deputy standing at the urinal said.

"No, not really," I said. "I look like something's wrong?"

"There's some kind of stomach flu going around. I thought you might have a touch of it, that's all."

"No, I'm feeling fine, Harry."

"That's good," he said, and glanced away from my face.

I went back inside the sheriff's office, opened the blinds, and watched the traffic on the street, the wind bending the tops of some myrtle trees, a black kid riding his bike down the sidewalk with a fishing rod propped across his handlebars.

I thought of the liberals I knew who spoke in such a cavalier fashion about pornography, who dismissed it as inconsequential or who somehow associated its existence with the survival of the First Amendment. I wondered what they would have to say about the film I had just watched. I wondered how they would like a theater that showed it to be located in their neighborhoods; I wondered how they would like the patrons of that theater to be around their children.

Finally I called Rosie at her motel. I told her where I was.

"Cholo Manelli gave me a pornographic film that you need to know about," I said. "Evidently Julie has branched out into some dark stuff."

"What is it, what do you mean?"

"It's pretty sadistic, Rosie. It looks like the real thing, too."

"Can we connect it to Balboni?"

"I doubt if Cholo would ever testify, but maybe we can find some of the people who made the film."

"I'll be over in a few minutes."

"Rosie, I—"

"You don't think I'm up to looking at it?"

"I don't know that it'll serve any purpose."

"If you don't want to hang around, Dave, just stick the tape in my mailbox."

Twenty minutes later she came through the door in a pair of blue jeans, tennis shoes, and a short-sleeve denim shirt with purple and white flowers sewn on it. I closed the blinds again and started the film, except this time I used the fast-forward device to isolate the violent scenes and to get through it as quickly as possible.

When the screen went blank I pulled the blinds and filled the room with sunlight. Rosie sat very still and erect, her hands in her lap. Her nostrils were pinched when she breathed. Then she stood and looked out the window a moment.

"The beating of those girls . . . I've never seen anything like that," she said.

I heard her take a breath and let it out, then she turned back toward me.

"They weren't acting, were they?" she said.

"I don't think so. It's too convincing for a low-rent bunch like this."

"Dave, we've got to get these guys."

"We will, one way or another."

She took a Kleenex out of her purse and blew her nose. She blinked, and her eyes were shiny.

"Excuse me, I have hay fever today," she said.

"It's that kind of weather."

Then she had to turn and look out the window again. When she faced me again, her eyes had become impassive.

"What's the profit margin on a film like this?" she said.

"I've heard they make an ordinary porno movie for about five grand and get a six-figure return. I don't know about one like this."

"I'd like to lock up Cholo Manelli as a material witness."

"Even if we could do it, Rosie, it'd be a waste of time. Cholo's got the thinking powers of a cantaloupe but he doesn't roll over or cop pleas."

"You seem to say that almost with admiration."

"There're worse guys around."

"I have difficulty sharing your sympathies sometimes, Dave."

"Look, the film was made around New Orleans somewhere. Those were the docks in Algiers in the background. I'd like to make a copy and send it to N.O.P.D. Vice. They might recognize some of the players. This kind of stuff is their bailiwick, anyway."

"All right, let's get a print for the Bureau, too. Maybe Balboni's going across state lines with it." Then she picked up her purse and I saw a dark concern come into her face again.

"I'll buy you a drink," I said.

"Of what?"

"Whatever you like."

"I'm all right, Dave. We don't need to go to any bars."

"That's up to you. How about a Dr Pepper across the street or a spearmint snowball in the park?"

"That sounds nice."

We drove in my truck to the park. The sky was filling with afternoon rain clouds that had the bright sheen of steam. She tried to pretend that she was listening to my conversation, but her eyes seemed locked on a distant spot just above the horizon, as though perhaps she were staring through an inverted telescope at an old atrocity that was always a-borning at the wrong moment in her mind.

I HAD TRIED several times that day to pursue Hogman's peculiar implication about the type of work done by DeWitt Prejean, the chained black man I had seen shot down in the Atchafalaya marsh in 1957. But neither the Opelousas chief of police nor the St. Landry Parish sheriff knew anything that was helpful about DeWitt Prejean, and when I finally reached the old jailer at his house he hung up the phone on me as soon as he recognized my voice.

Late that afternoon the sleeplessness of the previous night finally caught up with me, and I lay down in the hammock that I had stretched between two shade trees on the edge of the coulee in the backyard. I closed my eyes and tried to listen to the sound of the water coursing over the rocks and to forget the images from Lou's apartment that seemed to live behind my eyelids like red paint slung from a brush. I could smell the ferns in the coulee, the networks of roots that trailed in the current, the cool odor of wet stone, the periwinkles that ruffled in the grass.

I had never thought of my coulee as a place where members of the Confederate Signal Corps would gather for a drink on a hot day. But out of the rain clouds and the smell of sulfur and the lightning that had already begun to flicker in the south, I watched the general descend, along with two junior officers, in the wicker basket of an observation balloon, one that looked sewn together from silk cuttings of a half-dozen colors. Five enlisted men moored the basket and balloon to the earth with ropes and helped the general down and handed him a crutch. By the mooring place were a table and chair and telegraph key with a long wire that was attached to the balloon's basket. The balloon tugged upward against its ropes and bobbled and shook in the wind that blew across my neighbor's sugarcane field.

One of the general's aides helped him to a canvas lawn chair by my hammock and then went away.

"*Magnificent, isn't it?*" he said.

"*It surely is,*" I said.

"*Ladies from all over Louisiana donated their silk dresses for the balloon. The wicker basket was made by an Italian pickle merchant in New Orleans. The view's extraordinary. In the next life I'm coming back as a bird. Would you like to take a ride up?*"

"*Not right now, thanks.*"

"*A bad day for it?*"

"*Another time, General.*"

"*You grieve for your friend?*"

"*Yes.*"

"*You plan revenge, don't you?*"

"*The Lafayette cops are putting it down as a suicide.*"

"*I want you to listen to me very carefully, lieutenant. No matter what occurs in your life, no matter how bad the circumstances seem to be, you must never consider a dishonorable act as a viable alternative.*"

"*The times you lived in were different, General. This afternoon I watched a film that showed young women being beaten and tortured, perhaps even killed, by sadists and degenerates. This stuff is sold in stores and shown in public theaters. The sonsofbitches who make it are seldom arrested unless they get nailed in a mail sting.*"

"*I'm not quite sure I follow all your allusions, but let me tell you of an experience we had three days ago. My standard-bearer was a boy of sixteen. He got caught in their crossfire in a fallow corn-*

field. There was no place for him to hide. He tried to surrender by waving his shirt over his head. They killed him anyway, whether intentionally or by accident, I don't know.

"By evening we retook the ground and recovered his body. It was torn by miniés as though wild dogs had chewed it. He was so thin you could count his bones with your fingers. In his haversack was his day's ration—a handful of black beans, some roasted acorns, and a dried sweet potato. That's the only food I could provide this boy who followed me unto the death. What do you think I felt toward those who killed him?"

"Maybe you were justified in your feelings."

"Yes, that's what I told myself throughout the night or when I remembered the bloodless glow that his skin gave off when we wrapped him for burial. Then an opportunity presented itself. From aloft in our balloon I looked down upon a copse of hackberry trees. Hard by a surgeon's tent a dozen federals were squatting along a latrine with their breeches down to their ankles. Two hundred yards up the bayou, unseen by any of them, was one of our boats with a twelve-pounder on its bow. I simply had to tap the order on the telegrapher's key and our gunners would have loaded with grape and raked those poor devils through their own excrement. But that's not our way, is it?"

"Speak for yourself."

"Your pretense as cynic is unconvincing."

"Let me ask you a question, General. The women who donated their dresses and petticoats

for your balloon . . . what if they were raped, sodomized, and methodically beaten and you got your hands on the men who did it to them?"

"They'd be arrested by my provost, tried in a provisional court, and hanged."

"You wouldn't find that the case today."

His long, narrow face was perplexed.

"Why not?" he said.

"I don't know. Maybe we have so much collective guilt as a society that we fear to punish our individual members."

He put his hat on the back of his head, crossed his good leg across his cork knee, and wet the end of a cheroot. Several of his enlisted men were kneeling by my coulee, filling their canteens. Their faces were dusty, their lips blackened with gunpowder from biting through cartridge papers. The patchwork silk balloon shuddered in the wind and shimmered with the silvery light of the coming rainstorm.

"I won't presume to be your conscience," the general said. *"But as your friend who wishes to see you do no harm to yourself, I advise you to give serious thought about keeping your dead friend's weapon."*

"I have."

"I think you're making a serious mistake, suh. You disappoint me, too."

He waved his hand impatiently at his aides, and they helped him to his feet.

"I'm sorry you feel that way," I said.

But the general was not one given to debate. He

stumped along on his crutch and cork leg toward the balloon's basket, his cigar clenched at an upward angle in his teeth, his eyes flicking about at the wind-torn clouds and the lightning that trembled whitely like heated wires out on the Gulf.

The incoming storm blew clouds of dust out of my neighbor's canefield just as the general's balloon lifted him and his aides aloft, their telegraph wire flopping from the wicker basket like an umbilical cord.

When I woke from my dream, the gray skies were filled with a dozen silken hot-air balloons, painted in the outrageous colors of circus wagons, their dim shadows streaking across barn roofs, dirt roads, clapboard houses, general stores, clumps of cows, winding bayous, until the balloons themselves were only distant specks above the summer-green horizon outside Lafayette.

CHAPTER 17

On Monday morning I went to Lou Girard's funeral in Lafayette. It was a boiling green-gold day. At the cemetery a layer of heat seemed to rise off the spongy grass and grow in intensity as the white sun climbed toward the top of the sky. During the graveside service someone was running a power mower behind the brick wall that separated the crypts from a subdivision. The mower coughed and backfired and echoed off the bricks like someone firing rounds from a small-caliber revolver. The eyes of the cops who stood at attention in full uniform kept watering from the heat and the smell of weed killer. When the police chief and a captain removed the flag from Lou's casket and folded it into a military square, there was no family member there to receive it. The casket remained closed during the ceremony. Before the casket was lowered into the ground, the department chaplain removed a framed picture of Lou in uniform from the top and set it on a folding table under the funeral canopy. Accidentally he tipped it with the back of his hand so that it fell face-down on the linen.

I DROVE BACK home for lunch before heading for the office. It was cool under the ceiling fan in the kitchen, and the breeze swayed the baskets of impatiens that hung on hooks from the eave of the back porch. Bootsie set a glass of iced tea with mint leaves and a plate of ham-and-onion sandwiches and deviled eggs in front of me.

"Where's Alafair?" I said.

"Elrod took her and Tripod out to Spanish Lake," she said from the sink.

"To the movie location?"

"Yes, I think so."

When I didn't speak, she turned around and looked at me.

"Did I do something wrong?" she asked.

"Julie Balboni's out there, Boots."

"He lives here now, Dave. He's lots of places. I don't think we should start choosing where we go and don't go because of a man like that."

"I don't want Alafair around him."

"I'm sorry. I didn't know you'd object."

"Boots, there's something I didn't tell you about. Saturday a hood named Cholo Manelli gave me a pornographic video that evidently Balboni and his people made. It's as dark as dark gets. There's one scene where it looks like a woman is actually beaten to death."

Her eyes blinked, then she said, "I'll go out to

Spanish Lake and bring her home. Why don't you finish eating?"

"Don't worry about it. There's no harm done. I'll go get her before I go to the office."

"Can't somebody do something about him?"

"When people make a contract with the devil and give him an air-conditioned office to work in, he doesn't go back home easily."

"Where did you get that piece of Puritan theology?"

"It's not funny. The morons on the Chamber of Commerce who brought this guy here would screw up the recipe for ice water."

I heard her laugh and walk around behind me. Then I felt her hands on my shoulders and her mouth kiss the top of my head.

"Dave, you're just too much," she said, and hugged me across the chest.

I LISTENED TO the news on the radio as I drove out to Spanish Lake. A tropical storm off Cuba was gaining hurricane status and was expected to turn northwest toward the Gulf Coast. I glanced to the south, but the sky was brassy and hot and virtually free of clouds. Then as I passed the little watermelon and fruit stand at the end of West Main and headed out into the parish, my radio filled with static and my engine began to misfire.

The truck jerked and sputtered all the way to the entrance of the movie location at the lake. I pulled off the dirt road onto the grass by the security building where Murphy Doucet worked and opened the hood. He stepped out the door in his gray uniform and bifocals.

"What's wrong, Dave?" he asked. His glasses had half-moons of light in them. His blue eyes jittered back and forth when he looked at me.

"It looks like a loose wire on the voltage regulator." I felt at my pants pocket. "Do you have a knife I could use?"

"Yeah, I ought to have something."

I followed him inside his office. His work table was covered with the balsa-wood parts of an amphibian airplane. In the middle of the blueprints was a utility knife with a detachable blade inset in the aluminum handle. But his hand passed over it and opened a drawer and removed a black-handled switchblade knife. He pushed the release button and the blade leaped open in his hand.

"This should do it," he said. "A Mexican pulled this on me in Lake Charles."

"I didn't know you were a cop in Lake Charles."

"I wasn't. I was out on the highway with the state police. That's what I retired from last year."

"Thanks for the loan of the knife."

I trimmed the insulation away from the end of the loose wire and reattached it to the voltage regulator, then returned the knife to Murphy Doucet and drove into the grove of oak trees by the lake. When I looked in the rearview mirror Doucet was watching me with an unlit cigarette in his mouth.

The cast and crew were just finishing lunch by the water's edge at picnic tables that were spread with checkered cloths and buckets of fried chicken, potato salad, dirty rice, cole slaw, and sweating plastic pitchers of iced tea and lemonade. Alafair sat on a wood bench in the shade, next to Elrod, the lake shimmering behind her. She was dressed like a nineteenth-century street urchin.

"What happened to your clothes?" I said.

"I'm in the movie, Dave!" she said. "In this scene with Hogman and Elrod. We're walking down the road with a plantation burning behind us and the Yankees are about to take over the town."

"I'm not kidding you, Dave," Elrod said. He wore a collarless gray shirt, officer's striped trousers, and black suspenders. "She's a natural. Mikey said the same thing. She looks good from any camera angle. We worked her right into the scene."

"What about Tripod?" I said.

"He's in it, too," Alafair said.

"You're kidding?"

"We're getting him a membership in the Screen Actors Guild," Elrod said.

Elrod poured a paper cup of iced tea for me. The wind blew leaves out of the trees and flapped the corners of the checkered table covers. For the first time that day I could smell salt in the air.

"This looks like the good life," I said.

"Don't be too quick to judge," Elrod said. "A healthy lifestyle in southern California means running three miles on the beach in the morning, eating bean sprouts all day, and shoving five hundred bucks' worth of coke up your nose at night."

The other actors began drifting away from the table to return to work. Tripod was on his chain, eating a drumstick by the trunk of a tree. On the grass next to him was a model of a German Messerschmitt, its wooden fuselage bright with silver paint, its red-edged iron crosses and Nazi swastikas as darkly beguiling as the light in a serpent's eye.

"I gave her that. I hope you didn't mind," Elrod said.

"Where'd you get it?"

"From Murph, up there at the security building. I'm afraid he thinks I can get him on making props for Mikey or something. I think he's kind of a lonely guy, isn't he?"

"I don't know much about him."

"Alafair, can you go find Hogman and tell him we need to do that scene again in about fifteen minutes?" Elrod said.

"Sure, El," she said, swung her legs over the bench, scooped Tripod over her shoulder, and ran off through the trees.

"Look, El, I appreciate your working Alafair into your movie, but frankly I don't want her out here as long as Julie Balboni's around."

"I thought you heard."

"What?"

"Mikey's filing Chapter Eleven bankruptcy. He's eighty-sixing the greaseballs out of the corporation. The last thing those guys want is the court examining their finances. He told off Balboni this morning in front of the whole crew."

"What do you mean he told him off?"

"He said Balboni was never going to put a hand on one of Mikey's people again. He told him to take his porno actor and his hoods and his bimbos and haul his ass back to New Orleans. I was really proud of Mikey. . . . What's the matter?"

"What did Julie have to say?"

"He cleaned his fingernails with a toothpick, then walked out to the lake and started talking to somebody on his cellular phone and skipping rocks across the water at the ducks."

"Where is he now?"

"He drove off with his whole crew in his limo."

"I'd like to talk with Mr. Goldman."

"He's on the other side of the lake."

"Ask him to call me, will you? If he doesn't catch me at the office, he can call me at home tonight."

"He'll be back in a few minutes to shoot the scene with me and Hogman and Alafair."

"We're not going to be here for it."

"You won't let her be in the film?"

"Nobody humiliates Julie Balboni in front of other people, El. I don't know what he's going to do, but I don't want Alafair here when he does it."

The wind had turned out of the south and was blowing hotly through the trees when we walked back toward my truck. The air smelled like fish spawning, and clouds with the dark convolutions of newly opened purple roses were massing in a long, low humped line on the southern horizon.

LATER, AFTER I had taken Alafair home and checked in at the office, I drove to Opelousas to talk once again with the old jailer Ben Hebert. A black man raking leaves in Hebert's yard told me where I could find him on a bayou just outside of town.

He sat on top of an inverted plastic bucket under a tree, his cane pole extended out into the sunlight, his red bobber drifting on the edge of the reeds. He wore a crushed straw hat on the side of his head and smoked a hand-rolled saliva-soaked cigarette without removing it from the corner of his mouth. The layers of white fat on his hips and stomach protruded between his shirt and khakis like lard curling over the edges of a washtub.

Ten feet down from him a middle-aged mulatto woman with a small round head, a perforated dime tied on her ankle, was also fishing as she sat on top of an inverted bucket. The ground around her was strewn with empty beer cans. She spit snuff to one side and jigged her line up and down through a torn hole in a lily pad.

Ben Hebert pitched his cigarette out onto the current, where it hissed and turned in a brown eddy.

"Why you keep bothering me?" he said. There was beer on his breath and an eye-watering smell in his clothes that was like both dried sweat and urine.

"I need to know what kind of work DeWitt Prejean did," I said.

"You what?" His lips were as purple as though they had been painted, his teeth small and yellow as pieces of corn.

"Just what I said."

"You leave me the hell alone."

I sat down on the grass by the edge of the slope.

"It's not my intention to bother you, Mr. Hebert," I said. "But you're refusing to cooperate with a police investigation and you're creating problems for both of us."

"He done . . . I don't know what he done. What difference does it make?" His eyes glanced sideways at the mulatto woman.

"You seem to have a good memory for detail. Why not about DeWitt Prejean?"

The woman rose from her seat on the bucket and walked farther down the bank, trailing her cork bobber in the water.

"He done nigger work," Hebert said. "He cut lawns, cleaned out grease traps, got dead rats out from under people's houses. What the fuck you think he did?"

"That doesn't sound right to me. I think he did some other kind of work, too."

His nostrils were dilated, as though a bad odor were rising from his own lap.

"He was in bed with a white woman here. Is that what you want to know?"

"Which woman?"

"I done tole you. The wife of a cripple-man got shot up in the war."

"He raped her?"

"Who gives a shit?"

"But the crippled man didn't break Prejean out of jail, Mr. Hebert."

"It wasn't the first time that nigger got in trouble over white women. There's more than one man wanted to see him put over a fire."

"Who broke him out?"

"I don't know and I don't care."

"Mr. Hebert, you're probably a good judge of people. Do I look like I'm just going to go away?"

The skin of his chest was sickly white, and under it were nests of green veins.

"It was better back then," he said. "You know it was."

"What kind of work did he do, Ben?"

"Drove a truck."

"For whom?"

"It was down in Lafayette. He worked for a white man there till he come up here. Don't know nothing about the white man. You saying I do, then you're a goddamn liar." He leaned over to look past me at the mulatto woman, who was fishing among a group of willows now. Then his face snapped back at me. "I brung her out here 'cause she works for me. 'Cause I can't get in and out of the car good by myself."

"What kind of truck did he drive?" I asked.

"Beer truck. No, that wasn't it. Soda pop. Sonofabitch had a soda-pop truck route when white people was making four dollars a day in the rice field." He set down his cane pole and began rolling a cigarette. His fingernails looked as thick and horned as tortoiseshell against the thin white square of paper into which he poured tobacco. His fingers trembled almost uncontrollably with anger and defeat.

• • •

I DROVE TO Twinky Lemoyne's bottling works in Lafayette, but it was closed for the day. Twenty minutes later I found Lemoyne working in his yard at home. The sky was the pink of salmon eggs, and the wind thrashed the banana and lime trees along the side of his house. He had stopped pruning the roses on his trellis and had dropped his shears in the baggy back pocket of his faded denim work pants.

"A lot of bad things happened back in that era between the races. But we're not the same people we used to be, are we?" he said.

"I think we are."

"You seem unable to let the past rest, sir."

"My experience has been that you let go of the past by addressing it, Mr. Lemoyne."

"For some reason I have the feeling that you want me to confirm what so far are only speculations on your part." There were tiny pieces of grit in his combed sandy hair and a film of perspiration and rose dust on his glasses.

"Read it like you want. But somehow my investigation keeps winding its way back to your front door."

He began snipping roses again and placing them stem down in a milk bottle full of green water. His two-story peaked white house in an old residential neighborhood off St. Mary Boulevard in Lafayette was surrounded by spectacular moss-hung oak trees and walls of bamboo and soft pink brick.

"Should I call my lawyer? Is that what you're suggesting?"

"You can if you want to. I don't think it'll solve your problem, though."

"I beg your pardon." His shears hung motionlessly over a rose.

"I think you committed a murder back in 1957, but in all probability you don't have the psychology of a killer. That means that you probably live with an awful guilt, Mr. Lemoyne. You go to bed with it and you wake with it. You drag it around all day long like a clanking chain."

"Why is it that you seem to have this fixation about me? At first you accused me of being involved with a New Orleans gangster. Now this business about the murdered Negro."

"I saw you do it."

His egg-shaped face was absolutely still. Blood pooled in his cheeks like pink flowers.

"I was only nineteen," I said. "I watched y'all from across the bay. The black man tried to run, and one of you shot him in the leg, then continued shooting him in the water. You didn't even think me worthy of notice, did you? You were right, too. No one ever paid much attention to my story. That was a hard lesson for a nineteen-year-old."

He closed the shears, locked the clasp on the handles, and set them down on a glass-topped patio table. He poured two inches of whiskey into a glass with no ice and squeezed a lemon into it. He seemed as solitary as a man might who had lived alone all his life.

"Would you care for one?" he said.

"No, thank you."

"I have high blood pressure and shouldn't drink, but I put lemon in it and convince myself that I'm drinking something healthy along with the alcohol. It's my little joke with myself." He took a deep breath.

"You want to tell me about it?"

"I don't think so. Am I under arrest?"

"Not right now. But I think that's the least of your problems."

"You bewilder me, sir."

"You're partners in a security service with Murphy Doucet. A fellow like that doesn't fit in the same shoe box with you."

"He's an ex–police officer. He has the background that I don't."

"He's a resentful and angry man. He's also anti-Semitic. One of your black employees told me you're good to people of color. Why would a man such as yourself go into business with a bigot?"

"He's uneducated. That doesn't mean he's a bad person."

"I believe he's been blackmailing you, Mr. Lemoyne. I believe he was the other white man I saw across the bay with DeWitt Prejean."

"You can believe whatever you wish."

"We still haven't gotten to what's really troubling you, though, have we? It's those young women, isn't it?"

His eyes closed and opened, and then he looked away at the south where lightning was forking into the Gulf and the sky looked like it was covered with the yellow-black smoke from a chemical fire.

"I don't . . . I don't . . ." he began, then finished his whiskey and set his glass down. He wiped at the wet ring with the flat of his hand as though he wanted to scrub it out of the tabletop.

"That day you stopped me out under the trees at the lake," I said, "you wanted assurance that it was somebody else, somebody you don't know, who mutilated and killed those girls, didn't you? You didn't want that sin on your conscience as well as Prejean's murder."

"My God, man, give some thought to what you're saying. You're telling me I'm responsible for a fiend being loose in our midst."

"Call your attorney and come into the office and make a statement. End it now, Mr. Lemoyne. You'll probably get off with minimum time on Prejean's death. You've got a good reputation and a lot of friends. You might even walk."

"Please leave."

"It won't change anything."

He turned away from me and gazed at the approaching storm. Leaves exploded out of the trees that towered above his garden walls.

"Go do what you have to do, but right now please respect my privacy," he said.

"You strayed out of the gentleman's world a long time ago."

"Don't you have any sense of mercy?"

"Maybe you should come down to my office and look at the morgue photographs of Cherry LeBlanc and a girl we pried out of an oil barrel down in Vermilion Parish."

He didn't answer. As I let myself out his garden gate I glanced back at him. His cheeks were red and streaked with moisture as though his face had been glazed by freezing winds.

THAT EVENING THE weatherman said the hurricane had become stationary one hundred miles due south of Mobile. As I fell asleep later with the window open on a lightning-charged sky, I thought surely the electricity would bring the general back in my dreams.

Instead, it was Lou Girard who stood under the wind-tormented pecan trees at three in the morning, his jaw shot away at the hinge, a sliver of white bone protruding from a flap of skin by his ear.

He tried to speak, and spittle gurgled on his exposed teeth and tongue and dripped off the point of his chin.

"What is it, Lou?"

The wind whipped and molded his shapeless brown suit against his body. He picked up a long stick that had been blown out of the tree above him and began scratching lines in the layers of dead leaves and pecan husks at his feet. He made an *S*, and then drew a straight line like an *I*, and then put a half bubble on it and turned it into a *P*.

He dropped the stick to the ground and stared at me, his deformed face filled with expectation.

CHAPTER 18

THE CONNECTION HAD been there all along. I just hadn't looked in the right place. As soon as I went into the office at 8 A.M. the next morning I called the probation and parole officer in Lafayette and asked the supervising P.O. to pull the file on Cherry LeBlanc.

"Who busted her on the prostitution charge?" I said.

I heard him leafing back and forth through the pages in the file.

"It wasn't one officer. There was a state-police raid on a bar and some trailers out on the Breaux Bridge highway."

S.P. Yes, the state police. Thanks, Lou, old friend.

"Who signed the arrest report?" I asked.

"Let's see. It's pretty hard to read. Somebody set a coffee cup down on the signature."

"It's real important, partner."

"It could be Doucet. Wasn't there a state policeman around here by that name? Yeah, I'd say initial M., then Doucet."

"Can you make copies of her file and lock them in separate places?"

"What's going on?"

"It may become evidence."

"No, I mean Lou Girard was looking at her file last week. What's the deal?"

"Do this for me, will you? If anybody else tries to get his hands on that file, you call me, okay?"

"There's an implication here that I think you should clarify."

Outside, the skies were gray, and dust and pieces of paper were blowing in the street.

"Maybe we have a fireman setting fires," I said.

He was quiet a moment, then he said, "I'll lock up the file for you, detective, and I'll keep your call confidential. But since this may involve a reflection on our office, I expect a little more in the way of detailed information from you in the next few days."

After I hung up, I opened my desk drawer and took out the black-and-white photograph that Cholo Manelli had given me of Cherry LeBlanc and Julie Balboni at the beach in Biloxi. I looked again at the man who was reading a newspaper at another table. His face was beyond the field of focus in the picture, but the light had struck his glasses in such a way that it looked as if there were chips of crystal where his eyes should have been, and my guess was that he was wearing bifocals.

As with most police investigations, the problem had now become one of the time lag between the approaching conclusion of an investigation and the actual arrest of a suspect. It's a peculiar two-way street that both cops and criminals live on. As a cop grows in certainty about the guilt of a suspect and begins to put enough evidence together to make his case, the suspect usually becomes equally aware of the impending denouement and concludes that midsummer isn't a bad time to visit Phoenix after all.

The supervising P.O. in Lafayette now knew my suspicions about Doucet, so did Twinky Hebert Lemoyne, and it wouldn't be long before Doucet did, too.

The other problem was that so far all the evidence was circumstantial.

When Rosie came in I told her everything I had.

"Do you think Lemoyne will make a confession?" she said.

"He might eventually. It's obvious he's a tormented man."

"Because I don't think you'll ever get an indictment on the lynching unless he does."

"I want to get a search warrant and toss everything Doucet owns, starting with the security building out at Spanish Lake."

"Okay, Dave, but let me be honest with you. So far I think what we've got is pretty thin."

"I didn't tell you something else. I already checked Doucet's name through motor vehicle registration in Baton Rouge. He owns a blue 1989 Mercury. I'll bet that's the car that's been showing up through the whole investigation."

"We still don't have enough to start talking to a prosecutor, though, do we?"

"That's what a search warrant is for."

"What I'm trying to say is we don't have witnesses, Dave. We're going to need some hard forensic evidence—a murder weapon, clothing from one of the victims—something that will leave no doubt in a jury's mind that this guy is a creature out of their worst nightmares. I just hope Doucet hasn't already talked to Lemoyne and gotten rid of everything we could use against him, provided there is anything."

"We'll soon find out."

She measured me carefully with her eyes.

"You seem a little more confident than you should be," she said.

"It all fits, Rosie. A black pimp in the New Orleans bus depot told me about a white man selling dirty pictures. I thought he was talking about photographs or postcards. Don't you see it? Doucet's probably been delivering girls to Balboni's pornographic film operation."

"The only direct tie that we have is the fact that Doucet arrested Cherry LeBlanc."

"Right. And even though he knew I was investigating her murder, he never mentioned it, did he? He wasn't even curious about how the investigation was going. Does that seem reasonable to you?"

"Well, let's get the warrant and see what Mr. Doucet has to say to us this morning."

We had it in thirty minutes and were on our way out of the office when my extension rang. It was Bootsie. She said she was going to town to buy candles and tape for the windows in case the hurricane turned in to the coast and I would find lunch for me and Alafair in the oven.

Then she said, "Dave, did you leave the house last night?"

"Just a second," I said, and took the receiver away from my ear. "Rosie, I'll be along in just a minute."

Rosie went out the door and bent over the water cooler.

"I'm sorry, what did you say?"

"I thought I heard your truck start up in the middle of the night. Then I thought I just dreamed it. Did I just dream it?"

"I had to take care of something. I left a note on the lamp for you in case you woke up, but you were sound asleep when I came back."

"What are you doing, Dave?"

"Nothing. I'll tell you about it later."

"Is it those apparitions in the marsh again?"

"No, of course not."

"Dave?"

"It's nothing to worry about. Believe me."

"I *am* worried if you have to conceal something from me."

"Let's go out to eat tonight."

"I think we'd better have a talk first."

"A very bad guy is about to go off the board. That's what it amounts to. I'll explain it later."

"Does the sheriff know what you're doing?"

"He didn't ask. Come on, Boots. Let's don't be this way."

"Whatever you say. I'm sorry I asked. Everybody's husband goes in and out of the house in the middle of the night. I'll see you this afternoon."

She hung up before I could speak again; but in truth I didn't know how to explain to her the feelings I had that morning. If Murphy Doucet was our serial killer, and I believed he was, then with a little luck we were about to throw a steel net over one of those pathological and malformed individuals who ferret their way among us, occasionally for a lifetime, and leave behind a trail of suffering whose severity can only be appreciated by the survivors who futilely seek explanations for their loss the rest of their lives.

I lost my wife Annie to two such men. A therapist told me that I would never have any peace until I learned to forgive not only myself for her death but the human race as well for producing the men who killed her. I didn't know what he meant until several months later when I remembered an event that occurred on a winter afternoon when I was seven years old and I had returned home early, unexpectedly, from school.

My mother was not at work at the Tabasco bottling plant, where she should have been. Instead, I looked from the hallway through the bedroom door and saw a man's candy-striped shirt, suspenders, and sharkskin zoot slacks and panama hat hung on the bedpost, his socks sticking out of his two-tone shoes on the floor. My mother was naked, on all fours, on top of the bedspread, and the man, whose name was Mack, was about to mount her. A cypress plank creaked under my foot, and Mack twisted his head and looked at me, his pencil mustache like a bird's wings above his lip. Then he entered my mother.

For months I had dreams about a white wolf who lived in a skeletal black tree on an infinite white landscape. At the base of the tree was a nest of pups. In the dream the wolf would drop to the ground, her teats sagging with milk, and eat her young one by one.

I would deliberately miss the school bus in the afternoon and hang around the playground until the last kids took their footballs or kites and walked off through the dusk and dead leaves toward lighted houses and the sound of *Jack Armstrong* or *Terry and the Pirates* through a screen door. When my father returned home from trapping on Marsh Island, I never told him what I had seen take place in their bedroom. When they fought at night, I sat on the back steps and watched the sugarcane stubble burning in the fields. The fires looked like thousands of red handkerchiefs twisting in the smoke.

I knew the wolf waited for me in my dreams.

Then one afternoon, when I started walking home late from school, I passed an open door in the back of the convent. It was the music room, and it had a piano in it, a record player, and a polished oak floor. But the two young nuns who were supposed to be waxing the floor had set aside their mops and rags, turned on a radio, and were jitterbugging with each other in their bare feet, their veils flying, their wooden rosary beads swirling on their waists.

They didn't see me, and I must have watched them for almost five minutes, fascinated with their flushed faces inside their wimples and the laughter that they tried to hide behind their hands when it got too loud.

I could not explain it to myself, but I knew each night thereafter that if I thought of the dancing nuns before I fell asleep, I would not dream about the white wolf in the tree.

I wondered what kind of dreams Murphy Doucet had. Maybe at one time they were the same as mine. Or maybe it was better not to know.

I had no doubt, though, that he was ready for us when we arrived at the security building at Spanish Lake. He stood with his legs slightly spread, as though at parade rest, in front of the door, his hands propped on his gunbelt, his stomach flat as a plank, his eyes glinting with a cynical light.

I unfolded the search warrant in front of him.

"You want to look it over?" I said.

"What for? I don't give a good fuck what y'all do here," he replied.

"I'd appreciate it if you'd watch your language," I said.

"She can't handle it?" he said.

"Stand over by my truck until we're finished," I said.

"What do you think y'all gonna find?" he said.

"You never know, Murph. You were a cop. People get careless sometimes, mess up in a serious way, maybe even forget they had their picture taken with one of their victims."

Tiny webs of brown lines spread from the corners of his eyes.

"What are you talking about?"

"If I'd been you, I wouldn't have let Cholo take my picture with Baby Feet and Cherry LeBlanc over in Biloxi."

His blue eyes shuttered back and forth; the pupils looked like black pinheads. The point of his tongue licked across his bottom lip.

"I don't want *her* in my stuff," he said.

"Would you like to prevent me from getting in your 'stuff,' Mr. Doucet?" Rosie said. "Would you like to be charged this morning with interfering with a federal officer in the performance of her duty?"

Without ever removing his eyes from her face, he lifted a Lucky Strike with two fingers from the pack in his shirt pocket and put it in the corner of his mouth. Then he leaned back against my truck, shook open his Zippo lighter, cupped the flame in his hands, sucked in on the smoke, and looked away at the pecan trees bending and straightening in the wind and an apple basket bouncing crazily across a field.

On his work table were a set of X-Acto knives, tubes of glue, small bottles of paint, tiny brushes, pieces of used sandpaper, and the delicate balsawood wing struts of a model airplane pinned to a blueprint. Outside, Doucet smoked his cigarette and watched us through the door and showed no expression or interest when I dropped his X-Acto knives into a Ziploc bag.

His desk drawers contained *Playboy* magazines, candy wrappers, a carton of Lucky Strikes, a thermos of split pea soup, two ham sandwiches, paper clips, eraser filings, a brochure advertising a Teamster convention in Atlantic City, a package of condoms.

I opened the drawer of his work table. In it were more sheets of sandpaper, an unopened model airplane kit, and the black-handled switchblade knife he had lent me to trim back the insulation on an electrical wire in my truck. I put it in another Ziploc bag.

Doucet yawned.

"Rosie, would you kick over that trash basket behind his desk, please?" I said.

"There's nothing in it," she said, leaning over the corner of the desk.

My back was turned to both her and Doucet when I closed the drawer to the work table and turned around with an aluminum-handled utility knife in my fingers. I dropped it into a third plastic bag.

"Well, I guess this covers it," I said.

Through the door I saw his hand with the cigarette stop in midair and his eyes lock on the utility knife.

He stepped toward us as we came out of the building.

"What do you think you're doing?" he said.

"You have a problem with something that happened here?" I said.

"You planted that," he said, pointing at the bag with the utility knife in it. "You sonofabitch, you planted it, you know you did."

"How could I plant something that belongs to you?" I said. "This is one of the tools you use on your airplane models, isn't it?"

Rosie was looking at me strangely.

"This woman's a witness," he said. "You're salting the shaft. That knife wasn't there."

"I say it was. I say your fingerprints are all over it, too. It's probably going to be hard to prove it's not yours, Murph."

"This pepper-belly bitch is in on it, isn't she?" he said.

I tapped him on the cheek with the flat of my hand. "You say anything else, your day is going to deteriorate in a serious way," I said.

Mistake.

He leaped into my face, his left hand like a claw in my eyes, his right fist flailing at my head, his knees jerking at my groin. I lost my balance, tried to turn away from him and raise my arm in front of my face; his fists rained down on the crown of my skull.

Rosie pulled her .357 from her purse, extended it straight out with both hands, and pointed the barrel into his ear.

"Down on the ground, you understand me?" she shouted. "Do it! Now! Don't look at me! Get your face on the ground! Did you hear me? Don't look at me! Put your hands behind your head!"

He went to his knees, then lay prone with the

side of his face in the grass, his lined, deeply tanned neck oozing sweat, his eyes filled with the mindless light that an animal's might have if it were pinned under an automobile tire.

I slipped my handcuffs from the back of my belt and snipped them onto his wrists. I pulled his revolver and can of Mace from his gunbelt, then raised him to his feet. His arm felt like bone in my hand.

"You're under arrest for assaulting an officer of the law, Murph," I said.

He turned toward me. The top button of his shirt was torn and I could see white lumps of scar tissue on his chest like fingers on a broken hand.

"It won't stick. You've got a bum warrant," he said.

"That knife is the one you used on Cherry LeBlanc, isn't it?" I said.

Rosie walked behind me into his office and used his phone to call for a sheriff's car. His eyes watched her, then came back onto me. He blew pieces of grass out of his mouth.

"She let you muff her?" he said.

We brought him in through the back door of the sheriff's department, fingerprinted and booked him, let him make a phone call to an attorney in Lafayette, then took him down to our interrogation room. Personnel from all over the building were finding ways to get a look at Murphy Doucet.

"You people get back to work," the sheriff said in the hallway. "This man is in for assaulting an officer. That's all he's charged with. Have y'all got that?"

"There's three news guys outside your office, sheriff," a deputy said.

"I'd like to know who called them down here, please," he said.

"Search me," the deputy said.

"Will you people get out of here?" he said again to the crowd in the hall. Then he pushed his fingers through his hair and turned to me and Rosie. "I've got to talk to these reporters before they break a Jack the Ripper story on us. Get what you can from this guy and I'll be right back. Who's his lawyer?"

"Jeb Bonin," I said.

"We'll still have Doucet till his arraignment in the morning. When are y'all going to search his place?"

"This afternoon," Rosie said. "We already sent a deputy over there to sit on it for us."

"Was the blue Merc out at Spanish Lake?" the sheriff said.

"No, he drives a pickup to work. The Merc must be at his house," I said.

"All right, get on it. Do it by the numbers, too. We don't want to blow this one."

The sheriff walked back toward his office. Rosie touched me lightly on the arm.

"Dave, talk with me a second before we go inside," she said.

"What is it?"

She didn't reply. She went inside our office and waited for me.

"That utility knife you took out of his drawer,"

she said. "He was completely surprised when you found it. That presents a troubling thought for me."

"It's his knife, Rosie. There's no question about it."

"Why was he so confident up until that moment?"

"Maybe he just forgot he'd left it there."

"You got into that security building during the night, removed the knife, then replaced it this morning, didn't you?"

"Time's always on the perp's side, Rosie. While we wait on warrants, they deep-six the evidence."

"I don't like what I'm hearing you say, Dave."

"This is our guy. You want him to walk? Because without that knife, he's sure going to do it."

"I see it differently. You break the rules, you arm the other side."

"Wait till you meet his lawyer. He's the best in southwest Louisiana. He also peddles his ass to the Teamsters, the mob, and incinerator outfits that burn PCBs. Before he's finished, he'll turn Doucet into a victim and have the jury slobbering on their sleeves."

Her eyes went back and forth thoughtfully, as though she were asking herself questions and answering them. Then she raised her chin.

"Don't ever do anything like this again, Dave. Not while we're partners," she said, and walked past me and into the interrogation room, where Murphy Doucet sat in a straight-backed chair at a small table, surrounded by white walls, wreathed in cigarette smoke, scratching at whiskers that grew along the edges of the white chicken's foot embossed on his throat.

I stepped inside the room behind Rosie and closed the door.

"Where's my lawyer at?" he asked.

I took the cigarette from his fingers and mashed it out on the floor.

"You want to make a statement about Cherry LeBlanc?" I said.

"Yeah. I've given it some thought. I remember busting a whore by that name three years ago. So now y'all can tell me why I'd wait three years to kill somebody who'd been in my custody."

"We think you're a pimp for Julie Balboni, Mr. Doucet," Rosie said. "We also think you're supplying girls for his pornography operation."

His eyes went up and down her body.

"Affirmative action?" he said.

"There's something else you don't know about, Murph," I said. "We're checking all the unsolved murders of females in areas around highways during the time you were working for the state police. I have a feeling those old logs are going to put you in the vicinity of some bodies you never thought would be connected to you."

"I don't believe this," he said.

"I think we've got you dead-bang," I said.

"You've got a planted knife. This girl here knows it, too. Look at her face."

"We've not only got the weapon and the photo of you with the victim, we know how it happened and why."

"What?"

"Cherry LeBlanc told Julie he was a tub of guts and walked out on him. But people don't just walk out on Julie. So he got on the phone and called you up from the motel, didn't he, Murph? You remember that conversation? Would you like me to quote it to you?"

His eyebrows contracted, then his hand went into his pocket for a cigarette.

"No. You can't smoke in here," I said.

"I got to use the can."

"It's unavailable now," I said.

"*She's* here for another reason. It ain't because of a dead hooker," he said.

"We're all here because of you, Murph. You're going down hard, partner. We haven't even started to talk about Kelly Drummond yet."

He bit a piece of skin off the ball of his thumb.

"What's the bounce on the pimp beef?" he said.

"You think you're going to cop to a procuring charge when you're looking at the chair? What world are you living in?" I said.

"Ask her. She's here to make a case on Balboni, not a security guard, so clean the shit out of your mouth. What kind of bounce am I looking at?"

"Mr. Doucet, you're looking at several thousand volts of electricity cooking your insides. Does that clarify your situation for you?" Rosie said.

He looked into her face.

"Go tell your boss I can put that guinea away for twenty-seven years," he said. "Then come back and tell me y'all aren't interested in a deal."

The sheriff opened the door.

"His lawyer's here," he said.

"We're going to your house now, Murph," I said. "Is there anything else you want to tell us before we leave?"

The attorney stepped inside the room. He wore his hair shaved to the scalp, and his tie and shirt collar rode up high on his short neck so that he reminded you of a light-brown hard-boiled egg stuffed inside a business suit.

"Don't say anything more to these people, Mr. Doucet," he said.

I leaned on the table and stared into Murphy Doucet's face. I stared at his white eyebrows, the jittering of his eyeballs, the myriad lines in his skin, the slit of a mouth, the white scar on his throat that could have been layered there with a putty knife.

"What? What the fuck you staring at?" he said.

"Do you remember me?" I said.

"Yeah. Of course. When you were a cop in New Orleans."

"Look at me. Think hard."

His eyes flicked away from my face, fastened on his attorney.

"I don't know what he's talking about," he said.

"Do you have a point, Detective?" the attorney said.

"Your hired oil can doesn't have anything to do with this, Murph," I said. "It's between me and you now. It's 1957, right after Hurricane Audrey hit. You could smell dead animals all over the marsh. You remember? Y'all made DeWitt Prejean run with a chain locked around his chest, then you blew his leg out from under him. Remember the kid who saw it from across the bay? Look at my face."

He bit down on his lip, then fitted his chin on top of his knuckles and stared disjointedly at the wall.

"The old jailer gave you guys away when he told me that DeWitt Prejean used to drive a soda-pop truck. Prejean worked for Twinky Lemoyne and had an affair with his wife, didn't he? It seems like there's always one guy still hanging around who remembers more than he should," I said. "You still think you're in a seller's market, Murph? How long do you think it's going to be before a guy like Twinky cracks and decides to wash his sins in public?"

"Don't say anything, Mr. Doucet," the attorney said.

"He doesn't have to, Mr. Bonin," I said. "This guy has been killing people for thirty-five years. If I were you, I'd have some serious reservations about an ongoing relationship with your client. Come on, Rosie."

THE WIND SWIRLED dust and grit between the cars in the parking lot, and I could smell rain in the south.

"That was Academy Award stuff, Dave," Rosie said as we got in my truck.

"It doesn't hurt to make the batter flinch once in a while."

"You did more than that. You should have seen the lawyer's face when you started talking about the lynching."

"He's not the kind who's in it for the long haul."

As I started the truck a gust of wind sent a garbage can clattering down the sidewalk and blew through the oak grove across the street. A solitary shaft of sunlight broke from the clouds and fell through the canopy, and in a cascade of gold leaves I thought I saw a line of horsemen among the tree trunks, their bodies as gray as stone, their shoulders and their horses' rumps draped with flowing tunics. I pinched the sweat out of my eyes against the bridge of my nose and looked again. The grove was empty except for a black man who was putting strips of tape across the windows of his barbecue stand.

"Dave?" Rosie said.

"Yes?"

"Are you all right?"

"I just got a piece of dirt in my eye."

When we pulled out on the street I looked into the rearview mirror and saw the detailed image of a lone horseman deep in the trees, a plum-colored plume in his hat, a carbine propped on his thigh. He pushed up the brim of his hat with his gun barrel and I saw that his face was pale and siphoned of all energy and the black sling that held his left arm was sodden with blood.

"What has opened your wounds, General?"

"What'd you say?" Rosie asked.

"Nothing. I didn't say anything."

"You're worried about what Doucet said, aren't you?"

"I'm not following you."

"You think the Bureau might cut a deal with him."

"It crossed my mind."

"This guy's going down, Dave. I promise you."

"I've made a career of discovering that my priorities aren't the same as those of the people I work for, Rosie. Sometimes the worst ones walk and cops help them do it."

She looked out the side window, and now it was she whose face seemed lost in an abiding memory or dark concern that perhaps she could never adequately share with anyone.

Murphy Doucet lived in a small freshly painted white house with a gallery and a raked, tree-shaded lawn across from the golf course on the north side of Lafayette. A bored Iberia Parish deputy and a Lafayette city cop sat on the steps waiting for us, flipping a pocket knife into the lawn. The blue Mercury was parked in the driveway under a chinaberry tree. I unlocked it with the key ring we had taken from Doucet when he was booked; then we pulled out the floor mats, laid them carefully on the grass, searched under the seats, and cleaned out the glove box. None of it was of any apparent value. We picked up the floor mats by the corners, replaced them on the rugs, and unlocked the trunk.

Rosie stepped back from the odor and coughed into her hand.

"Oh, Dave, it's—" she began.

"Feces," I said.

The trunk was bare except for a spare tire, a jack, and a small cardboard carton in one corner. The dark blue rug looked clean, vacuumed or brushed, but twelve inches back from the latch was a dried, tea-colored stain with tiny particles of paper towel embedded in the stiffened fabric.

I took out the cardboard carton, opened the top, and removed a portable spotlight with an extension cord that could be plugged into a cigarette lighter.

"This is what he wrapped the red cellophane around when he picked up the girl hitchhiking down in Vermilion Parish," I said.

"Dave, look at this."

She pointed toward the side wall of the trunk. There were a half-dozen black curlicues scotched against the pale blue paint. She felt one of them with two fingers, then rubbed her thumb against the ends of the fingers.

"I think they're rubber heel marks," she said. "What kind of shoes was Cherry LeBlanc wearing?"

"Flats with leather soles. And the dead girl in Vermilion didn't have on anything."

"All right, let's get it towed in and start on the house. We really need—"

"What?"

"Whatever he got careless about and left lying around."

"Did you call the Bureau yet?"

"No. Why?"

"I was just wondering."

"What are you trying to say, Dave?"

"If you want a handprint set in blood to make our case, I don't think it's going to happen. Not unless there's some residue on that utility knife we can use for a DNA match. The photograph is a bluff, at least as far as indicting Doucet is concerned. Like you said earlier, everything else we've got so far isn't real strong."

"So?"

"I think you already know what your boss is going to tell you."

"Maybe I don't care what he says."

"I don't want you impairing your career with Fart, Barf, and Itch because you think you have to be hard-nosed on my account, Rosie. Let's be clear on that."

"Cover your own butt and don't worry about mine," she said, took the key ring out of my hand, and walked ahead of me up the front steps of the house and unlocked the door.

The interior was as neat and squared away as a military barracks. The wood floors were waxed, the stuffed chairs decorated with doilies, the window plants trimmed and watered, the kitchen sink and drainboards immaculate, the pots and pans hung on hooks, the wastebaskets fitted with clean plastic liners, his model planes dusted and suspended on wires from the bedroom ceiling, his bedspread tucked and stretched so tightly that you could bounce a quarter off it.

None of the pictures on the walls dealt with human subjects, except one color photograph of himself sitting on the steps of a cabin with a dead eight-point deer at his feet. Doucet was smiling; a bolt-action rifle with iron sights and a sling lay across his lap.

We searched the house for an hour, searched the garage, then came back and tossed the house again. The Iberia Parish deputy walked through the front door with an ice-cream cone in his hand. He was a dark-haired, narrow-shouldered, wide-hipped man who had spent most of his five years with the department as a crosswalk guard at elementary schools or escorting misdemeanor prisoners to morning arraignment. He stopped eating and wiped the cream out of his mustache with the back of his wrist before he spoke.

"Jesus Christ, Dave, y'all tore the place apart," he said.

"You want to stay behind and clean it up?" I said.

"Y'all the ones done it, not me."

"That's right, so you don't have to worry about it," I said.

"Boy, somebody didn't get enough sleep last night," he said. When I didn't answer he walked into the center of the room. "What y'all found in that trunk?"

When I still didn't answer, he peered over my shoulder.

"Oh man, that's a bunch of little girls' underwear, ain't it?" he said.

"Yes, it is," I said.

The deputy cleared his throat.

"That fella been doin' that kind of stuff, too, Dave?"

"It looks like it."

"Oh, man," he said. Then his face changed. "Maybe somebody ought to show him what happens when you crawl over one of them high barbwire fences."

"I didn't hear you say that, deputy," Rosie said.

"It don't matter to me," he said. "A fella like that, they's people 'round here get their hands on him, you ain't gonna have to be worryin' about evidence, no. Ax Dave."

In the trunk we had found eleven small pairs of girls' underwear, children's socks, polka-dot leotards, training bras, a single black patent-leather shoe with a broken strap, a coloring book, a lock of red hair taped to an index card, torn matinee tickets to a local theater, a half-dozen old photographs of Murphy Doucet in the uniform of a Jefferson Parish deputy sheriff, all showing him with children at picnics under moss-hung trees, at a Little League ball game, at a swimming pool filled with children leaping into the air for the camera. All of the clothing was laundered and folded and arranged in a neat pink and blue and white layer across the bottom of the trunk.

After a moment, Rosie said, "It's his shrine."

"To *what*?" I said.

"Innocence. He's a psychopath, a rapist, a serial killer, a sadist, maybe a necrophiliac, but he's also a pedophile. Like most pedophiles, he seeks innocence by being among children or molesting them."

Then she rose from her chair, went into the bathroom, and I heard the water running, heard her spit, heard the water splashing.

"Could you wait outside a minute, Expidee?" I said to the deputy.

"Yeah, sure," he said.

"We'll be along in a minute. Thanks for your help today."

"That fella gonna make bail, Dave?"

"Probably."

"That ain't right," he said, then he said it again as he went out the door, "Ain't right."

The bathroom door was ajar when I tapped on it. Her back was to me, her arms propped stiffly on the basin, the tap still running. She kept trying to clear her throat, as though a fine fish bone were caught in it.

I opened the door, took a clean towel out of a cabinet, and started to blot her face with it. She held her hand up almost as though I were about to strike her.

"Don't touch me with that," she said.

I set the towel on the tub, tore the top Kleenex from a box, dropped it in the waste can, then pulled out several more, balled them up, and touched at her face with them. She pushed down my wrist.

"I'm sorry. I lost it," she said.

"Don't worry bout it."

"Those children, that smell in the trunk of the car."

She made her eyes as wide as possible to hold

back the tears, but it didn't work. They welled up in her brown eyes, then rolled in rivulets down her cheeks.

"It's okay, Rosie," I said, and slipped my arms around her. Her head was buried under my chin. I could feel the length of her body against mine, her back rising and falling under my palms. I could smell the strawberry shampoo in her hair, a heated fragrance like soap in her skin.

The window was open, and the wind blew the curtain into the room. Across the street on a putting green, a red flag snapped straight out on a pole that vibrated stiffly in the cup. In the first drops of rain, which slanted almost parallel to the ground, I saw a figure standing by a stagnant reed-choked pond, a roiling myrtle bush at his back. He held himself erect in the wind with his single crutch, his beard flying about his face, his mouth an O, his words lost in distant thunder. The stump of his amputated right leg was wrapped with fresh white bandages that had already turned scarlet with new bleeding.

"*What are you trying to warn me of, General? Why has so much pain come back to you, sir?*"

I felt Rosie twist her face against my chest, then step away from me and walk quickly out the door, picking up her handbag from a chair in one smooth motion so I could not see her face. The screen door slammed behind her.

I put everything from Doucet's trunk into evidence bags, locked the house, and got into the pickup just as a storm of hailstones burst from the sky, clattered on the cab, and bounced in tiny white geysers on the slopes of the golf course as far as the eye could see.

THAT NIGHT THE weatherman on the ten o'clock news said that the hurricane was moving again in a northwesterly direction and would probably make landfall sometime late tomorrow around Atchafalaya Bay, just to the east of us. Every offshore drilling rig in the Gulf had shut down, and the low-lying coastal areas from Grand Isle to Sabine Pass were being evacuated.

At eleven the sheriff called.

"Somebody just torched Mikey Goldman's trailer out at Spanish Lake. A gallon milk bottle of gasoline through the window with a truck flare right on top of it," he said. "You want to go out there and have a look?"

"Not really. Who's that yelling in the background?"

"Guess. I can't convince him he's lucky he wasn't in the trailer."

"Let me guess again. He wants Julie Balboni in custody."

"You must be psychic," the sheriff said. He paused. "I've got some bad news. The lab report came in late this evening. That utility knife's clean."

"Are they sure?"

"They're on the same side as we are, Dave."

"We can use testimony from the pathologist about the nature of the wounds. We can get an exhumation order if we have to."

"You're tired. I shouldn't have called tonight."

"Doucet's a monster, Sheriff."

"Let's talk about it in the morning."

A sheet of gray rain was moving across my neighbor's sugarcane field toward the house, and lightning was popping in the woods behind it.

"Are you there?" he said through the static.

"We've got to pull this guy's plug in a major way."

"We'll talk with the prosecutor in the morning. Now go to bed, Dave."

After I replaced the receiver in the cradle I sat for a long time in the chair and stared out the open back door at the rain falling on the duck pond and cattails at the foot of my property. The sky seemed filled with electric lights, the wind resonant with the voices of children.

CHAPTER 19

THE RAIN WAS deafening on the gallery in the morning. When I opened the front door, islands of pecan leaves floated in muddy pools in the yard, and a fine, sweet-smelling, cool mist blew inside the room. I could barely make out the marsh beyond the curtain of rain dancing in a wet yellow light on the bayou's surface. I put on my raincoat and hat and ran splashing through the puddles for the bait shop. Batist and I stacked all the tables, chairs, and umbrellas on the dock in the lee of the building, roped them down, hauled our boats out of the water, and bolted the shutters on the windows. Then we drank a cup of coffee and ate a fried pie together at the counter inside while the wind tried to peel the tin roof off the joists.

In town, Bayou Teche had risen high up on the pilings of the drawbridges and overflowed its banks into the rows of camellia bushes in the city park, and passing cars sent curling brown waves of water and street debris sliding across curbs and lawns all the way to the front steps of the houses along East Main. The air smelled of fish and dead vegetation from storm drains and was almost cold in the lungs, and in front of the courthouse the rain spun in vortexes that whipped at the neck and eyes and seemed to soak your clothes no matter how tightly your raincoat was buttoned. Murphy Doucet arrived at the courthouse in a jail van on a wrist chain with seven other inmates, bareheaded, a cigarette in the center of his mouth, his eyes squinted against the rain, his gray hair pasted down on his head, his voice loud with complaint about the manacle that cut into his wrist.

A black man was locked to the next manacle on the chain. He was epileptic and retarded and was in court every three or four weeks for public drunkenness or disturbing the peace. Inside the foyer, when the bailiff was about to walk the men on the chain to the front of the courtroom, the black man froze and jerked at the manacle, made a gurgling sound with his mouth while spittle drooled over his bottom lip.

"What the hell's wrong with you?" the bailiff said.

"Want to be on the end of the chain. Want to set on the end of the row," the black man said.

"He's saying he ain't used to being in the front of the bus," Doucet said.

"This man been bothering you, Ciro?" the bailiff said.

"No, suh. I just want to set on the end this time. Ain't no white peoples bothered me. I been treated just fine."

"Hurry up and get this bullshit over with," Doucet said, wiping his eyes on his sleeve.

"We aim to please. We certainly do," the bailiff said, unlocked the black man, walked him to the end of the chain, and snapped the last manacle on his wrist.

A young photographer from the *Daily Iberian* raised his camera and began focusing through his lens at Doucet.

"You like your camera, son? . . . I thought so. Then you just keep it poked somewhere else," Doucet said.

It took fifteen minutes. The prosecutor, a high-strung rail of a man, used every argument possible in asking for high bail on Doucet. Over the constant interruptions and objections of Doucet's lawyer, he called him a pedophile, a psychopath, a menace to the community, and a ghoul.

The judge had silver hair and a profile like a Roman soldier. During World War II he had received the Congressional Medal of Honor and at one time had been a Democratic candidate for governor. He listened patiently with one hand on top of another, his eyes oblique, his head tilted at an angle like a priest feigning attentiveness to an obsessed penitent's ramblings.

Finally the prosecutor pointed at Doucet, his finger trembling, and said, "Your honor, you turn this man loose, he kills somebody else, goddamn it, the blood's going to be on our hands."

"Would counsel approach the bench, please? You, too, Detective Robicheaux," the judge said. Then he said, "Can you gentlemen tell me what the hell is going on here?"

"It's an ongoing investigation, your honor. We need more time," I said.

"That's not my point," the judge said.

"I object to the treatment of my client, your honor. He's been bullied, degraded in public, slandered by these two men here. He's been—" Doucet's lawyer said.

"I've heard enough from you today, sir. You be quiet a minute," the judge said. "Is the prosecutor's office in the process of filing new charges against the defendant?"

"Your honor, we think this man may have been committing rape and homicide for over three decades. Maybe he killed a policeman in Lafayette. We don't even know where to begin," the prosecutor said.

"Your sincerity is obvious, sir. So is your lack of personal control," the judge said. "And neither is solving our problem here. We have to deal with the charge at hand, and you and Detective Robicheaux both know it. Excuse my impatience, but I don't want y'all dragging 'what should be' in here rather than 'what is.' Now all of you step back."

Then he said, "Bail is set at ten thousand dollars. Next case," and brought his gavel down.

A few minutes later I stood on the portico of the courthouse and watched Murphy Doucet and his lawyer walk past me, without interrupting their conversation or registering my presence with more than a glance, get into the lawyer's new Chrysler, and drive away in the rain.

• • •

I WENT HOME for lunch but couldn't finish my plate. The back door was opened to the small screened-in porch, and the lawn, the mimosa tree, and the willows along the coulee were dark green in the relentless downpour, the air heavy and cold-smelling and swirling with mist.

Alafair was looking at me from across the table, a lump of unchewed sandwich in her jaw. Bootsie had just trimmed her bangs, and she wore a yellow T-shirt with a huge red and green Tabasco bottle on the front. Bootsie reached over and removed my fingers from my temple.

"You've done everything you could do," she said. "Let other people worry about it for a while."

"He's going to walk. With some time we can round up a few of his girls from the Airline Highway and get him on a procuring beef, along with the resisting arrest and assault charge. But he'll trade it all off for testimony against Julie Balboni. I bet the wheels are already turning."

"Then that's their decision and their grief to live with, Dave," Bootsie said.

"I don't read it that way."

"What's wrong?" Alafair said.

"Nothing, little guy," I said.

"Is the hurricane going to hit here?" she said.

"It might. But we don't worry about that kind of stuff. Didn't you know coonasses are part duck?"

"My teacher said 'coonass' isn't a good word."

"Sometimes people are ashamed of what they are, Alf," I said.

"Give it a break, Dave," Bootsie said.

The front door opened suddenly and a gust of cool air swelled through the house. Elrod came through the hallway folding an umbrella and wiping the water off his face with his hand.

"Wow!" he said. "I thought I saw Noah's ark out there on the bayou. It could be significant."

"Ark? What's an ark?" Alafair said.

"El, there's a plate for you in the icebox," Bootsie said.

"Thanks," he said, and opened the icebox door, his face fixed with a smile, his eyes studiously carefree.

"What's an ark?" Alafair said.

"It's part of a story in the Bible, Alf," I said, and watched Elrod as he sat down with a plate of tuna-fish sandwiches and potato salad in his hand. "What's happening out at the lake, El?"

"Everything's shut down till this storm blows over," he said. He bit into his sandwich and didn't look up from his plate.

"That'd made sense, wouldn't it?" I said.

He raised his eyes.

"I think it's going to stay shut down," he said. "There're only a couple of scenes left to shoot. I think Mikey wants to do them back in California."

"I see."

Now it was Alafair who was watching Elrod's face. His eyes focused on his sandwich.

"You leaving, Elrod?" she asked.

"In a couple of days maybe," he answered. "But I'm sure I'll be back this way. I'd really like to have y'all come visit, too."

She continued to stare at him, her face round and empty.

"You could bring Tripod," he said. "I've got a four-acre place up Topanga Canyon. It's right up from the ocean."

"You said you were going to be here all summer," she said.

"I guess it just hasn't worked out that way. I wish it had," he said. Then he looked at me. "Dave, maybe I'm saying the wrong thing here, but y'all come out to L.A., I'll get Alafair cast in five minutes. That's a fact."

"We'll talk it over," Bootsie said, and smiled across the table at him.

"I could be in the movies where you live?" Alafair said.

"You bet," Elrod said, then saw the expression on my face. "I mean, if that's what you and your family wanted."

"Dave?" She looked up at me.

"Let's see what happens," I said, and brushed at her bangs with my fingers. Elrod was about to say something else, but I interrupted him. "Where's Balboni?"

"He doesn't seem to get the message. He keeps hanging around his trailer with his greaseballs. I think he'll still be sitting there when the set's torn down," Elrod said.

"His trailer might get blown in the lake," I said.

"I think he has more than one reason for being out there," Elrod said.

I waited for him to finish, but he didn't. A few

minutes later we went out on the gallery. The cypress planks of the steps and floor were dark with rain that had blown back under the eaves. Across the bayou the marsh looked smudged and indistinct in the gray air. Down at the dock Batist was deliberately sinking his pirogue in the shallows so it wouldn't be whipped into a piling by the wind.

"What were you trying to tell me about Balboni?" I said.

"He picks up young girls in town and tells them he's going to put them in a movie. I've heard he's had two or three in there in the last couple of days."

"That sounds like Julie."

"How's that?"

"When we were kids he never knew who he was unless he was taking his equipment out of his pants."

He stared at the rain.

"Maybe there's something I ought to tell you, Dave, not that maybe you don't already know it," he said. "When people like us, I'm talking about actors and such, come into a community, everybody gets excited and thinks somehow we're going to change their lives. I'm talking about romantic expectations, glamorous relationships with celebrities, that kind of stuff. Then one day we're gone and they're left with some problems they didn't have before. What I'm saying is they become ashamed when they realize how little they always thought of themselves. It's like turning on the lights inside the theater when the matinee is over."

"Our problems are our own, El. Don't give yourself too much credit."

"You cut me loose on a DWI and got me sober, Dave. Or at least I got a good running start at it. What'd you get for it? A mess of trouble you didn't deserve."

"Extend a hand to somebody else. That way you pass on the favor," I said.

I put my hand on the back of his neck. I could feel the stiff taper of his hair under my palm.

"I think about Kelly most when it rains. It's like she was just washed away, like everything that was her was dissolved right into the earth, like she wasn't ever here," he said. "How can a person be a part of your life twenty-four hours a day and then just be gone? I cain't get used to it."

"Maybe people live on inside of us, El, and then one day we get to see them again."

He leaned one hand against a wood post and stared at the rain. His face was wet with mist.

"It's coming to an end," he said. "Everything we've been doing, all the things that have happened, it's fixing to end," he said.

"You're not communicating too well, partner."

"I saw them back yonder in that sugarcane field last night. But this time it was different. They were furling their colors and loading their wagons. They're leaving us."

"*Why now?*" I heard my voice say inside myself.

He dropped his arm from the post and looked at me. In the shadows his brown skin was shiny with water.

"Something bad's fixing to happen, Dave," he said. "I can feel it like a hand squeezing my heart."

He tapped the flat of his fist against the wood post as though he were trying to reassure himself of its physical presence.

LATE THAT AFTERNOON the sheriff called me on my extension.

"Dave, could you come down to my office and help me with something?" he said.

When I walked through his door he was leaned back in his swivel chair, watching the treetops flatten in the wind outside the window, pushing against his protruding stomach with stiffened fingers as though he were discovering his weight problem for the first time.

"Oh, there you are," he said.

"What's up?"

"Sit down."

"Do we have a problem?"

He brushed at his round, cleft chin with the backs of his fingers.

"I want to get your reaction to what some people might call a developing situation," he said.

"Developing situation?"

"I went two years to USL, Dave. I'm not the most articulate person in the world. I just try to deal with realities as they are."

"I get the feeling we're about to sell the ranch."

"It's not a perfect world."

"Where's the heat coming from?" I said.

"There're a lot of people who want Balboni out of town."

"Which people?"

"Business people."

"They used to get along with him just fine."

"People loved Mussolini until it came time to hang him upside down in a filling station."

"Come on, cut to it, Sheriff. Who are the other players?"

"The feds. They want Balboni bad. Doucet's lawyer says his client can put Julie so far down under the penal system they'll have to dig him up to bury him."

"What's Doucet get?"

"He cops to resisting arrest and procuring, one-year max on an honor farm. Then maybe the federal witness protection program, psychological counseling, ongoing supervision, all that jazz."

"Tell them to go fuck themselves."

"Why is it I thought you might say that?"

"Call the press in. Tell them what kind of bullshit's going on here. Give them the morgue photos of Cherry LeBlanc."

"Be serious. They're not going to run pictures like that. Look, we can't indict with what we have. This way we get the guy into custody and permanent supervision."

"He's going to kill again. It's a matter of time."

"So what do you suggest?"

"Don't give an inch. Make them sweat ball bearings."

"With what? I'm surprised his lawyer even wants to accept the procuring charge."

"They think I've got a photo of Doucet with Balboni and Cherry LeBlanc in Biloxi."

"*Think?*"

"Doucet's face is out of focus. The man in the picture looks like bread dough."

"Great."

"I still say we should exhume the body and match the utility knife to the slash wounds."

"All an expert witness can do is testify that the wounds are consistent with those that might have been made with a utility knife. At least that's what the prosecutor's office says. Doucet will walk and so will Balboni. I say we take the bird in hand."

"It's a mistake."

"You don't have to answer to people, Dave. I do. They want Julie out of this parish and they don't care how we do it."

"Maybe you should give some thought about having to answer to the family of Doucet's next victim, sheriff."

He picked up a chain of paper clips and trailed them around his blotter.

"I don't guess there's much point in continuing this conversation, is there?" he said.

"I'm right about this guy. Don't let him fly."

"Wake up, Dave. He flew this morning." He dropped the paper clips into a clean ashtray and walked past me with his coffee cup. "You'd better take off a little early this afternoon. This hurricane looks to be a real frog stringer."

IT HIT LATE that evening, pushing waves ahead of it that curled over houseboats and stilt cabins at West Cote Blanche Bay and flattened them like a huge fist. In the south the sky was the color of burnt pewter, then rain-streaked, flumed with thunderheads. You could see tornadoes dropping like suspended snakes from the clouds, filling with water and splintered trees from the marshes, and suddenly breaking apart like whips snapping themselves into nothingness.

I heard canvas popping loose on the dock, billowing against the ropes Batist and I had tried to secure it with, then bursting free and flapping end over end among the cattails. The windows swam with water, lightning exploded out of the gray-green haze of swamp, and in the distance, in the roar of wind and thunder that seemed to clamp down on us like an enormous black glass bell, I thought I could hear the terrified moaning of my neighbor's cattle as they fought to find cover in a woods where mature trees were whipped out of the soft ground like seedlings.

By midnight the power was gone, the water off, and half the top of an oak tree had crashed on the roof and slid down the side of the house, covering the windows with tangles of branches and leaves.

I heard Alafair cry out in her sleep. I lit a candle, placed it in a saucer on top of her bookcase, which was filled with her collection of Curious George and Baby Squanto Indian books, and got in bed beside her. She wore her Houston Astros baseball cap and had pulled the sheet up to her chin. Her brown eyes moved back and forth as though she were searching out the sounds of the storm that seeped through the heavy cypress planks in the roof. The candlelight flickered on all the memorabilia she had brought back from our vacations or that we had saved as private signposts of the transitions she had made since I had pulled her from the submerged upside-down wreck of a plane off Southwest Pass: conch shells and dried starfish from Key West, her red tennis shoes embossed with the words *Left* and *Right* on the toes, a Donald Duck cap with a quacking bill from Disney World, her yellow T-shirt printed with a smiling purple whale on the front and the words *Baby Orca* that she had fitted over the torso of a huge stuffed frog.

"Dave, the field behind the house is full of lightning," she said. "I can hear animals in the thunder."

"It's Mr. Broussard's cattle. They'll be all right, though. They'll bunch up in the coulee."

"Are you scared?"

"Not really. But it's all right to be scared a little bit if you want to."

"If you're scared, you can't be standup."

"Sure you can. Standup people don't mind admitting they're scared sometimes."

Then I saw something move under the sheet by her feet.

"Alf?"

"What?" Her eyes flicked about the ceiling as though she were watching a bird fly from wall to wall.

I worked the sheet away from the foot of the bed until I was staring at Tripod's silver-tipped rump and black-ringed tail.

"I wonder how this fellow got in your bed, little guy," I said.

"He probably got out of his cage on the back porch."

"Yeah, that's probably it. He's pretty good at opening latched doors, isn't he?"

"I don't think he should go back out there, do you, Dave? He gets scared in the thunder."

"We'll give him a dispensation tonight."

"A dis— What?"

"Never mind. Let's go to sleep, little guy."

"Goodnight, big guy. Goodnight, Tripod. Goodnight, Frogger. Goodnight, Baby Squanto. Goodnight, Curious George. Goodnight, Baby Orca. Goodnight, seashells. Goodnight—"

"Cork it, Alf, and go to sleep."

"All right. Goodnight, big guy."

"Goodnight, little guy."

In my sleep I heard the storm pass overhead like freight trains grinding down a grade, then suddenly we were in the storm's eye, the air as still as if it had been trapped inside a jar; leaves drifted to the ground from the trees, and I could hear the cries of seabirds wheeling overhead.

The bedroom windows shine with an amber light that might have been aged inside oak. I slip on my khakis and loafers and walk out into the cool air that smells of salt and wet woods, and I see the general's troops forming into long columns that wind their way into other columns that seem to stretch over an infinitely receding landscape of hardwood forests fired with red leaves, peach or-

chards, tobacco acreage, rivers covered with steam, purple mountain ridges and valleys filled with dust from ambulance and ammunition wagons and wheeled artillery pieces, a cornfield churned into stubble by horses' hooves and men's boots, a meandering limestone wall and a sunken road where wild hogs graze on the bodies of the dead.

The general sits on a cypress stump by my coulee, surrounded by enlisted men and his aides. A blackened coffeepot boils amidst a heap of burning sticks by his foot. The officers as well as enlisted men are eating honeycombs peeled from inside a dead oak tree. The general's tunic is buttoned over his bad arm. A civilian in checkered trousers, high-top shoes, braces, and a straw hat is setting up a big box camera on a tripod in front of the group.

The general tips his hat up on his forehead and waves me toward him.

"A pip of a storm, wasn't it?" he says.

"Why are you leaving?"

"Oh, we're not gone just yet. Say, I want to have your photograph taken with us. That gentleman you see yonder is the correspondent for the Savannah Republican. *He writes an outstanding story, certainly as good as this Melville fellow, if you ask me."*

"I don't understand what's happening. Why did your wounds open, what were you trying to warn me of?"

"It's my foolishness, son. Like you, I grieve over what I can't change. Was it Bacon that talked about keeping each cut green?"

"Change what?"

"Our fate. Yours, mine. Care for your own. Don't try to emulate me. Look at what I invested my life in. Oh, we were always honorable—Robert Lee, Jackson, Albert Sidney Johnston, A. P. Hill—but we served venal men and a vile enterprise. How many lives would have been spared had we not lent ourselves to the defense of a repellent cause like slavery?"

"People don't get to choose their time in history, general."

"Well said. You're absolutely right." He swings the flat of his right hand and hits me hard on the arm, then rises on his crutch and straightens his tunic. "Now, gentlemen, if y'all will take the honeycombs out of your faces, let's be about this photographing business. I'm amazed at what the sciences are producing these days."

We stand in a group of eight. The enlisted men have Texas accents, powder-blackened teeth, and beards that grow like snakes on their faces. I can smell horse sweat and wood smoke in their clothes. Just as the photographer removes his straw hat and ducks his head under a black cloth at the back of the camera, I look down the long serpentine corridor of amber light again and see thousands of troops advancing on distant fields, their blue and red and white flags bent into the fusillade, their artillery crews laboring furiously at the mouths of smoking cannon, and I know the place names without their ever being spoken—Culp's Hill, Corinth, the Devil's Den, Kennesaw Mountain, the

Bloody Lane—and a collective sound that's like no other in the world rises in the wind and blows across the drenched land.

The photographer finishes and stoops under his camera box and lifts the tripod up on his shoulder. The general looks into the freshening breeze, his eyes avoiding me.

"You won't tell me what's at hand, sir?" I say.

"What does it matter as long as you stay true to your principles?"

"Even the saints might take issue with that statement, general."

"I'll see you directly, lieutenant. Be of good heart."

"Don't let them get behind you," I say.

"Ah, the admonition of a veteran." Then his aides help him onto his horse and he waves his hat forward and says, "Hideeho, lads," but there is no joy in his voice.

The general and his mounted escort move down the incline toward my neighbor's field, the tails of their horses switching, the light arcing over them as bright and heated and refractive as a glass of whiskey held up to the sun.

When I woke in the morning the rain was falling evenly on the trees in the yard and a group of mallards were swimming in the pond at the foot of my property. The young sugarcane in my neighbor's field was pounded flat into the washed-out rows as though it had been trampled by livestock. Above the treeline in the north I saw a small tornado drop like a spring from the sky, fill with mud and water from a field, then burst apart as though it had never been there.

I WORKED UNTIL almost eight o'clock that evening. Power was still off in parts of the parish; traffic signals were down; a rural liquor store had been burglarized during the night; two convenience stores had been held up; a drunk set fire to his own truck in the middle of a street; a parolee two days out of Angola beat his wife almost to death; and a child drowned in a storm drain.

Rosie had spent the day with her supervisor in New Orleans and had come back angry and despondent. I didn't even bother to ask her why. She had the paperwork on our case spread all over her desk, as though somehow rereading it and rearranging it from folder to folder would produce a different result, namely, that we could weld the cell door shut on Murphy Doucet and not have to admit that we were powerless over the bureaucratic needs of others.

Just as I closed the drawers in my desk and was about to leave, the phone rang.

"Dave, I think I screwed up. I think you'd better come home," Elrod said.

"What's wrong?"

"Bootsie went to town and asked me to watch Alafair. Then Alafair said she was going down to the bait shop to get us some fried pies."

"Get it out, Elrod. What is it?" I saw Rosie looking at me, her face motionless.

"I forgot Batist had already closed up. I should have gone with her."

I tried to hold back the anger that was rising in my throat.

"Listen, Elrod—"

"I went down there and she was gone. The door's wide open and the key's still in the lock—"

"How long's it been?"

"A half hour."

"A half hour?"

"You don't understand. I checked down at Poteet's first. Then I saw Tripod running loose on his chain in the road."

"What was she wearing?"

"A yellow raincoat and a baseball cap."

"Where's Bootsie?"

"Still in town."

"All right, stay by the phone and I'll be there in a few minutes."

"Dave, I'm sorry, I don't know what to say, I—"

"It's not your fault." I replaced the phone receiver in the cradle, my ears whirring with a sound like wind inside a seashell, the skin of my face as tight as a pumpkin's.

CHAPTER 20

BEFORE ROSIE AND I left the office I told the dispatcher to put out an all-car alert on Alafair and to contact the state police.

All the way to the house I tried to convince myself that there was an explanation for her disappearance other than the one that I couldn't bear to hold in the center of my mind for more than a few seconds. Maybe Tripod had simply gotten away from her while she was in the bait shop and she was still looking for him, I thought. Or maybe she had walked down to the general store at the four-corners, had forgotten to lock the door, and Tripod had broken loose from the clothesline on his own.

But Alafair never forgot to lock up the bait shop and she wouldn't leave Tripod clipped to the clothesline in the rain.

Moments after I walked into the bait shop, all the images and fears that I had pushed to the edges of my consciousness suddenly became real and inescapable, in the same way that you wake from a nightmare into daylight and with a sinking of the heart realize that the nightmare is part of your waking day and has not been manufactured by your sleep. Behind the counter I saw her Astros baseball cap, where it had been flattened into the Buckboards by someone's muddy shoe or boot. Elrod and Rosie watched me silently while I picked it up and placed it on top of the counter. I felt as though I were deep under water, past the point of depth tolerance, and something had popped like a stick and pulled loose in my head. Through the screen I saw Bootsie's car turn into the drive and park by the house.

"I should have figured him for it," I said.

"Doucet?" Rosie said.

"He was a cop. He's afraid to do time."

"We're not certain it's Doucet, Dave," she said.

"He knows what happens to cops inside mainline jails. Particularly to a guy they make as a short-eyes. I'm going up to talk to Bootsie. Don't answer the phone, okay?"

Rosie's teeth made white marks on her bottom lip.

"Dave, I want to bring in the Bureau as soon as we have evidence that it's a kidnapping," she said.

"So far nothing official we do to this guy works. It's time both of us hear that, Rosie," I said, and went out the screen door and started up the dock.

I hadn't gone ten yards when I heard the telephone ring behind me. I ran back through the rain and jerked the receiver out of the cradle.

"You sound out of breath," the voice said.

Don't blow this one.

"Turn her loose, Doucet. You don't want to do this," I said. I looked into Rosie's face and pointed toward the house.

"I'll make it simple for both of us. You take the utility knife and the photo out of the evidence locker. You put them in a Ziploc bag. At eight o'clock tomorrow morning you leave the bag in the trash can on the corner of Royal and St. Ann in New Orleans. I don't guess you ought to plan on getting a lot of sleep tonight."

Rosie had eased the screen door shut behind her and was walking fast up the incline toward the house in the fading light.

"The photo's a bluff. It's out of focus," I said. "You can't be identified in it."

"Then you won't mind parting with it."

"You can walk, Doucet. We can't make the case on you."

"You lying sonofabitch. You tore up my house. Your tow truck scratched up my car. You won't rest till you fuck me up in every way you can."

"You're doing this because your *property* was damaged?"

"I'll tell you what else I'm going to do if you decide to get clever on me. No, that's not right. It won't be me, because I never hurt a child in my life. You got that?"

He stopped speaking and waited for me. Then he said it again: "You got that, Dave?"

"Yes," I said.

"But there's a guy who used to work in Balboni's movies, a guy who spent eleven years in Parchman for killing a little nigger girl. You want to know how it went down?"

Then he told me. I stared out the screen door at my neighbor's dark green lawn, at his enormous roses that had burst in the rain and were now scattered in the grass like pink teardrops. A dog began barking, and then I heard it cry out sharply as though it had been whipped across the ribs with a chain.

"Doucet—" I broke in. My voice was wet, as though my vocal cords were covered with membrane.

"You don't like my description? You think I'm just trying to scare you? Get a hold of one of his snuff films. You'll agree he's an artist."

"Listen to me carefully. If you hurt my daughter, I'll get to you one way or another, in or out of jail, in the witness protection program, it won't matter, I'll take you down in pieces, Doucet."

"You've said only one thing right today. I'm going to walk, and you're going to help me, unless you've let that affirmative-action bitch fuck most of your brains out. By the way, forget the trace. I'm at a phone booth and you've got shit on your nose."

The line went dead.

I was trembling as I walked up the slope to the house. Rosie opened the screen door and came out on the gallery with Bootsie behind her. The skin of Bootsie's face was drawn back against the bone, her throat ruddy with color as though she had a windburn.

"He hung up too soon. We couldn't get it," Rosie said.

"Dave, my God. What—" Bootsie said. Her pulse was jumping in her neck.

"Let's go inside," I said, and put my arm around her shoulder. "Rosie, I'll be out in just a minute."

"No, talk to me right here," Bootsie said.

"Murphy Doucet has her. He wants the evidence that he thinks can put him in jail."

"What for?" she said. "You told me yesterday that he'll probably get out of it."

"He doesn't know that. He's not going to believe anybody who tells him that, either."

"Where is she?"

"I don't know, Boots. But we're going to get her back. If the sheriff calls, don't tell him anything. At least not right now."

I felt Rosie's eyes on the side of my face.

"What are you doing, Dave?" Bootsie said.

"I'll call you in a little while," I said. "Stay with Elrod, okay?"

"What if that man calls back?"

"He won't. He'll figure the line's open."

Before she could speak again, I went inside and opened the closet door in the bedroom. From under some folded blankets on the top shelf I took out a box of twelve-gauge shells and the Remington pump shotgun whose barrel I had sawed off in front of the pump handle and whose sportsman's plug I had removed years ago. I shook the shells, a mixture of deer slugs and double-ought buckshot, out on the bed and pressed them one by one into the magazine until I felt the spring come snug against the fifth shell. I dropped the rest of the shells into my raincoat pockets.

"Call the FBI, Dave," Bootsie said behind me.

"No," I said.

"Then I'll do it."

"Boots, if they screw it up, he'll kill her. We'll never even find the body."

Her face was white. I set the shotgun down and pulled her against me. She felt small, her back rounded, inside my arms.

"We've got a few hours," I said. "If we can't get her back in that time, I'm going to do what he wants and hope that he turns her loose. I'll bring the sheriff and the FBI in on it, too."

She stepped back from me and looked up into my face.

"Hope that he—" she said.

"Doucet's never left witnesses."

She wanted to come with us, but I left her on the gallery with Elrod, staring after us with her hands clenching and unclenching at her sides.

IT WAS ALMOST dark when we turned off the old two-lane highway onto the dirt road that led to Spanish Lake. The rain was falling in the trees and out on the lake and I could see the lights burning in one trailer under the hanging moss by the water's edge. All the way out to the lake Rosie had barely spoken, her small hands folded on top of her purse, the shadows washing across her face like rivulets of rain.

"I have to be honest with you, Dave. I don't know how far I can go along with this," she said.

"Call in your people now and I'll stonewall them."

"Do you think that little of us?"

"Not you I don't. But the people you work for are pencil pushers. They'll cover their butts, they'll do it by the numbers, and I'll end up losing Alafair."

"What are you going to do if you catch Doucet?"

"That's up to him."

"Is that straight, Dave?"

I didn't answer.

"I saw you put something in your raincoat pocket when you were coming out of the bedroom," she said. "I got the impression you were concealing it from Bootsie. Maybe it was just my imagination."

"Maybe you're thinking too much about the wrong things, Rosie."

"I want your word this isn't a vigilante mission."

"You're worried about *procedure*. . . . In dealing with a man like this? What's the matter with you?"

"Maybe you're forgetting who your real friends are, Dave."

I stopped the truck at the security building, rolled down my window, and held up my badge for the man inside, who was leaned back in his chair in front of a portable television set. He put on his hat, came outside, and dropped the chain for me. I could hear the sounds of a war movie through the open door.

"I'll just leave it down for you," he said.

"Thanks. Is that Julie Balboni's trailer with the lights on?" I said.

"Yeah, that's it."

"Who's with him?"

The security guard's eyes went past me to Rosie.

"His reg'lar people, I guess," he said. "I don't pay it much mind."

"Who else?"

"He brings out guests from town." His eyes looked directly into mine.

I rolled up the window, thumped across the chain, and drove into the oak grove by the lake. Twenty yards from Balboni's lighted trailer was the collapsed and blackened shell of a second trailer, its empty windows blowing with rain, its buckled floor leaking cinders into pools of water, the tree limbs above it scrolled with scorched leaves. To one side of Balboni's trailer a Volkswagen and the purple Cadillac with the tinted black windows were parked between two trees. I saw someone light a cigarette inside the Cadillac.

I stepped out of the truck with the shotgun hanging from my right arm and tapped with one knuckle on the driver's window. He rolled the glass down, and I saw the long pink scar inside his right forearm, the boxed hairline on the back of his neck, the black welt like an angry insect on his bottom lip where I had broken off his tooth in the restaurant on East Main. The man in the passenger's seat had the flattened eyebrows and gray scar tissue around his eyes of a prizefighter; he bent his neck down so he could look upward at my face and see who I was.

"What d'you want?" the driver said.

"Both of you guys are fired. Now get out of here and don't come back."

"Listen to this guy. You think this is Dodge City?" the driver said.

"Didn't you learn anything the first time around?" I said.

"Yeah, that you're a prick who blindsided me, that I can sue your ass, that Julie's got lawyers who can—"

I lifted the shotgun above the window ledge and screwed the barrel into his cheek.

"Do yourself a favor and visit your family in New Orleans," I said.

His knuckles whitened on the steering wheel as he tried to turn his head away from the pressure of the shotgun barrel. I pressed it harder into the hollow of his cheek.

"Fuck it, do what the man says. I told you the job was turning to shit when Julie run off Cholo," the other man said. "Hey, you hear me, man, back off. We're neutral about any personal beefs you got, you understand what I'm saying? You ought to do something about that hard-on you got, knock it down with a hammer or something, show a little fucking control."

I stepped back and pulled the shotgun free of the window. The driver stared at my hand wrapped in the trigger guard.

"You crazy sonofabitch, you had the safety off," he said.

"Happy motoring," I said.

I waited until the taillights of the Cadillac had disappeared through the trees, then I walked up onto the trailer's steps, turned the doorknob, and flung the door back into the wall.

A girl not over nineteen, dressed only in panties and a pink bra, was wiggling into a pair of jeans by the side of two bunk beds that had been pushed together in the middle of the floor. Her long hair was unevenly peroxided and looked like twisted strands of honey on her freckled shoulders; for some reason the crooked lipstick on her mouth made me think of a small red butterfly. Julie Balboni stood at an aluminum sink, wearing only a black silk jockstrap, his salt-and-pepper curls in his eyes, his body covered with fine black hair, a square bottle of Scotch poised above a glass filled with cracked ice. His eyes dropped to the shotgun that hung from my right hand.

"You finally losing your mind, Dave?" he said.

I picked up the girl's blouse from the bed and handed it to her.

"Are you from New Iberia?" I asked.

"Yes, sir," she said, her eyes fastened on mine as she pushed her feet into a pair of pumps.

"Stay away from this man," I said. "Women who hang around him end up dead."

Her frightened face looked at Julie, then back at me.

Rosie put her hands on the girl's shoulders and turned her toward the door.

"You can go now," she said. "Listen to what Detective Robicheaux tells you. This man won't put you in the movies, not unless you want to work in pornographic films. Are you okay?"

"Yes, ma'am."

"Here's your purse. Don't worry about what's happening here. It doesn't have anything to do with you. Just stay away from this man. He's in a lot of trouble," Rosie said.

The girl looked again at Julie, then went quickly out the door and into the dark. Julie was putting on his trousers now, with his back to us. The walls were covered with felt paintings of red-mouthed tigers and boa constrictors wrapped around the bodies of struggling unicorns. By the door was the canvas bag filled with baseballs, gloves, and metal bats. Julie's skin looked brown and rubbed with oil in the glow from a bedside lava lamp.

"It looks like you did a real number on Mikey Goldman's trailer," I said.

He zipped his fly. "Like most of the time, you're wrong," he said. "I don't go around setting fires on my own movie set. That's Cholo Manelli's work."

"Why does he want to hurt Mikey Goldman?"

"He don't. He thought it was my trailer. He's got his nose bent out of joint about some imaginary wrong I done to him. The first thing Cholo does in the morning is stick his head up his hole. You guys ought to hang out together."

"Why do you think I'm here, Julie?"

"How the fuck should I know? Nothing you do makes sense to me anymore, Dave. You want to toss the place, see if that little chippy left a couple of 'ludes in the sheets?"

"You think this is some chickenshit roust, Julie?"

He combed his curls back over his head with his fingers. His navel looked like a black ball of hair above his trousers.

"You take yourself too serious," he said.

"Murphy Doucet has my daughter." I watched his face. He put his thumbnail into a molar and picked out a piece of food with it. "Did you hear what I said?"

He poured three fingers of Scotch into his glass, then dropped a lemon rind into the ice, his face composed, his eyes glancing out the window at a distant flicker of lightning.

"Too bad," he said.

"Too bad, huh?"

"Yeah. I don't like to hear stuff like that. It upsets me."

"Upsets you, does it?"

"Yeah. That's why I don't watch that show *Unsolved Mysteries*. It upsets me. Hey, maybe you can get her face on one of those milk cartons."

As he drank from his highball, I could see the slight tug at the corner of his mouth, the smile in his eyes. He picked up his flowered shirt from the back of a chair and began putting it on in front of a bathroom door mirror as though we were not there.

I handed Rosie the shotgun, put my hands on my hips, and studied the tips of my shoes. Then

I slipped an aluminum bat out of the canvas bag, choked up on the taped handle, and ripped it down across his neck and shoulders. His forehead bounced off the mirror, pocking and spiderwebbing the glass like it had been struck with a ball bearing. He turned back toward me, his eyes and mouth wide with disbelief, and I hit him again, hard, this time across the middle of the face. He crashed headlong into the toilet tank, his nose roaring blood, one side of his mouth drooping as though all the muscle endings in it had been severed.

I leaned over and cuffed both of his wrists around the bottom of the stool. His eyes were receded and out of focus, close-set like a pig's. The water in the bowl under his chin was filling with drops of dark color like pieces of disintegrating scarlet cotton.

I nudged his arm with the bat. His eyes clicked up into my face.

"Where is she, Julie?" I said.

"I cut Doucet loose. I don't have nothing to do with what he does. You get off my fucking case or I'm gonna square this, Dave. It don't matter if you're a cop or not, I'll put out an open contract, I'll cowboy your whole fucking family. I'll—"

I turned around and took the shotgun out of Rosie's hands. I could see words forming in her face, but I didn't wait for her to speak. I bent down on the edge of Julie's vision.

"Your window of opportunity is shutting down, Feet."

He blew air out of his nose and tried to wipe his face on his shoulder.

"I'm telling you the truth. I don't know nothing about what that guy does," he said. "He's a geek. . . . I don't hire geeks, I run them off. . . . I got enough grief without crazy people working for me."

"You're lying again, Julie," I said, stepped back, leveled the shotgun barrel above his head, and fired at an angle into the toilet tank. The double-ought buckshot blew water and splintered ceramic all over the wall. I pumped the spent casing out on the floor. Julie jerked the handcuffs against the base of the stool, like an animal trying to twist itself out of a metal trap.

I touched the warm tip of the barrel against his eyebrow.

"Last chance, Feet."

His eyes closed; he broke wind uncontrollably in his pants; water and small chips of ceramic dripped out of his hair.

"He's got a camp south of Bayou Vista," he said. "It's almost to Atchafalaya Bay. The deed ain't in his name, nobody knows about it, it's like where he does all his weird stuff. It's right where the dirt road ends at the salt marsh. I seen it once when we were out on my boat."

"Is my daughter there?" I said quietly.

"I just told you, it's where he goes to be weird. You figure it out."

"We'll be back later, Feet. You can make a lot of noise, if you like, but your gumballs are gone and the security guard is watching war movies. If I get my daughter back, I'll have somebody from the department come out and pick you up. You can file charges against me then or do whatever you want. If you've lied to me, that's another matter."

Then I saw a secret concern working in his eyes, a worry, a fear that had nothing to do with me or the pain and humiliation that I had inflicted upon him. It was the fear that you inevitably see in the eyes of men like Julie and his kind when they realize that through an ironic accident they are now dealing with forces that are as cruel and unchecked by morality as the energies they'd awakened with every morning of their lives.

"Cholo—" he said.

"What about him?" I said.

"He's out there somewhere."

"I doubt it."

"You don't know him. He carries a barber's razor. He's got fixations. He don't forget things. He tied parts of a guy all over a ceiling fan once."

His chest moved up and down with his breathing against the rim of the toilet bowl. His brow was kneaded with lines, his nose a wet red smear against his face, his eyes twitching with a phlegmy light.

I shut off the valve that was spewing water upward into the shattered tank, then found a quilt and a pile of towels in a linen closet and placed the towels under Julie's forearms and the quilt between his knees and the bottom of the stool.

"That's about all I can do for you, Feet. Maybe it's the bottom of the ninth for both of us," I said.

• • •

THE FRONT WHEELS of the truck shimmied on the cement as I wound up the transmission on Highway 90 southeast of town. It had stopped raining, the oaks and palm trees by the road's edge were coated with mist, and the moon was rising in the east like a pale white and mottled-blue wafer trailing streamers of cloud torn loose from the Gulf's horizon.

"I think I'm beyond all my parameters now, Dave," Rosie said.

"What would you do differently? I'd like for you to tell me that, Rosie."

"I believe we should have Balboni picked up—suspicion for involvement in a kidnapping."

"And my daughter would be dead as soon as Doucet heard about it. Don't tell me that's not true, either."

"I'm not sure you're in control anymore, Dave. That remark about the bottom of the ninth—"

"What about it?"

"You're thinking about killing Doucet, aren't you?"

"I can put you down at the four-corners up there. Is that what you want?"

"Do you think you're the only person who cares about your daughter? Do you think I want to do anything that would put her in worse jeopardy than she's already in?"

"The army taught me what a free-fire zone is, Rosie. It's a place where the winners make up the rules after the battle's over. Anyone who believes otherwise has never been there."

"You're wrong about all this, Dave. What we don't do is let the other side make us be like them."

Ahead I could see the lighted, tree-shadowed white stucco walls of a twenty-four-hour filling station that had been there since the 1930s. I eased my foot off the gas pedal and looked across the seat at Rosie.

"Go on," she said. "I won't say anything else."

We drove through Jeanerette and Franklin into the bottom of the Atchafalaya Basin, where Louisiana's wetlands bled into the Gulf of Mexico, not far from where this story actually began with a racial lynching, in the year 1957. Rosie had fallen asleep against the door. At Bayou Vista I found the dirt road that led south to the sawgrass and Atchafalaya Bay. The fields looked like lakes of pewter under the moon, the sugarcane pressed flat like straw into the water. Wood farmhouses and barns were cracked sideways on their foundations, as though a gigantic thumb had squeezed down on their roofs, and along one stretch of road the telephone poles had been snapped off even with the ground for a half mile and flung like sticks into distant trees.

Then the road entered a corridor of oaks, and through the trunks I saw four white horses galloping in circles in a mist-streaked pasture, spooking against the barbed-wire fences, mud flying from their hooves, their nostrils dilated, their eyes bright with fear against a backdrop of dry lightning, their muscles rippling under their skin like silvery water sliding over stone. Then I was sure I saw a figure by the side of the road, the palmetto shadows waving behind him, his steel-gray tunic buttoned at his throat, a floppy campaign hat pulled over his eyes.

I hit my bright lights, and for just a moment I saw his elongated milk-white face as though a flashbulb had exploded in front of it. "*What are you doing here?*" I said.

"*Don't use those whom you love to justify a dishonorable cause.*"

"*That's rhetoric.*"

"*You gave the same counsel to the Sykes boy.*"

"*It was you who told me to do it under a black flag. Remember? We blow up their shit big time, General.*"

"*Then you will do it on your own, suh, and without me.*"

The truck's front springs bounced in a chuckhole and splashed a sheet of dirty water across the window; then I was beyond the pasture and the horses that wheeled and raced in the moonlight, traveling deep into the tip of the wetlands, with flooded woods on each side of me, blue herons lifting on extended wings out of the canals, the moist air whipped with the smell of salt and natural gas from the oil platforms out in the swamp.

The road bent out of the trees, and I saw the long expanses of sawgrass and mudflats that spread out into the bay, and the network of channels that had been cut by the oil companies and that were slowly poisoning the marshes with salt water. Rosie was awake now, rubbing her eyes with one knuckle, her face stiff with fatigue.

"I'm sorry. I didn't mean to fall asleep," she said.

"It's been a long day."

"Where's the camp?"

"There's some shacks down by the flats, but they look deserted."

I pulled the truck to the side of the road and cut the lights. The tide was out, and the bay looked flat and gray and seabirds were pecking shellfish out of the wet sand in the moonlight. Then a wind gusted out of the south and bent a stand of willow trees that stood on a small knoll between the marsh and the bay.

"Dave, there's a light back in those trees," Rosie said.

Then I saw it, too, at the end of a two-lane sandy track that wound through the willows and over the knoll.

"All right, let's do it," I said, and pushed down on the door handle.

"Dave, before we go in there, I want you to hear something. If we find the wrong thing, if Alafair's not all right, it's not because of anything you did. It's important for you to accept that now. If I had been in your place, I'd have done everything the same way you have."

I squeezed her hand.

"A cop couldn't have a better partner than Rosie Gomez," I said.

We got out of the truck and left the doors open to avoid making any unnecessary sound, and walked up the sandy track toward the trees. I could hear gulls cawing and wheeling overhead and the solitary scream of a nutria deep in the marsh. Humps of garbage stood by the sides of the track, and then I realized that it was medical waste—bandages, hypodermic vials, congealed bags of gelatin, sheets that were stiff with dried fluids.

We moved away from the side of the road and into the trees. I walked with a shotgun at port arms, the .45 heavy in the right-hand pocket of my raincoat. Rosie had her chrome-plated .357 magnum gripped with both hands at an upward angle, just to the right of her cheek. Then the wind bent the trees again and blew a shower of wet leaves into a clearing, where we could see a tin-roofed cabin with a small gallery littered with cane poles, crab traps, and hand-thrown fishnets, and a Coleman lantern hissing whitely on a wood table in the front room. In the back were an outhouse and a pirogue set up on sawhorses, and behind the outhouse was Murphy Doucet's blue Mercury.

A shadow moved across the window, then a man with his back to us sat down at the table with a coffee pot and a thick white mug in his hands. Even through the rusted screen I could see his stiff, gray military haircut and the deeply tanned skin of his neck whose tone and texture reminded me of a cured tobacco leaf.

We should have been home free. But then I saw the moonlight glint on the wire that was stretched across the two-lane track, three inches above the sand. I propped the shotgun against a tree, knelt down in the wet leaves, and ran my fingers along the wire until I touched two empty Spam cans that were tied with string to the wire, then two more, then two more after that. Through the underbrush, against the glow of moonlight in the clearing, I could make out a whole network of nylon fishing line strung between tree trunks, branches, roots, and underbrush, and festooned with tin cans, pie plates, and even a cow bell.

I was sweating heavily inside my raincoat now. I wiped the salt out of my eyes with my hand.

One lung-bursting rush across the clearing, I thought. *Clear the gallery in one step, bust the door out of the jamb, then park a big one in his brisket and it's over.*

But I knew better. I would sound like a traveling junkyard before I ever made the gallery, and if Alafair was still alive, in all probability he would be holding a pistol at her head.

"We have to wait until it's light or until he comes out," I whispered to Rosie.

We knelt down in the trees, in the damp air, in the layered mat of black and yellow willow leaves, in the mosquitoes that rose in clouds from around our knees and perched on our faces and the backs of our hands and necks. I saw him get up once, walk to a shelf, then return to the table and read a magazine while he ate soda crackers out of a box. My thighs burned and a band of pain that I couldn't relieve began to spread slowly across my back. Rosie sat with her rump resting on her heels, wiping the mosquitoes off her forearms, her pink skirt hiked up on her thighs, her .357

propped in the fork of a tree. Her neck was shiny with sweat.

Then at shortly after four I could hear mullet jumping in the water, a 'gator flop his tail back in the marsh, a solitary mockingbird singing on the far side of the clearing. The air changed; a cool breeze lifted off the bay and blew the smell of fish and grass shrimp across the flats. Then a pale glow, like cobalt, like the watery green cast of summer light right before a rain, spread under the rim of banked clouds on the eastern horizon, and in minutes I could see the black shapes of jetties extending far out into the bay, small waves white-capping with the incoming tide, the rigging of a distant shrimp boat dropping below a swell.

Then Murphy Doucet wrote the rest of the script for us. He turned down the Coleman lantern, stretched his back, picked up something from the table, went out the front door, and walked behind our line of vision on the far side of the cabin toward the outhouse.

We moved out of the trees into the clearing, stepping over and under the network of can-rigged fishline, then divided in two directions at the corner of the gallery. I could smell a fecund salty odor like dead rats and stagnant water from under the cabin.

The rear windows were boarded with slats from packing boxes and I couldn't see inside or hear any movement. At the back of the cabin I paused, held the shotgun flat against my chest, and looked around the corner. Murphy Doucet was almost to the door of the outhouse, a pair of untied hunting boots flopping on his feet, a silvery object glinting in his right hand. Beyond the outhouse, by the marsh's edge, a blue-tick dog was tied to a post surrounded by a ring of feces.

I stepped out from the lee of the cabin, threw the stock of the shotgun to my shoulder, sighted between Doucet's neck and shoulder blades, and felt the words already rising in my throat, like bubbles out of a boiling pot, *Surprise time, motherfucker! Throw it away! Do it now!* when he heard Rosie trip across a fishline that was tied to a cow bell on the gallery.

He looked once over his shoulder in her direction, then leaped behind the outhouse and ran toward the marsh on a long green strip of dry ground covered with buttercups. But five yards before he would have splashed into the willows and dead cypress and perhaps out of our field of fire, his untied boots sank into a pile of rotting medical waste that was matted with the scales of morning-glory vines. A wooden crutch that looked hand-hewn, with a single shaft that fitted into the armrest, sprang from under his boot and hung between his legs like a stick in bicycle spokes.

He turned around helplessly toward Rosie, falling backward off balance now, his blue eyes jittering frantically, his right arm extended toward her, as though it were not too late for her to recognize that his hand held a can of dog food rather than a weapon, just as she let off the first round of her .357 and caught him right in the sternum.

But it didn't stop there. She continued to fire with both hands gripped on the pistol, each soft-nosed slug knocking him backward with the force of a jackhammer, his shirt exploding with scarlet flowers on his bony chest, until the last round in the cylinder hit him in the rib cage and virtually eviscerated him on the water's edge. Then he simply sat down on top of his crumpled legs as though all the bone in his body had been surgically removed.

When she lowered the weapon toward the ground, her cheeks looked like they contained tiny red coals, and her eyes were frozen wide, as though she were staring into a howling storm, one that was filled with invisible forces and grinding winds only she could hear.

But I didn't have time to worry about the line that Rosie had crossed and the grief and knowledge that dark moment would bring with it.

Behind me I heard wood slats breaking loose from the back of the cabin, then I saw metal chair legs crash through the window, and Alafair climbing over the windowsill, her rump hanging in midair, her pink tennis shoes swinging above the damp earth.

I ran to her, grabbed her around the waist, and held her tightly against me. She buried her head under my chin and clamped her legs on my side like a frog, and I could feel the hard resilience of her muscles, the heat in her hands, the spastic breathing in her throat as though she had just burst from deep water into warm currents of salt air and a sunlit day loud with the sound of seabirds.

"Did he hurt you, Squanto?" I said, my heart dropping with my own question.

"I told him he'd better not. I told him what you'd do. I told him you'd rip his nuts out. I told him—"

"Where'd you get this language, Alf?"

A shudder went through her body, as though she had just removed her hand from a hot object, then her eyes squeezed shut and she began to cry.

"It's all right, Baby Squanto. We're going back home now," I said.

I carried her on my hip back toward the truck, her arms around my neck, her face wet against my shirt.

I heard Rosie walking in the leaves behind me. She dumped the spent brass from the cylinder of her .357 into her palm, looked at them woodenly, then threw them tinkling into the trees.

"Get out of it, Rosie. That guy dealt the play a long time ago."

"I couldn't stop. Why didn't I stop shooting? It was over and I kept shooting."

"Because your mind shuts down in moments like that."

"No, he paid for something that happened to me a long time ago, didn't he?"

"Let the Freudians play with that stuff. They seldom spend time on the firing line. It'll pass. Believe me, it always does."

"Not hitting a man four times after he was going down. A man armed with a can of dog food."

I looked at the spreading glow out on the bay and the gulls streaking over the tide's edge.

"He had a piece on him, Rosie. You just don't remember it right now," I said, and handed Alafair to her.

I went back into the trees, found my raincoat, and carried it over my arm to the place where Murphy Doucet sat slumped among the buttercups, his torn side draining into the water. I took Lou Girard's .32 revolver from my raincoat pocket, wiped the worn bluing and the taped wooden grips on my handkerchief, fitted it into Doucet's hand, and closed his stiffened fingers around the trigger guard.

On his forearm was a set of teeth marks that looked like they had been put there by a child.

Next time out don't mess with Alafair Robicheaux or the Confederate army, Murph, I thought.

Then I picked up the crutch that had caught between his legs. The wood was old, weathered gray, the shaft shaved and beveled by a knife, the armrest tied with strips of rotted flannel.

The sun broke through the clouds overhead, and under the marsh's green canopy I could see hammered gold leaf hanging in the columns of spinning light, and gray shapes like those of long-dead sentinels, and like a man who has finally learned not to think reasonably in an unreasonable world, I offered the crutch at the air, at the shapes in the trees and at the sound of creatures moving through the water, saying, *"Don't you want to take this with you, sir?"*

But if he answered, I did not hear it.

EPILOGUE

I'D LIKE TO tell you that the department and the local prosecutor's office finally made their case against Julie Balboni, that we cleaned our own house and sent him up the road to Angola in waist and leg chains for a twenty- or thirty-year jolt. But that's not what happened. How could it? In many ways Julie was us, just as his father had been when he provided the town its gambling machines and its rows of cribs on Railroad and Hopkins avenues. After Julie had left town on his own to become a major figure in the New Orleans mob, we had welcomed him back, winking our eyes at his presence and pretending he was not what or who he was.

I believe Julie and his father possessed a knowledge about us that we did not possess about ourselves. They knew we were for sale.

Julie finally went down, but in a way that no one expected—in a beef with the IRS. No, that's not quite right, either. That ubiquitous federal agency, the bane of the mob, was only a minor footnote in Julie's denouement. The seed of Julie's undoing was

Julie. And I guess Julie in his grandiosity would not have had it any other way.

He should have done easy time, a three-year waltz on a federal honor farm in Florida, with no fences or gunbulls, with two-man rooms rather than cells, tennis courts, and weekend furloughs. But while in federal custody in New Orleans he spit in a bailiff's face, tore the lavatory out of his cell wall, and told an informant planted in his cell that he was putting a hit out on Cholo Manelli, who he believed had turned over his books to the IRS (which I heard later was true).

So they shipped Baby Feet up to a maximum-security unit at Fort Leavenworth, Kansas, a place that in the wintertime makes you believe that the earth has been poisoned with Agent Orange and the subzero winds blow from four directions simultaneously.

Most people are not aware of who comprises the population of a maximum-security lockup. They are usually not men like Baby Feet, who was intelligent and fairly sane for a sociopath. Instead, they are usually psychotic meltdowns, although they are not classified as such, otherwise they would be sent to mental institutions from which they would probably be released in a relatively short time. Perhaps they have the intelligence levels of battery-charged cabbages, housed in six-and-one-half-foot bodies that glow with rut. Often they're momma's boys who wear horn-rimmed glasses and comb their hair out on their frail shoulders like girls, murder whole families, and can never offer more in the way of explanation than a bemused and youthful smile.

But none was a match for Julie. He was a made guy, connected both on the inside and outside, a blockhouse behemoth whose whirling feet could make men bleed from every orifice in their bodies. He took over the dope trade, broke heads and groins in the shower, paid to have a rival shanked in the yard and a snitch drowned in a toilet bowl.

He also became a celebrity wolf among the punk population. They ironed his clothes, shampooed his hair, manicured his nails, and asked him in advance what kind of wigs and women's underthings they should wear when they came to his bunk. He encouraged jealousies among them and watched as an amused spectator while they schemed and fought among themselves for his affections and the reefer, pills, and prune-o he could provide to his favorites.

Perhaps he even found the adoration and submission that had always eluded him from the time he used to visit Mabel White's mulatto brothel in Crowley until he had Cherry LeBlanc murdered.

At least the psychologist at Fort Leavenworth who told me this story thought so. He said Julie actually seemed happy his first and final spring on the yard, hitting fly balls to his boys in the outfield, ripping the bat from deep in the box with the power and grace of a DiMaggio, the fine black hair on his shoulders glazed with sweat, his black silk shorts hanging on his hips with the confident male abandon of both a successful athlete and lover, snapping his wrists as he connected with the ball, lifting it higher into the blue sky than anyone at Leavenworth had ever done before, while all around him other cons touched themselves and nodded with approval.

Maybe he was still thinking about these things on the Sunday evening he came in from the diamond, showered, and went to the empty cell of his current lover to take a nap under a small rubber-bladed fan with the sheet over his head. Maybe in his dreams he was once again a movie producer on the edge of immense success, a small-town boy whose story would be re-created by biographers and become the stuff of legends in Hollywood, a beneficent but feared mogul in sunglasses and a two-thousand-dollar white tropical suit who strolled with elegance and grace through the bougainvillea and palm trees and the clink of champagne glasses at Beverly Hills lawn parties.

Or maybe, for just a moment, when a pain sharper than any he had ever thought possible entered his consciousness like a red shard of glass, he saw the face of his father contorted like a fist as the father held him at gunpoint and whipped the nozzle end of a garden hose across Julie's shivering back.

The Molotov cocktail thrown by a competitor for Julie's affections burst on the stone wall above the bunk where Julie was sleeping and covered his entire body with burning paraffin and gasoline. He erupted from the bunk, flailing at the air, the sheet dissolving in black holes against his skin. He ran blindly through the open cell door, wiping at his eyes and mouth, his disintegrating shape an enormous cone of flame now, and with one long bellowing cry he sprang over the rail of the tier and plunged like a meteor three stories to the cement floor below.

WHAT HAPPENED TO Twinky Hebert Lemoyne?

Nothing. Not externally. He's still out there, a member of a generation whose metamorphosis never quite takes place.

Sometimes I see his picture on the business page of the Lafayette newspaper. You can count on him to be at fundraiser kickoff breakfasts for whatever charity is in fashion with the business community. In all probability he's even sincere. Once or twice I've run into him at a crab boil or fish fry in New Iberia. He doesn't do well, however, in a personal encounter with the past. His manners are of course gentlemanly, his pink skin and egg-shaped head and crinkling seersucker suit images that you associate with a thoughtful and genteel southern barrister, but in the steady and trained avoidance that his eyes perform when you look into his face, you see another man, one whose sense of self-worth was so base that he would participate in a lynching because he had been made a cuckold by one of his own black employees.

No, that's not quite fair to him.

Perhaps, just like Julie Balboni, Twinky Hebert is us. He loathed his past so much that he could never acknowledge it, never expiate his sin, and never forgive himself, either. So, like Proteus rising from the sea and forever reshaping his form, Twinky Hebert Lemoyne made a contract of deceit with himself and consequently doomed himself to relive his past every day of his life.

At the crab boil in the park on Bayou Teche he inadvertently sat down at a wooden table under the pavilion not three feet away from me, Bootsie, and Alafair. He had just started to crack the claws on a crab when he realized who sat across from him.

"What are *you* doing here?" he asked, his mouth hanging open.

"I live in New Iberia. I was invited to attend."

"Are you trying to harass me?"

"I closed the file on the summer of 1957, Mr. Lemoyne. Why don't you?"

There was a painful light, like a burning match, deep in his eyes. He tried to break open a crab claw with a pair of nutcrackers, then his hand slipped and sprayed juice on his shirt front.

"Tell a minister about it, tell a cop, get on a plane and tell somebody you never saw before," I said. "Just get rid of it once and for all and lose the Rotary Club doodah."

But he was already walking rapidly toward the men's room, scrubbing at his palms with a paper towel, his change rattling in his pants' pockets, twisting his neck from side to side as though his tie and stiff collar were a rope against his skin.

WE TOOK OUR vacation that year in California and stayed with Elrod in his ranch home built on stilts high up on a cliff in Topanga Canyon, overlooking the Pacific Coast Highway and the ocean that was covered each morning with a thick bluish-white mist, inside which you could hear the waves crashing like avalanches into the beach.

For two weeks Alafair acted in a picture out at Tri-Star with Mikey Goldman and Elrod, and in the evenings we ate cherrystone clams at Gladstone's on the beach and took rides in Mikey Goldman's pontoon plane out to Catalina Island. As the late sun descended into the ocean, it seemed to trail ragged strips of black cloud with it, like a burning red planet settling into the Pacific's watery green rim. When the entire coastline was awash in a pink light you could see almost every geological and floral characteristic of the American continent tumbling from the purple crests of the Santa Monica Mountains into the curling line of foam that slid up onto the beaches: dry hills of chaparral, mesquite, and scrub oak, clumps of eucalyptus and bottlebrush trees, torrey and ponderosa pine growing between blue-tiled stucco houses, coral walls overgrown with bougainvillea, terraced hillside gardens filled with oleander, yucca plants, and trellises dripping with passion vine, and orange groves whose irrigation ditches looked like quicksilver in the sun's afterglow.

Then millions of lights came on in the canyons, along the freeways, and through the vast sweep of the Los Angeles basin, and it was almost as if you were looking down upon the end point of the American dream, a geographical poem into which all our highways eventually led, a city of illusion founded by conquistadors and missionaries and consigned to the care of angels, where far below the spinning propellers of our seaplane black kids along palm-tree-lined streets in Watts hunted each other with automatic weapons.

I thought in the morning mists that rolled up the canyon I might once again see the noble and chivalric John Bell Hood. Just a glimpse, perhaps, a doff of his hat, the kindness of his smile, the beleaguered affection that always seemed to linger in his face. Then as the days passed and I began to let go of all the violent events of that summer, I had to accept the fact that the general, as Bootsie had said, was indeed only a hopeful figment of my fantasies, a metaphorical and mythic figure probably created as much by the pen of Thomas Malory or Walter Scott as the LSD someone had put in my drink out at Spanish Lake.

Then two nights before we returned home, Alafair was sitting on the coral wall that rimmed Elrod's terrace, flipping the pages in one of the library books Bootsie had checked out on the War Between the States.

"What you doing in here, Dave?" she said.

"In what? What are you talking about, little guy?"

She continued to stare down at a page opened in her lap.

"You're in the picture. With that old man Poteet and I saw in the corn patch. The one with B.O.," she said, and turned the book around so I could look at it.

In the photograph, posed in the stiff attitudes of nineteenth-century photography, were the general and seven of his aides and enlisted men.

"Standing in the back. The one without a gun. That's you, Dave," she said. Then she stared up at me with a confused question mark in the middle of her face. "Ain't it?"

"Don't say 'ain't,' little guy."

"What are you doing in the picture?"

"That's not me, Alf. Those are Texas soldiers who fought alongside John Bell Hood. I bet they were a pretty good bunch," I said, and rubbed the top of her head.

"How do you know they're from Texas? It doesn't say that here."

"It's just a guess."

She looked at the photograph again and back at me, and her face became more confused.

"Let's get Elrod and Bootsie and go down to the beach for some ice cream," I said.

I slipped the book from her hand and closed it, picked her up on my hip, and walked through the canopy of purple trumpet vine toward the patio behind the house, where Bootsie and Elrod were clearing off the dishes from supper. Down the canyon, smoke from meat fires drifted through the cedar and mesquite trees, and if I squinted my eyes in the sun's setting, I could almost pretend that Spanish soldiers in silver chest armor and bladed helmets or a long-dead race of hunters were encamped on those hillsides. Or maybe even old compatriots in butternut brown wending their way in and out of history—gallant, Arthurian, their canister-ripped colors unfurled in the roiling smoke, the fatal light in their faces a reminder that the contest is never quite over, the field never quite ours.

Turn the page for a look at

FEAST DAY OF FOOLS

James Lee Burke's
masterful new novel
featuring Hackberry Holland

now available
from Simon & Schuster

SOME PEOPLE SAID Danny Boy Lorca's visions came from the mescal that had fried his brains, or the horse-quirt whippings he took around the ears when he served time on Sugar Land Farm, or the fact he'd been a middleweight clubfighter through a string of dust-blown sinkholes where the locals were given a chance to beat up what was called a tomato can, a fighter who leaked blood every place he was hit, in this case a rumdum Indian who ate his pain and never flinched when his opponents broke their hands on his face.

Danny Boy's black hair was cut in bangs and fitted his head like a helmet. His physique was as square as a door, his clothes always smelling of smoke from the outdoor fires he cooked his food on, his complexion as dark and coarsened by the sun and wind as the skin on a shrunken head. In summer, he wore long-sleeve cotton work shirts buttoned at the throat and wrists to keep the heat out, and in winter a canvas coat and an Australian flop hat tied down on his ears with a scarf. He fought his hangovers in a sweat lodge, bathed in ice water, planted by the moon, cast demons out of his body into sand paintings that he flung at the sky, prayed in a loincloth on a mesa in the midst of electric storms, and sometimes experienced either seizures or trances during which he spoke a language that was neither Apache nor Navaho, although he claimed it was both.

Sometimes he slept in the county jail. Other nights he slept behind the saloon or in the stucco house where he lived on the cusp of a wide, alluvial floodplain bordered on the southern horizon by purple mountains that in the late-afternoon warp of heat seemed to take on the ragged irregularity of sharks' teeth.

The sheriff who allowed Danny Boy to sleep at the jail was an elderly six-foot-five widower by the name of Hackberry Holland, whose bad back and chiseled profile and Stetson hat and thumb-buster .45 revolver and history as a drunk and whore-monger were the sum total of his political cachet, if not his life. To most people in the area, Danny Boy was an object of pity and ridicule and contempt. His solipsistic behavior and his barroom harangues were certainly characteristic of a wet brain, they said. But Sheriff Holland, who had been a prisoner of war for almost three years in a place in North Korea called No Name Valley, wasn't so sure. The sheriff had arrived at an age when he longer speculated on the validity of a madman's visions or, in general, the foibles of human behavior. Instead, Hackberry Holland's greatest fear was his fellow man's propensity to act collectively, in militaristic lockstep, under the banner of God and country.

Mobs did not rush across town to do good deeds, and, in Hackberry's view, there was no more odious taint on any social or political endeavor than universal approval. To Hackberry, Danny Boy's alcoholic madness was a respite from a far greater form of delusion.

It was late, on a Wednesday night in April, when Danny Boy walked out into the desert with an empty duffel bag and an army-surplus entrenching tool, the sky as black as soot, the southern horizon pulsing with electricity that resembled gold wires, the softness of the ground crumbling under his cowboy boots, as though he were treading across the baked shell of an enormous riparian environment that had been layered and beveled and smoothed with a sculptor's knife. At the base of a mesa, he folded the entrenching tool into the shape of a hoe and knelt down and began digging in the ground, scraping through the remains of fossilized leaves and fish and birds that others said were millions of years old. In the distance, an igneous flash spread silently through the clouds, flaring in great yellow pools, lighting the desert floor and the cactus and mesquite and the greenery that was trying to bloom along a riverbed that never held water except during the monsoon season. Just before the light died, like figures caught inside the chemical mix of a half-developed photograph, Danny Boy saw six men advancing across the plain toward him, their torsos slung with rifles.

He scraped harder in the dirt, trenching a circle around what appeared to be two tapered soft-nosed rocks protruding from the incline below the mesa. Then his e-tool broke through an armadillo's burrow. He inverted the handle and stuck it down the hole and wedged the earth upward until the burrow split across the top and he could work his hand deep into the hole, up to the elbow, and feel the shapes of the clustered objects that were as pointed and hard as calcified dugs.

The night air was dense with an undefined feral odor, like cougar scat and a sun-bleached carcass and burnt animal hair and water that had gone stagnant in a sandy drainage traced with the crawl lines of reptiles. The wind blew between the hills in the south and he felt its coolness and the dampness of the rain mist on his face. He saw the leaves on the mesquite ripple like green lace, the mesas and buttes shimmering whitely against the clouds, then disappearing into the darkness again. He smelled the pinyon and juniper and the scent of delicate flowers that bloomed only at night and whose petals dropped off and clung to the rocks at sunrise like translucent pieces of colored rice paper. He stared at the southern horizon but saw no sign of the six men carrying rifles. He wiped his mouth on his sleeve and went back to work, scooping out a big hole around the stone-like objects that were welded together as tightly as concrete.

The first shot was a tiny *pop*, like a wet firecracker exploding. He stared into the fine mist that was swirling through the hills. Then the lightning flared again and he saw the armed men stenciled against the horizon and the silhouettes of two other figures who had broken from cover and were running toward the north, toward Danny Boy, toward a place that should have been safe from the criminality and violence that he believed was threading its way out of Mexico into his life.

He lifted the nest of stony egg-shaped artifacts from the earth and slid them into the duffel bag and pulled the cord tight through the brass eyelets on the top. He headed back toward his house, staying close to the bottom of the mesa, avoiding the tracks he had made earlier, which he knew the armed men would eventually see and follow. Then a bolt of lightning exploded on top of the mesa, lighting the floodplain and the willows along the dry streambed and the arroyos and crevices and caves in the hillsides as brightly as the sun.

He plunged down a ravine, holding the duffel bag and e-tool at his sides for balance. He crouched behind a rock, hunching against it, his face turned toward the ground so it would not reflect light. He heard someone running past him in the darkness, someone whose breath was not only labored but desperate and used-up and driven by fear rather than a need for oxygen.

When he thought that perhaps his ordeal was over, that the pursuers of the fleeing men would give up and go away and allow him to return to his house with the treasure he had dug out of the desert floor, he heard a sound he knew only too well. It was the pleading lament of someone who had no hope, not unlike that of an animal caught in a steel trap or a new inmate, a fish, just off the bus at Sugar Land Pen, going into his first night of lockdown with four or five mainline cons waiting for him in the shower room.

The pursuers had dragged the second fleeing man from behind a tangle of deadwood and tumbleweed that had wedged in a collapsed corral dog-food contractors had once used to pen mustangs. The fugitive was barefoot and blood-streaked and terrified, his shirt hanging in rags on the pencil lines that were his ribs, a manacle on one wrist, a brief length of cable swinging loosely from it.

"*Donde esta?*" a voice said.

"*No se.*"

"What you mean you don't know? *Tu sabes.*"

"*No, hombre. No se nada.*"

"*Para donde se fue?*"

"He didn't tell me where he went."

"*Es la verdad?*"

"*Claro que si.*"

"You don't know if you speak Spanish or English, you've sold out to so many people. You are a very bad policeman."

"*No, senor.*"

"*Estas mintiendo, chico. Pobecito.*"

"*Tango familia, senor. Por favor. Soy un oberador, como usted.* I'm just like you, a worker. I got to take care of my family. Hear me, man. I know people who can make you rich."

For the next fifteen minutes, Danny Boy Lorca tried to shut out the sounds that came from the mouth of the man who wore a manacle and length of severed cable on one wrist. He tried to shrink himself inside his own skin, to squeeze all light and sensation and awareness from his mind, to become a black dot that could drift away on the wind and re-form later as a shadow that would eventually become flesh and blood again. Maybe one day he would even forget the fear that caused him to stop being who he was; maybe he would even meet the man he chose not to help and be forgiven by him and hence become capable of forgiving himself. When all those things happened, he might even forget what his fellow human beings were capable of doing.

When the screams of the tormented man finally softened and died and were swallowed by the wind, Danny Boy raised his head above a rock and gazed down the incline where the tangle of tumbleweed and deadwood partially obscured the handiwork of the armed men. The wind was laced with grit and rain that looked like splinters of glass. When lightning rippled across the sky, Danny Boy saw the armed men in detail.

Five of them could have been pulled at random from any jail across the border. But it was the leader who made a cold vapor wrap itself around Danny Boy's heart. He was taller than the others and stood out for many reasons, as though the incongruity of his appearance only added to the darkness of his personae. His body was not stitched with scars or chained with Gothic-letter and swastika and death's-head tats. Nor was his head shaved into a bullet or his mouth surrounded with a circle of carefully trimmed beard. Nor did he wear lizard-skin boots that were plated on the heels and tips. His running shoes looked fresh out of the box; his navy-blue sweatpants had a red stripe down each leg, similar to a design a nineteenth-century Mexican cavalry officer might wear. His skin was clean, his chest flat, the nipples no bigger than dimes, his shoulders wide, his arms like pipe stems, his pubic hair showing just above the white cord that held up his pants. An inverted M-16 was cross-strapped across his bare back; a canteen hung from a web belt on his side, and also a hatchet and a long thin knife of a kind that was used to dress wild game. He leaned over and speared something with the tip of the knife and lifted it in the air, examining it against the lights flashing in the clouds. He cinched the object with a lanyard and tied it to his belt, letting it drip down his leg.

Then Danny Boy saw the leader freeze, as though he had just smelled an invasive odor on the wind. He turned toward Danny Boy's hiding place and stared up the incline. "*Quien esta en la oscuridad?*" he said.

Danny Boy shrank down onto the ground, the rocks cutting into his knees and the heels of his hands.

"You see something up there?" one of the other men said.

But the leader did not speak, either in Spanish or English.

"It's just the wind. There's nothing out here. The wind plays tricks," the first man said.

"Ahora para donde vamos?" another man said.

The leader waited a long time to answer. *"Donde vive la Magdalena?"* he asked.

"Don't fuck with that woman, Krill. Bad luck, man."

But the leader, whose nickname was Krill, did not reply. A moment that could have been a thousand years passed, then Danny Boy heard the six men begin walking back down through the riverbed toward the distant mountains from which they had come, their tracks cracking the clay and braiding together in long serpentine lines. After they were out of sight, Danny Boy stood up and looked down at their bloody handiwork, scattered across the ground, in pieces, glimmering in the rain.

PAM TIBBS WAS Hackberry's chief deputy. Her mahogany-colored hair was both white and sunburned on the tips, and hung on her cheeks in the indifferent way it does on a teenage girl. She wore wide-ass jeans and half-topped boots and a polished gunbelt and a khaki shirt with an American flag sewn on one sleeve. Her moods were mercurial, her rhetoric often confrontational. Her potential for violence seldom registered on her adversaries until things happened that should not have happened. When she was angry, she sucked in her cheeks, accentuating a mole by her mouth, turning her lips into a button. Men often thought she was trying to be cute. They were mistaken.

At noon she was drinking a cup of coffee at her office widow when she saw Danny Boy Lorca stumbling down the street toward the department, his torso bent forward, as though he were waging war against invisible forces, a piece of newspaper matting against his chest before it flapped loose and scudded across the intersection. When Danny Boy tripped on the curb and fell hard on one knee, then fell again when he tried to pick himself up, Pam Tibbs set down her coffee cup and went outside, the wind blowing lines in her hair. She bent down, her breasts hanging heavy against her shirt, and lifted him to his feet and walked him inside.

"I messed myself. I got to get in the shower," he said.

"You know where it is," she said.

"They killed a man."

She didn't seem to hear what he had said. She glanced at the cast-iron spiral of steps that led upstairs to the jail. "Can you make it by yourself?"

"I ain't drunk. I was this morning, but I ain't now. The guy in charge, I remember his name." Danny Boy closed his eyes and opened them again. "I think I do."

"I'll be upstairs in a minute and open the cell."

"I hid all the time they was doing it."

"Say again."

"I hid behind a big rock. Maybe for fifteen minutes. He was screaming all the while."

She nodded, her expression neutral. Danny Boy's eyes were scorched with hangover, his mouth white at the corners with dried mucus, his breath dense and sedimentary, like a load of fruit that had been dumped down a stone well. He waited, although she didn't know for what. Was it absolution? "Don't slip on the steps," she said.

She tapped on Hackberry's door, but opened it without waiting for him to answer. He was on the phone, his eyes drifting to hers. "Thanks for the alert, Ethan. We'll get back to you if we hear anything," he said into the receiver. He hung up and seemed to think about the conversation he'd just had, his gaze not actually seeing her. "What's up?" he said.

"Danny Boy Lorca just came in drunk. He says he saw a man killed."

"Where?"

"I didn't get that far. He's in the shower."

Hackberry scratched at his cheek. Outside, the American flag was snapping on its pole against a gray sky, the fabric washed so thin the light showed through the threads. "That was Ethan Riser at the FBI. They're looking for a federal employee who might have been grabbed by some Mexican drug mules and taken to a prison across the border. An informant said the federal employee might have gotten loose and headed for home."

"I've heard Danny Boy has been digging up dinosaur eggs south of his property."

"I didn't know there were any around here," Hackberry said.

"If they're out there, he'd be the guy to find them."

"How's that?" he said, although he wasn't really listening.

"A guy who believes he can see the navel of

the world from his back window? He says all power comes out of this hole in the ground. Down inside the hole is another world. That's where the rain and the corn gods live. Compared to a belief system like that, hunting for dinosaur eggs seems like bland stuff."

"That's interesting."

She waited, as though examining his words. "Try this: He says the killing took fifteen minutes to transpire. He says he heard it all. You think this might be the guy the feds are looking for?"

Hackberry bounced his knuckles lightly up and down on the desk blotter and stood up, straightening his back, trying to hide the pain that crept into his face, his outline massive against the window. "Bring your recorder and a pot of coffee, will you?" he said.